ONE PLUS ONE

ONE PLUS ONE

TONY FAGGIOLI

Atticus Creative

ISBN 978-0-9978974-6-3 print edition
ISBN 978-0-9978974-7-0 ebook edition

For my mother...here's hoping that heaven is as sweet as the laugh you left behind.

CHAPTER 1

Detective Evan Parker advanced past the crime scene tape, up the driveway and through the front door of the Fasano residence in La Canada, California with a focused determination to keep it together. Getting here had not been easy.

The drive here from Beaury had been the longest in his life, even though he'd done it at over a hundred miles an hour, the desert landscape blurring into a shit smear of nothingness as he advanced after a madman who was somehow mixed up the investigation of Caitlyn Hall.

Murillo had already told him to expect the worst when he got there, but it still didn't help when the moment finally arrived.

It was obvious that the attack had taken place in the foyer, right inside the entrance of the front door, and that it had been a violent one. There was a shattered painting against the wall. Beneath it a metal-framed table had been collapsed, its glass shelf now in shards across the floor along with a broken ceramic vase, the daisies it once held having fallen in a small arc, like a yellow and white rainbow that would've almost been beautiful if not for the streaks of blood that were cast like red crescents alongside it.

Shit.

Tamara Fasano had put up one hell of a fight. Parker suddenly remembered his partner, Detective Napoleon

Villa, now missing and presumed dead, though Parker knew better. After they'd come to the Fasano residence looking for Kyle Fasano as a suspect in the Caitlyn Hall case, they'd instead been stuck interviewing Tamara, his wife, who was nobody's wilting flower. Nap had been impressed, and afterwards he told Parker that it seemed like Tamara was a "good wife."

That was true. But she evidently was an even better Mama Bear too.

On the wall near the floor was a bloody handprint, female in size, finger streaks forming "s" shapes on the way down. There were scratches in the paint. She'd not stayed down easy; evidently she'd tried to claw her way back to her feet. The crime scene guys were already on scene, planting evidence markers everywhere, with the majority of the foyer and hall now taped off as well. One tech crouched with a digital camera, aiming carefully, his flash firing repeatedly.

Parker looked down and felt his heart seize. There, marked crime scene item #32, was a Welch's Flavor Blast juice box, its tiny straw bent in half.

"Jesus," Parker whispered, shaking his head. The kids. He'd hoped they hadn't been home when this happened, that maybe they were at school or with some friends.

"Jesus is your friend and mine, brotha."

Parker recognized the voice immediately. "Murillo."

The man who shook his hand was short and a bit on the heavy side, with big hands and a face that usually held an even bigger smile. He wasn't smiling now, but he looked encouraged.

"And he was a friend to these kids too. They're good, man. In the backyard."

Parker sighed. "You're serious?"

Rubbing his hand over his full mustache and down his goatee, Murillo shook his head. "A hundred percent. We just found them a little while ago and it was total chaos once we did."

"Yeah?"

"Yep. Fireman, paramedics, the forensic guys, you name it, we were all scrambling. Klink's in the backyard now, trying to get information from them as best he can."

"Where were they?"

Murillo's face was tinged with a bit of awe. "Smart kids, man. They hid from this guy in the tool shed out back. The girl used a shovel to bar the doors from inside."

Parker shook his head in amazement.

"Yep. Close. Very close. He was after them for sure, told them he was going to take them for a 'swim' in the pool."

A chill spilled down Parker's back. "Sick bastard."

"Yep. No doubt. From the looks of it, though, the mom wasn't so lucky."

"Any witnesses to what happened?"

"No. But it's obvious that he took her afterwards. You said his name was Troy Forester?"

"Yeah. Bread deliveryman in Beaury. Body counts over eighty."

Murillo's face went slack. "Bull… shit."

"Got the trophies to prove it, hair tassels from the vics, and I think an equal number of bodies down a ravine in the mountains out there." Parker ran his hand through his hair and shook his head again. "By the time we tracked him down, he had two more in the garage."

"Alive?"

"Yep. Though the county sheriff may pay the price for getting there before we did."

"May?"

Parker could still remember when Kendall had asked one of the volunteer deputies to drive Parker back to his hotel. As they'd pulled away from Troy Forester's house, Kendall's sad and shocked expression hadn't changed a bit as Conch was loaded into the ambulance and driven away, with two paramedics and an EMT still working on him feverishly. "Yeah. He's not dead, at least not last I heard, but his heart stopped twice before they could even get him in the ambulance."

"Damn," Murillo said.

"Can I see the kids?"

Murillo grimaced. "You know, Park, technically you're still suspended. You shouldn't even be here."

Parker dead-eyed him. "And?"

Murillo thought for a second and then shrugged. "And you're now the best lead we have on this case… so screw it. Go ahead. I'll explain to the captain when he gets here."

"The cap's coming here?" Parker asked as he followed Murillo through the kitchen, past the dining room table, where Parker and Napoleon had interviewed Mrs. Fasano not that long ago, then into the den and out through a pair of sliding glass doors that led to the patio and pool beyond.

"Yep. On his way now."

"That explains it."

"Explains what?"

"Why he was blowing up my cell on the drive here."

"You gonna wait for him?"

"Screw him. He wants my help on this case going forwards? He'd better reinstate my ass."

"Hmm. Well, I know you're a newbie, but the guys would still love to have you back."

As they walked out onto the patio, a group of three uniformed cops parted, like a wall of LAPD blue, and let them past. Beyond them stood Klink and…

When Parker saw the two children, his heart broke; the little boy, about seven, was clutching a stuffed animal to his chest, evidently still in shock. A cellophane blanket had been draped over his shoulders by the paramedics, and his little eyes stared blankly into the pool. The little girl, about ten or so, was rambling and in a panic. "You have to help my mom!" she yelled.

"We know that, Janie. We're trying. But we need your help too," Klink was saying, his normally deep voice softened for the kids. When Parker walked up, Klink stood. They nodded at each other.

"Parker," Klink said with a grim smile, his pale white face shiny in the waning light of the day, his thinning blond hair making a last stand against premature baldness.

"Klink."

"You doing okay?"

"Yeah. Do you mind?" Parker asked, nodding towards Janie.

Klink fixed his blue eyes on Parker for a moment, then nodded.

He extended his hand to the little girl. "Hi… Janie, right?"

The little girl nodded but wouldn't look at him.

"My name is Det… my name is Mr. Parker."

"I know who you are," Janie said, still looking at the ground. "You're the detective who came here that night with the other detective and upset my mommy."

There was an awkward silence. Parker nodded for a second or two. He could almost feel every cop in the vicinity thinking about Napoleon: Where was he? What happened to him? Had Parker told the truth about that night? Was he hiding something? Finally, mercifully, one of the uniforms cleared his throat.

"Yes. I am. I mean… I was. I'm sorry about that. I didn't mean to upset your mom that night."

Janie kept her head down, her fingers playing ceaselessly with a strand of her long hair.

"We were trying to figure out what happened to someone."

"Like what's happened to my mom?" Janie asked, finally looking up at him.

Parker wished she hadn't. The conviction in her eyes was almost piercing. He nodded.

"Will you find her?"

Parker knew the stock answer. The trained answer. He ignored it. "Yes."

Klink shuffled his feet and Murillo folded his arms, their body language trying to remind him not to make promises that he might not be able to keep.

"Okay. You have to," she said, and her lower lip trembled as she added, "because the man that took my mommy wasn't normal."

"Janie, listen—" Klink tried to say.

"No! I won't listen. *You* listen!" she screamed, and then she began to cry.

"Shhhhh… hey, hey, come here," Parker said as he knelt down and put out his arms.

She shook her head the whole time she shuffled towards him. When she was within reach, Parker rested his hands on her tiny shoulders, which were covered by light-green cotton pajamas.

"Calm down. You can tell me, okay? What is it, Janie?"

"I've been telling them, but they won't listen to me," she sobbed.

"Tell *me* then," Parker replied.

"You won't believe me either. You won't!"

"Try me."

She stopped crying and took a deep breath before fixing her eyes on Parker with a poker stare that was beyond her years. "It was a monster," she said, her voice cracking momentarily. Her eyes grew big as they filled with the memory of whatever she'd seen. After a second or two she added, "A devil-monster."

The uniforms, Murillo, Klink and Parker remained silent; the only sound remaining was that of the pool filter as it gurgled and churned nearby.

Janie turned her gaze back to Parker, fear now filling her face. "You don't believe me either, do you?" she cried.

Parker leaned back. He glanced at Murillo briefly, then back to Janie, as his own eyes filled with tears. He couldn't help it.

"Oh, I believe you," Parker said, taking little Janie's hands between both of his and squeezing gently. "I... don't... doubt... you... one bit."

"You promise?" she squeaked.

Parker leaned into her face and then cupped her round cheeks in his hands. "I swear."

Just then, his cell phone rang. It was Deputy Kendall.

"I'll be right back Janie. Okay?"

She nodded.

He stepped away and answered on the third ring. "Hello."

"Parker?"

With all he'd already been through in his life, Parker knew the tone of someone about to bear bad news. So he braced himself and forced the question out of his mouth. "Yeah, Kendall?"

The deputy's voice shook as he struggled to say the words. "He didn't make, Parker. The sheriff's dead."

Parker was surprised at how weak he felt all of a sudden, like maybe his legs might give out on him, right there in front of everyone. All he could think about was Sheriff Conch and his wife, Mandy, bantering over the pie she'd made the night they'd all stayed at the station house in Beaury trying to work the case. She was worried about his weight. Sheriff Conch was worried about his retirement.

"Dammit," Parker replied, the word coming out of his mouth so weakly that it was barely a whisper. He cleared his throat and tried again. "Kendall. I'm so sorry."

"It's okay, man," Kendall said, but the words were hollow. Because it wasn't okay. Because they both knew they were sharing a moment between them that would change them forever.

Parker had been to this place, before the immensity of death, many times, and each time he told himself that the next time it would be easier. But it never was.

"Parker? You there?"

"Yeah. Sorry, man. I'm just… I don't know what to say, Kendall."

"Not what you were expecting, huh?"

Rubbing his hand over his eyes, Parker replied, "No. I thought he'd pull through. I really did."

"Yeah. So did most everyone here. But Mandy, she seemed to know something we didn't."

"How's that?"

"I dunno man. I ain't much of a churchgoer, but she didn't leave his side the whole time. And when she was here, she just prayed and prayed and prayed."

"Did his kids make it before he…"

"Only his son and two of his grandkids. The rest were on their way but they live kinda far off. They didn't make it. But you won't believe who else made it."

"Who?"

"Ashley Barton's mom. You remember her?"

"I never met her."

"Oh. That's right. Well, anyway, she fainted at the crime scene the morning her daughter disappeared. Took it hard. So you can imagine how happy she was when we found Ashley alive."

"Yeah?"

"Lost her mind with joy, because Ashley's was pretty much unharmed, but then she heard what happened with the sheriff. She rolled up in here with her entire church congregation practically. Prayer circles in shifts, between Ashley down the hall and the sheriff, back and forth."

"Wow."

"Yeah. I ain't seen nothing like it. We're a small town, Parker. The nurses on shift knew him. One of the doctors remembered when he was younger, how the sheriff helped him with some bullies. Oh, man..." And now he was crying.

"Hey, you okay?" It was Murillo, grabbing Parker by the shoulder as Parker's own eyes began to water. He nodded, and then remembering that the kids were standing right there, Parker composed himself and walked further away, towards the corner of the patio, each step feeling like an out of body experience.

He wanted to say something, but the words that came to mind seemed far too small. So he waited, and after a bit, Kendall spoke again. "They prayed and prayed, man, but it just wasn't enough."

Parker thought of Kamdesh, and Fallujah, the second time around, when the body counts and the prayers seemed to tally against each other, like some mad, insane sort of math. All of it senseless and futile. "Yeah. Sometimes it isn't, Kendall."

"But Mandy… man, Parker, she's a mess but she's holding it together. She wanted me to tell you something."

"What's that?"

"To not be blinded by vengeance now, when you go after this guy. To be careful. Can you believe that? I mean… man."

It wasn't the common response, that was for sure. How many guys had Parker seen, filled with rage over the death of a buddy, who had advanced too far ahead of the platoon, or up a flight of stairs, or through the desert, thirsty for revenge and left only drinking their own blood? Too many. Parker had done the same, but had been lucky to live to tell about it. Though not lucky enough to be able to forget it.

"Tell her I'll be careful, Kendall."

"I will. I gotta go now, my wife just got here. But, Parker? One more thing?"

"Yeah, Kendall. You name it."

"I ain't Mandy, you hear? Do it for me. Kill that fucker."

The line went dead.

Parker sighed. He didn't really believe that Kendall meant that. They both were men of the law, and that meant resisting the urge to act outside of it, even when you really wanted to.

He leaned against a wooden beam that supported the patio roof and again rubbed his eyes.

Evidently he'd gotten closer to Sheriff Conch than he was aware of. How couldn't you? The old man had grit, and a sweet wife and a simple life. How he was ever put in a place where he had to deal with Troy Forester was beyond

Parker's comprehension, and it made him angry. God himself should've prevented such a thing from happening.

It was too much sometimes, which is why he'd spent most of his life just not thinking about it. He remembered Martinez with his Bible and his rosary under that hot desert Afghani sun, smiling amid the sorrows. He remembered Napoleon Villa's face as he looked at the man in gray with such awe before they both disappeared to wherever. And he remembered the angel by the side of the road at that car crash.

How did any of that make sense when a monster like Forester was allowed to kill all those girls, kill Conch, ravage the Fasano home, abduct Tamara and scar the Fasano children for life?

Then Parker imagined Ashley Barton's mom and the army of the Beaury Baptist Church, shuffling up and down the hall of the hospital, back and forth, praying just as hard for both, between one person who would live, and another who would die.

How was one to make sense of it all?

God help him, but Parker felt like he knew the answer: you didn't.

CHAPTER 2

KYLE STOOD MOTIONLESS ON the hillside, his hands on his hips, trying to find the right words to say, his shock at what he'd just heard filtering through his mind like water through charcoal. "This can't be. It can't."

"I'm afraid it is." The Gray Man's voice was barely more than a whisper.

Kyle's gaze darted in panic across the ground as if he could find a switch down there in the dirty brown grass that he could flip to go back in time, to pretend none of this had ever happened. "*What* did you say?"

"I'm sorry…"

"You're *sorry*? That's all you've got?" Kyle said, the words echoing with accusation.

"We had no way of…"

"We?" Kyle interjected flatly. "How is it 'we'?"

"Don't forget, Kyle. Things turned on a dime. We both knew the risks back when this began, when I abandoned your training to go and try and protect Tamara."

"And now we can see how that worked out, can't we?"

"I wanted to be there with you, at the end, to make sure you made it. In hindsight, I should've stayed with you and made sure that you were ready to confront Victoria. If I had, maybe none of this would've happened."

Kyle said nothing.

A short silence waited between them. Then The Gray Man nodded, his face painted in distress. "But there's no way of really knowing. Yes. Tamara's in trouble now. But she was in no less danger before. At first they sent a lesser demon after her, which attacked her in her sleep. I dispatched it. That's when I became aware that she was a target, right before I talked with you and we made our pact."

"Then?"

"You proceeded on, and I fell back. And I watched and waited. There was a shift of some kind, in her reality, right about the time she began driving to Monterey to try and save you."

"Oh my God," Kyle murmured, putting his hands on his head. "She came to *help* me?"

After a moment of silence, Detective Villa walked over, his hands in his pockets, and spoke. "Yeah. She managed to put it all together somehow, about the same time my partner and I did. She knew where you were headed and who you were trying to get to."

Kyle felt his face knot with confusion.

The Gray Man sighed. "Along the way, two more came after her, a mother and her spawn. They attacked her at a truck stop."

Detective Villa's head snapped in The Gray Man's direction. "Truck stop? You mean the one outside of Barstow?"

"Yes."

"One came after me there too."

The Gray Man nodded. "Yes. It makes sense. A portal has been established there, by the other side. It was a logical point of intercept, as it was the road you were both most likely use to get to where you were going, and the only stop for miles. You were a nuisance, though. *She* was their first order of priority."

Kyle shook his head slowly. The whole world seemed to be immersed in a fog. "So what happened next?"

"I waited until they fully materialized, when they were most vulnerable, and then I dispatched them."

"What about the one who attacked me, in the John Deere cap?" Napoleon asked.

This time it was Kyle's turn to snap his head. "John Deere cap?"

"Yeah," Napoleon said. "Why?"

"I ran into one wearing a John Deere cap too, at the Denny's in Beaury."

The Gray Man cleared his throat. "It was the same one. He's a more serious threat."

"Serious?"

"Hell has rank: minor demons, major demons, and those evolving or devolving between the two. Here on earth a person can become possessed." The Gray Man looked from Napoleon to Kyle. "Like Caitlyn or Victoria. They weren't entirely lost yet, to the darkness. You saw that with Caitlyn in the hotel room, Kyle, when she was struggling on the edge of the bed, fighting the urge to kill you when you came back from the bathroom."

The memory came back to Kyle as clear as the day before them; Caitlyn rocking back and forth, talking to the carpeted floor, sounding so… afraid.

The Gray Man continued, "And you saw it with Victoria, right at the end, when you shared your memories of your time together with her. Even at that advanced stage of possession, salvation was still in her grasp. I was stunned by that, Kyle. I really was."

"Why?"

"Because I knew you had the power to save the boy, to save Sebastian. But I never imagined you could save her too. Now it makes more sense."

Kyle sighed. "What does?"

"My orders were clear: tell you to save your first love from committing the same mistake you had. I did so, in faith, even though I knew that she wasn't the one you'd actually be saving."

"So I was tricked?"

"No. I knew that you'd never be willing to take on the mission, deal with what was coming, the struggle and the fight, for a boy you didn't even know, who'd foolishly convinced himself that sleeping with a married woman would be a good thing. But I knew you'd do it for her."

"You did trick me."

The Gray Man shook his head again. "Kyle. I know you can't see the full picture now, with what's happened. But let's clear that up before we proceed, okay? Because we must—"

"There's no time for—"

"—or our efforts to save Tamara now could fail completely. You need to understand, Kyle. You must."

Fixing his jaw in frustration, Kyle put his hands on his hips again. "Fine. Spit it out."

"The boy could only be saved by a millionth. Why? We may never know. It simply isn't part of our mission. But regardless, that millionth was you. The second hand of the universe turned into position and the precise second that you gave yourself to Caitlyn, and took her for yourself, you were the one."

"Luck of the draw," Detective Villa said dryly and out of nowhere.

The Gray Man looked back at him intently. "Luck? Really? Do you think that luck had anything to do with the incredible—some might say, one in a million—odds, that the boy who would need to be saved would choose as his target for adultery the first love of the one-in-a-million man who had already committed that very same sin, six hundred miles away?"

Detective Villa grew quiet. The Gray Man went on. "The odds are nearly incalculable. That's when you know the Father is at work, as best He can be, amidst all the math of human free will. In the end, the boy still chose to try, and almost paid for it with his life. If not for Kyle, he would surely be dead now. And in the end Victoria still chose the darkness, though she had one, final chance at the light. If not for Kyle, she never would've had that chance. That means something."

"And me? What did it get me?" Kyle asked defiantly.

The Gray Man looked at Kyle with a look of intense disappointment. "What did it get you, Kyle? You mean, besides forgiveness for what you did? To that girl? To your wife? To your children? To yourself? And what of this man here? This detective? Or his partner? All these lives, forever altered, by the chain reaction of your decision at a bar in that hotel? One selfish decision after many others."

Kyle said nothing.

"Feeling guilty, now, Kyle?" The Gray Man asked in nearly a whisper, sounding a bit emotional himself.

Kyle simply nodded.

"The Lord was working on you too, Kyle Fasano."

"How?" Kyle asked, looking away across the hillside at a swaying branch on a tree in the distance. He couldn't look at The Gray Man. Couldn't bear to hear what he might say.

"You knew you had work to do, Kyle. On yourself. In yourself. That very first time Tamara took you to church. You felt it. Too much of your life had been about you. You asked God to forgive you, but then you had to take the next step: you had to forgive yourself too. And you couldn't. It's a frustrating hypocrisy of humanity. One of many, really. But, in truth, when you get right down to it, we're most unwilling to forgive ourselves. For the hurts we've caused, the damage we've done, the hearts we've broken."

"Stop…" Kyle murmured, putting up his hand.

"You never forgave yourself, Kyle, for what you did to Victoria when you left for college, and for what—"

"Gray. Please. Stop."

"—you did to Vinnie."

Pain blossomed like a vicious flower that had been planted right between Kyle's lungs.

"When we don't forgive ourselves, Kyle, do you know what happens?" The Gray Man said, stepping forwards and putting an arm on his shoulder.

Struggling to maintain his composure, Kyle shook his head.

"We damn ourselves, long before hell ever gets a chance."

The hillside grew quiet again. The sky over and around them was large and foreboding, a pale blue canvas with only a few small wisps of white clouds that had been torn apart and contorted by a wind high up in the atmosphere.

"Now what?" Detective Villa asked, pulling a hand free from his pants pocket to scratch at his chin.

For the first time Kyle really looked at him, seeing that the detective's dark eyes were not only piercing but almost always squinting, as if he were a man who never stopped questioning things. The wrinkles around his eyes said he'd been squinting and questioning things for a long time. But right now it was obvious: he was stepping in to bail Kyle out, and Kyle was thankful for it.

The Gray Man took a deep breath and gave Kyle some space. "I think it's clear, for both sides, really. A millionth comes to pass. One side seeks the success of his or her mission; the other side seeks his or her destruction. At first they just wanted to stop Tamara from helping Kyle, but then you, Detective Villa, began to figure some things out that you shouldn't have, so you became a target too."

"But I wasn't attacked at the truck stop," Napoleon said calmly.

"No. You were deemed the lesser threat for the moment. The goal was to scare you away."

"So... Tamara was a bigger threat then? Why?" Kyle asked.

The Gray Man looked at Kyle hesitantly. "Why, love, of course."

Kyle swallowed hard. "Love?"

"Yes, Kyle. She had the power to help you. Had she found you first, told you that she'd forgiven you for your sin, perhaps even encouraged you on your mission, it would've only made you more focused and more powerful when you finally confronted Victoria."

Kyle felt exhausted. "But that didn't happen."

"No. They impeded Detective Villa and Tamara, even diverted me away, just enough to leave you exposed for defeat. But they underestimated your power. They should've seen it, at least a little bit, with how well you were doing so early in your training. But they didn't. Then, when I went after you, I assumed you'd shifted the battle completely to hell. But every action has a reaction. You know this from your earthly science, at the most rudimentary of forms, but it's a truth that holds firm even at the highest levels. So they decided to counter your victory as a millionth by not only trying to trap you in hell, but by also coming after that which you held most dear here on earth."

"Okay," Napoleon said firmly. "So here we are now. Again, what next?"

"You're sure my kids are safe?" Kyle asked.

"Yes," The Gray Man replied. "They're with the police. Actually, with Detective Villa's partner."

Napoleon looked out over the horizon with a small nod. "Good job, Parker."

"You should know that he checked in twice with your nephew, by phone, right after your disappearance, Detective Villa. He was going to try and see him, but then he was drawn back into this."

"I want to see my kids," Kyle said.

"There isn't time," The Gray Man said sternly.

Kyle spun on The Gray Man and grabbed him by the shirt. "I want to see my kids!"

"Tamara could die, Kyle, if we don't move to get to her as soon as possible."

Kyle cursed and released his grip, his knuckles going from white to soft pink as he did so. "What?"

"The monster that has her is of an evil the likes of which I've never encountered."

"Just do that travel-thing you do, to get us to where she is then. Now," Kyle begged.

"You cannot travel to a destination you do not know, Kyle. He's obscured their retreat somehow, probably with the aid of his sponsor."

"His... what?" Detective Villa asked.

"The man who has taken Kyle's wife is in training too."

Kyle was shocked. "What? Are you kidding?"

"No. The process works both ways, and the major demon in hell that is behind this man is very powerful. It's going to take both of us to stop them."

"So how do we find her?" Kyle asked.

"We have markers, intermittent points of contact that

we can use to pierce the darkness and ascertain where they were at a particular point in time."

"And?"

"When he abducted her from your house, they headed north."

"But we have no way of knowing where they were actually headed?" Detective Villa asked.

"Not yet."

"You said my partner was watching the kids. Does that mean he was on this guy's tail?"

"Yes. He was closing in on him with local law enforcement in Beaury."

"So they have Mrs. Fasano. Will they still go after the kids?"

"At this point, anything's possible," The Gray Man said grimly.

"My God. Tamara. The kids. This is insane. What do I do?" Kyle asked, staring up with dismay at the sky.

"This is simple," Napoleon said, walking up to Kyle.

"Simple?" Kyle nearly choked on the word.

"You and our gray friend go after your wife. I'll go to protect my partner, and by default your kids, since he has them."

Kyle thought about it quietly. "You're sure?"

"It makes sense," The Gray Man interjected.

Kyle nodded and then stuck his hand out to Napoleon. "I don't know anything about you except that you came to hell to help save me. I'll never forget that."

"We all need a little saving sometimes," Napoleon said, shaking Kyle's hand.

"My kids?" Kyle asked worriedly.

Napoleon nodded. "Parker and I have got this. You just get to your wife. I have no idea where we are though. Any help?" he said, looking to The Gray Man.

Time held still for a moment, and then it began to spin in rapid succession. The Gray Man looked at Kyle. "I'll be right back."

Then he and Napoleon blinked away in a soft light that left behind a faint hiss. A minute later, The Gray Man returned. That is, it seemed like just a minute to Kyle, but he could sense that time was warping. He wondered how long The Gray Man had really been away but was too upset to really care right now.

Kyle looked at him. "I'm still pissed at you."

"I know you are."

"But… this is… all of it, is my own fault anyway."

"You did well, Kyle. You achieved your mission."

"No," Kyle said firmly. "Not yet. Not until my wife's safely back with my children will I have achieved anything at all. I don't want to be a millionth or anything else, this side of heaven or the other, until that happens. Do you understand that?"

The Gray Man looked at Kyle. "I understand."

Then the sky around them began to warp into a tunnel of warmth and light, and Kyle closed his eyes.

CHAPTER 3

THE DRIVE THEY WERE on was made up of a series of bumps and turns. The soundtrack had switched from country to heavy metal music that was so loud it reverberated to Tamara's cramped space in the trunk in relentless waves, screeching guitars and wailing lyrics bouncing around like marbles and beating against her aching head.

She tried to count the turns and stops. That's what they did in the movies. But then she realized that only worked if you were awake when the drive began. Who knew how much of the drive she'd missed from the time they left the house, when she was unconscious? So she gave up on that idea. The inside of the trunk still smelled like polyester carpet and blood, but now another smell had joined in: her sweat.

Her eyes were now fully adjusted to the darkness of the trunk and it was obvious he was no fool. There was nothing, not one damned thing, that she could use as a tool to work her way free. No tire iron, no wrench, no odds or ends.

The trunk was bare, except for a roll of plastic sheeting that was near her head. She knew what that was for: to wrap her up in after he was done with her.

She thought of him there at the steering wheel, that psychopath, not ten feet from her, and she was suddenly thankful that she was in the trunk instead of the back seat, where he could look over his shoulder and leer at her with those eyes full of madness.

Just keep driving. I don't care where. Just don't stop the car.

She kept pulling and tugging against the rope around her wrists.

I'm not ready to die yet.

Her sense of consciousness seemed more rooted, more sure of itself, and this was a relief. Twice now she'd faded in and out of reality, and it was not only frightening but very disorienting. Each time she awoke, she had to struggle to piece back together what had happened all over again, as if she were sketching her existence with a broken-tipped pencil. Now, with a firmer grip on things, she was able to move past the agony of her memories, and the fear of what was next, by devising a plan.

Any plan would do, as long as it fulfilled only one objective: killing him before he killed her. Because common sense dictated that he was going to kill her. Eventually. He might play with her, rape her and torture her before he did, but eventually he would—if she didn't do something about it.

Again she worked her wrists and forearms against the rope, in figure eight patterns, feeling her skin chaffing and cutting, her tendons rubbing against her bones beneath the firm, scratchy fibers. She had to be careful not to damage her hands so badly that she left herself defenseless, ruining the only weapons she still had besides her feet.

He'd hog tied her up good and this was going to take forever. The trunk was shrinking again.

She closed her eyes and stilled her panic.

Be patient. Be patient. There's enough play around your hands to maybe get one of them free, and that's all you need. Just one.

"You can do this," she whispered to herself. Positive reinforcement. A trick from her days on the volleyball team.

The car suddenly swerved hard to the left, as if maybe he was trying to avoid something on the road, and this shifted her position enough to give her a better angle on her bindings. Again she set about working on them. The ones around her ankles were the tightest, and one of her feet had gone numb with all her efforts. That couldn't be a good thing. Especially if she got the chance to bolt out of the trunk and run at some point.

Trying to get her hair out of her face, she whipped her head to the side, which caused her to go woozy for a second.

No! I can't pass out again.

She waited. Nothing happened. But the near miss only increased her sense of desperation.

The next thought that came to her was from a dark, unwelcome place.

My children are probably dead.

It was like a gunshot, and it dropped her instantly.

She stopped struggling and grew still, moaning softly against the despair that began to envelope her. Why fight? Who cared anymore? She wanted to die. Without her babies, what was the point? To live the whole rest of her life knowing that she'd failed to protect them? No. Forget it.

No. Stop. You don't know that for sure.

It was true. She had no way of knowing if they were really dead. That was the main reason to push on.

But she felt another reason inside of her.

God would not let that happen. Not after the sacrifice Kyle made. And what about The Gray Man? Hadn't he already come, three times, to help?

If the devil could send creatures after them at the market and from under their beds, could not God send someone else to help the kids? Yes.

"Lord," she whimpered, "please, Father. Please show me a sign." And the prayer, even when whispered so meekly, seemed to cocoon the trunk in silence and stillness.

She looked to the sliver of light in the trunk lid again. The sun's rays, shining through in tiny, piercing lines, began to widen and pulsate ever so briefly, and her mind was filled with images that she knew did not come from her imagination.

She was back in her house. As the monster advanced on her babies, they had fled. But in the wrong direction—towards the kitchen.

Where a larger monster awaited. A beast.

A beast in the lantern.

Inside the lantern Ben had given her.

There on the counter, and directly in their path, it erupted with color, and a voice came out of it that froze Janie in her tracks, causing Seth to bowl into her and knocked them both over.

The voice was so horrible that the monster in the hall grabbed Tamara and fled the house, half-carrying, half-dragging her unconscious body to his car, where he tied her up and threw her in the trunk, gasping in panic as if he were afraid that what was in the house might come outside and get him.

Why? Because he'd screwed up somehow. He was a failure.

She was above it all and in it all, the moment at her house, as if she were a ghost traveling back in time.

Surely this was a dream. She had a concussion or something. This was her mind concocting a theory, a coping mechanism to help her deal with her situation.

But she knew… *knew*… it was real.

She was awake, stone cold conscious, and this was exactly what she had asked for: an answer to her prayer. A vision. The kids had managed to flee the house, out of the sliding glass door to the patio. They'd gotten away.

Oh God, thank you so much. Thank you, Lord.

As the trunk hummed along the asphalt road, Tamara felt herself growing warm as she forced her mind to be at peace.

She felt the kids were safe now. And this gave her a newfound sense of strength.

Because if her babies were alive?

Then she needed to stay alive for them.

* * *

Parker stood on the patio with Murillo and gazed absent-mindedly across the pool in the backyard of the Fasano house. It was growing dark. An errant leaf had fallen from the hibiscus tree, that stretched out over patio, down into the water, and it was now spinning in sporadic circles as it was carried by an eddy towards the pool filter. "So? What now?"

Murillo shrugged. "House didn't have security cameras, so we got nothing on tape. Based on your description of this guy and what the kids have confirmed, we know who we're after—"

"But we got dick on which way he went."

Murillo nodded as he hunched his shoulders and rolled them. "Freakin' stress, Parker. Got my neck so tight I can barely take it."

"Where's Cap?"

"Running and ducking, like he has been since Nap went Area 51 on everybody."

Parker chuckled bitterly. "Yeah, like he gives a rat's ass about Nap."

"Or you," Murillo said as he too now watched the leaf in the pool.

Parker sighed. "It's a miracle he let me in here."

"He didn't. Klink and I figured this was a gimme. I mean, you're the one who called us. We had nothing, otherwise."

"We still have nothing."

The leaf swung wide right and then slightly left as it was finally pulled into the tide of the pool filter and disappeared.

"We got a perp. We got the make and model of his car. No plate yet, but we can dig it up, put out an APB… and we can look for info on any friends or family he might run to."

Parker said nothing for a minute, then replied, "We got a guy smart enough to kill over eighty women, across five different counties, over God knows how many years, is what we got. A guy too smart to keep that car for long, or to not have false plates stashed that he's probably switched to by now, and a guy who probably is such a lone wolf that he either has no friends or family to turn to or wouldn't if he did."

Murillo pursed his lips at this and looked at Parker. "He wasn't smart enough to get past that small-town sheriff in Beaury."

The offense Parker felt at hearing Conch called this must have been telegraphed to his face, because Murillo instantly backtracked.

"Sorry, Park."

"It's okay. You don't know, but that old man had more skills than the two of us put together."

"Had?"

"He's dead, Murillo."

"What?"

The sun was bowing out. A daily routine. Probably a pretty sight across most of the city, but from the backyard of the Fasano home, which was smothered under an ominous weight, it just looked like a big yellow bomb falling into darkness.

"Bastard stabbed him ten times."

Murillo rubbed his temple with his left hand, his wedding ring glistening for a moment in the light. "Shit."

Looking around, Parker saw that the techs were gone, leaving the house yellow taped in front and back. Neighbors had gathered at a house on the hill just behind the backyard, some of them brave enough to peak their heads over to snoop.

The Fasano children were seated beneath the patio roof on a lawn chair huddled closely together, each of them wrapped in blankets, seemingly shifting in and out of shock. Right now they both had the same blank stares on their faces. And who could blame them? They'd already lost their father, and now they'd lost their mother too. Parker shook his head.

He imagined the little girl playing soccer a month ago, and the little boy drawing crude sketches in some class at a nearby school in this idyllic little neighborhood.

Now? It was likely they were both orphans.

Through the sliding glass doors of the patio, Parker saw him coming: the captain, a small entourage of uniformed officers and Sergeant Decker in his trail. Klink saw them too, and he immediately walked over to Parker and Murillo, the three of them forming a small wall against the reality about to confront them.

At first the captain didn't see Parker, but when he did, a look came over his face not unlike the look a person gets when confronted by an inconvenient truth.

"What the hell are you doing here?" the captain asked, his eczema-ridden face redder than usual, his pure white hair looking greasy.

"We asked him to—" Murillo tried to interject.

"Oh!" the captain exclaimed, his blue eyes widening. "You guys *asked* him to be here? I'm sorry. I had *no* idea. In that case I guess it's okay that we have a suspended officer standing in the middle of a fucking crime scene then, right, Murillo?"

Parker didn't know Sergeant Decker very well beyond his name and the fact that he was supposed to be a hard-ass. Right about now, though, he looked like he'd rather be anywhere else than here. Then it was Klink's turn to try to say something. "Cap. We shoulda called you—"

"Yeah? Ya *think*? I mean, for a second there I thought you got promoted over me, Klink."

"But the scene was active and it was Parker who called it in."

The captain turned his icy glare to Parker. "So what the fuck are you—"

Parker held his hand up for him to stop. He intentionally waited a few seconds until rage crossed the captain's face before Parker nodded slightly in the direction of the children. Once the captain saw them and realized he was muzzled, he only looked more enraged. Then Parker finally spoke. "I found some stuff out in Beaury."

"Jesus, Mary and Joseph. Where you decided to go... under *whose* authority?"

Perhaps it was the events of the day, the bleakness of the situation, or the contrast between this asshole standing upright while a good man like Sheriff Conch was in a morgue only two hours away, but Parker just wasn't going to have it. He took a step towards the captain and eyed him hard. "Listen. Listen to me good," he said.

A wave of stunned disbelief spread from Klink to Murillo to the uniforms and to Sergeant Decker, who looked as if he were ready to intervene.

The captain squinted back hard at Parker as he continued. "You want my fucking badge, Cap? Take it. I don't give a shit. I was in Beaury with the permission of Sheriff Conch, assisting him with an investigation, on my own free time and of my own free will."

The air between them froze. The captain nodded gently, almost mockingly, but said nothing.

"I've been an exemplary officer since I made the force. You know my history, here and in the military. I know the chain of command and I usually respect it. Shit, out of respect for your orders I didn't even contact my union rep, and you know damn well I could've."

Silence held court for a few moments. The captain seemed to be chewing on something. "Go ahead," he finally said, puffing up his chest. "You wanna say your peace, say it."

"Peace? I haven't had peace for one night, not even one half a day, since this case started. My partner is gone"—Parker grunted out the words, fighting his emotions—"I was there and I couldn't do a thing to stop it. I don't know where he is but he could be dead. Then? I stumble into a hornets' nest in Beaury that's somehow, against all odds, connected to this case. I then get to find a mountain of bodies in a fucking ravine, then see a good man, a good cop, stabbed to death by this fucking psychopath."

The captain looked stunned. "He's dead?"

"You're damn right he is!"

"Parker—" Murillo said, trying to stop him.

Parker shook his head firmly and continued. "No one on this entire planet wants this guy more. Not a soul. But I'm not going after him, at least not yet. Do you wanna know why?"

The captain grimaced. "Sure, after you tell me how I'm gonna tell the DA that you being here traipsing around hasn't somehow put this case in jeopardy. After you—"

"Do you want to know *why*?" Parker said again, barely able to contain himself.

Again, the captain just stared at him.

"Because of them," Parker said, nodding towards the children. "Because right now they have no one and—"

"And Child Protective Services will be here any minute to—"

"To hear me tell them that I'll watch them until next of kin arrives."

"And who would that be?" Sergeant Decker interrupted, but his tone was supportive, not accusatory. Decker was on his side somehow, or was probably just trying to defuse the situation.

Parker struggled for a minute, trying to come up with what to say or how to say it. He didn't know why, but something in him, deep inside, was telling him not to let the children out of his sight. He hadn't even started this argument with them in mind at all, and he was just about to concoct a lie when the little girl, Janie, spoke up.

"My aunt Trudy!" she said, wiping tears off her cheek. Perhaps it was the way she said it, as a desperate plea smothered in fear, but it calmed the moment instantly.

The captain, being a coward at heart, saw his out and took it. He turned to the little girl. "Your aunt?"

"Yes. She lives in San Francisco. She just left here yesterday. Her number will be in my mommy's cell phone."

Klink looked at the captain, who hesitated a minute before he nodded his permission for him to go find the number.

"Decker?" the captain said firmly.

"Yes, sir."

"Sheriff Schmidt is our counterpart here. La Canada is their jurisdiction but we've agreed to treat this as a joint investigation for now. Ask them to help you get this house cordoned off and to get the damn BBQing looky-loos up on the hill there away from the fence. They're taking damn cell phone photos, for shit's sake!"

"Got it." Decker and the uniformed cops fanned out to follow orders. With Klink gone inside the house, it was only Murillo, Parker and the captain now.

"Murillo?"

"Yeah, Cap?"

"I should be telling you to arrest Parker for interfering with a police investigation, but we both know I'm not gonna do that."

"Yes, sir."

"But what is going to happen is this: Parker and I are going to have a little sit down, right over there at the patio table, you got it?"

"Yes, sir."

"You stay here and let CPS do their job when they arrive, but don't let them take the kids yet, got it?"

Murillo nodded.

"Okay, Parker? You up for a chat?"

Parker was beyond surprised, but he nodded.

CHAPTER 4

As he travelled, cocooned in white, with The Gray Man, Kyle's eyes grew heavy. The weight of his escape from hell and the disaster of what he'd returned to finally began to overtake him. Nodding off, he asked himself to find something in his mind to ease his anxiety, a happy moment to escort him to sleep. At first nothing happened and then…

They had sat beneath a maple tree on a hill in the park near the apartment she'd shared with her three roommates, and Kyle was impressed by the picnic she'd laid out, unabashedly old school, with a large checkered blanket and a picnic basket that seemed bottomless. From its depths she produced cheese, crackers and wine at first, then homemade sandwiches and a mini cheesecake.

He was nervous, and not a little bit scared, about the feelings he was beginning to have for this new girl in his life, this Tamara Fitzgerald, with her playful spirit and deep, rich laugh. He watched as she neatly laid everything out, admiring the curves of her body, which she still hadn't given to him, and the way her eyes glistened in the sunlight when she looked out over the grass to the children at play and the old people on their walks. She was observant and not a little bit sappy.

In that, she had something that he was lacking, and he sensed its pull but denied it, determined for once to get things right, to not kidnap the strengths of someone he claimed to love but rather to simply to acknowledge them.

They talked as they ate, about her plans to get her MBA and his plans to forge out into the world of sales with only his undergraduate degree. This being their fourth date (their third only happening two days before) it felt like they'd reached a point where it was time to start letting their guards down—when you go from sharing your dreams and ambitions to sharing your hopes and fears.

As his dream translated the memory, Kyle became aware that he could recall what was said, but there was no sound. Just pictures, vacillating in his mind: a red Frisbee gliding through the air, ducks combing along the shore of the park's man-made lake, an old man with a redwood cane navigating a nearby set of steps, and a group of boys nearby playing Whiffle ball, the yellow bat matching the color of the sun overhead, the day so warm Kyle didn't want it to end.

He gathered it all in before his eyes found their way again back to Tamara, seated, smiling, looking at him now like she had been looking at the children at play and old people only moments before—studying him, appreciating him. He avoided her eyes because of the depth of the vulnerability that they stirred in him.

A warm breeze moved momentarily across the grass, stirring a few napkins on the picnic blanket and making the maple leaves whisper overhead.

After the cheesecake, she cracked a joke about needing to be rolled out of the park she was so stuffed, and then she moved closer, leaned against him and rested her head just below his chin. That was it, really, the feeling of her head against his chin, that made him realize that for the first time in his life, he was truly in love. Not "maybe" in love, not "kinda" in love, but "done for" in love.

She was right, from the very first beer at the dinner party they'd met at, because the moment she spoke, the moment she moved her hands around to make a point, or shook the hair out of her eye to ponder an idea, she rendered him immobile. His heart, his soul, his body... they all took notice, and then could do no more. He had looked. And then? He simply could not look away.

He teased her when he felt her politely stifled burp against his chest, and she pinched his ribs in embarrassment.

"We've already reached that point, have we?" he pressed.

"Oh, please," she said mockingly. "I'm sorry. I left my tiara in the car."

"It's okay," he said, wrapping one arm around her. "I think the slipper still fits."

"Pfft! Stop now, sir, or risk my lunch coming back up."

It was her voice, and more particularly her laugh, that finally brought sound to his dream and cracked it wide open. He'd noticed many times by then that she had a laugh pregnant with potential, a laugh that wanted to be happy but was still guarded against sadness. In its inflection she could both reach out and pull away, at nearly the same time. But now... at this moment... he could tell: she was reaching out to him, all the way, with her arms wide open.

She laced the fingers of her left hand through the fingers of his right, their thumbs locked for a moment, but it felt wrong for some reason. They'd already confessed their past hurts to each other, and the clingy grasp of their thumbs seemed like a reminder of past mistakes.

Instinctively, as if that ability that all serious couples have—that ability to finish each other's sentences or know each other's thoughts—was already sparking, they playfully loosened their fingers, thumb wrestled until they laughed, then simply let their hands come together of their own accord.

The fingers of her hand were closed, save for her index finger, which was playfully dancing on his bent knee. Without thinking, he reached out and crossed it with his own index finger. They both saw it immediately; their fingers had formed a plus sign, and then remained still.

After a moment she giggled and said, "One…"

Without hesitation he smiled and replied, "Plus one."

From that day forwards, it was their thing. Yes, they said "I love you" from time to time too, but more often than not they eschewed it in favor of their secret phrase, which reminded them of the day even their hands knew they were meant to be together.

Not to grip, but to hold.

Not to subtract, but to add.

* * *

They traveled across the sky amid the clouds. It was a different mode than how Napoleon had traveled with The Gray Man in hell, much lighter, but it was no less awe-inspiring. The sun was hovering above the clouds, tingeing their tops orange and yellow.

Napoleon had forgotten the feeling of the wind on his face and how beautiful the sky looked. A part of him felt dirty, as if hell had permanently stained him with soot he couldn't see.

He still didn't feel right in his head, and the sense of living a life permanently inserted into the surreal was beginning to overtake him; he'd been from here to hell, from hell and then back again. The visages of angels and demons, forces that until now he couldn't have been sure were real, now left him feeling confused, overwhelmed and small.

The talk on the hill with Kyle Fasano hadn't helped any, either. Napoleon had put on a brave face, but inside he was baffled by it all: Parker getting pulled back into Beaury, Tamara Fasano being abducted. Everything that happened after he'd left with The Gray Man was insane, and though they'd escaped hell, the actual place of the damned, it felt like it had only followed them back to earth.

But now that he was here, there was only one thing on his mind, and he wasn't going to be able to focus on anything else until he dealt with it.

"Hey..." he said.

The Gray Man turned his head slightly. "Yes?"

"I know there's not much time, but I need a favor."

The Gray Man paused, blinked and then looked at Napoleon with understanding. "Your nephew?"

Napoleon sighed. "Yes. Please."

"I understand. . . . he's important to you. I will divert our course and drop you off there," The Gray Man said, then added, "There's no school this week. He's at the park playing."

Napoleon swallowed, feeling a lump in his throat at just knowing that Efren was still okay. Before long they descended lower to the ground and their surroundings were impossible to miss: East Los Angeles. Boyle Heights. Scoops of graffiti on brick walls between bent fences and dirty alleys. Home. He wished they had time to hit up Los Cinco Puntos for some carnitas and nopales.

They went down Cesar Chavez to Evergreen, past the cemetery, and then circled around to the left to Guirado Street and the elementary school, the small dots of people below slowly becoming recognizable as children playing basketball.

As they grew nearer it was their sounds, the shouts and giggles and screams of children at play, that brought an overwhelming sense of joy to Napoleon's heart. He was certain that if not for the wind blowing in his eyes, he would've cried. All he could say was, "Man."

"Yes," The Gray Man replied. "Of all the sounds of earth that I miss the most, this is it. There can be no purer joy than that which we feel as children."

They landed on the walkway between the basketball court and the old recreation room where Napoleon had played countless board games on rainy days as a child himself, decades before, and there was no mistaking Efren, in his slightly over-sized Lakers t-shirt, running a fast break with another boy down the court, dribbling the ball with one hand while trying to fend off another boy with the other.

He was, for all intents and purposes, the most beautiful thing Napoleon had seen in a very long time. Safe. Healthy. Precious.

"Does he see us?" Napoleon asked.

"No. We're concealed. Do you want him to?"

Napoleon nodded.

"It's the least I can do for the help you've given our cause, Villa. Go. Stand over there next to those trees by the fence so you will both have some privacy. When you get there, I will send him. Then I must get back to Kyle, okay?"

Napoleon did as he was asked.

After a few minutes and five or six baskets later, the boys stopped for a breather. Watching from a distance Napoleon could see Efren's head turn, first in one direction and then the other, as if he were looking for something. Then, quite firmly, his gaze fixed in Napoleon's direction. At first his face was painted in shock, then he bounced the ball to one of his friends, subbing him in for the next game, and quickly left the court.

He walked at first, in seeming disbelief, and then, with a smile as wide as hope can be deep, he shouted "¡*Tio!*" and broke into a dead run towards Napoleon.

His breath catching in his throat. Napoleon was sure that if he'd died right that second, he would have been the happiest man on earth.

CHAPTER 5

THEY HAD STOPPED SOMEWHERE in the desert. That was all Tamara could tell of the place. He'd built a fire and she could make out the outlines of a few Joshua trees nearby. Beyond them the sky was pitch black, the stars across it looking like spilled grains of salt.

He sat near the fire, with his back to her, about fifteen feet away from the car. This left her halfway between warm and freezing cold, depending on which way the wind blew, and even when the heat of the fire blew her way it was a mixed blessing, as it also carried smoke that made her cough.

When he'd pulled her out of the trunk she'd gotten another good look at him. He was calmer, more sedate, but the black of his eyes held the same hopelessness they had when he'd been beating her senseless with a sneer on his face. He was still crazy, but the madness had just retreated to his pupils and curled up there like a snake.

She begged him to let her pee, which he did, but he wouldn't look away as she squatted and he barked orders at her to hurry up. Every muscle in her body stiff, she nearly fell over twice into her own puddle of piss before she finished emptying her bladder.

He dragged her back to the car to her current position, where she now sat on her hip with her wrists tied in her lap, a length of chain going from them to some point just underneath the front bumper. She tried twice to quietly pull on it, only moving the chain a few links at a time across the sand so he wouldn't hear. But it was no use.

She was chained like a dog.

He had pulled a bag out of the car, absentmindedly tossing a bottled water and a bag of Fritos into her lap, before he'd set up the fire and began to heat a can of SpaghettiOs over the open flame.

He said nothing and sat nearly motionless, occasionally stabbing a stick in and out of the fire, his long, tousled hair going in all directions.

His silence was unnerving, so she tried not to focus on it.

Instead she ate her chips and drank the water and thanked God for saving her babies. She believed in her heart now that He had, so much so that she hadn't bothered to ask Him to save her yet. If this were her fate then she would accept it. All that mattered was that Janie and Seth were okay.

That left only one dangling thread in her life: Kyle.

After everything they'd been through, it was almost incomprehensible to her that she might die without ever knowing what had finally happened to her husband. Had he died in hell? Could someone actually survive such a place? What forces were their simple, puny, human lives caught up in anyway? And why? Sure, Kyle had been unfaithful. But hadn't countless other husbands, and wives? Why Kyle? What made his sin so unique that he'd become the plaything of the Gods?

She chastised herself for the blasphemy. It was "God," not "Gods," and He did not play with us.

"He loves us," she whispered softly, closing her eyes to remember her husband's face.

"No He doesn't." The monster's voice was hoarse and broken, and it startled her.

She looked up to see that he'd turned his head slightly to the side, as if he were looking back over his shoulder at her.

"How did you hear me?" she asked. "I barely even heard myself."

He shrugged. "I'm changing. I'm hearing things better, seeing things better."

"What?"

"But I'm not… understanding things much better."

Tamara had no idea what he was talking about, but she finally saw a chance to communicate with him, so she took it. "Listen. You don't want to hurt me. Please don't. Just let me go."

Turning his gaze back to the fire, he said nothing.

"I promise, I won't tell anyone about you. Not a thing."

Silence. He was back to poking his stick in the fire.

Tamara tried to speak with confidence, but she could also hear a tone of desperation creeping into her voice that she didn't like. "Listen. Please. I don't know why you've done this, but I don't care either. Just let me go."

At first he remained motionless. Then he shook his head.

"Why? Why can't you just let me go?"

"Because."

"Because why?"

"The scales must be balanced. Blood for blood."

"No."

"Yes," he said before adding words that were music to Tamara's ears. "It's bad enough I let your stupid kids get away."

She couldn't help herself. Her relief was so great she began to cry softly, pressing her chin against her breastbone as her lungs squeezed air into her emotions.

"Yes. Go ahead and cry. Sure. I fail on part of my mission, and while you beg for your life, you cry happy tears at my expense."

This time it was her turn to remain speechless.

"Admit it. You're happy, you dumb cow."

Tamara wondered if maybe she should just try to anger him into killing her, to end it, to end it all as quickly as possible. She was just beginning to contemplate what to say and how to say it when he spoke again and ruined it all.

"But don't be too happy. The master will find a way to get your kids. He's already sending others to finish the job."

The entire sky came crashing down upon her. "W-what did you say?"

Still with his back to her, he looked down and his head began to bob, slightly at first and then a bit more. At first she couldn't tell what was happening and then she heard his stifled laughs. He was chuckling. The bastard thought all this was funny.

Rage boiled into her. "Fuck you! Fuck you, you sonofabitch!"

"Shhhhhhhh..." he said, whipping his head to the side. Then again, "Shhhhhh."

Tamara yanked hard on the chain. It was no use, but she managed to get to her knees. "Let me go! Now!"

Again, he laughed.

"You tell your master, or whatever the hell he is, to leave my children alone."

He stretched, the bones in his back crackling like the dry desert wood on the fire, and spun around towards her, his physical presence suddenly ominous. "You don't listen very well, do you, cow?"

Tamara was aghast. "What?"

"Didn't you hear me!? I was trying to tell you, earlier.

I said, 'I'm not understanding things much better.' I'm just not."

"Not understanding what?"

"Why he won't let me."

"Let you do what?"

He stood up straight and looked down on her, whatever it was inside him looking as if it was barely contained again, and she wished he'd never turned around from his fire and his stupid SpaghettiOs, because what he said next left her colder than the desert ever could.

"I've asked him three times now if I can kill you, cook you and eat you," he said, reaching down to lift her chin and look at her, the snakes in his eyes now slithering back and forth as he gazed at her with a sad look on his face and added, "But he won't let me."

* * *

The captain sat at the patio table, one leg crossed over the other, his arms folded across his chest with a scowl on his face that was more weary than angry. After appearing to size Parker up for another moment, he sighed and finally spoke. "So. You want back in on this or not?"

Parker didn't hesitate. "Depends."

"Don't get cute, Parker."

"I'm not. It's just—"

"Just what?"

"It's a mess. All of it."

"No shit."

Parker shifted in his chair and cleared his throat. "I want in, but I don't at the same time."

"Understandable."

The kids were in the house with Murillo having Bomb

Pops from the freezer. Klink was walking the property for any clues. Besides them, it was just him and the captain. All the LAPD officers had gone back to the city, leaving behind a handful of La Canada sheriffs.

Before they'd had a chance to sit down, the watch commander had arrived on scene and talked briefly with the captain about this and that protocol, one or another agency now involved, paperwork and a whole host of other shit that bored Parker to death.

He walked away and sat down at the table and listened to the birdsong in the trees behind the Fasano residence and tried to tell himself to quit thinking. It hadn't worked. Now, with the captain sitting here wanting to talk, it only felt worse.

He was thinking about what he was and wasn't supposed to say. He and Tamara had made a deal, there in front of the Brasco home, seemingly a century ago. Should he have made that deal with her? Was all this his fault somehow? If they had come clean, up front, would any of this have happened?

The captain pressed him. "So?"

"Here's the thing. I didn't think it could get any worse than what happened to Nap. I really didn't."

"Mm-hmm. And we still don't know what that 'what' actually was."

Parker played along. "Right."

The captain nodded again. Parker continued.

"Then I get a call from Sheriff Conch asking me to informally help with his investigation in Beaury."

"Why and how?"

"He thought Fasano had backtracked his way through Beaury after disappearing in Monterey."

"Why?"

"Conch had a missing girl, which is major news in a

small town like that. He failed to see it as a coincidence that less than a week before she goes missing, we just happened to arrive looking for Kyle Fasano, who was wanted for what happened to Caitlyn Hall."

"Okay. Still. Murder and abduction, though not mutually exclusive, do not automatically make for a connection."

"I know. Of course. But again. Two major events in a small town like that... folks are going to automatically link them."

"Fair enough."

Parker leaned on the table with his hands folded in front of him. "Then it got weird. Fast."

"How?"

"At the workplace of the girl who went missing we find a business card defaced in the same way as one that Nap and I found in Monterey outside Victoria Brasco's wine shop."

"And I didn't get a call?"

"Conch told me he called you."

"He did. But only to tell me that he was working on something and 'might' be needing your help. I told my assistant to call him and tell him fine. You were on suspension. Your time was your time. But I thought he meant he'd be *calling* you, not pulling you into an active role in his investigation."

"Well. Shit took off fast."

"Yeah?"

"Yeah. Next thing we know we have a second girl go off the radar. Except this one was different."

"How so?"

"This was a girl Nap and I had actually interviewed, and she'd ID'd Fasano."

A grim shadow came over the captain's eyes. "And you didn't call me immediately?"

Parker sighed. This was the part he knew was bad for him. "Look. I'm not going to lie. I was afraid to."

"What?"

"I was afraid that once you heard the possible connections were strengthening, you'd yank me out of Beaury and send in someone else."

"You're damn straight I would've. You were already suspended for what happened in Monterey. Or didn't happen."

"Exactly. I knew you wouldn't trust me."

"Incorrect," the captain said firmly, unfolding his arms and placing them on the armrests of his chair. "Look. Parker. You're a good cop and you might still have a future as a good detective. But common sense, to any DA that could be roped into this thing, is to keep a suspended officer off any other case that could tie back to the case he was suspended from. You get that, right?"

Parker nodded.

"It's nothing personal."

"It isn't?" Parker said in an accusatory tone, remembering the conversation he'd had with Napoleon in front of Larry Klein's residence in La Jolla, the "lay it all on the table" chat. Nap had tried to talk him into leaving the case, because it was a dog that would destroy Parker's young career. Nap was close enough to retirement age to not care. But they'd both decided that the captain didn't have either of their backs. Not one bit.

"Why would you think that?"

"You sent us on a fucking US Marshall's goose chase, that's why, and then rode us when we didn't get results fast enough for anyone to realistically be able to expect them."

"Look—"

"Cap. Please. Let me finish."

The red was back in his cheeks, but the captain motioned for Parker to go on.

"We made mistakes because we were so rushed. Mistakes that cost us."

"What kind of mistakes?"

"You've read the report, dammit! The red herrings Fasano placed in the computers at the Beaury Public Library. The bus ruse. The calling card. I may be new on the job, but Nap? There's no way we play the Keystone Cops like that, no way we fail that badly, if we weren't set up to fail in the first place."

"Listen. If you're saying what I think you're saying? Get up and walk the fuck outta here. Go to your union rep. Get a transfer and never speak to me again, because I would never…"—his jaw tensed hard as he leaned across the table and pointed an angry finger in Parker's face—"… ever set my people up to fail. So fuck you for saying it."

In the backyard, there was a whir of leaves in the trees and the soft drone of very distant traffic. No matter where you went in LA, it sounded like traffic. Parker thought of walking away, but that would get him nowhere, especially with protecting the kids, which he had to do until they at least got into their aunt's hands. Also, a part of him felt he was owed an explanation, so he went for it.

"Fine, Cap. Then tell me: why?"

The captain had evidently expected him to get up and storm off, because he blinked in surprise and bit down on his lip as his face contorted in preparation for another outburst. Instead, suddenly, his expression melted, the anger dripping off him like butter as his eyes grew suddenly soft.

"Look, Parker," he tried to begin, and then he leaned back in his chair and stared into the pool with a look of resignation before trying again. "Look. This case has been a bucket of hot grease since the moment it was opened."

Parker said nothing as the captain loosened his tie and rubbed at his neck. The eczema had spread down over his Adam's apple. "When you and Nap started on the case I thought we had a plan, an operable way to get this guy quick, and the heat I put on you two, I swear, it was one tenth the heat I was getting from the DA and City Hall. I mean, they went apeshit over this. Hall's dad had more friends than you can imagine, fucking power whores, all of them. I couldn't leave my office to take a dump without that phone ringing with someone pushing or pulling on me."

"That makes it right?"

"No. Of course it doesn't. You'll see someday that sometimes the circumstances of your situation… shit, I'll just say it: they overwhelm you."

Parker waited to get angry, but he didn't. Something in him reminded him of the kid in Kamdesh who took his bullet in the back and the feeling of constantly being the next domino in an endless row of falling blackness. The captain was wrong. Parker didn't need to wait until "someday" to know what it felt like to be overwhelmed by your circumstances.

The captain sighed, suddenly looking like a frail old man, as human and messed up as the next. "You understand?"

"I do." And then, in semi-disbelief that he was actually saying it, Parker told him about the boy. Again, he was being guided by something inside of him. His conscience, maybe? Who knew. But it was the same something that had told him to look to the side of the road on his drive up to Beaury, after that horrible car accident, when he'd seen that angel.

It was a something that told Parker that right now, at this moment, he needed to tell the captain something truthful, something important. And since he still felt like he couldn't say a word about what really happened to Napoleon, he chose the only great truth he had left, the truth of his greatest sin.

When he was done the captain glanced away and then back at him quickly. "So you *do* get it."

"Yeah, man. I do. Please. Reinstate me. Let me get to work on this."

The words crossed the table, the pleas like punches from one beaten man to another.

The captain looked solemnly at Parker and then nodded. "Done. Now, let's talk. What next?"

Parker felt his insides shift again. It was clear what he was supposed to do: protect the children. It was counter-intuitive to every fiber in his being that screamed for him to go after Troy Forester, for what he'd done to Conch and what he may have already done to Tamara Fasano. But he just knew that wasn't what he was supposed to do.

"I gotta believe that Fasano, at some point, is going to come home. I think, for now at least? I stay here."

The surprise on the captain's face was almost comical. "What?"

"Think about it, Cap. This bastard has been one step ahead of us the whole way. Instead of chasing him, maybe it's time to stop and just wait for him."

"Go on."

"We have to assume that he's still out there somewhere. He's gonna hear what happened here, that his wife's missing, abducted by some psychopath."

"Assuming he doesn't already know said psychopath."

Parker shook his head. "No way."

"So you're going with coincidence on this? Did Napoleon ever tell you his theory about coincidences?"

"He thought they were all bullshit."

"Exactly."

"I agree. Ninety-nine percent of the time, they are. But nothing in the universe is absolute." Parker thought of The Gray Angel in front of the Brasco house that had been so bright he'd nearly struck Parker blind. He knew in his heart, beyond a shadow of a doubt, that somehow, Fasano and Troy Forester were connected, just not in the way that the captain was thinking.

"So after all I've just shared with you, you're asking me to ride with the one percent odds?" the captain said with a chuckle and a look of dismay.

"No. I want you to ride with the fact that this guy, if he's still alive? He's gonna come for his kids. He'll have to. What father wouldn't? I can almost guarantee it."

Parker noticed a squirrel doing four-legged ballet moves across the top of the neighbors' wrought iron fence. The Fasanos also had a lemon tree in the backyard that he hadn't noticed until now. Meyer lemons. His favorite. He waited.

He'd been here before, many times, in this place of "patient reserve," usually when they were on point in the hills, when the platoon would fan out, some to his left, others to his right, and wait for the moment to present itself. There was nothing more to do but wait for it. It would come. One way or another, it always did.

Finally, the captain grunted and said, "Fine. You're on the children."

Parker would've smiled if not for an intense feeling of relief that nearly made him nauseous.

Because his gut told him that it wasn't Fasano who was coming for the kids, but something else.

And he wasn't sure he wanted to find out what.

CHAPTER 6

IT WAS LIKE WATCHING the world on fast forward—blurred landscapes, open desert to rolling hills of shrubbery, across small towns and through streets—until they finally came to a stop at a mailbox on the corner. The Gray Man seemed to be studying something in the dirt near it, tire tracks perhaps, or a spot of fresh oil, before the video wound forwards, again and again, to the train car McDonald's in Barstow, then to another spot, Schat's Bakkery, where they made the best jalapeno cheese bread in the world and which was barely more than a smudged image as they zipped along to a gas station, then a four-way stop beyond that, and finally a hard left out of town and back to the open road.

Each time they came to a stop The Gray Man focused on something, or picked something up, or stared off into the distance, as if the clues were all around them now, on hairs accidentally caught in the wind or in dust motes that had settled on something seemingly inconsequential.

Kyle realized with a measure of fascination that The Gray Man really was a kind of heavenly detective, and that he was teaching Kyle to become one too. Already he felt… more in tune… with space and time, in what The Gray Man was doing, how he was doing it and why. If it weren't for his incessant worry over Tamara's safety, Kyle might have actually been able focus on it all.

They were heading north-east, across the open desert, when the video finally stopped and the world around them crystalized to something that felt more like reality.

The Gray Man looked confused.

"What's wrong?" Kyle asked.

"I've lost it."

"Lost what?"

"His trail. Or rather, the markers that make up his trail."

"What now?"

"We exercise patience. We wait. Something will be revealed in time."

"But Tamara—"

"Yes. I know," The Gray Man said with a sigh. "But we cannot act on information that we don't have yet, Kyle."

They stood in silence for a moment as a lizard scrambled by, over a small rock and then up the face of large bolder, its greenish-brown scales flat and dull beneath the setting sun.

"What was all that, what we just did?"

"We're tracking, Kyle. Much like the hunters in your world do each day. But on a much finer scale."

"You mean, like by scent?"

"Not really. More like… by what you would call 'aura.'"

"Hmm."

"Each of you has one. The next time we stop in a populated area, take a quick moment, call on the blue and reach out with it."

"Reach out?"

"Yes. With your mind this time, though. Not how you've been doing it: with anger or fear, to attack or defend. Instead, calm your heart and mind, and instead of lashing out with it, let the blue simply emanate outward."

"Emanate?"

"Yes. Like ripples. Small waves will push out of you and you will see them, the hues and colors that tell you who a person is, what they're made of and the mood that they're in. Three colors that will rotate in fairly rapid succession."

"Really? That sounds incredible."

The Gray Man removed his hat and wiped his sleeve across his brow. He was squinting into the distance as he spoke. "It is. At first you will be amazed and thrilled, but I think it's okay to warn you that, eventually, you're just as likely to see it as a terrible gift."

Kyle was perplexed. "How so?"

"In our world, in the world you are slowly becoming a part of, you can see it."

"See what?"

"Sin. How it has corrupted someone, and the propensity a given person has to engage in it. As such, you see the creatures that are tormenting them, mostly minor demons of temptation, from the place we just escaped."

"Then what? You step in and destroy them?"

The Gray Man chuckled sadly and shook his head. "No, unfortunately. The amazing thing about humanity, about being human, is that the creatures are almost always there by your own invitations."

Kyle said nothing. Instead he took note of the wrinkles in The Gray Man's forehead, which were more pronounced now.

"What you all do with your free will… the way you torment yourselves? It's tragic. But if we stepped in and intervened every time? You'd have no free will."

Kyle decided that it was time to ask. "You were human too, once, right?"

The Gray Man nodded. "Yes. But one man's misery, contained within the capsule of his own lifetime, is one thing. Being raised to a state where you can see such miseries from person to person, soul to soul, across hundreds and thousands of lives? It's almost too much to bear."

For some reason Kyle felt dizzy. Perhaps the aftereffects of the travel they'd just engaged in. "Then why do it?"

The Gray Man raised his eyebrows. "Because some of us are meant for it."

"Am I meant for it?"

"No," The Gray Man said, shaking his head firmly. "You were called for it."

"There's a difference?"

"Oh, yes. A vast one."

"How so?"

Again The Gray Man shook his head. "Another time, perhaps. That, for now, you do not get to know."

Kyle nodded reluctantly. "Okay then. So? Teach me. You're tracking their… auras, their hues or whatever, now?"

"Trying to. But they've faded."

"I had ideas while we were traveling, about hair and dust in the air?"

"Yes. Biological residue is harder to track but sometimes necessary."

Kyle knitted up his brow. "But what could possibly be on dust?"

The Gray Man smiled. "He sneezed."

"What?"

"The man we're after, the one who has Tamara? He sneezed. His DNA was on the dust."

Kyle was dumbfounded.

"The problem is that dust travels, swiftly and far. So we must then ascertain when he sneezed and at what distance."

"You can do that?"

"Manipulate time? Very little. But as you've noticed in the past, when you've been attacked, like with the boy on the bike, how things slow down?"

Kyle nodded as he stretched. He'd lost weight. A lot of it. His belly felt tight beneath his shirt. "Yeah. I remember."

"That's the effect of my world engaging directly with yours, and it leaves a wrinkle in time, a crease of sorts."

"And you can see that too?"

"Yes. So, I can roughly estimate that he was through here, this area, about twelve hours ago."

"That doesn't help much."

"No," The Gray Man said with a nod, "it doesn't. And the sample size of the dust was too old to get a more accurate reading. The distance it travelled, though, wasn't far, based on the windage on it the past twelve hours, and the fact that the particular sample we found was stuck to something."

"What?"

"That mailbox."

"Which leads us to do what, now?"

"If we were in a large city? Not much. We'd be relying more on auras there than we can here, and less on the biological clues. In cities the auras are reflected and re-reflected, in building windows, across car windows, in chrome fixtures and metallic frames. They're embedded, albeit briefly, in such things, far better than they are out here, in the open sky and desert. Since that's our situation, we need something else to drift our way or catch our eye."

"But that could take hours."

The Gray Man held up his hand in a quieting gesture, nodding softly for a brief moment before he fixed his attention once again on the horizon. As restless and desperate as Kyle felt, he sensed it would be no use to protest.

And it did take hours. Just over two of them, actually. The sun set and the desert sky turned a cobalt blue before The Gray Man's head suddenly snapped up and his jaw stiffened.

"What is it?"

"Words."

Kyle was stunned. "What? What words?"

The Gray Man hesitated, as if he didn't want to answer.

"Gray?"

"She's praying, Kyle. I can hear her."

"She's alive?" Kyle felt his chest burst with relief as he leaned over and put his hands on his knees. "Oh, thank God. Thank God."

The Gray Man nodded. "Yes. Amen. I couldn't hear her before, her proximity to him being the likely cause."

"What do you mean?"

The Gray Man sounded concerned. "His evil, his state of being, it is a darkness so great that it stifles the light and mutes her prayers."

"So how did you finally hear her?"

"He must have fallen asleep."

A semi rolled down a highway road in the distance.

"We're still very far behind them," The Gray Man said, shaking his head.

"Why do you say that?"

"Because this prayer was from last night. She's referenced the moon and the stars. She was thanking Our Father for the light they were giving her…" He paused, tilting his head back and then forwards in deep concentration. "She was contemplating a way to escape and asking for his help, but more than that—"

The Gray Man stopped as a look of love and sorrow, mixed twins, wrestled in his face.

"What? Tell me, Gray. What?"

He put his hands on his hips and nodded softly, his hat tipping a bit over his forehead. "She was praying, above all, for Janie and Seth."

Kyle felt his emotions beginning to overwhelm him. Tamara. His girl. She'd always been his girl, but then she'd become the mother of his children, and in so doing, the math that made her so special a woman only multiplied. How had he been so blind? So stupid? To risk her. To risk it all for nothing, really? "My God. Gray. What have I done?"

The Gray Man turned to Kyle and put a hand on his shoulder as the air around them grew warm and the video began to play again, a click and a whir as they lifted off the ground.

"Many are the men who make grave mistakes and carry them to their graves, Kyle. But it is a rare man who faces them head on and seeks redemption. Do not lose heart."

Tears were filling Kyle's eyes. "Why? Why shouldn't I?"

The Gray Man looked at him solemnly.

"Because she was also praying for *you*, Kyle."

* * *

They sat together in the tall grass, the smell of dirt filling their nostrils, as Napoleon deflected Efren's questions about where he'd been and instead got the boy talking about himself. About the simplest, most beautiful things in life: schoolwork, his little league team, the newest Goldfish crackers (Flavor Blasted Extreme!) and the dark-haired girl that he liked in his class. Napoleon hadn't been gone that long since the Fasano case first came across his desk, but it felt like centuries.

Once past his joy at seeing Efren, Napoleon knew he had to do the unthinkable: ask him to lie.

"*¿Por qué, Tio?*"

"Because, *mijo*. No one can know that I'm back. Not yet. I'm on a very secret mission. You could put people in danger, do you understand?"

Efren nodded as he pulled his jersey up to wipe the sweat off his face. "But you're coming home soon, Tio. Right?"

"Absolutely," Napoleon said. "Why is school out, anyway?"

"Flex schedule. We didn't even go that long and now we're off again."

"You keepin' busy?"

"Yeah. Friday we have a special double header at the park for Cinco de Mayo. First game's at ten. I wish you could come, Tio."

"Okay, *jefe*, I'll do my best."

An old man was rolling a fruit cart down the cement path that divided the park. A piece of cantaloupe with some chili powder sounded beyond good right now, but Napoleon knew there wasn't time. Parker was in trouble, and so was Mrs. Fasano. This moment was a gift, but it was one meant to be enjoyed only briefly.

Efren suddenly got to his knees, leaned over and hugged him. Napoleon could feel the boy's ribs through his shirt, small and fragile, and cupping the small of his back, Napoleon pulled him close and squeezed him hard. They stayed that way as a breeze swept over them both and Napoleon whispered words of advice to his nephew as his heart swelled: Don't swing at the outside pitches, stay focused on your grades, tell her how you feel because not knowing is the worst kind of knowing of all.

"You know, when you disappeared, Tio?"

"Yeah?"

"Mom started taking us to church. Philomena's."

His sister was never one for religion. Napoleon was genuinely surprised. "Really?"

"Yeah. Me and Mom? We've been lighting candles for you, Tio. I been praying every day, in the morning and the night and at every meal. I even know the Lord's Prayer now."

Napoleon felt his legs going weak. He couldn't speak.

"I been asking God to please bring you back... and look! He did, Tio! He did!"

Napoleon swallowed hard, forcing his Adam's apple back down his throat. He couldn't cry. It would freak Efren out for sure. He felt panicked, unsure of what to do or say next.

"Yes, *mijo*. He did. And He'll bring me back again. But I gotta go now, *jefe*, okay?"

Efren nodded. As they separated, Napoleon looked one last time into his nephew's big brown eyes. They were wide-awake with trust and happiness.

A lady in a white hat was walking her poodle in the distance, negotiating the open space between two kids who'd just finished playing catch with a football. The air and trees seemed to paint the moment in Napoleon's mind. He messed Efren's hair and then got up and began to walk away. After a few steps he turned back.

"Hey, buddy?"

Efren, who was already jogging back to the basketball court, stopped and turned. "Yeah?"

"What's her name?"

Efren smiled sheepishly. "Catalina."

Napoleon smiled and nodded before turning again to leave. He made his way through the trees and out onto the street before he finally lost it and the tears came. Leaning on a light post, he took a few deep breaths, his lungs unable to hold the air properly. Before long he felt a sort of peace come over him, as if he weren't alone, as if someone were there.

He didn't dare, but then he did. "God?" he cried. "It hurts… and I shouldn't have done that. I shouldn't have promised him that I'd be back. Because what if I'm not?"

Silence. But it was not a still silence; it was active, alive, aware.

"Help me to fulfill that promise, Father. Please."

A gust of wind rushed over Napoleon in a blanket of comfort, drying his tears as it separated his eyelashes and dried them to his cheeks.

CHAPTER 7

MORNING SPREAD LIKE SPILLED orange juice across the blue sky. Tamara had to blink more than once to take it in. She'd cried herself to sleep under the weight of pure exhaustion; her eyes felt swollen and her head hurt.

She'd experienced the kind of sleep one might expect when someone who wanted to kill and eat you was only ten feet away: light and guarded, a barely-happening sort of sleep that left you weaker than when you first went to lie down. But, still, it was better than nothing.

Behind the sunrise, the moon was still holding court in the sky, refusing yet to step off the stage of the world. She sighed. What was she going to do? How was she going to survive this?

She heard him before she saw him. He was jabbing a stick at the fire again, this time trying to bring it back to life, a camping pot over the now weak and desperate embers.

Seeing her awake, he smiled. "Good morning."

She said nothing, because there was nothing to say.

"That's it? No 'hello'? No 'top of the morning to ya'?" He chuckled, shaking his head. "That's not very nice now, is it?"

She tried to speak but her voice was jammed. Clearing her throat she finally replied, "Would it make any difference if I was? Nice, I mean?"

He looked at her, but somehow, now, amid the light, he did not seem nearly as ominous. Just a man. A skinny man with a mop of dark hair, hallowed cheeks and a week's worth of beard.

She pressed. "I mean, does it ever do any good to be kind to your kidnapper?"

He raised his eyebrows, pursed his lips and gave a quick nod. "No. I suppose not."

"You're going to kill me one way or the other, right?"

Again, he nodded.

"So," Tamara said, gritting her teeth, "why bother with all the pleasantries?"

He chuckled again and stood up, the legs of his dirty jeans scraping against one another as he did. "Fair enough."

Perhaps it was the sunrise, or the fire, but for a split second she was in Bolivia again, a child, with her parents.

As missionaries they often dealt with the ebb and flow of participants who wanted to hear The Word. Sometimes her father would be preaching it to fifty people, sometimes ten. Her parents told her that it didn't really matter. The Lord brought to their camp, there on the edge of a meadow that was stamped between their village and the jungle, whomever He knew needed to hear her father's words, when they needed to hear them. "Tam," her dad had said one day, "it's not the count that matters, but the heart that does the counting."

It was a frequent refrain of her father's: the focus on inward perception over outer.

She looked at the ground, feeling the chains around her wrists grating against the bumper of the car, and wondered silently what her dad would think of this situation.

Then, quickly, she realized the answer: he would focus on having heart. To endure. To overcome. No question about it.

Somehow, she had to find the heart to get out of this, for the kids, yes, but the new day brought with it a few rays of brutal honesty. She wanted out for herself too. She wasn't ready to die yet. She still had a lot of living to do, many things to see and experience before her end.

She had to find the heart, but also the will. To survive.

"Not a problem," she whispered.

"What was that?" he said tersely.

"Nothing. Just rambling."

He grunted and turned to face her, and she noticed he was wearing a Def Leppard t-shirt. That was an '80s band, before her time, which made him older than her probably. His shoulder blades were jabbing at the stitching in the shirt and she tried to guess his weight. He was heavier than her, for sure, but not by a whole lot. It wasn't like she was going to have to face off with Vin Diesel if she got a chance to fight him.

She wondered if it was okay to pray for the opportunity to kill someone and decided that it probably wasn't.

"So what's for breakfast?" she asked with a yawn, trying to act calm even as she began to shiver a bit against the morning air.

"Coffee," he said, pointing at the pot, "and I got a bag of Hostess Crumb Donettes over here. But who says you're getting any?"

She shrugged. "You've kept me alive this long for a reason."

"No, I haven't."

"Okay. Then whoever you have to answer to has."

"And?"

"How can I stay alive if you don't give me any food or water?"

He squinted at her, hard and cruel. A wave of shivers rolled over her that had nothing to do with the morning air. "You'd be surprised how long you could last," he said with a sneer.

She looked away from him, and then reminded herself to have heart, to have will, and looked back. "Okay then. Well. Fuck you too."

He gave her a stunned look, and then began to laugh, softly at first, before it grew into a full-blown cackle. "Oh, man. This is gonna be fun!"

You didn't have to be a genius to know that knowledge was everything in this situation. Seeing her chance to get some, she took it. "What is?"

"Your ending. My beginning."

"Yeah?"

"Yeah. I just don't know why it's taking so long to get the command."

Tamara set her chin for a second. *Shit. He's a complete wing nut.* "Command?"

He nodded, then suddenly seemed confused, lost almost, in his thoughts. Then, tentatively, almost like a child, he said, "I think it's a test."

Just keep him talking. "A test?"

"Yes. To see if I'm ready, ya know. For the next step. Do you know what I mean?"

Tamara shook her head.

"You regular people don't realize it but there are some of us in the world… we just choose this path, ya know?"

"Choose what path?"

"Evil."

A bubble of silence formed between them for a few seconds. She bit her lip, and then popped it. "Really?"

"You think I'm kidding, don't you?" he said, smiling again. His teeth were yellow and she noticed that one of his ears was deformed. Seeing her look at it, he reached up to caress it.

"He was evil too, ya know."

"Who?"

"My dear old dad." He chuckled. "He did this to my ear, in case you're wondering, for not taking out the trash."

Bit by bit he was revealing things, like a crossword puzzle in faded ink.

"I'm sorry," she said, in spite of herself.

"Oh, don't be," he replied with a shrug. "He helped make me the man I am today."

She struggled for words, but it was no use, they weren't coming, so she just waited for him to continue.

"It was really the only time he ever touched me. Mom drew the line there. Moms usually do," he said before looking at her in a different light now, a sliver of pity holding firm in the tilt of his eyebrows. "Like you and *your* kids, ya know? You put up a big fight back there. You sure drew the line, I'll give you that."

She switched gears, knowing that she needed to exploit his pity as quickly as she could, because it probably wouldn't last long. "So… tell me something."

He lifted his chin to her. "Shoot."

"My kids. Please tell me you didn't hurt them before they got away, did you?"

He looked away, out over to the horizon, before looking back at her. "No."

Relief washed over her. "Thank God."

Suddenly his face went hard again. Like a rock. "See. You've chosen too."

"What?"

"Your puppet master. Your… 'God .' You've chosen Him over my master, the True Master. Do you understand?"

Oddly, she did. Who else could a sick bastard like this be serving besides the devil himself? "Yeah. I guess I do."

"I see that pretty silver cross around your neck and I promise, I will feed it to you right before the end, okay?"

His eyes were back to being filled with cruel intent, forcing her to divert her gaze. She noticed a scorpion moving lazily over a boulder behind him. Sadly, in the wrong direction. She felt scared and vulnerable.

Have heart, you must have heart. Make your stand.

"Fine," Tamara said, holding her lower lip in check. "But only if I don't kill you first, okay?"

He blinked again and tilted his head to the side, as if studying her. Rubbing his chin with his left hand, he squinted at her. "Wow. Ya know, I've had a lot of girls talk tough before, it's a defense mechanism kinda thing, I think. But they don't mean it. They're fronting. I can tell. But you? Hmm. You're different. Bitch, I think you mean it."

Walking over to the fire he pulled open a duffel bag and produced two coffee cups. He whistled softly as he poured them each a cup and then he produced the magic packet of Donettes. Her stomach rumbled at the sight of them as he split the pack open and set three aside for himself before bringing the packet and a coffee cup over to her.

He fed her the Donettes one by one, lifting the coffee cup up to her lips for each sip, not giving her the chance to throw something hot into his face, whistling the whole time. The coffee was black, and burned her parched throat, but she drank it, the strength of the caffeine offset by the sweetness of the Donettes. She tried to ignore his fingers as he ran them softly over her lower lip or caressed her cheekbones. When she was done he cupped his hand under her chin, lifted it gently and looked at her intently. "You're special," he said in a dreamy voice.

When he stood up to walk away, she noticed something that made her stomach turn.

He had an erection.

* * *

Trudy O'Hara was almost exactly what Parker expected. He'd grown up in an Irish neighborhood. Be it first generation or fifth, the Irish girls were almost always spitfires. Straight from central casting, Trudy had sharp green eyes and deep-red hair that matched the small spattering of freckles over each cheek.

She came into the Fasano home hell-bent on getting to the children, with most everyone moving quickly out of her way when she spat Murillo's name or asked to speak with Captain Bennett.

Only one poor bastard, a La Canada sheriff with a close-cropped haircut, tried to cut her off and all that got him was a holy fit. Trudy threw her purse to the floor and let loose a deluge of longshoreman-worthy expletives the sheriff was evidently not accustomed to hearing, at least from a woman. He backed up, stunned, and puffed out his chest in some sort of instinctive reassertion of his alpha male status, but it was too late. He'd been demoted down to gamma or some other letter in the Greek alphabet that no one knew about. Parker almost felt sorry for him; the other two sheriffs present would eat him alive at the station later.

"I want to see the kids, right now!" she yelled, shock and horror from seeing the disarray inside the house still plastered on her face.

Parker had gone along with a rep from Child Protective Services to a nearby women's shelter overnight. This morning they'd come back to the house to meet Ms. O'Hara because she had insisted that she knew where a copy of the Fasanos' will was, naming her as guardian if anything happened to them, and so she could pack up stuff for the kids if that were the case. CPS had thought it a bad idea to bring the kids back into the home, so they were outside in their caseworker's blue minivan awaiting the outcome.

The crime scene techs had cordoned off entire sections of the inside of the house before they'd left the day before, so Ms. O'Hara was channeled by yellow tape, plastic sheeting and fate directly towards Parker.

Taking his life in his hands, Parker decided that he too would try and step in front of her.

She was fit, about five foot seven, with taut arms. She was wearing black yoga pants, white tennis shoes and a pale blue Nike sweatshirt top that reached to just below her pants. Her jaw dropped as she saw Parker in her way.

The eye roll to the heavens that followed told Parker he was in for it. She fixed her glare on him and was no doubt just about to explain to him how seriously his life was at risk when he cut her off. "Ms. O'Hara?"

She paused, took a deep breath and tersely replied, "Yes?"

"I'm Detective Parker, with the Los Angeles Police Department."

"Are you in charge here?"

"No ma'am, but I—"

"Then why in the hell am I talking to you?"

"Listen—"

"I just took the first flight in from San Francisco this morning; I grabbed a rental and was on the phone the whole way here. Screw this. Where's Detective Murillo or Captain Bennett? That's all I want to know and the only people I want to talk to."

"The captain's not here," Parker said truthfully before he tossed in a little white lie because he wanted her to himself for a bit, "and Detective Murillo is currently unavailable, but I'm allowed to take you to the kids."

Body language told you a lot. She took a small step back and put her hands on her hips. "So?"

"Before I do, I have a few questions to ask though, all required." Another lie.

This prompted a small shake of her head as she folded her arms across her chest. "Listen, Detective… what was it again?"

"Parker."

"Parker. Yes. Okay. Let me make this clear. My best friend has been kidnapped or something." And with that, her voice momentary stuttered, as if she might've felt that by saying it she was somehow now risking darker thoughts. It took two seconds, tops, for her to get back her fury. "And her children, who are like my children too, need me. Do you understand?"

"Yes, but—"

"But my ass," she said, hands back on her hips, but balled up into fists this time. "I'm not answering shit until I see them and know they're okay. Are. We. Clear?"

Parker scratched his temple as his will drained out of him. This was cruel, and stupid. What he had to know he could find out later, and the earnest, almost desperate look on her face now was more than he could take. She looked like she was about to cry, and well, when Irish girls cried people were almost guaranteed to get physically hurt, usually bad. Holding up his hands in a "whoa" sort of gesture, he nodded and said, "Follow me."

They moved from near the patio to back inside the house and away from the news helicopter that had arrived about an hour ago and was still buzzing overhead like a fat metal bee in the blue sky.

As he led her through the kitchen he remembered the odd behavior of the kids the night before—how Janie had nearly tripped herself and the policeman next to her up as she made a sharp, urgent attempt to avoid an old rusted lantern that was sitting on the kitchen counter. The policeman had caught her before she fell and tried to make a joke of it, totally clueless as to what had suddenly spooked her. But Parker had seen it, clear as day.

The second odd behavior manifested itself a few minutes later as the same poor policeman, Officer Wall, had naturally assumed that the kids might want to go to their bedrooms for pajamas or something. The kids had both stopped in the hall, frozen stiff and staring at the girl's bedroom door, eyes wide, Janie clutching at Seth as the little boy clutched his stuffed animal.

Officer Wall had looked back at Parker with bewilderment in his eyes. Deciding to help, Parker simply asked the kids if they'd rather pass on pajamas. They did.

But it was all a bit odd. A lantern and a room, each separate from the foyer, where their mother had been attacked and taken from them. As they left the house for the ride to the shelter Parker couldn't shake the feeling that something else was going on.

Now, as he led Ms. O'Hara back out to the front driveway he sensed an odd pressure in the house, as if a cloud or heavy fog had settled into the rafters and the walls. It didn't give him an immediate sense of danger, but rather a permeating sense of unease. The place didn't feel haunted or anything. It felt… occupied. Haunted houses were scary. This house was different. This one felt… threatening.

Ms. O'Hara was riding his hip out the front door and down the driveway, pissed that the kids were in a vehicle she'd just walked past on the way in, before she bypassed

Parker entirely, nearly shoving him out of the way, her right hand pressing at his forearm with a strength that seemed beyond her size. Adrenaline. She advanced to the minivan, deliberate and determined.

She hesitated though, for just a split second, when she grabbed the door handle, and then she opened the door.

When the kids saw her it was as if an angel of heaven had descended into their midst. She nearly stumbled as they leapt into her embrace and the three of them clutched each other and broke into tears, which became sobs and then a series of garbled questions and concerns.

Parker only caught one of them, little Seth, begging for Trudy to tell him that his mother wasn't dead. That's when Parker decided that he could take no more. He motioned for one of the sheriffs to come watch over them and then, not having anything to do for a bit, Parker decided he might as well go to Janie's bedroom and poke around.

CHAPTER 8

THEY WERE IN A ghost town, plain and simple. A dozen buildings, squat and dilapidated, in various stages of rot, stood like markers from a distant past, their wood exposed and almost moaning beneath yet another brutally hot day, after enduring thousands of days just like it.

To Kyle's left were four buildings, only one of which still had faded signage to identify it as an old tack and feed shop. To his right were five more buildings and a monument made of an old stone and mortar block with wagon wheels affixed to either side. Walking over to investigate it closer, Kyle read the plaque on the monument that identified the place as an old watering hole, located next to the Carson River and used in the mid-1800s by settlers traveling west on the California trail. There was a sign mounted on a single wooden post at the entrance, giving the place a name: Ragtown.

Meanwhile, oddly, The Gray Man remained standing directly in the center of the old dirt road, frozen in place, as he had been since they'd arrived five minutes earlier.

Finally, Kyle couldn't take it anymore. "Gray?"

"Many of them didn't make it," he replied.

Kyle was confused. "Who?"

"The settlers that came through this place. It was a forty-mile haul with no water holes just to get here. Many died along the way. Many took ill and were left behind. If we traveled east, we could see them still."

"See what?"

"The shallow graves across the terrain, still visible after all this time."

"How?"

"Some go into the ground more beaten than they could ever become after death," The Gray Man said sadly. "As such, their graves seep with sorrow that no amount of dirt, no amount of time, could ever hide."

"And those that did make it here?"

"A brief respite, at best, to pour water down their parched throats and to clean their dust-encrusted clothes. Hence the town's name."

Motioning Kyle to come closer, The Gray Man put his arm over his shoulder and leaned in. "Like I told you earlier: call on the blue. But do so softly, almost pleadingly. Demand nothing."

Kyle was afraid. It didn't matter how many times he called on the force now within him, he wasn't getting used to it. It was a power that brought with it the heavy weight of responsibility. It also felt like a little bit of himself disappeared each time he used it.

Nonetheless, as per The Gray Man's instructions, he called on it now. He breathed in softly through his nose and exhaled deeply through his mouth, almost trembling when the warmth arrived in his chest. But this time it did not spread to his arms and hands. It simply settled there, in his lungs, like menthol.

"Good," The Gray Man encouraged softly. "Now, push it upwards this time, to your eyes, and beyond them to your mind."

At first Kyle couldn't get the warmth, the feeling of the blue, to move at all. It simply wouldn't budge. Then it began to, with a wisp of energy that pulled behind it more of itself, working its way up through his throat and jaw. He'd closed his eyes, but when the blue reached them and then hopscotched to his mind, they were forced open again, and he caught his breath in wonder at what he saw.

"Keep calm," The Gray Man said. "This is the power, manifested as awareness."

Kyle blinked. The world around him was now an electric blue of various shades. The buildings and a nearby cactus were outlined in bold, and the day sky and night sky were no longer divorced but merely one blue template laid over another, so that the sun and moon were married with the clouds and stars. Again, Kyle became aware of just how limited human perception was. A sudden wave of panic hit him, as if a part of his mind were trying to revolt.

"Focus! Ignore your fears and ignore everything your mind is telling you right now. Focus on the blue. Don't let go of it, let it spread."

Kyle's breathing was shallow but he did as he was instructed. "O-okay."

"Pull the lens of your mind back. Your focus is too wide now."

"How?"

"Do you feel it? That pressure just inside your forehead?"

Kyle did. Like a rubber band pulled tight, one end affixed just above his nose and the other end attached to somewhere in his brain. "Yes. I do."

"Focus on releasing that tautness."

Kyle obeyed and it almost felt as if something inside him, inside the blue, or perhaps whatever had sent the blue in the first place, was helping him. The Gray Man had used the perfect word: lens. As he took the picture of the world around him and pulled it in; the images became closer, more localized and more pertinent to the area around his body.

But the picture he was now presented with was no less overwhelming.

"Do you see them?" The Gray Man coaxed.

Kyle could barely speak. "Oh, God. Y-yes."

All around them were shirts, pants, towels and table-cloths, strung out and over the surrounding bushes, trees and cacti. And Kyle understood. From a distance, to those parched and defeated souls on their way to whatever better life they were hoping for out west, it was a sea of rags, white and blue cottons, laundry as an oasis. A sign of life. A sign of water. Ragtown.

Stillness enveloped them, and Kyle felt The Gray Man helping him now too. The rubber band in Kyle's mind was rejiggered again.

Wagons materialized, followed by horses and donkeys. Signs appeared on the buildings and Kyle noticed the three nameless buildings to his left were once a market, a livery and a blacksmith shop. The buildings to his right were once a small hotel, a saloon, a post office, a stable and a warehouse.

With these images Kyle was fine, but when the people appeared, in soft hues of see-through blue, like human jellyfish, moving about and living their lives from an age past, he felt himself grow very dizzy.

"Hold on, it'll pass," The Gray Man said gently.

"Gray. Make it stop. Let's just go find Tamara. This isn't important."

"Oh," The Gray Man said, "but it is. Trust me. Focus."

Black specks came over Kyle's eyes, and then faded as he resumed breathing deeply. In and out, firm breaths, each one soothing him some.

Mothers in sleeveless dresses and sandals, their feet as worn as their faces, each of them with their hair pulled up to fend off the heat, were moving across the town. Some of them had children in tow, and some had infants or groceries in their arms. All of them were outlined in blue. The men, in their trousers and shirts, sleeves rolled up past their elbows, appeared next. Almost all of them wore hats, some of which were firmly affixed straight, others tilted to one side or the other. One man, coming up suddenly behind Kyle, walked right through him and on into the town, spitting tobacco along the way, his essence a lingering tingle over Kyle's body.

But one thing was noticeably absent.

"Why is there no sound?"

"That's a harder discipline," The Gray Man answered. "Our eyes have seen a lot of things that our ears have never heard."

Kyle nodded, still looking across the town with wonder, and furrowed his brow in confusion.

"With those we love, those we are closest to in our turn at existence, it is often just the opposite. You can almost always remember the voice—"

"Yeah," Kyle said, "like with my dad. But it's harder to remember his face."

The Gray Man smiled. "Yes."

"Why is that?"

The Gray Man shook his head gently. "Later. For now, I want you to focus: this time on your own. No help from the spirit or me. What you're seeing is a fixed point in time, *before* your time. Look at the town and command it to now, to this day in your life, but don't let go of the blue."

It was harder than Kyle imagined. With no help, his mind kept overcompensating, back and forth, from the town to the horizon beyond and back again. Distractions and denials impeded his perception. Wagons rode into town and then out again. Occasionally he would advance the image but to the wrong decade; a 1972 Chevy truck, brand new, had once driven through here with a bed full of desert firewood.

But slowly, as he focused more and more, he began to feel as if he was getting the hang of it. When he looked harder with what felt like the outside of his eyes, he moved forwards in time, and when he strained with the bottom and center of his eyes, just the opposite.

Before long his mind, his eyes and the blue felt almost perfectly calibrated.

He felt himself shift back to the present day.

And that's when he saw them: a teenage boy with a little girl off to his right, hiding between the feed shop and the livery, and an old man, crouching ominously to Kyle's left, as if trying to approach him without being detected.

Kyle looked directly at him and the man seemed to realize that Kyle could see him, so he stood up straight.

"What's going on, Gray?"

"Ghosts, Kyle. The ones left behind who've refused to leave, for over a century now."

The kids suddenly came out of hiding as well. The boy jumped up on an old wooden container affixed to the livery, the container so old that one of its four sides had collapsed in on itself.

"Ghosts?"

"Yes."

The man began to approach them now, his eyes fixed firmly on Kyle.

"Are they going to be a problem?" Kyle asked warily.

Removing his arm from around Kyle's shoulder, The Gray Man returned to his spot in the middle of the street and replied, "That remains to be seen."

* * *

Napoleon had walked east from the park and a good three miles up Boylston, determined to get to his apartment, where he could sort out a plan of action. A rent notice was on the door, which was ironic. In the hood they didn't care if you were missing or presumed dead: rent day was rent day. He'd come inside to a wall of stale air, opened the windows, had a Dr Pepper and sat down on his couch, and was debating with himself on how to contact Parker on the down low when…

A horn outside blasted and he looked up, completely dumbfounded.

It was already morning. He'd fallen asleep. And from the feeling in his head it had been a long, solid sleep. His stomach was growling too.

After taking a piss he allowed himself a good, hot shower, which felt like heaven, before he changed clothes, shaved and made himself some coffee with toast, using bread a week past the expiration date, which he consumed while sitting in his boxer shorts and a t-shirt.

His iPhone was gone, lost somewhere in hell. He wondered if he opened his laptop and used Find My iPhone if it would actually come back with the location: "Hell. Tenth Level." This made him laugh for the first time in ages. It was okay. He could be happy. He was back, alive, and with a chance to get his life right this time.

There was no one in the world he felt comfortable contacting right now besides Parker, but reaching him was going to be an issue. Napoleon had never bothered with a landline in his apartment, and didn't know Parker's number offhand. He couldn't call him from a neighbor's phone without word getting out that he was back.

And he sensed that this would be a very bad thing. Not necessarily for nefarious reasons, but for the simple facts that a chain of events would then unfold: being brought in, interviewed, debriefed, grilled… all so he could say what, exactly? He could never tell them the truth, and any story he concocted would need to be exhaustive to get them to leave him alone. Then? The press would be all over him.

In short, it was a mess he was going to have to deal with eventually, but not one he wanted to deal with when he was supposed to be getting to Parker and helping protect the Fasano kids.

So, he'd have to call the station and get to Parker that way. A pay phone would do. They were rare as Indian head nickels these days, but they were around. Still. If he were going to go down that route, he would need to call from a place where he could melt away afterwards, in case his cover was blown. Union Station would be perfect. Tourists, travelers and commuters, in and out, all day long, in hundreds of directions. With his car still at the police station, he'd have to walk the hour or so it would take to get there.

He finished his breakfast and downed two more cups of coffee, wanting to enjoy them more but feeling pressed to get moving. He threw on some jeans before sliding his feet into a pair of Nikes, a welcome change from the work outfit he'd worn to hell and back, which was now in the trash. Then he reloaded his 9 mm, strapped on his holster and threw on a windbreaker jacket to conceal it.

Then he cautiously stepped out of his apartment, dodged his way past the manager's office and set out for Union Station.

Thirty minutes later he was deep in thought about what to do next and how, when he realized he was way off course.

He'd somehow walked the wrong way, miles further than planned, and stood now at 1812 Riggins Street, just north of Downtown Los Angeles, at an old beige apartment complex. The lawn out front was completely dead and the shrubs against the building were barely standing. In this way, the landscape outside was not unlike the lives of most of the tenants within. This was White Fence territory: a small, but vicious gang that had repeatedly fragmented and reformed over the years, leaving bodies here or there like so much discarded trash, and families grieving in the aftermath.

But this address was more than that. It was, or had once been, the home of Joaquin Murietta.

What in the world was he doing here?

He'd entirely forgotten this place. At least he thought he had.

Just being here, standing in the memory of what this building meant, in such close proximity to where too many little girls were brought, for a snack of all things, before being taken off somewhere else to be raped and strangled to death, was eerie.

"Some places you leave behind for a reason," he whispered to himself.

Napoleon was about to lash out in frustration. He didn't have time for this, but something told him that he had to find the time. There was something here, a familiar feeling, something to solve.

A few kids jetted by on Razor scooters. Napoleon noticed they were already wearing gang attire: black pants, pure white t-shirts. All of ten years old, it wouldn't be long now before they were indoctrinated into a way of life that could very well lead them to that dark realm of hell that Napoleon had just escaped. The thought pained him.

Napoleon followed behind them, fighting the urge to leave before forcing himself to take it all in: the weeds in the cracks of the sidewalks, the half-shredded rap concert poster stapled to the telephone pole, the smell of the oil-stained asphalt from all the leaking late-model cars, the beeping of a delivery truck in reverse. It all rooted him in this world as much as those dandelions were rooted in the ground, and it felt oddly reassuring.

But his comfort evaporated as soon as he entered the wrought iron gate of the apartment complex, which was still black, still creaky, and still corrupted with rust and foreboding.

Napoleon stopped in front of the wall of aluminum mailboxes in the lobby.

The first girl was the key. They had him, but they didn't. No priors. No witnesses. Murietta had fairly decent alibis that checked out. His employer, a local marketing warehouse, had him in that neighborhood that day, hanging a double billing of Dominos and Subway flyers door by door. An old lady confirmed that after work he'd come by her house and mowed her lawn.

The little girl disappeared after school that day, on her walk home, when Murietta was supposedly checking in to end his shift—the manager saw him. After that he'd gone to Pep Boys to buy a gas cap. The clerk there remembered him too, because he accidentally bought a locking cap and brought it back in a minute later to exchange it for a normal one. Both places were at opposite ends of town. From there he supposedly went home, though nobody saw him.

They could've dug deeper. But the obvious answers were too easy to grab at; they already had a good half-dozen registered sex offenders who lived in the area, one of whom was much more likely to be their guy.

Napoleon shook his head and began to walk into the complex, past one flight of stairs and to a second. When he came to the door of Murietta's old apartment he stopped cold, recalling a moment from over a decade before as if it were yesterday.

"Apartment nine," Napoleon said with a sigh. The door stood there, as if it were looking back and taunting him. It was the same, practically unchanged, the "9" still tilted slightly to the right. Ten years and the landlord hadn't even bothered to straighten out a door number.

They found out later that Murietta brought the girl here after grabbing her on the drive from his work site to the Pep Boys. Bastard had locked her in the trunk while he went in to shop for his gas cap.

"Quit calling her that," he said to himself firmly, boxing with his mind. "She's not 'the girl.' She had a name."

Napoleon put an arm out to the wall to steady himself, but his emotions still choked him. He didn't want to say it. Their names made it personal. Their names made it, made *them,* more real. But feeling the overwhelming need to, he mustered the courage. "Esmerelda. Esmerelda Trejo."

The day grew still. A cat skittered through the weeds to his left.

He'd made them watch Disney movies between assaults, and then fed them applesauce. "Disney movies," Napoleon said. "My God."

The pain in his heart was almost crippling.
He fought it, but in the end it was no use.
Some places you leave behind for a reason.
And oftentimes the reason is wrong.

CHAPTER 9

After breakfast the monster stuffed her back into the trunk like so much luggage, being careful, Tamara noted, with how he approached her and held her. She tried at first to put up a fight, before he bear hugged her from behind, picked her up and shook her a few times like a rag doll. This made Tamara think the better of it. There would come a time for a fight, but it was not here and now.

Once she was back in the trunk he forced her head down into one of the corners, the heel of his hand pressed meanly into that soft space between her shoulder blades and just below her head. "I'll snap your neck if you move, you understand?"

"Why? Why are you doing this?" she cried out.

"Just shut up!" he screamed as he tied her up again.

"Please don't tie my hands to my feet again, it hurts too much." She felt pathetic for pleading with him, but the small of her back still ached horribly from being hogtied the day before

He paused. She felt the trunk carpet tickling her lower lip.

"Fine. But if we stop and you start kicking around back here? I swear…"

She nodded meekly and then studied his actions: he moved very quickly to tie her up the rest of the way. Even with her wrists and ankles bound, he then checked and double-checked the ropes, as if he had OCD or something. No. It wasn't that. She recalled his sudden agitation and realized something astonishing: he was afraid.

On some level he was afraid of her. Perhaps it was because he remembered the solid shot she'd delivered to him in the foyer back at the house, when she'd been off by just an inch, one inch that could've prevented all of this, and he knew it. She could hurt him. She'd proven it. And so now he was going to be careful whenever he came near her or removed her ties.

But that was okay. No one could be careful all the time.

After a few minutes she heard sounds of him packing the car. He was mumbling to himself again, something about not wanting to let someone down, about doing a good job and about being a good boy. She strained to listen to the words before deciding it was useless to try to interpret crazy talk.

The car sank a bit when he got in, then she jumped when the motor started and music began blaring. Black Sabbath. Great.

The car made a U-turn to the left, the tires digging into the desert dirt, and then it was back onto the bumpy road to the highway. She took a deep breath and wondered where they were off to next, but this only started a chain reaction of questions. What would he do when they got there? What if he wasn't alone in this? Would he rape her? If there were others, would she be gang raped? Was he going to kill her? Was she actually going to die this way? How in her life could she ever have foreseen this as her end? Each thought another brick, building in her a wall of panic.

So she stopped herself, and again, she prayed. A simple prayer of the Franciscan order that her father had taught her in Bolivia.

Most High, Glorious God,
Enlighten the darkness of our minds.
Give us a right faith, a firm hope and a perfect
Charity,
So that we may always and in all things act
According to Your Holy Will.
Amen.

It was as if the prayer were a gateway to the past. Instantly, desperately, she was thirteen again, in the jungle with her father, meditating as they waited for a few people from the village to visit them before they were to go and forage for mushrooms and chickpeas.

"Dad? Why are we saying a Catholic prayer?" she asked.

He smiled warmly, as he almost always did when she was curious about things. "As Christians we acknowledge the true prayers of other believers of Jesus Christ, as well as our own."

"Really?"

"Yes, Tamara. Think about it. We do the same with our music too, don't we? We have our hymns that we treasure, sure, but don't you also love 'Ave Maria'?"

Tamara nodded.

"Because it's beautiful, right?"

"Yes," she replied, then thought for a moment about why it was beautiful, before adding, "Because I feel God in that song."

"Exactly. So? Did you feel God in this prayer?"

She let out a small laugh. "Yeah. Actually, I did."

The birdsong of the jungle, normally chaotic and overwhelming, waned a bit as she watched a dragonfly cross between them and then down into a thicket of grass, the sunlight caught in its wings and gathered to the metallic green tint of its body.

Her father watched it too before he continued. "As you get older, remember that: not to turn away from anything that you feel God in, be it a song or a prayer or, especially, a person. God talks to us in many ways, at many times and in many situations."

His brown hair was partially windblown and his light brown eyes were wrinkled deeply at the edges, his cheeks tan beneath a stubbly beard. Tamara had always wondered at her father's eyes, always searching and yet always seeing somehow. There in the jungle that day he was more alive than she'd ever seen him, his faded blue t-shirt and tan shorts cast against the deep green of the jungle leaves and surrounding foliage. She realized then that you could love someone forever, really, without even trying.

They practiced the prayer a half-dozen more times and, for whatever reason, it was one of the easiest ones she'd ever memorized.

Because it spoke to her, there that day beneath the harsh Bolivian sun as much as it was speaking to her now, in the trunk of a car that belonged to some psychopath.

"God speaks to us in all situations," she whispered into the dark.

And boy, she was in quite the situation now.

Somehow the darkness of the trunk had grown deeper, not lighter, in the face of the prayer. The music blared and before long the madman was singing along, occasionally shouting a profanity or two for no good reason, as they sped down the highway.

After a while she began to slip into despair, worried that maybe this was it, that God had simply forsaken her or that she'd used up all her "God chips" to save the kids, and she was fine with that, if that was the case, but still, it was sad to die this way. This was a horrible thing that happened to other people, not you.

Why? Why has this happened, God?

Then she felt it: a fourth presence, there in the car, with her, the madman and God. It was a dark and foreboding presence, like an unwelcome guest at the table. From it emanated a profound hopelessness and a tempting call to revisit bad times and sad memories, and its attendance seemed to envelope the car in an evil cloud that permeated the trunk and scraped at her skin. Whatever it was, it was now riding shotgun to wherever they were headed.

They rolled to a stop, but only briefly, before the car turned right and accelerated again. Tamara shuddered in relief. *Just keep driving, you crazy bastard. Don't pull over. Because I know for a fact that I don't wanna see who you're with.*

She was cold and her fear only multiplied when she suddenly heard something up front: there was a second voice now.

She strained as hard as she could to hear it over the droning tires and her own labored breathing, and when she finally did, her heart sank.

It was singing.

Singing right along with the monster.

* * *

Parker approached the bedroom door and then, for no good reason, he hesitated, staring blankly at the doorknob. Droplets of doubt and hesitation sprinkled through his mind haphazardly, mixing with a strong sense of foreboding.

It was the same feeling you had when going door to door with your M16 through some shit-small village in country. Which door was the enemy behind? What did it matter when your mind felt like it could be any door and every door at the same time? But he wasn't in country, he was in a house in a well-to-do neighborhood in Los Angeles, and this wasn't a reconnoitered location where the Taliban were thought to be holed up, but a little girl's bedroom.

Yes… but the same bedroom that the little girl herself had gone to great lengths to avoid entering earlier, not even wanting to grab a change of clothes. Why?

He stood still, listening at the door, feeling ridiculous and stupid and yet totally justified on some level with his behavior.

A lot a shit had gone down that made little or no sense, most of it bad. Still. The only way to get past being frozen like this was to reach, turn the doorknob and open the door. So he did.

It swung open quietly and something struck Parker immediately: the light from the hallway outside seemed to enter the room and disappear into the inner darkness, instead of illuminating anything. The sense of foreboding he'd felt seconds earlier was now expanding. The soldier in him screamed danger and the cop in him told him to draw his weapon. He was just about to do so when he heard Trudy O'Hara's voice from the other end of the hall.

"Detective?"

He knew it was rude, but his instincts were in control of him now: he answered her without looking her way, keeping his focus on the inside of the bedroom. "Yeah?"

"The kids want to leave."

To the left he could make out the far corner of a dresser. Toys and stuffed animals were on the floor and a white bookcase stuffed end to end was to his right. He focused his attention around the room like a laser. Something wasn't right, but he couldn't get a fix on it.

Then he noticed them: the bedsheet and comforter were on the floor between the door and the bed, but not tossed there haphazardly as if perhaps the little girl had been lying on the floor playing at some point. No. They were strung out and twisted tightly, as if a struggle had ensued in here, with one end of the comforter disappearing under the bed.

"Detective?" Ms. O'Hara's voice was firmer this time, but laced with something too: a bit of desperation that forced him this time to glance her way. When Parker did, he immediately noticed Janie Fasano; she'd wrapped herself almost entirely around Ms. O'Hara's waist, her little arms gripping her tight, one eye peering out at Parker in terror from behind Ms. O'Hara's jacket.

Parker knew better, but he had to ask. He just had to. "Janie? What happened in here?"

Instead of answering, Janie suddenly released her grip and bolted out of the hallway and into the living room. Ms. O'Hara was about to say something when her eyes suddenly widened and diverted to the open bedroom door that Parker was standing in front of.

He never should've looked away.

When the door slammed in Parker's face he immediately jumped backwards, drawing his handgun instinctively and blindingly fast. Then, like an idiot, he just stood with his gun pointed at the door.

"What the hell?" Ms. O'Hara let slip.

Parker blinked and took a deep breath. Something was behind the door, he could feel it, but the last thing he needed to do was look like a nutjob or scare Ms. O'Hara and the kids. On that last point though, at least with Ms. O'Hara, it was probably too late now.

He spoke firmly. "Nothing. Just a window left open. With what's gone on in this house though, I'm obviously a little bit jumpy. Sorry, Ms. O'Hara."

She blinked at him twice before saying, "It's Trudy." Then she went after Janie.

Parker gathered himself together but, now alone, still didn't holster his weapon.

There was no open window in the bedroom. No way. No how. Something had closed the door. Sometimes you just had to walk away, but now was not that time. What if that sick bastard Troy hadn't fled the house? What if he'd beaten Tamara Fasano senseless, given up on getting the kids and dragged her in there? The odds were long, and in his heart Parker sensed it not to be true. Surely Murillo, Klink and the arriving officers had swept the home yesterday. But he had to verify, because, well, bedroom doors didn't just close themselves.

There was a small group of LAPD officers on scene to help secure the home.

"Officer Meyer!" Parker shouted.

It took a second, but Meyer called out from what sounded like the kitchen, "Yes, Detective?"

"You got any more uniforms out there with you?"

A few seconds hesitation and then, "Yeah. Two here with me and two on the porch."

Parker pointed his gun at the door again, just in case whoever was in there was listening and decided to run out.

"I want the two on the porch to circle around outside the girl's bedroom window. Second bedroom from the front of the house. You three come here. Now."

This time there was no hesitation. Just a flurry of activity. When the three officers turned the corner and saw that Parker had drawn his weapon they all did the same, their looks of confusion erased by concern.

"Is this why the lady and kids just ran outside?" Meyer whispered.

Parker nodded. "I was about to go in when it slammed shut on me. Maybe the window in there is open… the wind… or…"

"Or maybe we got someone in there," one of the uniforms added. It was not a question. Her badge read "Benitez."

"I dunno how, Beni," Meyer whispered. "We cleared it earlier."

"Crawl space, maybe? Or an attic door in the closet?" she replied.

Parker made eye contact with each of them, gave the silent finger count to three, and then opened the bedroom door and charged in, Meyer, Benitez and the other cop fanning out behind him in a semicircle. Benitez checked behind the door and cleared it before Parker and Meyer cleared the inside of the closet. The third cop, tall with blond hair, advanced past them all and to the window. "Locked," he said flatly.

The room being cleared, they all lowered their weapons.

But, looking down, Parker's blood went ice cold: the sheet and comforter that had been twisted on the floor were now gone.

He was about to say something but he bit his tongue. They'd think he was crazy, for sure. He'd just gotten back into the captain's good graces; the last thing he needed now was a report, or worse, rumors, spreading that he'd gone Section 8. Instead, Parker waved his hand to get everyone's attention and pointed to the bed.

They looked skeptical, and rightfully so, because the space between the bed frame and the floor wasn't all that wide. But from his employee photo, Troy was a real skinny bastard too. It was possible.

Reaching down in one fluid motion that was full of adrenaline, Parker grabbed the edge of the bed frame and yanked the bed, box, mattress and all, up and over.

The four of them stood with their guns fixed on a poorly vacuumed patch of carpet and nothing more.

"No one ever cleans under the bed," Benitez said sarcastically.

Feeling just a tiny bit like an ass, Parker holstered his weapon as the other officers followed suit. On the other side of the bedroom window Parker could see the shadows of the two officers that he'd foolishly pulled into this exercise.

The tall blond cop, Parker now noticed that his badge said "Shaw," walked over to the door and checked the hinges. "Maybe they're in tight or something?"

"Yeah," Meyer said with a shrug.

Shaw opened the door a few times but it refused to move an inch, much less close itself.

It was time for damage control. "Hmm," Parker said, "musta just been a freak thing."

"Yeah?" Benitez asked warily, glancing at Parker as if she were sizing him up a bit.

"The O'Hara lady was here when it happened too," Parker added for insurance. "Whatever. The room's clear obviously. Let's hit it."

The uniforms filed out of the room ahead of him, and as Parker followed, he looked back one more time.

There had been a bed sheet and comforter on that floor. There had been.

He was as sure of it as he was sure the sky was blue and that babies crapped their diapers.

And he was just as sure, damned near positive in fact, that he knew where they'd gone.

Something under the bed had taken the sheets.
And it wasn't dust bunnies.

CHAPTER 10

Kyle noticed that if the man had still been alive, he would've most certainly been bleeding everywhere; most of his insides were missing and a few ribs were blown outward. As he approached them cautiously, his dead eyes turned to The Gray Man. His body shuffled awkwardly, like a deck of cards, one shoulder corkscrewing grotesquely higher than the other with every third or fourth step. Off to the left, the teenage boy hopped off the box in front of the livery and waved his arm at the little girl to stay where she was.

A gust of wind blew down the street, kicking up a dirt devil that spun haphazardly down the road, through all three ghosts, around The Gray Man and right into Kyle.

Silence formed all around them.

When The Gray Man finally spoke, Kyle jumped, then felt immediately embarrassed.

"What do you want?" The Gray Man asked, a mix of concern and compassion in his voice.

"Nuttin' you don't, Agent," the old man replied, his voice raspy.

"Which is?"

"Just peace and quiet."

The Gray Man glanced around. "I wonder," he said with a sigh, "how peaceful this lonely place is for the children."

The old man looked towards the kids and then back to The Gray Man, his eyes like little dark beads in the midst of his pale white visage. "Dey here of dey own vo-lition," he said, swinging his chin back and forth as if he were chewing imaginary tobacco. "Dey my little ones."

Kyle cleared his throat, but everyone ignored him, including the little girl, which only increased his unease.

Not seeming to buy the old man's statement at face value, The Gray Man looked to the children. "Is this true?"

"Yah, mister. You leave our pop alone," the boy said with the hesitant bravado of a teenager. "He done nothin' to you or yer friend."

The Gray Man waited, his eyes fixed on the little girl, a sad look on his face. Finally, evidently realizing that he was waiting on her, the little girl also replied. "Das my daddy," she said nodding. "Please don hurt 'im."

"What's your name?" The Gray Man said, turning back to the old man.

"Solomon," the old man answered, then pointing to the kids he added, "This here is Andy and Margie."

"Nice to meet you. This is Kyle."

Only the teenage boy felt the need to ask, "And what's your name, mister?"

"Andy!" Solomon spat under his breath, "Don't. You don' ever ask one such as 'im 'is name. Not'n'less he offers it."

"But—"

Solomon shot him a harsh gaze that made the boy's mouth clamp shut like a bear trap. What few remaining doubts that Kyle had about him really being their father disappeared entirely.

"Why?" The Gray Man asked, relaxing his stance.

Solomon placed his hands on his hips, his one shoulder popping in its socket. "Why what?"

"Why linger?"

"Why go, Agent?"

"Because what waits cannot be any worse than this, Solomon."

"For them, maybe," Solomon said, nodding his head in the direction of the children.

The Gray Man nodded, and then shook his head. "Always the same; always the fear."

"You don' know nuttin' 'bout me," Solomon said with a sneer.

"No. I don't," The Gray Man agreed. "But I also don't know anything that can't be forgiven."

Margie's canary-like voice chirped. "Papa?"

"You be quiet now, girl. Papa's busy," Solomon replied.

Still refusing to take his eyes off The Gray Man, he stepped forwards quickly. Kyle instinctively did the same, surprised as much by his instinct to protect The Gray Man as he was by the notion that The Gray Man needed protecting.

"Now listen. Whyn't you just leave and take yer friend with you?"

The two of them stood like that for a long time, The Gray Man not answering and Solomon not budging.

Awkwardly, Kyle asked, "What happened to you?"

Solomon shot a look at Kyle and then returned his stare to where it had been before answering out of the corner of his mouth with a tone dripping with bitterness. "Dynamite. Charge got away from me. We were tryin' to blast a hole in the ground to find a new well."

"You died instantly," The Gray Man said flatly.

Solomon nodded.

Again The Gray Man looked at the children, except this time it was with pity. "Then the children's mother—"

"Then their mother was kidnapped and taken away by bad men," Solomon said firmly, cutting The Gray Man off.

Kyle watched as for the first time a look between them was not based on confrontation, but rather understanding.

The Gray Man lowered his voice. "You stayed… for them."

Taking another step forwards, Solomon nearly dropped his voice to a whisper. "Yes. To protect 'em. When she ran off and left 'em behind, right after I died."

"But don't you see—"

"I told 'em what I did to protect 'em, after I came back." The old man looked to the ground. "After I let 'em see me."

"Before the typhoid came."

Solomon nodded, his face wrought with pain and sorrow. "I tried to protect 'em, but this place, with no mother and no father? Can you even imagine?"

The Gray Man now also looked to the ground. "No. I can't."

"I kept whisperin' to other families, especially the other mothers in town, tryin' to move 'em to pity, to take my children on to California. Sometimes it worked but then their men folk would reverse their minds. Another mouth to feed from here to there was too much to even consider, much less *two* mouths."

"What happened next?" Kyle interjected.

"Someone brought it into camp. The sickness spread quick-like. Most folks fled and moved on, but for those who were already sick? It was too late."

"And?"

"And it was a merciful thing. At least for my babies. It was a most merciful thing to be spared the horrors this town had in store for 'em, and the hard, bitter life that would've awaited 'em afterwards, even if they'da survived."

"That's why they're still the ages they are?" Kyle said, getting it.

Solomon swallowed hard, shifted his weight on his boots and then looked back at The Gray Man. "You should go."

"Yes. We will. But first, a few questions."

"What?"

"We're looking for a man. An evil man. You really couldn't miss him. He has my friend's wife."

"He was in one of the metal wagons that roars," Solomon said with a nod. "Painted black as night."

"Then you saw him?"

"Barely. The wagon window was only half down. But it didn't matter. We hid. You woulda too if you saw him."

"I doubt that," The Gray Man replied.

"Yah. I'm sorry. The likes of you, no, you wouldn't hide."

"Did you see the woman?"

"No," Solomon said, shaking his head. "I could sense 'er though."

"Sense her?" Kyle asked.

Solomon looked at Kyle and then looked away again, seemingly out of shame for his next words. "I could feel 'er despair. She was very much in despair."

The weight that kept visiting Kyle's chest returned now, a tightness in him that would not leave. The thought of his wife in danger, no doubt in fear for her life, and his inability to be there for her was becoming a lingering dread that refused to evaporate.

"How long ago?" The Gray Man asked.

"A day's length, maybe a little more," Solomon answered.

"Did they stay here at all?"

"No. I think 'e sensed us somehow. He got out, threw a piss and then got back in and drove off. That's it."

The Gray Man nodded firmly. "Okay then. Thank you."

"Yer welcome."

"Papa?" the little girl chimed in again, kicking a toe at the dirt, her dirty brown dress a shade of white in spots. "Does the man know what ever happened to Mama?"

Solomon shook his head ever so slightly at The Gray Man.

"They should know," The Gray Man said encouragingly.

"No," the old man said, an intense look in his eye. "It would break them."

"Quite the opposite, my friend: it would free them."

"No."

"They're staying for you, Solomon, and for no other reason."

"And what about it?"

"You love them. I can tell. I can also assure you that heaven most certainly awaits them."

Solomon's face seemed to drop. *If ghosts could cry,* Kyle thought.

"I know it's you who's afraid of what's next, and only you and God can take that inventory of your life and have that discussion."

His shoulders slumping, Solomon seemed to sway a bit.

Putting out a hand to steady him, The Gray Man continued, "But you've been a fine father. For many years. Your life *after* your life, in its own way, was a repentance of sorts."

"What're you saying?"

"No guarantees, Solomon. It's not my place. But answer me something."

"What?"

"What is the risk of going to hell if it means getting your children to heaven?"

Solomon reached out, leaned on The Gray Man like a blown-over tree and shook.

It appeared that, in their own way, ghosts could, indeed, cry.

The old man looked up into The Gray Man's eyes and said one word. "Yes."

The Gray Man stepped back suddenly and waved a hand across the three ghosts, left to right, in a movement so sudden that Kyle barely had a chance to understand what was happening.

In an instant, they were gone, leaving Kyle and The Gray Man alone in the street.

"What just happened?" Kyle asked, dumbfounded.

"They were sent on their way, at long last."

As the air around them grew warm, signaling yet another leg on their travels, Kyle couldn't help himself. "I have to know," he said.

The Gray Man had evidently read his mind again, that or he just knew to expect the question. "Of course you do."

"What happened to him?"

"I'm not supposed to say, Kyle."

Welling up with emotion from all sides for reasons he couldn't understand, Kyle pressed. "Please."

As the sky and sun around them warped into glops of paint drops, The Gray Man replied. "Kyle. After a hundred years of watching over them, protecting them and loving them, even if Solomon had it wrong at times, do you honestly think that God would forsake him? He's in heaven with his babies, Kyle. Their loneliness is no more."

There was a falcon in the distance flying lazy curves in the sky.

As the world melted away, Kyle sighed in relief.

* * *

Napoleon stood by the pool of the apartment complex. It was all that was left to go to after he'd finished walking through the entire complex, his eyes hazy at times, looking at things but not really, as he worked his way down a memory lane that was one part "dead man's curve" and one part just plain "dead end."

But, he told himself, *everything happens for a reason. Focus.*

The two levels of the apartment complex housed maybe a total of forty units. The rain gutters along the rooftop were rusted and worn, the distressed metal having given way and bent back in places. Some units had plants in front of them, others small signs of greeting or hope. One apartment actually had a Christmas wreath still up in the window, even though the holiday was long past.

They tried. God bless them, they tried to make it like a home. For some of them it was, and for some of them it was even a happy home.

But to Napoleon the idea was beyond comprehension. This whole place, to him, would always be where a killer lived, once upon a time. They could strip it, replaster it or rename it and it would make no difference. They could even burn it to the ground and rebuild it and somehow that bastard's ghost would find its way back into the rafters.

The pool water, still and flat, was clear enough to see through to the bottom, which was partially covered with algae and dead leaves that had made the dive down. The number markers for depth were faded, and mosquitos were brazenly swimming in threatening pirouettes along the surface.

Another bad thought, another urge to resist it. But instead, something told him to let it go, so he did, in a whisper. "He let them play in the pool before he killed them. He would threaten to hurt them, or to hurt their families, unless they did as he said."

He felt cold and sweaty. Not good. But he pressed on. "He would bring them to the apartment and have them watch those cartoons while he picked out which bathing suit he wanted them to wear. He had a whole plastic tub of them that he bought from Target."

Napoleon's stomach rolled, but held.

A small flock of birds landed in a tilted tree at the end of the property and began to debate with one another in sharp tones.

Don't say it. Don't say it. Don't say it.

"He confessed later that he had Esmerelda take a swim first, in a bikini, because she was overdeveloped for her age."

He turned immediately and stumbled to a bush nearby and vomited until his stomach was empty and it was bile that scalded his throat on the way out.

Calm down. Get your shit together.

He had to get away from the memories for a moment, so he forced himself to focus on his surroundings.

The traffic beyond the apartment complex wasn't too heavy, but it still offered up the occasional sound of distraction: a beeping horn, the rumble of a passing cement truck, the protesting cry of a motorcycle in the wrong gear.

But he couldn't help himself; Napoleon pushed past them all, past the sounds of today and back to the interview room so many years ago, with its white tiled floor and walls painted mint green, to the cold metal interview table and the man that was seated opposite him, after they'd brought him in for the third time.

"His face wasn't right. During the whole interview, his face just wasn't right."

And it was true. There was no remorse, no fear of incriminating himself, no pity. He wasn't prideful but he wasn't regretful, either. Once he knew the gig was up he just rolled over and started talking, telling them how he grabbed her, brought her here, dressed her up in that little red bikini and then just watched her swim around awhile.

"Poor thing knew she was in trouble. She was smart enough to try and befriend him, to ask him to get in and swim with her, to play with some silly plastic blue ball that was in the pool that day."

Napoleon pulled himself back by focusing on the smell of his puke, which nearly made him vomit again. How long before someone in the apartment complex called the police to report some haggard looking old dude walking around the complex talking to himself? The thought made him shake his head. No one in this neighborhood called the police, unless someone was dead or about to die.

Looking around, he watched as the birds shifted branches in staggered lines, their clustered bodies like tiny music notes.

That day, after Murietta had finished telling them how he liked to watch them swim, or get changed, or rinse off in the shower before he raped them because it was fun to "screw with their minds before he screwed them," it had taken both he and the other interviewing detective, Reyes, who was female, all the strength they had not to lose it and beat him. Screw the law they were sworn to uphold. If the DA hadn't been watching it all from the other side of the double glass with two other detectives, they would've. Napoleon still wished he had.

The truth was that most abductors killed their victims within twenty-four hours. But not Murietta. No. He kept them two, sometimes three days; always grabbed them on a Friday so he'd have something to do on the weekend.

The birds fell silent, which only made Napoleon sadder. "He killed her three blocks from here, near the train tracks, in the middle of the night, on a Sunday." The option to vomit now gone, it was replaced with a strong desire to cry. "He strangled her with the bikini top." A tiny sob broke through, insistent, desperate, as if his body were trying to shut his mouth for him. It didn't work. "He buried her in a shallow grave beneath an abandoned development project near the tracks, after wrapping her in some carpenter's plastic he found inside. The dogs got to her a few times before we found her. We had to turn her face sideways for the ID photo for the parents because we just couldn't put them through that, ya know?"

He couldn't tell if he was still talking to himself or to God.

Napoleon eased his head against a nearby stairway railing, stuffed his hands in his pockets and sighed.

The birds in the tree took flight, up and off into the sky, speaking back and forth with renewed fervor.

It was time to go, so he did, walking past the pool, past the apartment units and back out through the lobby and to the street beyond.

There was no telling how many little girls they saved when they caught Joaquin Murietta. But one more died when he got off on a technicality. Napoleon's technicality. One.

Esmerelda.

In the distance a train whistle sounded, from those tracks, nearby and yet so far away, a place where a ten-year-old girl said goodbye to the world in a most terrible way. Had she prayed too? Why weren't her prayers answered? Or those of her parents when she first went missing?

His mind was going numb. The street was jammed with parked cars, not unusual for an area like this, which mostly housed the unemployed or underemployed.

Then he saw it.

There on the wall, perched quietly, staring intently at him, was a single black crow.

He turned and began walking down the street in the direction of his apartment and, as he did out of the corner of his eye Napoleon noticed the crow.

It had lifted off the brick wall and into flight… right behind him.

That's when he realized that The Gray Man was right: the thirst for vengeance was useless. He'd gone all the way to hell to exorcise a demon that was already damned.

And now a little piece of hell had followed him home.

CHAPTER 11

IT WAS THE LONGEST drive of her life, trapped as she was in the darkness, and she spent most of it counting bumps in the road. Eventually they pulled off the road and coasted to a stop. She heard him get out of the car and walk off, his shoes crunching in the dirt and gravel outside, far and near, then far and near, as if he were checking the area to make sure no one was around. Finally, and mercifully, he popped the trunk lid. Fresh air poured over her as he yanked her forwards and removed the ropes.

They were at a rest stop. Tamara looked inside the car to see if anyone else was there with them. There was no one, which meant earlier he'd just been talking to himself, but how was that possible? She was sure she'd heard a second voice and this realization caused a crease of goosebumps to climb her arms, despite the desert sun.

"I gotta pee," she said, feeling embarrassed.

"Make it count, 'cause we got a long haul from here."

She nodded and began walking stiffly. When he tried to follow her into the bathroom she told him she had to go number two, not number one. He was wearing a faded Anaheim Angels cap, which he pulled down hard across his forehead. Looking at her suspiciously, he nodded and said, "Fine. Don't get slick, or I may bust up that pretty face of yours some more."

It wasn't like there was anywhere to go. The rest stop bathrooms were enclosed in a squat building made of thick bricks painted an ugly tannish-brown that matched the surrounding terrain. For both the men's and ladies' rooms there was only one way in, and one way out. He seemed to surmise this because as she walked into the restroom he took up a nonchalant pose, his shoulder propped against a metal post with an "Area Safety" sign on it, one foot over the other, and began whistling softly.

When she was finished she went to the sink, washed her hands and then scooped big handfuls of water over her face and through her hair, the coolness both refreshing and exhilarating. She was frightened by the red hue of the water as she washed all the blood from her facial wounds, using her fingernails to scrape away the dried up bits, before the water went pink and then clear. She felt a cut on her cheek and one over her eye; they were raw, but closed.

Sighing, she took a few deep breaths and thought about what she'd seen on the way in.

Besides the rest stop there was nothing else around them but fields of rocky desert and near-dead foliage. No other cars were here, and she could hear no coming or passing traffic. She had hoped the rest stop would be near a camping ground of some kind, but she hadn't seen any RVs or campers either, nor the smoke from any campfires, which made sense since it was the middle of day.

There was a payphone mounted against a boundary wall outside, but it looked shaky at best. She realized she had no change in her pocket and then remembered that 911 was a free call, even from a payphone. But there was no guarantee the phone worked at all. Down the road, in one direction or the other, there was bound to be a call box of some kind, but who knew how many miles away.

She wondered if he had a cell phone and then figured he had to. Who didn't, these days?

And that brought her back, full circle, to him.

It was going to come down to him, sooner or later. The question was: was that time now?

To use his cell phone or the payphone, or to get to a call box, either on foot or in his car… all of these scenarios required one thing: overpowering him.

As if sensing that she was thinking of him, he suddenly shouted from outside. "Hey. What's taking so long?"

"Almost done. Just had to clean up a bit," she shouted back as she leaned over the sink and looked into the scratched piece of sheet metal that served as the bathroom's mirror.

The woman looking back at her was a mess. Her face was gaunt, with hardly any color, and her hair was matted flat in sections from sweating so much in the trunk. Her eyes were sunken, with bags beneath them that were discolored and swollen with fatigue. Her left eye was still black from when he'd punched her and her upper lip was swollen badly.

Bastard messed me up good, she thought. *But it isn't over yet. Not yet.*

She ran her tongue over her teeth, feeling the blood that had dried between them, and quelled her emotions again. That was the last thing she needed now; if she let them, her emotions would only give birth to fear, and she knew, absolutely knew, that fear would be what got her killed, because she could tell that this sick pervert fed off it.

If that's what he needed then she had to find a way to marshal her inner-self to only give it to him in metered doses, to string his sorry ass out as long as she could, until she found a way to escape, or help came. Surely, by now, someone had discovered what had happened at the house. Janie would've called for help, or gone to the neighbors for it. The police would be involved and then…

Then what? How in the world would they ever know whether he'd gone south to Baja, north to Alaska or wherever?

How would they even know what his car looked like?

She cursed herself for not putting in the security cameras that were offered when they'd had the alarm system installed a few years back. They'd at least have given the police the make and model to go off. But no, for some reason she and Kyle had decided to save the money. A measly few hundred bucks.

Life was funny. Back then, how could they've known that just a few hundred bucks might save her life someday?

Bringing her focus back on point, she asked herself if this was the place to make her stand, and just as quickly, it was obvious to her that it was not. If there were a few cars around, or a campsite with other people who could hear her scream—anything really, besides just barren desert and a blacktop road disappearing in each direction to separate, lonely horizons—then maybe.

She was determined to take him head on and do him some harm, but he was bigger and stronger and, more importantly, crazier than her. So if the battle went against her she needed the option of escape too. In short, she needed a place with more than the single option of fight or die. At the very least she needed fight, flight or die.

"Quit dicking around!" he yelled, making her jump. His feet shuffled at the entrance, as if he was getting ready to come in. She saved him the trouble by walking out confidently, noticing his eyes combing over and lingering on her chest.

A sudden sense of empowerment came over her. But of course. Until now she'd worried about whether or not he would rape her, but really, if his desires to do so opened up yet another front in her battle against him, then fine. Fear and lust. They were his two vulnerabilities. One was based in need, the other in want. She was playing a dangerous game, but really, what other game was there left to play?

She stretched in front of him, pushing out her chest a bit, but not enough to be obvious about it. "Please..."

"Shut the fuck up," he said, grabbing her at the elbow.

Instinctively she wanted to resist. Instead, she complied as he walked her to the trunk. He pushed a button on his key fob and it popped open. Then he made her sit on the bumper.

Same as last time. One step, two step, three step... four.

He reached down and grabbed the ropes, which were just inside the trunk near the bumper. She rubbed her wrists and moaned as he brought the ropes up to tie them. "They hurt," she said with a pout.

Saying nothing, he grabbed her arms, forced them together and tied them tightly. *But not as tightly as before.* He was already starting to get sloppy. She smiled on the inside.

This time he moved just as quickly, but a few times he lingered, just a bit. At one point she could feel him push his cheek quickly into her hair before he pushed her back into the trunk and tied her ankles.

Matted, sweaty hair? Really? Okay then, she thought.

As he gagged her again, she forced herself to look up into his merciless, crow-like eyes and blink pitifully, again, not heavy handedly, just sadly.

Next time I hope you smell my hair a little longer, you son of a bitch.

When he closed the trunk a studious look was on his face, as if she'd caught his attention.

Because next time? I'll make sure those ropes are pushed back a little deeper into the trunk, so that you have to reach in, past me, to get to them.

The trunk went dark as the latch locked with a loud click.

And then I will jump off that bumper and push you forwards just enough to slam that trunk lid... right... into the back... of your miserable... skull.

* * *

Murillo looked perplexed. "So. You're taking them *where*, again?"

Parker was annoyed at being held up, but he understood protocol, and he had to sell this the right way. "The Travel Lodge in Eagle Rock, off Los Feliz Boulevard."

"And Social Services?" Murillo asked with a sigh, rubbing his left hand over his face as he looked over at Trudy and the kids, who were standing by Trudy's rental car, a white Honda CRV, which was parked in the driveway.

"Look. The kids are beyond spooked that this guy's gonna come back for them, and I doubt anyone wants to force them to choose between staying in the house where their mother was beaten and abducted or going off to foster care."

"Procedurally, though, Parker—"

"I talked to the cap. He cleared it because, at this point in the case, police protection is a good idea anyway. Quite frankly, the little girl in particular is starting to come unwound."

"Yeah?"

"And Ms. O'Hara provided the guardianship paperwork signed by the Fasanos a few years back naming her for custody anyway," Parker said with a shrug, remembering how Trudy had whipped out the sheet of paper from a desk drawer in the house, as if she were flashing a badge of her own at him.

He glanced over at her and the kids. He had to hurry this up, or she was going to bail without him if she could. She hadn't been keen on the idea of Parker tagging along in the first place, but something had told him then, as it was telling him again now, not to let the kids out of his sight, no matter what. Sure. He could tail the three of them all over the city if he had to, but it would be easier to protect them if he were with them.

Murillo finally gave a nod of resignation. "Fine. Hit it then, *guero*. But please, Parker, go there and stay put. You know Social Services. If they go there to check on the kids and you're not there then they'll throw a big baby fit, and I just know it will somehow fall in my damn lap, okay?"

"Deal," Parker replied, slapping Murillo on the shoulder as he walked past him and to the car. Looking at Trudy he said, "We're good to go."

"About time," she said impatiently. "I'll drive. Where did you say we're going?"

"A motel near here."

She looked like she was about to protest, so Parker cut her off at the pass. "Social Services will have to certify everything with the court before you can take them out of the city. Police protection is your best bet right now. If they want to play hard ball? Social Services can keep the kids until the court reviews everything, which could take days. The case worker doesn't want to traumatize the kids any further by keeping them from you right now, but still, it's probably best not to push it."

"Great."

Parker realized that his words had unsettled the kids even more, so he moved to fix that. "Besides. There's still a good chance Mrs. Fasano will be found and brought home anyway. They've set up roadblocks now and it's on the news. Every major station. Someone's bound to see her out there."

If she's not already dead, Parker thought before forcing the idea out of his mind.

"Fine," Trudy said curtly, looking at Parker and discretely rolling her eyes in the direction of the children. "It's really best if we just get going."

Parker nodded.

They loaded into the CRV and headed down the driveway, where a police cruiser was parked and partially blocking the exit. As they slowed to a stop and Parker motioned for a uniformed officer to move the car, a tall young man in tan chinos and a blue Izod shirt stepped from the curb and walked up to the car on Parker's side. Evidently seeing Parker's immediate concern at his approach, the man put his hands out and said, "I'm not with the press. I'm a family friend."

"Yeah?" Parker said flatly. He didn't like the guy, even before he knew his name.

"My name's Ben," the man said. "Ben Weisfeld."

The kids said nothing from the back seat, but Parker felt Trudy stiffen next to him.

"Well, Mr. Weisfeld, I wish we could talk, but this is an active investigation, so there's really nothing—"

"Are the kids alright?" Mr. Weisfeld said, moving closer to the car.

There was nothing about his body language or tone

of voice that said danger, but Parker felt it nonetheless.

"Sir. Please," Parker said, holding his hand up for him to stop approaching.

He complied, but only barely, and even then it was obvious that he was trying to see past Parker and into the car. The back windows being rolled up, he had no other way to answer his own question.

"Please. I work with Tamara. I just wanted to make sure they're okay."

"Do you know this guy?" Parker asked Trudy under his breath.

"Know *of* him," she replied in a hushed tone. "He works at Tamara's company. On her project team, I think."

You live enough, you don't have to be a cop or a war veteran to know when someone is telling you half-truths. Trudy had answered his question, but Parker could tell that she'd left something out.

"The kids are fine, Mr. Weisfeld."

He let out a big sigh, but to Parker it seemed a little too big—as in fake. "Oh, man. That's great to hear."

First the sigh was too big, now the relief was too small. The hair on Parker's arms began to stand up. Weisfeld was only about six feet from the window. If he was up to no good he'd be a damn fool to try something here, but still, Parker did not like being vulnerable, seated in the car the way he was.

"How about Tamara?" Weisfeld asked in that same flat tone.

"Mr. Weisfeld, as I said, this is an active investigation. We cannot comment on anything at this time."

"Is she dead?"

Parker's patience had been reached. He looked over

at Trudy and then at the police cruiser, which was now pulling out of the way. "Mr. Weisfeld. Leave. Now."

Peering into the back seat of the car again, he was, incredibly, about to say it again, right in front of the kids. "Is she—"

"Mr. Weisfeld, if you have information that you think can help the investigation then tell that uniformed officer right over there," Parker ordered, his voice firm as he pointed at a thin brown-haired La Canada deputy who was standing guard nearby and chewing a toothpick. "And he can put you in touch with one of the investigating detectives."

"But—"

"But nothing. We're done here," Parker cut him off, waving Trudy forwards.

As they pulled down the street a pocket of silence filled the car.

"Head down to the end of the road and make a left. That'll take us to Angeles Crest Highway. Make another left there and then we'll catch the 210 to the 2 south, okay?"

Trudy nodded, and then quietly added, "I can tell you more about him later."

Parker nodded in return and looked out over the road ahead. Traffic was light. A trash bag had gotten wrapped up in a stack of weeds at the base of a nearby telephone pole. A bus stop bench, no doubt put there to ship in the immigrant maids and nannies that serviced the affluent homes in the area, displayed an ad for a local Realtor with a Photoshopped smile. A man in a sweat suit was jogging in place at a red light, and a mom with a double stroller was navigating the hilly curb nearby.

Domestic bliss.

Just a quarter mile from where a brutally violent crime

occurred. Go figure.

Parker chewed on his lower lip and squinted against the sunlight. He wanted very much not to give up on the entire human race. Lord knew he'd seen enough to be granted the right. But that would mean giving up on himself, and right now, even more importantly, giving up on Trudy O'Hara and the Fasano kids, and that just wasn't an option.

After a while, as they made their way down the 2 Freeway, one of the kids finally spoke up. It was the little boy, Seth.

"We knew that man," he said in a soft voice.

"You did?" Parker asked.

"Yeah," the boy answered.

Then it was Janie's turn to speak. "He's the one that gave Mommy the lantern."

"Lantern?" Trudy asked.

"Yeah," Parker said. "It was on the counter in the kitchen."

"There was something bad in the lantern," Seth said, way too calmly, like he was commenting on the weather.

The road moved past them in a blur as a few seconds went by. Parker didn't know what to say. Evidently neither did the only other adult in the car, as Trudy was also silent.

Then Janie spoke again, just as calmly, but with a voice tinged with fear. "We felt it when we were running past it to get away..."

"... until we got to the shed," Seth finished.

Trudy glanced at Parker, then back to the road. "Then what happened?"

"We started saying one of the prayers Mommy taught us," Seth said, "and I think God maybe kinda heard us."

"Why do you think that?" Trudy asked.

"I didn't hear anything, but Seth says someone spoke in his head."

Parker was confused. "Spoke in your head?"

"Yeah. He spoke in my head and told me."

"What did he tell you, my man?" Parker said, feeling reality beginning to teeter.

Seth said nothing, so Janie spoke up again. "He told my brother that someone would be coming to protect us."

"He did, huh?"

"Yeah," Seth said. "A man who used to be a soldier. Is that you?"

The 2 Freeway dipped down into a valley. Their exit was a good five miles away.

Parker was speechless.

CHAPTER 12

KYLE STOOD ALONGSIDE THE Gray Man as they both looked down at the burned-out campfire that was in the middle of nowhere. He didn't need anyone to tell him that his wife had been here; he could feel her somehow, as if people left behind a bit of their essence wherever they went that forever changed a place.

No, Kyle, you have that a bit backwards.

Kyle looked at The Gray Man in annoyance. "I'd forgotten how much I disliked having you bouncing around inside my head."

"I'm sorry. The truth is, it's part of the process of you and me growing closer. I have so much to teach you before you're done."

"Done?"

"Yes."

"I thought I *was* done? Shit! Haven't I done enough?"

The Gray Man glanced out over the horizon with a pained look on his face and sighed.

"What?" Kyle asked with irritation.

"I told you, in the beginning, at the diner, right after the event."

"What event? What did you tell me?"

"The death of Caitlyn Hall. That event," The Gray Man answered deliberately, looking at Kyle. He continued, "I told you that you had a mission."

"Yes. And I guess I achieved it, right? As best I could, anyway. I stopped Victoria from killing that guy."

"You did something far more important than that: you prevented her from taking his soul."

Kicking at the desert sand, Kyle put his hands on his hips and replied, "Same difference."

"No. It's not. There's a huge difference. This world is crawling with people who have saved their lives and yet surrendered their souls."

"And what does that have to do with me?"

"You're a millionth, Kyle." The Gray Man paused for a long while before adding, "Like me."

The morning was long gone and now the sun, having made its menacing ascent, was so intense that it felt like it could penetrate the sand. The cacti and Joshua trees around them seemed to be held in suspended animation, sleepy in their stillness, their quills and branches unwilling to move.

Overcoming his shock, Kyle looked The Gray Man in the eye. "You're a millionth too?"

The Gray Man nodded. "I was. A long, long time ago. Then came my training and first assignment. As it will with you."

Kyle turned away from him. "No. Man. I told you. I'm not sure I'm made for this job."

"Yes, you are. You were created to be special, to live your life and then go on to great things."

"You mean—"

"Yes, Kyle. After death. You were destined for great things. All of you are created that way: with a destiny. Sadly, you assume from nearly the very moment you realize you have free will that your destiny is here, on this planet."

"And it's not?"

"No. You will have a temporary existence of sorts, a life in which you will live and learn and evolve. You may call that a destiny of a kind, I suppose, but in truth it's merely training for what comes next. All of it."

Kyle swallowed hard. "Training?"

"Yes. For how to love and transcend; for how to be more than conquerors. Sadly, you all get stuck conquering something here. And more often than not, that something conquers you."

The Gray Man's face had gone soft. Kyle studied him but said nothing.

"You, Kyle, decided to conquer yourself by sleeping with a woman who was not your wife. A destiny in heaven traded for a carnal indulgence."

"She was just as much to blame as me."

"She was fighting the same demons you were, Kyle. She was. Yes, before she met you they took up residence within her, where they tortured her and toyed with her mind, using her past against her like a blunt instrument, but it was you, Kyle, *you* who let them out."

Kyle shook his head. "No. That can't be right. My free will. Her free will. We're all accountable for our own actions."

In reply, The Gray Man did the oddest thing: he smiled. Looking up to the sky he said, "Now I know, Father, in your wisdom, why I was given him. He reminds me so much of myself."

Perplexed, Kyle ran his fingers through his hair and shook his head. "What are you talking about, Gray?"

Looking back at him, The Gray Man nodded with sympathy. "I made the same mistake you did, Kyle."

There were small lizard tracks in the sand, crisscross patterns of claws and tails that snaked back and forth between a group of large bushes nearby. After a while Kyle could only manage a weak reply. "Unbelievable."

"Yes and no. Who better to aid the man with a weakness for whiskey than the man who has himself swam in the bottom of a bottle? God is always at work, Kyle. Often, He uses those who have been down a certain path to help those stumbling right along behind them."

"That's all well and good, but we need to find my wife, Gray."

"In a way, we already have."

"How?"

"You noticed her essence. You thought she had affected this place. I told you no, because that is counter to your training. You're in training now, like it or not, so listen carefully. When she left she took this place *with her.* She took it in the form of memories, which are harder to trace, and in the form of ashes, from this fire, unique with the wood and plants used to fuel it. Now, put your hand in the ashes."

Kyle looked at The Gray Man as if he were crazy, but then did as he was told, tentatively at first. The ashes were gray and black on top, but there was no saying that there wasn't red hot embers just below the surface. Yet, as his fingers divided the ash and penetrated its depths, he felt nothing but cold.

"Further," The Gray Man ordered.

Finally, as he pushed nearly all the way to the ground, he felt a small remnant of heat.

"It's been a while since they were here. So they're still quite a way ahead of us," The Gray Man concluded.

"Yeah. It looks that way."

"Please note that I have shown you now two different instances of using the physical elements of this world to your advantage."

Kyle stood up and brushed the ash off his hands.

"First the dust, now the ash. One to determine distance, the other to determine time."

"Okay," Kyle said with a nod.

"That's how it works here, on this plane of existence. You know that: time and space. On other planes, other rules apply."

"What about her prayers? The ones you heard?"

"That's a different plane entirely, but you've visited it before. Prematurely, but visited it still."

"When?"

"When we were in Monterey and you were healing; when you listened to my companions and I speaking, when you saw the veil of stars around us and realized that you'd been transported somewhere else. Also, when you manifested 'the blue' so early and so powerfully. Those are forms of hearing, seeing and knowing that you should be cycles away from. But you're not."

"So? What does that mean?"

"I don't know, except that I have to accelerate your training as a result."

A bank of clouds had moved in from the west, partially obscuring the sun and leaving a dull, flat glare of weak light and discounted warmth. Turning and walking around the area, The Gray Man continued, "Don't forget, you've also done something that no one before you ever has."

"Which is?"

"Gone to hell and returned," The Gray Man said in a tone of near disbelief. "Villa and I may have helped, but I have an odd feeling you would've gotten out regardless."

Kyle chuckled grimly. "Yeah. Uh. No. I don't think so."

"Michiko came to you, Kyle. She wanders those lands in search of love, lands that would be the last place in any of the universes you could hope to find it. She wanders in the name of love. She is a legend in heaven, Kyle. And she found you."

"She said that you sent her."

"I prayed for her help, yes. But that's all. I had no way of knowing if a prayer could ever stand a chance of surviving in that place, much less reach its intended recipient."

"I couldn't have made it without her," Kyle said.

The Gray Man paused, bent down and picked something up off the ground. "Funny," he muttered softly. "She told me that you hardly needed her."

"No way," Kyle replied.

"She said that you carried within you a love that left her in awe."

Then, The Gray Man took what was in his hand, dusted it off, and raised it up for Kyle to see. It was an earring; a small gold hoop with pale green stones.

Kyle recognized it immediately. It was part of a set that he'd given Tamara a few years ago for Christmas.

The Gray Man stepped towards Kyle, then added, "She said you had a desire to seek forgiveness from the one you loved that was so strong, even the devil himself couldn't stop you."

The sky around them began to change, and as The Gray Man dropped the earring into his palm, Kyle thought of Tamara. Of her beautiful face and soft laugh and gentle touch.

And how, whenever she used to hold his hand, he never felt stronger.

* * *

It was supposed to be simple: get his ass to Union Station as soon as possible and make a phone call to Parker, who was with the Fasano kids, and limit any more collateral damage.

Instead, it had become a visit to a child-murdering psychopath's old apartment and now this, a kindergarten game of follow the detective, with a damn crow of all things.

But he knew that wasn't correct. The crow was obviously more than just a bird by the way it abandoned any attempt whatsoever to hide that it was following Napoleon, hopping from tree branch to tree branch, mostly behind him, occasionally in front of him, and sometimes squawking a few times, as if mocking him.

Napoleon turned and went one way, then the other and then back again, just to make sure, and without fail the crow shadowed him.

For a second Napoleon had déjà vu: hadn't it been like this when he'd first entered hell with The Gray Man? When they'd been chased by that wave of crows that had peeled off that wall of dead souls at the entrance? If this was a member of that same flock, where were the rest?

Trying to calm down, he reminded himself of something: *I've already survived hell. What could possibly be worse than—*

They arrived almost instantly; the world around him began to flicker in torn images. Of here. Now. And here from another time, maybe long ago, or in the future.

Reality wasn't supposed to work this way. But maybe this was the *real* reality. Maybe what he'd called reality all his life was the unreality, the clouded image, the distorted view.

The place that flickered into his vision felt like doom... and the bodies only cemented the feeling.

"Oh my God," Napoleon said.

The picture of the world around him was peeled back, in strips, to reveal another world entirely.

Around him was a field of dead angels, wings torn asunder, eyes ripped out, mouths agape in horror. They were everywhere; to the right, the left, cast in various poses of death. Back and forth the images flickered. One second a series of altars with broken-winged bodies over them, the next the image was gone, replaced with a line of parked cars.

What's going on?

And then it struck him: the crow was doing this.

He'd never felt so hopeless in all his life. If he drew his gun and tried to shoot it then he would no doubt cause panic, and he couldn't be dragged in to the station now. Trying to explain all that had happened to him would only lead to a visit to the psych ward, and far worse, it would leave Parker without any help. But if this wasn't a hallucination of some kind, what was he to do?

The images kept splicing. A tipped-over Rubbermaid trash can next to a patch of brown grass near the curb turned slowly into a lava flow on which the body of a demon floated by, its head rolled back and the tips of its horns melting like wax.

Whatever happened there, in the other world that had overlaid his own, it was a bloodbath. Open combat. Napoleon's brain began to get that feeling of complete overload, as if once more he was seeing things not meant for a human being to see, comprehending things not yet meant to be comprehended.

Then he noticed that each time his world came back into view, the shadows of the trees and cars and nearby stop sign grew darker.

And were moving… coming alive.

Shit.

He was in a mental fog, feeling around for focus, when he finally saw that the distance between the creatures in the shadows and him was narrowing by the second; they were taking on more solid form, and moving towards him.

He looked for a way out, seeing only one: a small gap between a blue Honda and white, late model Lincoln to his left, which led to a brick wall and long alley beyond.

He was beginning to shuffle his feet in that direction when he felt the crow slam into the side of his head and neck. Instinctively he reached up to slap it away, but it was fast and pecked hard at his hands. It managed to grab hold of his index finger, then planted its talons into his wrist and began pulling as hard as it could at it, as if to sever his finger completely.

Napoleon balled up his other hand and punched the crow three times before he finally dislodged it. He grabbed at it, almost catching it by a wing, before it retreated backwards and up out of reach, where it hovered for a second, cawing angrily, its wings flapping wickedly as it moved in semicircles, first left, then right, as if probing for another chance to attack.

The shadows were still shifting around him. It was now or never. The crow was like the trucker back in Barstow: present in this world and physical. But the shadows were game changers from that other world, intent on dragging him there.

Without Kyle or The Gray Man he was a goner, for sure, if they came completely to life.

He bolted for the gap between the cars and made it just as the crow swooped in for another shot, missing him as he skittered to the sidewalk and cut hard to his right, towards the alley, where it missed him again, its beak clipping at his ear as Napoleon cut hard left and began running full speed down the alley, dodging piles of discarded trash, water puddles and oil slicks along the way. There was one good thing about crows: they were slow.

Its wings flapped laboriously behind him as he pushed on, knocking over some metal trash cans and instinctively grabbing one of the lids so he'd have a shield of some kind. When he slowed to negotiate a street corner up ahead his idea worked, the crow came at him again. It pecked at the back of his scalp a few times before Napoleon brought the trash can lid up and over his head, hitting the bird in the process.

There were shadows everywhere, in the alley and the street beyond. But they were fixed. Normal. The moving shadows had been left behind.

It was just him and the crow again, which was a good thing.

He slowed to a walk as the crow flew off, up ahead a good fifty feet. In front of Napoleon, on the sidewalk, a small group of old ladies were walking in jogging suits. "*¿Es loco?*" the fattest one of them said to him as she looked at the trash can lid in his hand.

He remembered that he didn't want to attract any more attention than he already had. Thinking quickly, Napoleon answered in Spanish, telling the ladies that there was a nasty dog in the alley behind him and he'd used the lid to protect himself. It was a racial stereotype of his people, sure, but it was a true one; most of the older generation Mexicans did not like dogs. At all. Heeding his warning, they crossed instantly over to the other side of the street, their eyes looking warily at the alley the whole time, as if they expected a Stephen King monster to come trotting from its depths.

If only they knew, Napoleon mused. He tossed the trash can lid aside and marched down the street.

The crow went back to tree branch hops with short duration flights, methodically trailing him. That's when the idea occurred to Napoleon that something, or someone, was telling it what to do.

Great.

He'd thought he was free and clear. Back to the land of sinners and the saved, to help rescue a family and then get back to his life. What a fool.

His life would never be the same.

CHAPTER 13

TAMARA HAD GIVEN UP trying to figure out where they were headed. There was a left turn, then a right turn. They'd gone straight for a long while and then at some point she'd nodded off, exhausted, only to awaken as they made a U-turn.

Her head and face were throbbing in pain from her wounds. She was lucky that she didn't have a concussion, but she was pretty sure she'd give just about anything right about now for a handful of Advil.

Or Percocet. A handful of those and this whole nightmare could be over.

The worst part about her predicament was her vacillating mood swings: from defiant to defeated, from depressed to hopeful, from brave to terrified. Her mind was a spilled box of toys, her emotions like playthings, some broken, some running low on batteries, others offering the fantasy of escape.

Right now it was surrender that was the doll of choice, and suicide was the pretty outfit she was dressing it up in.

Was there a way she could just kill herself? She could provoke him, but that would be a horrible death, ultimately inflicted upon her by a man she already despised. Wasn't suicide supposed to be about going on your own terms? Maybe at the next stop there'd be traffic. Running was a more viable option when the idea wasn't to get away, but instead just about getting to a certain point.

Like the middle of the road.

In front of a rolling semi.

She could close her eyes and picture the kids in her mind, and before the monster got to her, it would be over. Who knew. Maybe in trying to get to her he'd get hit too and she could leave this earth with some small satisfaction.

Then another thought occurred to her: what if he didn't chase her? Or what if he did but didn't get hit too?

That would mean he'd still be left behind. Angry. Defeated. Bitter.

Vengeful.

She sighed heavily, her breath bouncing back into her face from the trunk lid. He'd go after the kids. She was almost sure of it. And she was sure of something else too: this all had something to do with Kyle. The phantom that had visited her in her sleep, the horrid mother and daughter in that rest stop bathroom, the creatures under Janie's bed and then later at the park and in the market, and even this man driving the car now? All of it was tied to Kyle somehow, by what he'd done here on earth or was doing in hell.

If he wasn't dead already. There was that possibility too. But she switched that notion off like a light.

She made herself think of the reality of all of this. Amazing things were happening, all of them validating her notions of good and evil, and at the same time revealing the horrible truth about them. There was no denying it anymore: every decision in life was important, and everyone did have to face an afterlife. It wasn't theory, nor did it require blind faith to believe. You had to do your best to live for the next life, and even then there were no guarantees in this one. Random evil roamed the earth. She knew this now. She only had to look around the cramped space of the trunk to confirm it.

The car took another sharp turn, this time to the right. The movement mercifully shifted the weight off her left hip, which had partially fallen asleep, and it screamed in relief as she rolled partly onto her back, her shoulder blades popping stiffly in the process.

A whiff of exhaust fumes crept into the trunk somehow. She coughed lightly, feeling her throat parched again. She'd have to find a way to convince him to leave her with bottled water next time. Because she decided once and for all that there would be a next time. As long as he was alive and had any chance at all of running off to hurt the kids? Suicide was off the table.

The car began to bounce in a rapid-fire sequence. Confused at first, she couldn't equate the sound with what it reminded her of, and then it came to her: he was driving on the lane dividers. She feared he'd fallen asleep at the wheel, but the pattern was steady and long, not an intermittent or back-and-forth sound. After a long while, just when her head began to split from the noise and she began to grow nauseous, he suddenly turned down the death metal music on the radio and blurted out, "Hey? Did you like that? Thought you might need a little massage!" Then he cackled, pulled the car off the dividers and mercifully back onto the road.

The pain in her skull had spread to the back of her eyeballs. She took some deep breaths, over and over again, a good dozen times, and forced herself to relax. She needed an out. Someplace to go that wasn't here.

Bolivia called again, so she answered…

Her mother used to like to wear flower print blouses, some blue and purple, others orange and yellow, that she would buy from the local markets on their days off, usually a weekend a month. In them, her mother looked small and pretty, her face and smile a blossom rising from the folds of colored cotton fastened one button shy of her neck. When she was younger, Tamara, like any girl, would mirror her mother and dress similarly. But as she got older, she'd changed. Wanting to be taken seriously, she'd dressed in serious colors: flat navy blue or bland tan. No flowers. No patterns. She didn't want to be girlie, but worldly. She wanted out of Bolivia and to go back to the States, where the bands she could only listen to on fading AM radio actually played concerts in arenas and stadiums.

And she wanted to have a Big Mac, every day, not just once every three or four months when they left the village to go to Brazil or home to California during the holidays to see family. Her mother would tell her that such a diet would only make her horribly fat, and yes, Tamara knew that, of course, but fat and alive was better than skinny and alone.

In her teen years the village had grown too small and stifling. There was randomness to their work that was frustrating; people found God and were saved, then found the world again and fell away. The huts and tents, boxed in by dirt roads and left behind by the passing centuries, left no room for anyone to be anything.

"To *become* anything," she whispered into the darkness of the trunk.

They were the exact words she'd said to her mother one day while they were grinding flour together, the muscles in her mother's forearms flexing in the sunlight. It was a spring day in full flourish, the tree line of the forest behind her painted in shades of fresh green and cropped in a sea of yellow flowers that, in short order, would become dandelion seed heads waiting to explode into the wind of a future day.

"Oh, Tamara," her mother replied in an impatient tone. "What is it with you and this longing to become 'something'?"

"What's wrong with that, Mom? Really."

"Why can't you just be happy with what you already are?"

"Oh, please."

"What's wrong with that? Seriously. What you are is already so beautiful, honey."

She rolled her eyes. "Mom."

"I mean it."

"I'm nothing here. I'm the pastor's daughter. I do laundry and homework and cook."

"Do you really believe that's *all* you do?"

"What else, then? Oh, yeah. I help with the food or fires. Big deal."

"And just what do you think you'd be doing that's so much better back in the States?"

Tamara shrugged in mock dismay. "You mean besides having *fun*, Meredith? Meeting new people? Doing *exciting* things?"

Meredith. Her mother's name. Gone now. The breast cancer took it, along with her smile and her pretty brown hair, which had fallen smooth and straight to the center of her back until the chemo—when it fell off like the leaves of fall.

"Don't start with the name calling," her mother chastised. It was something they'd already spoken about—a bad habit Tamara had gotten into of trying to address her mother as an equal by calling her by her first name when they would argue.

"Mom! I'm serious."

"And so am I, Tamara. You just don't understand yet. You're only fifteen."

"A woman, according to everyone here."

Now it was her mother's turn to roll her eyes. "Ah. So I see. Then you don't mind this place when its definitions serve your purpose."

Bits of chaff wafted up from their grinding bowls, catching in the air and spinning in some invisible vortex. They were quiet for a while before Tamara's mother spoke again. "Honey. Please listen to me, okay?"

"No."

"Yes. Just listen. You being who you *are*? That's far more important than chasing this someone that you *want* to be. Do you understand?"

"No."

Tamara's mother shook her head softly. "Yes you do. You're smart enough to know exactly what I'm saying. You're just being stubborn."

"Oh, please, Mom. What am I then? Do tell."

"You're the girl that every little girl in this village looks up to. Don't you see it in their eyes, especially at Sunday school? And not just the little ones, either. The big ones too. They want to braid your hair or come to you for advice about boys."

"Mom..."

"No, Tamara. Just hear me out. If you left, even if you didn't intend for them to take it that way, they'd feel like you were leaving *them*, as if they weren't good enough somehow."

Tamara stopped to rest her hands. Grinding wheat always made her fingers hurt. "How?"

Her mother slowed her pace and looked at Tamara. "Honey. When you say someplace is better than where you are, it's the same as telling people that where they are isn't good enough."

She'd looked at her mother and—

His voice boomed through the car.

"Hey, sweet cheeks! How about a love song?!"

And with that she heard 'Stand by Me' playing on the radio, a song she'd always loved. If she survived this, she'd never be able to listen to it again. He'd ruined it.

Just like she'd ruined that simple, understated hope her mother had that Tamara could become a woman who was content in serving God; a woman who could find happiness in flower print blouses and the bright smiles they brought to people who started each day with very little reason to smile at all.

Because Tamara *had* left the village, shortly thereafter.

And she'd been leaving it every, single day ever since.

* * *

After a few moments of silence, even though he felt ridiculous about it, Parker finally asked, "What did he tell you about the soldier?"

Seth hesitated, so again Janie answered for him. "That he would protect us and help us."

"Anything else?"

"And that we could trust you," Seth added. "I told my sister right after, when we were hiding. And then later, when you came to our house and we heard one of your detective friends telling one of the other policemen that you fought in the war, we knew."

The inside of the car felt suddenly stuffy. Trudy glanced over again at Parker, but he didn't acknowledge her as he lowered his window halfway down, the warm late afternoon air flowing in and only making it feel worse somehow. Cool air. He needed cool air or cool water, because this was all getting a bit too weird.

Parker cleared his throat. "Did he say anything else?"

"That we should tell you that we still weren't safe. He said you might not believe us. So we were supposed to tell you a name, that's all." There was a sweet innocence to Seth's voice, as if a voice in your head saying such things was no great miracle at all. Just another day of childhood.

Some questions you know you should ask, but you don't anyway, maybe for self-preservation reasons, maybe due to just plain instinct. Parker wanted to know the name, actually tried to move his lips to ask it, but something in him, perhaps the last bit of his rational mind going down with a fight, wouldn't let him.

To his shock, it was Trudy who asked it. "What was the name, honey?"

"Wa-heeb?" Seth answered hesitantly, sounding a bit confused. "I think that's how you say it, right?"

Moments have weight to them. Parker had known this all his life. There's the moment just before your first kiss, and before countless others that follow; there's the moment before the first live rounds of combat whiz by your head, when you can swear you "feel" the bullet coming. Moments upon moments, some sit still and others shift around, some are light and airy, others, like this one right now, were unbearably heavy. Parker could barely breathe, but Seth's question was just hanging there in the car, fluttering around in the wind rushing in through the window, so Parker forced a reply. "Yes. Yes, that's right."

"What—" Trudy said, only the first word of the question able to escape her mouth before Parker shook his head.

Jesus. Jesus. Jesus. This isn't happening. I'm not in this car. We're not going down this road.

This road...

He blinked and the 2 Freeway melted before his eyes and became Madagan Pass, a single dirt road framed on each side by dry brush and desert bushes, pockets of cacti populating the right side of the road far more so than the left. It was the only road that connected Kamdesh with Arotchi, a small village to the south, and it had become more heavily trafficked after a larger road nearby had been subjected to heavy snipering.

They were on a supply run. Two Humvees and a cargo truck. A shipment of food, ammunition and—most importantly—mail was awaiting them in Arotchi, along with four new grunts for the platoon, who were guarding the shipment.

Waheeb wasn't even supposed to be on the ride. As a local enlisted to be a translator, he was off duty that day, but bored. He'd waved off the translator who was supposed to be going and hopped into Parker's Humvee to ask him more questions about American women. Over the past eight months, he and Parker had formed a close friendship. Waheeb, being barely eighteen, had a curiosity about Western society that centered mostly on pretty girls and short skirts.

Dark skinned with thick black hair, Waheeb was considered handsome by the local village girls, but was already committed to marrying the daughter of his father's best friend, who was the head of a local tribe in the hills that had, up to now, managed to play things as close to neutral in the war as possible—which was to say they played both sides of the fence, depending on which side suited them best at the time. Waheeb's father, being a lower ranking member of the Kamdesh council, did not approve of Waheeb helping the Americans, but being sickly, he understood the army pay his son brought home as being good enough to support the family.

That was mostly Afghanistan for you: no friends and shifting enemies, with nothing in between but discrimination of facts and needs.

The I.E.D. on Madagan Pass was incapable of discrimination though. It blew up what it blew up, and on that day it blew up the Humvee in front of theirs, detonating late for some reason and catching the rear end of the vehicle. Parker had no idea if this was due to a trigger man in the hills who'd gotten the yips or maybe a bad transmitter, but it didn't matter, a piece of shrapnel ripped through the gas tank and the combined explosion of that and the I.E.D. blew with enough force to lift their vehicle, and with enough debris to shatter the front windows, killing Corporal Timmy Anderson, twenty, who was driving, and Corporal Billy Fenn, nineteen, who was riding shotgun.

That left Parker, Waheeb and Crp. Freddie Bastone, twenty, to flee out the side door and into a barrage of gunshots that rained down on them from what felt like all sides.

At twenty-five, Parker was the old man of the crew. He glanced quickly back at the supply truck and was pleased when he remembered that Perez was driving it. There was no way he would abandon them, and Parker was relieved to see the supply truck gun forwards, its engine revving loudly, as Bastone screamed into his radio back to base for help.

That help was three miles away. You could jog there in twenty minutes. Drive there in under five. But in this situation it might as well have been across the Atlantic.

A self-propelled rocket grenade hit the supply truck from a nearby hill, blowing the side door, Perez and his Holy Bible to smithereens.

Without hesitating, even as the blast force blew over and by him, Parker brought his M16 up and shot the Taliban soldier who'd fired the rocket in the head, just above his left eye, a pink plume of brain and blood misting out the back of his skull.

Waheeb was screaming, in Arabic, for them to stop, pleading for mercy, fantasies of girls in short skirts now giving way to the reality of death in short seconds.

Bastone had pulled his M30 from inside the Humvee and spun around with it on his hip, firing a string of spitting three-inch rounds into the hill on their side of the vehicle, cutting two more Taliban nearly in half and clipping a third in the thigh, his leg bone bending and then snapping beneath him as he screamed in pain.

"Parker?"

It was Trudy O'Hara, from someplace very far away.

"Yeah?" he replied in a daze, the fingers of the memory still clutching him.

"What exit did you say?"

"Verdugo Road. Turn right. Travel Lodge."

"Are you okay?" she asked softly, worry in her voice.

"Are you okay?!" Bastone shouted at him. "Parker?"

"Yes! Everyone is down but us, you got that, Bastone?"

Bastone nodded as he swung the M30 to the front of the vehicle and laid down a line of fire, which momentarily stopped the firing from that direction. Parker meanwhile used the grenade launcher on his rifle to fire rounds off over the back of the car at random to try and quiet the enemy behind them. The grenades exploded and shouting echoed through the canyon.

He had a few precious seconds to assess their situation, determine their options and to make a decision. In the meantime, Bastone was back on his radio.

"Mr. Parker. Please don't leave me," Waheeb screamed, clutching at Parker's chest and shoulder. "You know what they'll do to me."

Parker pushed him back but made the mistake of looking into Waheeb's eyes; they were filled with horror.

"I won't leave you, man," Parker said.

"Please, sir. Please don't!" Waheeb pleaded, his face melting in desperation.

"Don't worry," Parker said, "I swear. Bastone? What's the word?"

"They're on their way. We got lucky. They decided to send another Humvee shortly after we left to send Starett along. One of the greenhorns we were supposed to pick up has a fever or some shit."

Parker nodded. Starett was the company medic. But if they didn't get here quick, his services wouldn't be needed.

The fire from the position behind them had nearly ceased. That meant one of Parker's grenades had randomly found their mark. Lucky.

Still. They were far too outnumbered to make a stand here.

"You got a plan?"

The sun was high, a melon ball burning too bright directly over their heads. "Yes! But we're fucked if we don't get to that ridge!" Parker shouted, pointing left with his hand while he used his eyes to indicate they would be going right. Immediately both he and Bastone laid down fire as they bolted to the right, hell bent on a dead run for a small hill about thirty yards away.

Tactics 101: visibly point left, then go right. The enemy will waste a second or so firing in the wrong direction. It was an old trick, but soldiers knew it well.

But Waheeb was not a soldier. Taking Parker literally, he bolted left like a scalded dog, his joints fueled by panic, and directly into the line of fire.

Parker glanced over his shoulder just in time to see Waheeb take five or six bullets to his lower extremities and one to the shoulder.

He fell in a heap, very much alive, screaming, his hand outstretched to Parker.

Bastone, moving ahead with ferocious determination, screamed at Parker to follow, but Parker stopped. He'd made a promise.

Then? Their luck ran out.

A hail of bullets so thick that it felt like a hot waterfall separated Parker from Waheeb. Parker hit the ground, rolled behind a large boulder to his left and tried twice more to advance to Waheeb to get him out. But it was no use.

Suddenly, out of nowhere, three Taliban appeared next to Waheeb and dragged him away as he screamed in terror. Parker emptied his clip trying to stop them but it was no use.

Often now, whenever Parker visited a nightmare in his sleep, what awaited him was the image of Waheeb's face at that very moment they dragged him away. It was a face that still pleaded for the great and mighty American with all his manly stories of conquered women to rescue him.

Parker had sat in shock behind the boulder as Bastone hunkered down in relative safety on the ridge and laid down more suppression fire. He was still sitting in the same spot when the other Humvee arrived and two Black Hawk helicopters swooped in from the west, guns screaming.

But the Taliban had heard the rotors coming long before and had already melted away into the mountains, their day a big success, and though they had all searched for him, Waheeb's body was never to be found.

A month later, Parker and the rest of his unit were shipped home.

That was the last time he ever made a promise to anyone about anything.

Until now.

All Parker could think of as they pulled up to the Travel Lodge was that he'd done it again—this time for the kids.

He'd done it by the pool at the Fasano house without a second's thought or hesitation.

Just like the voice that spoke to Seth hoped he would. But it also left behind a little reminder, a single name, for Seth to pass on: Waheeb.

To remind Parker that this time?

This time he had to get it right.

CHAPTER 14

Kyle somehow saw them before The Gray Man did: shimmers that became cuts and then violent cracks in the sky off to their left. Again he was struck by the utter facade of everyday life, how the trees and sidewalks, and now even the sky, were like painted images on rice paper that could be easily tossed aside by forces beyond human comprehension, forces of good and evil who wandered in and out of the world as if it were a spare room.

There were three of them, blackish-gray demons, with ears like bats that sprung outward from the sides of their heads. They were about half a football field away, and even from this distance he could tell that they were large and muscular.

"Hey, Gray!" Kyle shouted.

From within their cocoon of light, traveling at the speed they were moving, they sped quickly past the creatures. The demons angled their bodies and banked hard to the left as they fell through the sky, swooping in behind Kyle and The Gray Man.

"I see them," The Gray Man said.

"What are they?"

"I have no idea. But we've come to someone's attention and—"

Kyle craned his neck over his shoulder to track the flight of the demons, but just as he realized they had no wings, they crossed into the tunnel of light that he and The Gray Man were traversing in and seemed to completely short circuit it. The Gray Man's sentence was cut off and Kyle realized, to his horror, so was their method of travel.

They were in free fall, from a good five thousand feet up in the sky.

The Gray Man tried to grab him but it was no use. Kyle was out of his reach. He was on his own now. There was no two ways about it.

This feeling was only compounded when all three demons immediately set upon The Gray Man, a blackish cloud of limbs and gnashing teeth enveloping him as he looked towards Kyle with a haunted expression.

Kyle panicked. He didn't know how to fly, or coast, or travel the way The Gray Man did. He had no parachute, no anything. As he fell, his lungs compressed in his chest and he spun his arms wildly. Then it was obvious what he had to do: he called on the blue.

It came to him as if a levee had finally given way; it coursed through his body wild and free, hard and pure, instantly stabilizing his fall and leaving him stunned and breathless before launching him to where he told it he wanted to go: towards The Gray Man.

By the time he was close enough to see that The Gray Man was shaking his head at him, it was too late. Kyle crashed into the falling group with such force that it temporarily separated everyone. Then, like magnets, the demons seemed to snap right back upon The Gray Man, except this time one of them grabbed a hold of Kyle too.

He felt hell, the place he'd barely escaped, there in his mind, like a new horizon, like a confirmed destination. He felt it in the desperate mental pleas of The Gray Man, who was shouting in his head. *Kyle! Break loose. Get away!*

And there was still time for that, still an opportunity. The demon that had grabbed him was barely hanging on. One burst of the blue into his face and maybe, just maybe, he could get away.

Which of course would mean condemning The Gray Man to the same fate that he had actually rescued Kyle from in the first place.

Logic tried to join the fall, clouds zipping past them like so many gobs of melted marshmallows. Wasn't that the point? Wasn't Kyle supposed to be some sort of chosen one? Or rescued one? Wouldn't The Gray Man himself, if given the luxury of one more quiet chat over a cup of coffee and a warm slice of blueberry pie, tell Kyle that he should escape, that the whole point of all of this was him and his evolution, or whatever it was? Wouldn't The Gray Man insist that his own sacrifice was a very small price to pay for that?

Kyle was never good with logic. He usually relied on his emotions and his feelings, and they'd mostly served him well, until the day he'd cheated on his wife. Then they'd proven to be not so reliable. But now? He was going to follow them anyway; he cared too much about his friend. And he was not going to allow this to happen.

The blue exploded out of his hand in a thin burst that struck a glancing blow across the neck of the demon latched onto his ankle, partially severing its head. The force of the fall and the pressing wind caught the lip of the wound and slowly tore its head the rest of the way off. It was a moment of hope. Now, two on two, they'd have a better chance.

When the sky ripped again it was with a sharp crack that split Kyle's eardrums. A larger hole this time. They all fell through.

Instinctively Kyle let loose with a body-wide burst of the blue that diverted their course across the great expanse on the other side of the portal, an expanse that seemed to be a black, far-off section of the universe, and away from a small supernova nearby, which Kyle instinctively knew was some sort of gateway to hell the creatures intended them for.

They careened wildly towards a large meteor, ashen and barren, below and to the right of them. It was there that The Gray Man seemed to gain some leverage on the two remaining demons as he slowed their descent and then steered them all to the surface of the meteor. It wasn't a gentle landing though. The four of them bounced and rolled, all in separate directions, Kyle feeling the skin of his left temple grind across the fine sandpaper surface of the meteor, skin giving way in sheets of pain. He reached out to try to stop his motion, and was finally able to grip a small section of rock that held firm, stopping his roll.

The first thing he realized was that he could still breathe. How? Then he felt it: in his lungs and veins and heart. The blue had spread through him internally, like a second system of blood. He could've never imagined such a thing, and therefore he could've never called it into action, which meant that something, somehow, was protecting him even when he didn't know how to protect himself. He wondered if maybe the blue was alive in a way, with cognitive powers all its own.

Standing on wobbly knees he saw The Gray Man rise as well. The two remaining demons seemed momentarily confused.

Then, The Gray Man's voice was in his head: *They're not as strong here.*

I know, Kyle thought back. It was obvious that words would do no good in a place that carried no sounds.

Keep them at a distance, The Gray Man ordered.

The demons turned and faced them. They were at least twelve feet tall. Their eyes, red beads swimming in opaque circles, were slanted downward and reached almost to their ears. Their mouths were pulled back in grimaces, exposing small piranha-like teeth.

It's an even fight, Kyle said. *You take the one closest to you and I'll take the one closest to me.*

In a bar, back in the real world, it would've made perfect sense.

But in this place, with who they were up against, not so much.

As Kyle watched in stunned disbelief, the creatures craned their necks, as if popping a few vertebras to release some tension after a long day, and then proceeded to reach up to their faces. As they did so, their hands became more elongated and their fingertips much sharper.

Then, with zero hesitation, they simply dug their fingers into their faces, through their own skin, their cheekbones splitting first, then their noses and eye sockets, then as one hand pulled upwards through their skulls, the other pulled downwards through their torsos. And slowly, deliberately, every bone in them gave way as they tore themselves completely in half.

The Gray Man, either sensing something was coming or just trying to jump on a tactical advantage, leaped forwards to attack but was repelled by an unseen force field. Kyle, taking his cue, fired a bolt of blue at them, but it simply careened off into space where it disappeared among some stars.

Still, it made no sense. Kyle wondered why their opponents were killing themselves.

Because they aren't, The Gray Man said. He was becoming more of himself around Kyle now, even though Kyle wished he wasn't, because his voice was tinged with deep concern.

In front of them, the creature-halves held static in the air and then, like an Etch-A-Sketch moving with a laser dot and at top speed, Kyle watched in awe as each half restored itself in zipping lines of crisscrossing currents.

The two were now four.

* * *

Napoleon made his way methodically down the street, one step at a time and with a wary eye in the crow's direction. The damned thing had evidently gotten a good taste of that trash can lid, because it was keeping its distance now. At present, it was on a telephone wire overhead, doing a little hop-skip down the line in that ominous, mischievous lurch characteristic of crows. Unlike with other birds, there was nothing graceful about crows, nothing hopeful. This one was no different. It occasionally came close enough for Napoleon to see its flat black eyes, contrasted against the sheen of its shiny black feathers.

If Napoleon advanced twenty feet or so, it would retreat an equal distance, as if it were mocking him with the obviousness of its intent to continue watching him.

And that's when it dawned on Napoleon that going to Union Station right now and calling Parker was the worst idea ever. He would lead whatever forces behind this bird right to them—to Parker and the Fasano children.

He was so disappointed by this thought that he hadn't realize he'd slowed his pace. He thought of stopping altogether. Surely this would force the crow's hand and maybe even make it go back on the attack again. If so, maybe he could kill it and then be free to get to Parker.

It was odd, because he was used to being the one doing the following. But he was also used to the notion of not making it obvious. That was the whole point, really, seeing where your target was naturally headed. But whoever was guiding the crow was not interested in stealth or deception.

Which meant that it either already knew where Napoleon was going or didn't care.

After another four blocks he reached Boylston, which was busy with traffic in both directions. There was a liquor store on the corner nearest him and a Shell gas station across the street. With no cell phone he couldn't call Uber—something he had just learned how to do from the pimply-faced rookie at the reception desk a few months back—but up ahead there was a bus stop. He could ask the driver for the right lines to take, but now something else was going on: his gut was churning. A sort of urgency had developed there, and was spreading to his nerves.

Parker needed him. In a bad way. He could flat out feel it.

He looked over at the gas station and noticed a red, white and blue Independent cab gassing up, its rates spelled out in faded decals on the rear door. The cab had seen better days, probably back in the '90s, and it looked like one could say the same for the cabbie. He was leaning against the back edge of the car, staring at the ground, one hand resting on the nozzle.

Reaching into his pockets, Napoleon found a wrinkled five; not enough for a cab. But he still had his badge. That would get him what he wanted. He darted across the street and approached the cabbie. "Hey!"

The cabbie was Middle Eastern with a worn face and graying beard, which he scratched at as he looked towards Napoleon. "What's up?"

"I need a ride."

"Not really on the clock yet, but since my wife's the boss and fetches the calls from home, she won't mind. Where to?"

That's the million dollar question, Napoleon thought. Instead he said, "Doesn't matter," and flashed his badge at the cabbie. "I'm being followed and I need a ride out of this area. Now."

The cabbie's suddenly bunched up face made it clear that he thought Napoleon was on crack. "Yeah, right, buddy. Funny joke. What are you, homeless or something? You find that on the street or what?"

Thinking quickly, Napoleon replied succinctly and firmly. "Look. I've been undercover. It's gone upside down on me. Look at the photo closely; you'll see it's me."

The cabbie squinted at the ID, his eyes dancing to Napoleon's face a few times. It was a little disconcerting. Did he really look that much differently now? Evidently, yes.

Meanwhile, the crow had landed on the air/water machine nearby and was bobbing its head in a "yeah-yeah" sort of movement.

Napoleon gritted his teeth. *Fucking crows.*

"Look buddy—" the cabbie began.

But Napoleon was in no mood. His gut was churning even worse now. "'Look buddy' nothing. I'm a police officer in need of your car. You can just give me a ride and be on with your day or I can take it and call the number on the side to tell your wife where I've left it and screw you out of a day's worth of fares. You decide."

The man looked at Napoleon angrily as he chewed on his lower lip, which was dry and cracked. "Fine. Shit. Okay."

He pulled the nozzle out of the car and re-racked it before he got behind the wheel. Napoleon climbed in the backseat.

"Where to?" the cabbie asked again.

"Just get on the freeway," Napoleon said.

He was getting old, he was tired and he'd just gotten back from hell, so he wanted to cut himself a little slack for not being the stupidest man alive as he watched the cabbie grab his cell phone off the dashboard, evidently to make a call, probably to the wife.

He didn't know Parker's number by heart and he didn't dare call the station to ask for it. They would flip and lose their minds if they knew he was back.

But, then again, it didn't have to be *him* who was calling…

"Give me that!" Napoleon commanded.

"What?"

"I gotta call the station. You just get on the freeway before…" He had to get this guy moving, so Napoleon let his imagination take it from there. "Before the guys after me shoot us both."

It worked. The cabbie practically tossed him the phone while he put the car in gear and pealed out of the driveway. A block later they merged onto the ramp of the 10 Freeway.

Napoleon saw the crow following behind, flying furiously to keep up, but it worked: slowly but surely it became a receding black dot over the freeway behind them.

Napoleon sighed in relief and dialed the station house. After three rings, the clerk at the front desk of the station answered.

Napoleon smiled at the irony. It was Cooper. The kid who had taught him about Uber. Damn. Now he would have to disguise his voice. Muffling his mouth, Napoleon leaned towards the back window of the cab, which he lowered a bit for background noise. "Who's this again?" he asked.

"Officer Cooper. How can I help?"

"Cooper, it's Detective Arias. I'm in the field and I need some help. Can you get me the cell phone number for Detective Parker?"

There was a short hesitation that felt like a trip to the damned ballet.

"Uh. Sure thing, Detective. But you know the scoop. I need your badge number before I can just go handing out that information."

Well, at least he hadn't recognized Napoleon's voice. Still. What now?

"Shit, Cooper. C'mon. I can never remember that. You know me." Napoleon thought of Arias and then went with it. "I'm about six-two. The other guys call me slugger? Best guy on the squad softball team? And I know you. Blond hair. You like the Red Sox, even though you're originally from Philly. Fuck. Do I have to go on? I'm pressed here."

"Hey, Arias. Okay. I hear ya. But you sound different. You got a cold or something?"

Napoleon rolled his eyes. "Yeah. Bad one too." A few coughs would've sounded too fake, so instead he cleared his throat for effect.

"Got it. Here it is."

As he read off the number Napoleon tapped the cabbie on the shoulder and motioned for a pen and paper so he could write it down. Then he thanked Cooper for the number, thanked God that Arias wasn't on shift at the moment and hung up.

As the car wove its way through traffic on the 10, Napoleon dialed Parker's number and looked out the window.

The crow was still there in the sky, wings flapping furiously to keep up.

They were in LA, which meant traffic and more traffic, but maybe if they could get to the 2 Freeway he could tell the cabbie to open it up.

He didn't know how fast a crow could fly, but no crow could outfly a car.

Apprehension filled him from head to toe as Parker's phone rang.

It rang three times before it went to voicemail.

CHAPTER 15

THE MOTEL ROOM WAS small, but not as small as the trunk. Tamara sat on the edge of the bed while the monster sat in a corner of the room in a cloth chair, next to a small round table that was partially lit by one of the nightstand lamps he'd turned on. A pop-up advertisement card for the local Applebee's was standing at attention, casting a shadow across his forearm. Except for the soft hum of the air conditioning unit, the room was quiet and still.

She surmised that he'd picked the deadest motel around and asked for a room at the back of the complex, because when he parked and pulled her out of the trunk, there were no other cars around and not even the motel office was in sight. He'd backed the car up to the ground level room door, grabbed her out of the trunk and carried her rapidly six feet or so into the room, like a piece of luggage. He was bold. And reckless. And seemingly invincible. But not stupid. He'd made sure her gag was stuffed even tighter into her mouth than usual before he did any of it.

The room wasn't cold, but she was shivering from nerves. A motel room. Her on a bed. Him nearby. This couldn't turn out well.

He'd been silent for a good twenty minutes now. She knew that because the digital alarm clock on the nightstand, which said 3:40 when they arrived, now read 4:00.

At times she could hear him murmuring quietly, the words sharp one moment, pleading another, as if he were arguing with himself but unable to keep the dialogue contained in his head.

Shit. The waiting is the worst.

But she knew that was a lie. When he raped her? That would be the worst. No point in trying to deny it.

As if reading her mind, he finally spoke. "Take off your clothes."

She welled up. At some point you cry because that's all there's left to do. "No," she said softly, as if she had an option.

"Don't make me say it again, bitch."

She shook her head.

In one fluid motion he stood, took two steps towards her and slapped her, hard, across the face with the back of his hand. Spittle flew from her mouth as she recoiled in shock.

Jesus. No. This isn't happening. Please tell me this isn't happening.

He was on her in a second. Grabbing her by the shoulders, he threw her on her back, then sat on her stomach and forced her arms over her head. "Don't… you… *ever*… tell me 'no,' bitch. You understand?"

She grimaced in defiance. Her clothes were still on. He'd have to let go of her arms or try to hold them both with one hand in order to take them off of her, and then she was going to attack him with all she had. "I'm not going to let you do this."

He chuckled. "Do what? Oh, *that*? Yes you will, for the sake of your little ones. Best thing that ever happened was your kids getting away from me. Had I killed them already, I'd have nothing to bargain you down with, would I?"

"You won't go back there. You can't now. They're safe."

"You're right. I can't... now. But all I gotta do is go into hiding, wait a while, maybe six months, maybe a year, until everyone relaxes. They always do, ya know? I mean, do you have any idea how many girls I've killed already? Some weeks apart. Some years and years apart."

Her heart sank as her breathing became labored. His weight on her was too much, but his words were even worse. He meant it. He was talking in a slightly different tone now, with the voice of a man at a job interview, establishing his qualifications.

"No. They're safe. You'll never get to them."

No chuckle this time; instead he laughed. Hard. "Please. Who's going to stop me? The police? They haven't been able to stop me all this time."

"Somebody will."

"Who? That detective friend of yours? The wetback?"

Tamara blinked. How did he know about Napoleon Villa?

"Or maybe your husband, Tamara? Maybe him?"

A chill came and nestled itself in that soft space between her neck and chest, like a winter bird hunkering down in a storm. Kyle? He knew about Kyle too? How?

He rolled off of her stomach and reclined next to her like a lover, his head propped up on his elbow, relaxed and gazing at her face. With his other hand he began to gently stroke her cheek. "Pooooor honey-pie. You just don't know what you've gotten yourself into, do ya?"

Confusion swam over her. "What're you talking about?"

Then he uttered two words that knocked her clear into outer space. "They're alive."

She tried to speak, but couldn't.

"They're back, honey-bee. Back home. Safe and sound. Driveling pieces of shit that they are."

Kyle was back? And the detective too? "How?" she forced herself to ask.

"Oh. You know, that hubby of yours is quite special. Oh yes. First he wins, then kinda loses, then ends up in a place where no one wins, but fucking ends up winning anyways. It's really incredible, ya know."

"Oh my God. Kyle!" she cried, relief flooding her veins.

The hand caressing her cheek suddenly gripped her throat, so tight she was certain that this was it, that he was going to kill her by crushing her windpipe. "Don't you ever, *ever*, mention that pig's name in front of me again." Then, just as quickly, he released her.

She coughed in a series of phlegm-filled hacks, her throat trying to realign itself as the air moving in and out of her lungs wreaked havoc going both ways.

"So. Here we are," he continued. "First, he upsets my master. Then he upsets my master's master. Not good, that last part. Some masters you don't want to upset. Here. Let me show you why."

He reached out and gently laid his hand on the soft space between her breasts, and his touch brought with it a flood of pictures.

Images of the sins of her life came upon her like a thousand rapists, each taking turns. Each moment of lust, shame, fear, anger, vengeance, slander, every bad thought, spiteful word, disgraceful act and shame again, more and more shame, a triple scoop of it, so that all the things she'd hid in her life, the scars that never mended, the bruises that never healed, began to open and throb in pain, all those secrets that she'd tucked away in her mind so very well, or so she'd thought, now let loose to run around inside her skull, a wild stampede of mistakes and sorrows.

Then, for some reason, she thought of Ben.

"Ahhh," he moaned in suppressed ecstasy. "Thank you, master," he said. "It *is* better than sex." And he rolled onto his back and closed his eyes before speaking again, now with bated breath. "So, honey bunny, you get it now? You're little boyfriend there from work? The one you wanted to have in your mouth, the one you thought of having all over that office desk, the one—"

"Stop it!" Tamara cried.

"Oh no, I won't. Fuck you. This is all *your* fault. I was happy just doing my thing there in my little no-name town. Just like that sheriff I had to kill. Both of us like opposite sides of the same boring coin. But I was content. All you had to do was screw that horny boy and that would've succeeded in turning the tables a bit. The echo of that sin woulda found its way to your hubby's ears at the crucial moment, when he was fighting his first love—how Shakespearean, no?—and then maybe, just maybe, he woulda slipped up and failed completely in his damnable mission. But no. Nope. Nope. Nope. You had to keep them legs closed, didn't you, whore? You had to be *faithful*."

The last word seemed so disgusting to him that he spat on her after he said it, twice, the wetness erupting on her check and forehead.

Tamara couldn't have cared less. Her shock was in full bloom. Her mind, expunged of all the evil deeds in her life, both large and small, was like jelly. To counter the thoughts of Ben, she thought of Kyle. "He's alive. He's okay," she whimpered.

"Yes, he is." He laughed. "And don't worry, Maid Marian, your Robin Hood is coming for you."

She froze.

"And we'll be waiting for him when he does, won't we, master?"

The room seemed to tilt. Tamara blinked. There was no one with them, so who was he talking—

"Look in the mirrors, honey baby," he whispered.

When she did she saw him: a man in a black wool coat, black sweater and a black scarf wrapped a few times around his neck, the ends dangling over his chest. He had no face, or rather, his face was completely wrapped in black cotton swaths that seemed to be matted to his features, so that you could barely make out the outline of his nose, mouth and eye sockets. On his head he wore an old top hat.

She shrieked in horror, but the cry was stifled by the crazy man's hand, which clamped down over it instantly. From her spot on the bed she could see the creature in the mirror over the dresser, but she could also see into the bathroom nearby, and he was there too, in the mirror over the sink. She had a feeling that if there were more mirrors in the room that she would see him in all of them, his horrible image emanating nothing but hate and rage in alternating but equal proportions.

Then she noticed that in one hand he was holding, of all things, a lantern.

Just like the one Ben had brought to her home, as a gift.

As if reading her mind again, the monster lying next to her spoke into her ear. "You're getting it now, aren't ya, honey bunny? Benny-boy. He's still out there, back home, isn't he? So, you see? I don't have to go back to get your babies." He chuckled, sweet and long. "*He'll* do the job just fine."

She screamed against his palm and closed her eyes as he slid his tongue into her ear.

* * *

After they'd checked in, Parker notified Murillo that they were safe and sound. Trudy washed up while the kids watched cartoons, but before long they began to protest that they were hungry.

They'd passed a 7-Eleven that was just a mile down the road before they'd checked in, so they decided to make a run and load up on food and snacks to get through the night and, most importantly to Parker, to get a large coffee with four shots of caffeine booster. Anything he could do to erase the images of Kamdesh and Waheeb. It seemed that, as of late, he was having a hard time controlling his memories. As if the PTSD was making a comeback.

Parker felt his phone vibrating in his pocket, but he had a problem.

He'd noticed the guy in the John Deere cap the minute they got out of the car and began making their way into the store. He was what Parker's mother used to call "husky," but he wore that look at an easy six foot three. He stood near a large tree near a short wall that separated the 7-Eleven from the car dealer next door. His face was covered in a full beard and his blond hair hung to his shoulders. But it was his eyes, that seemed red at first but were now squinted nearly shut and staring, that caught Parker's attention first. Parker looked away, took a few more strides towards the entrance and then looked back: he was still staring at them.

After the promise of candy brought at least a small squeal of happiness out of the kids, Parker had agreed to this stop, but now something about the John Deere man made Parker regret that decision. The kids were to Parker's right, flanked by Trudy, which at least meant Parker was squarely between them and this guy, but that was assuming that he was alone.

Scanning the area, Parker noticed that he wasn't. A skinny man was near the entrance, wearing a Lynyrd Skynyrd t-shirt and a black beanie that was far too hot for a day like today. He had one foot up on the wall, just kicking back, and was smoking a cigarette.

And glaring at Parker as well.

Parker could feel his phone vibrating madly again. Whoever it was, they'd have to wait. He wasn't done sizing these two up yet.

The little boy was ambling a few feet away from them, excited to get his candy. Instinctively Parker reached out, grabbed his shoulder and gently guided him closer to Trudy.

Parker felt the weight of his 9 mm tucked there safely in its holster against the small of his back. He also had a small .22 strapped against his sock on the inside of his left ankle.

Who the hell are these guys? And what the hell is going on?

The two questions banged like gongs in his head the entire walk to the door, over and over again. His muscles tensed. This whole situation was fluid, in a bad way, as if things could go upside down at any moment, from any direction, for no reason.

But, for now, John Deere stayed put and so did the kid with the beanie. Only once did they divert their gazes, quickly towards one another and then back to center again, like lizards, and that was all the confirmation Parker needed that they were together. A pair. Two pals. Like two guys at the bar who had decided they didn't like the way that Parker looked or something.

Once inside, Parker exhaled a bit. It was busy, with five customers lined up at the counter with their Slurpees, Slim Jims or Red Bulls. Parker noticed that one guy even had a Ne-Mo's Banana Bread cake in his hand, Parker's favorite.

"Can I get a Big Gulp?" Janie asked excitedly.

"Sure, honey," Trudy answered, smiling weakly at her.

"I want M&M's!" Seth yelled. Trudy's smile grew a little bigger and Seth ran off down the candy aisle.

There were two Pakistanis behind the counter in 7-Eleven smocks. Parker knew this because he knew the accent and because there was never going to be another day of his life that he ran into anyone looking or sounding even slightly Middle Eastern that he wasn't going to immediately, at least for a second, be on guard against. They were young guys. Their dad probably owned the store. He relaxed a bit.

"What should we get?" Trudy asked him, lightly touching his forearm.

Parker shrugged. "The usual artery cloggers, right? Let's get them pizza slices now, Hot Pockets or something for later. Hopefully the room has a microwave."

Trudy was watching Seth turn his permission for one candy into a lottery session that included Sour Patch Kids, a 3 Musketeers bar and three different colored Twizzlers. "I just don't want them loading up on candy," she said.

"Shit," Parker replied, "after what they've been through? I'd let them have whatever they want."

Trudy nodded. "Only because you won't be the one stuck up with them until two in the morning on their sugar highs."

"Oh, yes I will," Parker said matter-of-factly.

Trudy raised her eyebrows. "You're planning on staying in one room?"

"Yes. Yes I am."

"That's not necessary."

"Look. I'll sleep on the floor or in the bathtub. Whatever. But something's going on and I'm not going to leave the three of you alone."

"You'd be just next door or across the hall."

Parker looked at Trudy firmly. "Which, I have a feeling, could still be too far away, okay?"

He thought she was going to argue further, but instead she just nodded gently, as if she were relieved by his protests. "You don't have to sleep on the floor or"—she rolled her eyes—"in the bathtub. We have a room with two beds. Me and the kids take one, you take the other."

Parked nodded. "Fair enough."

As she took the display tongs and loaded six pieces of pizza into a to-go bag, Trudy surprised Parker with what she said next. "Is something wrong?"

"Yes."

"What?"

"Did you notice the two guys on the way in?"

"No. Who?"

"The scrawny guy with the black beanie by the door, and the big guy in the baseball cap near the tree at the edge of the driveway."

Trudy squinted out the window, and then looked confused. "I don't see them. Where?"

Looking out the store windows to the parking lot, Parker's heart sank. John Deere had moved from his original position near the driveway and was now standing in the parking lot. Right next to their car. "Shit."

"What?"

"The big guy is standing by your car now. Do you see him?"

Trudy's face darkened. "Yeah. Where's the other one?"

Parker scanned the parking lot again until he noticed the beanie opposite the other side of the entrance now, near a USA Today stand. "You can barely see him, the right edge of the window."

Trudy looked and nodded as worry lines scattered from her eyes and across her forehead.

Janie made her way back to the counter with a Slurpee cup that was damn near the size of her head. She looked at Parker sweetly. "Raspberry and Cola! Yummy."

Parker didn't want to alarm the children so he forced himself to chuckle and say, "It must be."

Trudy played along. "I got pizza. Why don't you guys grab some Gatorade and chips for later? I'll get some Hot Pockets or something."

As the kids ran off again to gather the goods, Trudy turned to Parker. "What do we do?"

"We could call the police," Parker replied wryly.

"You *are* the police."

"Yeah. I know. That was me being a smartass. Still, backup wouldn't be a bad idea."

Trudy sighed, but it was a sigh of fear. It rattled out of her not in a single breath, but in stages. "They haven't done anything yet but stare at us."

"Maybe they think you're hot, or maybe I remind them of someone that used to beat them up when they were little."

Trudy nodded again. "Yeah. Well, no offense, but I'm not sure too many guys have ever beat up on the big dude."

Parker was tired and irritable, so he let it slip in spite of himself. "Fuck him."

As Trudy walked off to get the Hot Pockets, he walked over to the coffee island, glancing repeatedly outside as he made his coffee. Their two new friends had stayed put, which was a relief, because for some reason Parker suspected that, if given the chance, John Deere would flatten their tires with whatever knife he had on his person, because a guy like that always carried a knife.

Once everyone had what they wanted, they got in line at the cash register.

Parker thought again about calling for backup, but that would be overreacting a bit, and there was a chance he'd end up looking jumpy after just returning to active duty. Plus, if he were honest, he had a burning in his chest right now for a fight. With someone. Anyone. Sometimes putting a beating on an asshole or two was the best kind of stress relief.

He was beginning to imagine how he'd do it, how he'd take out John Deere's left kneecap first, then deal with the scrawny classic rock fan next, when his phone went off. Again.

Pulling it out of his pocket, he checked the caller ID, not recognizing it. He decided not to answer again, but then something told him he should. "Hello?"

"Parker?"

The voice was unmistakable. Parker was so stunned that he had to lean against the counter.

CHAPTER 16

Kyle wondered if these things could just keep doing this: splitting and multiplying. If so, then what? They had now instantly gone from an even match to being outnumbered two to one. This might only get worse if they didn't find a way to kill them.

Widen your blasts! The Gray Man commanded. He stepped back and brought both his hands forwards in front of his face and quickly swept them down and out to his sides. Two white crescent-shaped lines cut free of his hands and carved through the air towards the two demons nearest him. One missed by a large margin but the second, in mid-air and evidently still under The Gray Man's control, suddenly spun sideways, catching the demon it was intended for just below both knees, severing its legs completely. It let loose a silent scream and toppled forwards, face first, into the dirt, its claws clutching at the ground in pain.

Meanwhile, the demons nearest Kyle had closed in. He almost panicked before realizing that maybe this was a good thing, because the closer they got the easier they would be to hit. They charged in hard, zigzagging back and forth, and before long they were within twenty feet. Kyle's first blast incinerated the taller of the two and he puffed out of existence in a spray of orange and red ash. But the second demon, seeing what was coming, stuttered in the air again, a good half dozen times, moving through the dark creases one by one, like a child weaving in and out of the clothes racks in a department store, until he was close enough to reach out and grab Kyle.

Instinctively, Kyle brought both his hands up to his chest to defend himself, his left hand blocking one of the claws while the blue shot out of his right hand at a downwards angle, disemboweling the creature with a round blue hole about eight inches in diameter.

Two down, one dead, one still…

Kyle looked up to see that The Gray Man and the final demon were grappling with each other, the demon stepping back at times to unleash a flurry of blows to The Gray Man's head, the punches landing clean and hard. The Gray Man would try to back away and get some distance before the creature would charge and grab him again. Kyle was just beginning to wonder what The Gray Man's strategy was when it became apparent: by retreating and keeping the demon on the attack, he was keeping the creature from splitting itself again.

Kyle moved to help but was grabbed around the waist by the demon he'd felled. Its claws dug into his sides, the death grip of a dying creature, knocking Kyle to one knee. It died just as it tried pulling itself up to Kyle's face, its fangs gnashing with wet, bloody spittle.

Immediately Kyle felt the evil in it trying to pierce through his wounds, to infect him with the germs the creature had carried with it all the way from hell. Reaching down, Kyle ripped the creature's hands free, screaming as the claws tore at his skin. He was bleeding, badly, which surprised him because the wounds didn't seem to be that severe. Taking a deep breath and putting one hand over each wound, Kyle cauterized them with the blue, again aware that he was doing things that no one had taught him.

Looking up, Kyle noticed that the demon The Gray Man had taken out at the knees was beginning to reach up to tear itself apart again. Wasting no time, Kyle blasted it in the chest, just below the throat, and it toppled over with a wide-eyed death stare.

Meanwhile, the final demon was in the last seconds of its life as well. The Gray Man's white force pulsed down his wrists and into the forearms of the creature that was gripping him. Kyle watched in awe as the white spread throughout the creature in fine woven lines, like a spider's web, cutting into and bursting it from the inside out, its limbs exploding in four different directions as its head melted into its chest cavity.

Kyle ran and half-stumbled his way to The Gray Man, who seemed completely spent by the battle.

Are you okay? Kyle thought the question.

Leaning over, The Gray Man nodded but said nothing.

What now?

The Gray Man held up a hand, as if asking Kyle to wait, then after a moment he replied, *We've got to get out of here. The enemy dominates this place to such an extent that we might as well be in hell again. It's almost worse, I think.*

Worse?

Yes, the creatures here, there are more of them, various species. I can feel their thoughts. They're all on their own. There's no order here, no control. It's just a plane of madness that's infected everything.

Well, what do we do next then? It's not like I can get us out of here, said Kyle.

You're going to have to.

Kyle was shocked. *How?*

You have to learn to traverse.

What?

You remember, when we first met. We talked about it.

We did?

Yes. The drawing you made in class, the one Victoria noticed. You titled it 'Traversing the fields,' remember? You drew it on your note book. It's a concept that's been within you from the beginning, Kyle. You knew it. Felt it. What it was. You just didn't know how to use it.

Okay. I remember.

Reach to that moment within you. Pull on it.

I don't understand.

That's the problem. Quit trying to apply your reason to things. Have faith and apply that, nothing more. Just do it.

Kyle was about to argue, but instead he slowed his thoughts and took a deep breath. He needed to get this right. The Gray Man needed him this time. It wasn't the other way around for once and Kyle didn't want to fail him.

So Kyle let go again, let himself be seventeen again… in Econ class with his wobbly desk and the prettiest girl in the world sitting right next to him. He'd drawn a road disappearing off into the distance, to a flat line horizon with shadowy edges and…

Something inside him shifted and brushed against his soul, like an instinct that had been hiding in the shadows, and the blue came alive again, emanating from him in a soft circle, first only around his own body before he willed it to reach out towards The Gray Man. Kyle began to wonder how it all worked, what would happen next, and then noticed that the very act of breaking his concentration made the circle retract, inches at first, then a few feet, so he forced himself to refocus and let the process unfold.

The Gray Man was leaning on one elbow, nodding encouragingly, and yet there was a look on his face of near surprise, as if he'd expected this process to take longer. Kyle surmised that, once again, he was proving to be quite the gifted student.

The circle expanded, enveloping The Gray Man, and then held static before it began to hum, softly at first, then louder. Kyle had the distinct impression that he'd grabbed a bull by the horns as the ground began to shake and everything around them, things seen and unseen, from the canyons on the meteor's surface to the molecules in the air next to his face, began to vibrate rapidly. *Gray?* he said, his voice trembling.

Now. Think of where you want to go.

What?

Where is it that you want to go, Kyle?

Shit. Earth I guess.

No. Not specific enough. We could end up anywhere if you think that, from a ranch in Wyoming to a buoy in the middle of the Indian Ocean. Focus.

Okay. Tamara. I want to go where Tamara is.

The Gray Man nodded again, but then began coughing. Kyle realized that he was wounded somehow, and this idea broke his concentration again. The humming began to fade and the glow of the circle pulsed high and low, like a light bulb just before it goes out.

Kyle!

I know. I know. I'm focusing again.

Where Tamara is, her exact location, is being blocked from us, remember?

Kyle nodded. *Yeah. Right. Okay. Then I want to go where she... was.*

Was... last.

Got it. Was... last. I want to go where my wife was last. Where my wife... and just thinking about Tamara wrenched at his heart, again breaking his concentration, as he worried where she was now, and if she was okay, and if the man that had her was hurting her.

The circle began to recede again.

Kyle lowered his head. This was all his fault. All her pain and suffering, what had almost happened to the kids. His heart sank in his chest as guilt and sorrow rode through him like twin trains, rattling the rails of his convictions.

Somewhere far off in the distance he heard The Gray Man screaming. *Kyle! Snap out of it! Kyle!*

Kyle wanted to ignore him, but there was something new to The Gray Man's voice. Something different: a tone of desperation.

Kyle lifted his head and opened his eyes just in time to see it cresting over a ridge far off in the distance: a massive black centipede-like creature with red eyes, cruising along the meteor's surface as if it were swimming towards them, its venomous claws snapping.

And it was closing fast.

If he thought hard, if he focused quickly, maybe they could—

Kyle blinked. It was too late. The circle around them disappeared with a pop, and the look on The Gray Man's face now was one that Kyle never imagined he would ever see: terror.

CHAPTER 17

SHORTLY AFTER HIS COMMENT about Ben, the mad man went into some sort of trance. Tamara was convinced that he was going to rape her, but instead, in stunned disbelief, she listened as he slowly fell asleep next to her. When she finally allowed herself to breathe again it was in tiny, measured breaths for fear that she would wake him.

Here was her chance, but it seemed too good to be true. How could he fall asleep and leave her completely untied? Terrified, she glanced at the mirror over the dresser, and her heart sank. The creature in the hat was still there, watching her. She forced her eyes away from his visage, which wasn't an easy task because his image deadened her mind with a murmuring sound not unlike buzzing bees.

When she looked away the sound stopped instantly, but when she looked back it would start up again. Whatever that thing was, he emanated ruthlessness and a power that trumped anything she'd encountered thus far, even more than the clown creature under Janie's bed, with its gnashing teeth, which she would've never thought possible.

But this creature didn't need teeth. He was powerful enough to make a person eat themselves. One tiny morsel at a time.

She was shivering, frozen in place, but this was her chance. She had to take it, mirror creature or not. Feeling her breathing becoming too rapid, she calmed herself. *Focus. Focus.*

She was clothed, though she had nothing else. They were on the ground floor of the motel. It looked like it was dark outside. If she got past the door she could run to the front desk.

She rotated her head, ever so slowly, to the right side of the bed, looking past the monster's face to the nightstand for his keys.

They weren't there.

Using the same slow incremental process, she craned her neck backwards to look at the nightstand behind her. They weren't there either.

Or on the dresser. Or the desk. He probably had them in his pocket, or maybe—

When she saw the small silver glitter on the chair next to the desk her heart leaped. She focused her attention and confirmed that they were keys. Three of them, on a small key chain with what looked like a Chevy logo, cast beneath the desk light in partial shadow.

She'd have to make her way off the side of the bed without waking him somehow. From there she could probably reach the keys quickly on a dead run for the door. But what were the odds of getting to the car, getting inside and locking it, all before he reached her? Not high. He was a quick, shifty bastard, and he was much stronger than he looked.

But she could fight back. She would fight back. With all she had. Because more than anything, even more than the fear of what was in that mirror, was the terror of going back into that trunk. How many more times would she see that lid close over her head before it closed for the last time?

She looked towards the bathroom for a weapon, regretting so instantly as once again the creature in the mirror greeted her, the rags that covered his face in no way hiding the fact that he was staring at her, intently. Regardless, there was nothing in the bathroom or anywhere else in the room that she could use as a weapon. So hand to hand it might have to be.

It occurred to her to think this out, very carefully. So she began to do so, then realized almost immediately that all her thoughts were trying to talk her *out* of doing it.

So, in direct disobedience of her own mind, she sat up, slid off the edge of the bed and ran for the keys.

The room, the air around her, held still and silent, pregnant with doom. Reaching the chair and grabbing the keys, she laced them in the gaps between her fingers, making a claw fist with which she could gouge out his eyes when the time came. He was behind her, she could feel it, but as she spun to face him she was stunned yet again. He was still on the bed, still sound asleep.

Joy, relief and hope rolled over her in waves as she changed her approach from a chaotic escape to a stealthy one. She crept across the carpet of the room on the balls of her feet, slowly turned the lock on the door and opened it carefully, wincing as it creaked ever so slightly.

She stepped into the dead of night, the cold air flooding her again in shivers. She turned to close the door for fear the cold air would rush into the room and wake him.

One last glance: he was still as he was except now she swore she could even hear him snoring.

Shifting the keys in her hands she felt the small plastic key fob. It was a good idea to close the door behind her, because the sound of the car unlocking could still awaken him. She would get as close to the car as she could before she unlocked it. After pulling the door shut, she turned towards the car with purpose.

When she saw them she was shocked, but not entirely surprised.

It had all been too easy.

And now she knew why.

Here was more proof that the sermons her father taught under the hot Bolivian sun, all those years ago, of angels and demons being around and among us, were true.

Except here, now, there were only demons. Five of them.

The first one, nearest her, was wearing a black trench coat. His face looked like old, dried leather and he had sunken red eyes. He was leaning against the ice machine just outside the room, chewing on the nail of his left index finger, looking at her in a bored sort of way, as if he were a security guard waiting out his shift.

Two more creatures, with coyote-like faces, long snouts and beady eyes, and with mangled human bodies, were actually at the car: one on the hood, reclining backwards with his shoulders and head against the windshield, as if he were taking a nap, the other seated on the roof with his legs hanging off the side and over the driver's window. The fourth one was tall, with a wide chest and a face that was almost all teeth, his smile like that of an exaggerated clown's, stretching from just above his chin and out, nearly touching the base of each ear. He stood at attention, feet spread shoulder-width apart, hands clasped behind his back, his black leather hat shiny beneath the moonlight.

She noticed a shiny pin on each shoulder and Tamara realized that the creature near the ice machine had them too: SS pins. They were Nazis, and not the pretend kind. They were the real ones, who gassed and carved people up for the fun of it. When he saw Tamara look at him he smiled and licked his lips.

"You are very perceptive, young lady," the fifth and final demon said softly. She was leaning against the railing of a nearby stairwell that had rust stains smeared down the sides. It was the old woman from the park, who'd been watching her and the kids that day.

Tamara stood in defeat. Fighting the monster in the room was one thing, but who could possibly overcome the one in the mirror and these demons whom, she firmly believed, he commanded. Five guards stationed outside their room so that the monster could get some sleep. She was crushed.

So. Yes. All those sermons were true. Demons and angels roamed the earth.

But it had been a long time since she'd seen any angels.

* * *

Parker knew the answer but had to ask the question. "Who is this?"

"It's me, numb-nuts."

Parker smiled. "Where are you? What the hell is going on?"

"Nice slip of the tongue. Well, I'm not *there* anymore." He chuckled. "Are you okay?"

"Yeah."

"You're with the Fasano kids?"

"Yeah," Parker replied, more than a little stunned. "And their… aunt. How'd you know that?"

Parker heard an audible sigh from the other end of the line.

"Where are you, Nap?"

"In a cab on the 2 Freeway, trying to get to *your* sorry ass."

"Me? Why?"

There was a lengthy silence, where all Parker could hear through the phone was the hum of traffic through a car window before Napoleon spoke again. "Look. I don't expect you to believe all I'm about to say, but you've seen enough, more than most, to believe enough, okay?"

"Spit it out, Nap."

"Okay… screw it, I'll just say it… Demons… demons are going to be coming after you."

Parker didn't smile. Instead he looked long and hard at the two men out on the parking lot as his jaw tightened. "Come again?"

"Listen." And now his partner's voice cracked with emotion. "It's all real, man, all the angels and demons, good and evil stuff? It's all real, Parker. Real as the day is long. You saw what happened at the Brasco house. You *know* where I went."

He couldn't believe he was doing it, but Parker was nodding. It was time to just admit it. "Yeah. I know. I believe you."

"Thank God." Napoleon sighed. "They're after the Fasano kids, Parker." The way he said it was unsettling.

"How'd you know that?"

"Parker. I just do. I'll explain later, when I get to you. Where are you now?"

"At a 7-Eleven in Los Feliz. Corner of Rowena and Hyperion."

Trudy was looking at Parker as if she were trying to figure out who he was talking to as he listened to Napoleon giving the cabbie directions.

"Okay, man, I'm on my way. Don't leave."

Parker chuckled, again looking at the two men in the parking lot who were waiting for them to come out. "I couldn't even if I wanted to."

"Why?" Napoleon asked, his voice sounding grave.

"There are two guys here, out in the parking lot. They watched us on the way in and I think they're waiting for us to come out."

"What do they look like?"

Parker gave him the descriptions, but when he described the John Deere guy he thought he heard Napoleon audibly gasp. "Watch that fucker," Napoleon commanded. "He's a big problem, Parker. We're on our way. Cabbie says ten minutes tops. Stall. Heat up a few burritos, lose yourself in the lotto section, whatever you gotta do, okay?"

Parker felt the world slipping away again, like that hot-wax feeling in his brain that day on the freeway when he'd seen the car accident and its aftermath. "Nap?"

"Yeah?"

"You and I, we've been through a lot together. I hear you, loud and clear."

"Good."

Then the line went dead.

"Are we ready to go yet?" Janie whined, her lips stained a bluish-red from her Slurpee.

Seth was quietly working his way to the bottom of his bag of Doritos, but Parker was stunned to see that the boy was staring right at Beanie as he chewed.

"We good?" Trudy asked as she looked intently at Parker.

Parker nodded. "We gotta buy some time," he replied, looking firmly into Trudy's eyes, "so my partner can get here."

Her look said that she understood. "Hey kids, let's go pick out some magazines for the room. Maybe they have coloring books or something."

"There's a toy section too!" Seth shouted.

"Yeah. Great honey. Let's go."

They killed time as best they could for the next ten minutes until Parker saw him, past the parking lot and across the street, getting out of a cab. It still felt unreal.

"Okay guys, time to hit it."

Trudy seemed nervous, but she rounded the kids together and walked them out of the store, keeping them slightly behind her as she walked next to Parker. "What're we waiting for?" she finally whispered as they stepped off the concrete steps in front of the store and onto the black asphalt of the parking lot.

"Listen," Parker whispered, reaching back to grab the handle of his 9 mm. "Your only job now?"

"Yeah?"

"No matter what happens, get to the car with the kids and get the hell out of here. Got it?"

"What about y—"

"Don't worry about me. This is all about the kids, you got it?"

Trudy nodded, but seemed pissed, like she was ready to throw down with someone if shit went south and being told that she couldn't wasn't sitting well with her.

Once on the parking lot, Beanie immediately left his post and came up behind them as John Deere craned his neck from side to side as they approached. Close enough now to see his face clearly, Parker noticed that he had beady eyes, set close together, and he was chewing on, of all things, a Slim Jim.

Something in Parker's heart sank. He'd had this feeling before a few times during the war, while on foot patrol. It was a sense that something was wrong, right when things were about to go off. There were just two of them, and he had sixteen shots—fifteen in the clip and one in the chamber. And now help had arrived. How in the hell could this go wrong?

Then he realized how: the enemy had too many target options. Trudy. Each child. Beanie and John Deere had already split up, one in front and one behind them, trapping them in, so that Parker had to be able to defend their front and rear, and if they attacked at the same time…

Parker sighed. They were still at a good distance. He knew how to choose his target order. No human could cover the distance either of them needed to get to the kids.

That's the problem dumb ass. Just admit it. Because you know they're not human. You knew it the minute you saw them. Even before Napoleon said what he said.

He felt silly and stupid and crazy all at the same time. But worse than all that? He felt helpless.

This wasn't going to go well.

And that's when he looked up to see the man coming across the driveway into the parking lot. He looked like he'd lost weight and hair was disheveled, but there was no mistaking him.

Even until now Parker was afraid to believe, but it really was Napoleon Villa.

In the flesh.

And he was drawing his weapon.

CHAPTER 18

THE CREATURE SWEPT OVER them, casting a shadow so dark that it was like being drenched in ink, a shriek emanating from its underside that rocked Kyle backwards and had The Gray Man covering his ears in agony.

Kyle waited for it to bite at them, or for its legs to grasp them, but no. Nothing. Just the shriek. But when he looked over at The Gray Man it was obvious that the sound was far worse for him; it was going to kill him. Cracks of light were beginning to burn through The Gray Man's suit, and he was shriveling up, as if his soul were being sucked out of him.

No. His *spirit.*

Fighting this thing was out of the question. Kyle again called on that moment back in school and the half-dreaming state it induced, and called once more upon the blue, called for a transversion of thought and place: *where Tamara was last.*

For a second or two nothing happened, and then, in a snap and shudder, the circle formed around him and The Gray Man again. The world around them began to melt away in dripping colors, like crayons over an open flame, and the creature's sound was muted as they began to whisk across the surface of the meteor, away from it and back out into the solar system. Before long the circle began to move so fast that the stars blurred into white lines and space itself seemed to warp.

Kyle stood in the center of the circle, his arms out in front of him, trying to figure out how to steer them somehow, but he felt like a child clutching at a steering wheel as The Gray Man lay beneath him, barely conscious.

That was close. Real close, Kyle thought. *If The Gray Man had died . . .* He let the thought end there.

Before long they were surrounded by light blue sky and white clouds. Earth. And then a few seconds later they were over the ocean, then the surface of the desert and then, finally, over a faded highway road with fresh yellow stripes before they finally began to slow.

When they came to a stop the circle around them seemed to fade just as quickly as it had formed and they were set down gently in the dry, rocky soil next to an old rest stop.

Tamara had been here; he could smell her somehow. You love somebody long enough, and even the smell of their sweat becomes distinct enough to remember and even cherish. But she wasn't here. They were too late. What if she was dead?

Tears filled his eyes. *No. Don't think like that. She's not dead. You can still find her. There's still time.*

"Yes," The Gray Man mumbled aloud beneath him. "There is. But we have to hurry."

"Are you okay?"

The Gray Man nodded gently, but didn't rise. Instead he rubbed at his forehead with one hand while the other lay limp at his side.

"What was that thing?"

"I have no idea," The Gray Man said, sounding exhausted. "I'm just relieved that you got us out of there."

"So what now?"

The Gray Man looked at him with irritation. "Kyle. Just as with the circle a minute ago, you know what to do. Just do it!"

"Okay, okay," Kyle answered. "Calm down. Shit."

"I'm going to stay here and keep an eye out... and rest. I must rest. Do you understand?"

"Yeah. I do. I'm gonna... take a look around."

"Remember your training."

Kyle nodded and walked to the entrance of the rest stop. The remnant of her presence was stronger here. Kyle took a deep breath and closed his eyes. This was a place that had a name, but more importantly, a place that held within it lingering memories. He had to reach out to those memories... and sift through them. Like flour.

A family of three had been here a few hours earlier. Two adults, one child. One of them had been carsick. The child. A little boy. He'd vomited into the toilet of the ladie's room for a good half-hour, the mother rubbing his back while the father checked his cell phone for emails from work before they'd resumed their journey.

A half-day before that a loner on his way back home to New Mexico had pulled through, driving drunk on whiskey and still missing the girlfriend who had dumped him years ago.

The moments flashed on the inside of Kyle's eyelids like tiny, faint movies that held still for a second and then disappeared to the right or left of his eyeballs and out of sight. It was maddeningly frustrating; he had to focus to keep them still, but if he did so too hard he would actually chase the image away quicker than it would disappear if he left it alone.

So he held his concentration, resisting the urge to force it when the screens of his eyes went black. He waited.

Before long, more moments came. Some from weeks ago, others days ago. Up and down the time scale. Another couple, this time with three children. They'd taken a break to eat lunch out of the back of their SUV before they moved on. A couple, young and in love, stopped to fill their water bottles from the tiny water fountain framed between the bathrooms. A group of four guys on their way to a bachelor party at a nearby Indian reservation, loaded up on beer, stopped here to change a tire and see who could piss the longest. The images faded. Nothing. He wished The Gray Man were the one doing this. He knew what he was doing. This was wasting time and—

When the vision of his wife, beaten, bloody and tied up, flashed into his mind, Kyle was wounded. "No," he whispered.

The man who had taken her was blurred out, like a water stain. But Tamara had been here. She was tired and scared. Dried blood was on her face, framing her terrified eyes. Dust was on her shirt. The man untied her and she had thought briefly of escape.

The image began to fade as Kyle's rage began to build. His emotions were like bright lights in the dark room of his mind, ruining all the pictures. He couldn't help it. This was his wife. Savaged. One eye half swollen. Her hair matted to her forehead. He wanted to kill the smudged man, tear him limb from limb and crush his bones.

The Gray Man was in his mind in an instant. *Focus, Kyle. Focus.*

Kyle nodded and paced his breathing.

The man had let her wash up a bit. She was so thankful for cool water on her face that it was the strongest memory that lingered. Relief. Blissful coolness. Framed in fear, yes, but it was what it was.

A wind blew over the desert like a hand growing heavier by the moment. The air was metallic. A storm was coming. Maybe an hour or two away. His focus wandered and now he could sense a plane far overhead, up beyond the clouds, loaded with people and all their worries.

He was losing control. He felt The Gray Man right there, ready to speak again, but Kyle pushed him away somehow, with his mind. He wanted to figure this out on his own. Slowly, with great effort, he pulled his mind, literally, out of the clouds and back to the rest stop.

Back to the smell of his wife.

Soft sweat, like when after they made love, when words gave way to sounds and scents. She'd been here and she'd been thinking of something.

Kyle smiled when it came to him.

His wife was a fierce one. Kyle knew that already. But this was an encouraging bit of proof.

Tamara had been planning on how to kill the man. Even as he tied her up and put her back into the trunk of his car.

Then they had driven off and Tamara had been thinking one word.

"East," Kyle said aloud. "She must be tracking where the sun is rising or setting."

When he opened his eyes The Gray Man was standing right next to him, still not looking a hundred percent, but at least looking a bit better.

He smiled softly. "Very good, Kyle."

* * *

Napoleon looked across the street and saw Parker, a woman and the Fasano kids coming out the double doors of the 7-Eleven.

He gritted his teeth, searching among the cars on the lot for the guys Parker had described. Nothing. He wasn't going to lie, a part of him was relieved. Maybe they'd left. Hopefully. Because he was exhausted to the bone, and really, even at full strength, John Deere had nearly kicked his ass last time around.

The day was the color of flat, gray paint. No sun. Very little light. It was as if he were in an old black and white TV show. *The Rifleman*, perhaps, or, more likely *The Twilight Zone*.

He made his way cautiously across the street, and that's when he noticed him: the bastard from the rest stop in Gorman who'd attacked him in the bathroom, wearing the same John Deere cap. He was turned sideways, standing near a white CRV, feet shoulder-width apart, thumbs hooked into his jeans pockets as he stared intently at the entrance of the store.

When the doors of the 7-Eleven had swung open and Parker stepped out it was like finding the last piece of a jigsaw puzzle; Napoleon was surprised, but not by much. His partner looked a bit older. Of course he did. Napoleon had missed quite a bit while he was away, most of it stressful it seemed. But he would not miss this.

"They'll be time for catching up later," Napoleon said into the wind as he crossed the street in long, deliberate strides, glancing to make sure there was no traffic. His path was clear.

He and Parker barely had time to make eye contact before John Deere reached behind his back for something, and a split second later that something came into view: a gun.

Napoleon steadied his breathing. Reaching for his weapon was like second nature, and felt long overdue.

There were about a half-dozen cars in the parking lot, and at this point no other people—except the punk wearing a black beanie to the left of the door who Parker had also described.

After a second, and as Napoleon hit the slight slope of the 7-Eleven driveway, his knee bending the wrong way for a second, it was obvious that neither of them had seen Napoleon.

Beanie pulled a hunter's knife from his belt and began advancing towards the kids.

So this was it then. Time to play. Like the old days, on the streets, when he was young and would get giddy with nerves right before a brawl. Napoleon couldn't help himself. "*¡Que onda, vatos!*" he screamed.

John Deere partially turned and Beanie glared his way.

Napoleon drew his weapon and walked with purpose straight at John Deere. "Parker!" he yelled. "You got the skinny one!"

There was no head snap of surprise, no shock or delay of action. Parker simply spun and drew down on Beanie.

John Deere, meanwhile, turned to draw on Napoleon.

Good. I was hoping you'd do that, Napoleon thought. *I've got a score to settle with you, puto.* Then he squeezed three shots in a tight grouping right into the center of Deere's chest. He never had a chance. His eyes, which had already registered Napoleon's arrival, now filled with rage as he fell against the car and a red blot began to fill his shirt.

You go to hell, you see things. So Napoleon was not impressed when John Deere's face went slack, then began to flicker in and out with the image of a goat head, front teeth exposed and gnashing at the air.

The creature fell to its knees and then quickly bounced

back up, stumbling towards Napoleon as it dropped its gun. Funny thing about guns: they're hard to fire with claws. Evidently the thing hadn't thought of this before it morphed into what it really was.

Another gunshot rang out across the lot. Parker had dropped Beanie at a distance of about fifteen feet, with one shot to the head. Napoleon raised his eyebrows; Parker had a good aim. Meanwhile, the woman with him, a red head, was making a beeline to the white CRV with the kids.

But, again, something was off. Napoleon wondered what it was, and then he realized there were no other sounds. Gunfights caused all sorts of shit: panic and chaos to name a few. Yet there were no screams, no shouts or yells, no screeching tires, no people diving for cover inside the 7-Eleven. Nothing.

It was like they'd transitioned from the black and white TV program to a silent movie.

Beanie and John Deere flickered and then just disappeared, dead in whatever way their kind could die. But Napoleon suspected that after failing on their mission like this, they were probably destined to spend eternity as a few new bricks in that wall of flesh at the entrance of hell, where all the crows fed, day and night.

"So?" Parker half-shouted across the lot as he approached Napoleon. "Nice of you to finally come back from vacation."

Napoleon grinned. "Blow me, smartass."

CHAPTER 19

THE OLD LADY WAS quite reasonable for a demon who, Tamara could sense, would've much rather have just ripped out Tamara's spinal cord. "No trying to run. It won't work, you know."

"Why are you doing this? Why is any of this happening?"

"Things happen, young lady. Lives are taken and given, found and lost. Sacrifices are made. Your world and our world are on a collision course, and until then, well, the game goes on."

"What if I don't want to play?" Tamara asked.

The old woman was about to reply but was cut short when the monster grabbed a handful of Tamara's hair from behind and yanked her back into the room like a caveman.

He spun her around viciously and grabbed her by the throat. "I should kill you now."

Tamara swallowed hard against his grip and choked out the words, "But you won't. You can't. You piece of shit!"

He punched her in the temple, making her woozy, then slapped her across her cheek twice. But his free hand didn't concern her nearly as much as the one around her throat; it was gripping tighter and tighter.

"Do it," she said, her voice barely a squeak now. "Just kill me then."

A grimace cut across his face as he gritted his yellow teeth and his eyes bore a hole into her. It looked like his rage had reached a tipping point.

That's when the fear hit. The death Tamara had been trying to avoid these past few days was now finally upon her. She was unable to stop the wave of sadness that came over her when visions of all the moments she would never see now flashed before her eyes: Seth's first little league game, the kids graduating from high school, Janie's face when she got her first college acceptance letter. They tumbled down on her like boulders, moments out there in the ether that was supposed to be their future. What of wedding days and grandchildren? What of her own marriage and the man she still loved, in spite of what he'd done?

The monster snapped his head towards the mirror, as if he'd been called. "No!" he said, frustration swimming back and forth across his face. "I'm going to do it. She's mine! I don't care anymore what you say!"

With that, an unseen force ripped him away from her so hard and fast that she could feel his fingernails cutting into her neck. Her eyes widened with horror as he was tossed against the opposite wall, down to the carpet, up to the ceiling and down again to the floor before he was held levitating in the air. The defiance from only a moment before was gone now, replaced with a look of terror and dread. "Please!" he pleaded. "No!"

The cuts began to appear on his forehead at first, and then, like a school of anchovies, thin and dark, they swam over his face, down his neck, under his shirt and back out where she could see them on his forearms. It was as if he were being attacked by a hundred knives, all at once.

All the noise, all the screaming, surely someone would hear. Someone would come to help.

She scoffed at her thoughts. Of course they wouldn't. The things outside would stop them or, more likely, this entire moment was just outside the borders of normal reality, like in the market that day: no one else could see the demon creatures at all, except Tamara and the kids.

Without warning the monster dropped to the floor in a heap, the force in the room left and everything grew still. Then, to Tamara's amazement, the monster began to cry. Deep, sorrowful, tormented cries as snot and tears rolled off his face and down into the carpet. He was bleeding from everywhere, in obvious agony.

If she were like him, she would kill him where he lay. But she wasn't, and despite her resistance to it, a deep sense of pity came over her. Yes, he'd just punched her in the face, and right about now she could settle the score, but then what? The thing in the mirror might do the same to her, or those things outside might just come in and do worse.

She'd heard before, on TV or some place, that the only way to help yourself in a situation like the one she was in was to get your abductor to see you as a human being, and to identify with them somehow. He was obviously on someone's leash, or some*thing's* leash—something that had just finished jerking him around quite hard. Maybe this was her opening.

"What the hell was that?" Tamara said as she sat cross-legged against the wall.

He didn't answer, but instead tried to roll over onto his back before crying out in pain. "You… still… can't… get away," he moaned, the words like food stuck in his teeth, as he took deep breaths. "They won't let… you… get… away."

Tamara nodded. "I know that."

For a minute or two they remained quiet. Then Tamara spoke again. "What's your name?"

He blinked and made a dismissive gesture with one hand. "What do you care, you crazy bitch."

Again, she had to fight the urge to attack him.

"I'm gonna get something to help," she said. Standing cautiously, she made her way to the bathroom, where she closed the door and glanced quickly in the mirror, a little terrified of what she might see there. Even though her image frightened her, it was still far better than seeing the thing in the mirror. It was gone. She exhaled and told herself to get it together. She took a washcloth, soaked it in warm water and went back into the room.

He was still on the floor, moaning softly now. She knelt carefully next to him. Repulsed by her own actions, but determined to carry them out anyway, she began to wipe the blood off his face, noticing that all the wounds had somehow already sealed and were beginning to scab.

Shit. He even has small cuts on his eyelids. What the hell...

He suddenly spoke up. "Troy."

"What?"

"My name is Troy. Or was. Whatever."

She nodded grimly as she continued wiping gently at his face.

He winced. "My mother used to do this, when I had a fever. She used to use a cool cloth though, it was kinda scratchy, and..."

His eyes closed. She wondered for a second if he'd died, the possibility bringing conflicting emotions of relief and worry to mind. Then she heard him snoring softly. He'd passed out.

With this many wounds, who could blame him?

She thought of the mirror behind her and, though she was sure it would be empty, she decided that, having no real need to look, she'd take a pass.

Well, he had a name now. That was something. Troy. She preferred calling him "the monster."

She wondered how many other women had faced this monster, and shuddered.

"Psst."

She looked over at him, startled to see that his eyes, trance-like and glassy, were half open. He forced a small smile to his face, breaking one of the cuts on the corner of his mouth; a little blood trickled out, down his chin and over his neck.

"What?" she said.

"Don't think by being nice to me it can change anything." Another threat, but this one was different than all the rest. It was tinged in defeat and sadness. "It's just not how it works."

"Really?" she said, her voice sounding pitiful to her.

"I hate him, you know."

"Who?"

"My master. I hate him. Look at me," he murmured, tears filling his eyes. "I've always followed instructions. Done what I was told. Still. Look what he did to me."

Tamara nodded. "I know. I'm sorry."

His eyes filled with shock. "You're sorry? No you're not."

"Yes I am," Tamara said. "What he did was mean."

For a second he looked skeptical but then, maybe due to the pain, his face turned soft. He'd bought it.

"Yeah. It was. But he's gone now. Even from my head. I think he went off somewhere. So I'm gonna tell you a secret, if you promise not to tell."

Tamara said nothing. Instead she looked him in the eye and waited.

"The millionth is coming."

"The… what?"

"The millionth. Your husband. He's coming."

Tamara's heart swelled and she took a deep breath. It couldn't be, could it? "That's not true, Troy. Don't lie to me, okay?"

Like a little child, he scrambled to convince her. "No, no, no. I mean it. I do. He's coming, and you wanna know what?"

"What?"

"My master?"

"Yeah."

"He's afraid of him."

* * *

They stood outside Room 317 of the Travel Lodge in Los Feliz, leaning against the balcony railing. Parker still couldn't believe his eyes. Napoleon looked leaner, as if he'd lost a good twenty pounds, and older, his face taut and dry. He hadn't even been gone all that long.

They'd agreed to save the chitchat for later and get the hell out of the 7-Eleven parking lot as soon as time caught up with them and the world began to work at normal speed. Now, with Trudy inside napping as the kids watched Nickelodeon, Parker gave himself the luxury of wonder. His partner was alive. Standing right here. It didn't seem possible. Napoleon, meanwhile, was munching his way through a Hot Pocket as he looked out over the city, as if waiting for Parker to break the silence. So Parker did.

"What happened after you disappeared with the gray guy?"

Napoleon chuckled and answered with his mouth half full. "Pwhy-we went to fhell! Phatswhat."

"Hell? Really?"

He finished his bite. "What else did you expect me to say? You were right there when I made the decision to go."

Shaking his head, Parker looked at the ground. "I dunno. I guess I was holding out for the possibility that the guy was an alien or something."

"Would that've somehow been better?" Napoleon laughed. Then he chased another bite of his Hot Pocket with the Mountain Dew he'd bought in the vending machine down the hall.

Instead of answering, Parker just shrugged.

"Hmm," Napoleon said, then looking at Parker he added, "Why man? You got a problem with God?"

You have no idea, Parker thought. But this wasn't a time for confessions, so he dodged the question. "Don't we all?"

Napoleon nodded and drank more of his soda. He looked a few more seconds at Parker and then back out over the city.

It felt like the sun was setting in protest. Parker was exhausted but he couldn't help but notice the world in orange, glints of red and yellow vibrating through from the horizon line and bouncing off the city skyscrapers in the distance. The air had cooled and was now dancing on the edge of chilly.

A silence visited them, but it was a comfortable one. Both of them seemed to need a little time to wrap their heads around their reunion. When Napoleon finally spoke, his words were heavy and still tinged with what sounded like dazed amazement.

"It's real, Parker. Hell is real. It's not some fantasy, it's not some myth created to control people. I saw it. Another land, another world, that you don't even want to know about."

Parker didn't know what to say, so he just nodded for Napoleon to go on.

"I'd like to be able to describe it better but... man. . . horrifying is just not a good enough word. I mean, the best I can do is this: imagine being in a place where you feel hunted, every second... hunted... and it never ends. You can't relax, you can never let your guard down, there is absolutely zero peace of mind to be found."

"Shit."

Napoleon's eyes had gone from wild to lost. "Yeah. For eternity. An eternity of non-stop, relentless fear."

"How'd you get out?"

"We found Fasano, that's how. Barely, and almost after it was too late."

"Where is he now?"

"With the... gray guy, as you call him. Trying to find his wife."

Parker was surprised. "She's still alive? I wasn't betting on that, to be honest."

"Why?"

"You want to talk about monsters? The guy that has her? He's earned the title."

Napoleon blinked. "Yeah?"

"There's over eighty bodies in various stages of decomposition in a mountain ravine outside of Beaury that can attest to it."

Napoleon looked stunned. "What?"

"Yeah. He's been hunting a long time, Nap. Hunting girls from Beaury who dared to move away, or offend him, turn him down for a date, whatever the fuck."

"Well, I imagine he's not working alone."

"No. He's a solo act. I think we can confirm that."

"That's not what I meant."

Parker glanced over the railing. A few cars were parked below, but beyond them, the Travel Lodge was slow today.

He had an idea what Napoleon meant, but he didn't want it confirmed. Napoleon confirmed it anyway.

"His side is helping him, Parker. This angel, or whatever, that has helped us, that was helping Fasano the whole time? He's part of only half the story. It only makes sense it can happen in reverse, right? You go bad, maybe you start getting some help too. Maybe you end up with a demon friend to lead you along the wrong path. I'm willing to bet that this guy…"

"Troy Forester."

"Has help."

"You mean, like, horns and a forked tongue kinda help?" Parker said, feeling silly for saying it.

There was no humor from Napoleon. Not a drop. "Worse," he said, taking another swig of his Dew. "Way, way worse."

"How so?"

"You don't wanna know."

"Man. I need a drink."

"You and me both."

"But we can't leave them alone," said Parker with a nod to the other room.

"No."

"That's why you're here, isn't it?"

Napoleon stuck out his chin, stretched his neck and nodded.

"The thing you think is helping Forester may be after the kids, right?"

"He and the ones that serve him, yes."

Parker stepped back from the railing, crossed his arms and shook his head. "I'm sorry, man, but this all sounds *Looney Tunes* crazy, dude."

A seagull, miles from the ocean, sailed by overhead as a kid skateboarded down the street below them, the wheels banging over the cracks in the sidewalk as he shifted his book bag from one shoulder to the other. Napoleon had never seemed like the touchy-feely kind, so Parker was surprised when he reached out and put his hand on Parkers shoulder. “No, Parker. I get it now. Not all of it, but a lot of it. It’s not crazy at all. It’s a truth we all believe at some level, even when we think it’s the biggest lie ever. A part of us already knows there’s more to this world than meets the eye.”

“I dunno, man…”

“Yes. You do. The shit we’ve seen on the streets as cops? The shit people do to each other? Hated rivals or people in love, man, it doesn’t matter. You know what I’m saying, right?”

Parker was frozen. He looked at Napoleon and the gaze from his partner was so intense he could not look away.

“You and I, we’ve made a living looking for proof. Of who killed someone, or raped someone, or stabbed their boss. We look for proof of crimes committed. That’s our job, but these very same crimes?”

“Yeah?”

“They’re proof that the place I went to not only exists, but is alive and well in helping all those horrible atrocities to be committed in the first place.”

“Good and evil?”

Napoleon nodded. “And us in the middle.”

“Like pawns or something?”

“We may be pawns, but don’t kid yourself. We move *ourselves*, Parker, one square at a time, in one direction or the other.”

A gray late-model Ford Mustang came rolling into the Travel Lodge parking lot, bumping rap music through its closed windows. The sun had finally pulled the horizon up over itself like a blanket. Parker cleared his throat as a bus growled by in the distance. "So, what do we do now?"

Napoleon acted like he didn't hear the question. "Parker. You've had to have seen some shit by now."

You mean like an angel with a dead man by the side of the road? Parker thought. Instead he said, "Yeah. I think I have."

"Tell me about it," Napoleon said.

Parker sighed. Why not? So he did.

When he was done, all his partner said was: "Anything else?"

Parker thought hard for a moment. "Only a feeling. At the Fasano house today. Something wasn't right in the whole place, but especially in the little girl's bedroom."

"Like?"

Parker spat the words out like black licorice. "Something was under the bed."

"Did you see it?"

"No. But I felt it. And then there was that Sebastian kid at the Brasco house. The night you disappeared?"

"Mm-hmm."

"He came running out the front door like a man fleeing the devil himself, babbling, terrified. He's still a mess. He's locked up in the psych ward up in San Francisco."

"Damn."

"Yeah. Damn is right. He's twenty-three."

"Casualties."

The word immediately set Parker on edge. "Yeah. And there's one I haven't told you about yet."

"What?" Napoleon replied, a look of concern on his face.

"Sheriff Conch is dead."

Napoleon's face went slack.

"Forester killed him, on the way out of town."

"How?"

"Stabbed him to death."

Napoleon put his hand over his face. "Dear Jesus." When the hand came away he looked more tired than ever.

"So," Parker pressed, unable to help himself, "what about God and casualties now?"

"Nothing's changed."

"Casualties are what happen during a war, Nap."

"I know. And this is one. A spiritual one, all around us. For some reason we *make* it a war, Parker. We do."

"What are you saying?"

"With our choices, our free will and the consequences that follow. I still don't understand it all, Parker. But after what I've seen? The really sad thing?"

"Yeah?"

"I don't think there'd even be a hell at all, without us."

CHAPTER 20

THEY TRAVERSED THE FIELDS of earth on a road not unlike the one he'd drawn on his notebook back in high school, all those years ago. It wasn't hard once you got the hang of it. You just had to draw with your mind.

Kyle balanced himself and The Gray Man within the circle and realized that the view as the driver on one of these journeys was much different. As a passenger it was all blurs and colors, almost like you were a kid in a car, looking out the side window as you buzzed down the highway with a parent driving. Now though, looking out the front window, controlling the speed and direction, the world ahead was clear and concise even though it was still moving by at incredible speed. Light beige desert gave way to darker sand with patches of weeds and thickets of Joshua trees, then paved highways and a small town with faint lights and a Chevron gas station before more desert, this time rockier and relieved of flat oblivion by a few rolling hills and a distant mountain.

Tamara was out there, somewhere, and Kyle was determined to get to her, to hold her again, to tell her face to face how sorry he was, for what he'd done and for all that had happened, even though he was sure beyond a shadow of a doubt that she would probably spit on him and curse his name. And who could blame her when she did? This thing he'd done. How could he? He'd sacrificed so much, for so little, and most of it—like a loving wife's peace of mind or the safety of his children—he had no right to sacrifice in the first place. His mood began to darken.

"There's no point to it, Kyle," The Gray Man said softly.

"Point to what?"

"Kyle. If only you knew how many times across the centuries a man has traded everything he has for something he'll never have."

"I thought we agreed a long time ago that you'd stay out of my head."

"I am. It's in your aura. The colors tell me all I need to know."

Kyle glanced over briefly at The Gray Man. "Yeah?"

"Yes. It's how you will truly 'see' people eventually. How you will know when they need us, or need to *believe in* us. It's also how we know when they're about to do wrong, or something evil. The colors never lie. They reflect the emotions within, purely and completely."

"Us? You mean… like angels?"

"Angels are part of it, but keep in mind that 'us' in heaven is a very large contingent."

"Huh?"

"Surely you don't believe that you're an angel, do you, Kyle?"

"No," Kyle replied.

"Okay. Well, soon, you'll be able to see the colors too. At the rate you're evolving, you'll be experiencing many new things before long."

"Like what?"

"In due time. But as for right now? I think we're here."

Kyle controlled the orb's descent, slowing it and then lightly touching the ground. When it was almost at a complete stop, it popped softly like a bubble, dropping them to their feet.

The world around him told Kyle that, again, they were too late.

It was a motel of some kind, with old wooden staircases and an ice vending machine against a wall nearby. The door they stood before was painted mint green.

She'd been here, but so had many others. Kyle could still feel them. "Good Lord."

"She's been assigned a guard. Five of them."

"Is that what I feel?"

"Yes. It is. Things have changed some. The man who took her is hurt."

"He is? Badly?"

"Not badly enough to stop him. He was…" The Gray Man closed his eyes and lifted his head slightly to the sky. "Disciplined."

"Disciplined? By who?"

"His master."

"Why?"

The Gray Man said nothing.

Then Kyle had an idea. "Was he having second thoughts? Was he gonna let her go?"

Again, The Gray Man remained silent, but a stern look came over his face.

"Gray?"

"No. He wasn't trying to let her go."

"What then?"

Shaking his head, The Gray Man answered in a flat tone, "He was trying to kill her… too early… before he was meant to."

"What?"

"I'm sorry, Kyle."

"Too early? What the hell does that mean, Gray?"

"It means he is going to try again. It's just a matter of when."

"Oh my God. Does this ever end?" Kyle bent over with his hands on his knees, then stood up straight and looked up into the sky. "Why? What did she ever do to deserve this, Gray? How could God—"

"Kyle, don't—"

"No! This isn't fair. She's paying, she's suffering, for *my* mistakes."

"Calm down, son."

"No. I won't. This is insanity, I accept full responsibility but it makes no sense, it—"

"Kyle. The reality of free will, the ultimate, ugly truth of it, is the unintended consequences that it has. It is both a glorious and a horrible gift. Your kind chose it, and all pain and suffering that can come with it. God's work now is to affect upon it a purpose."

"What?!"

"The world acts upon us, but the way it changes us depends on how we react. But since God created the world and everything in it, He can bring good from it all."

Shaking his head, Kyle turned on his heel and walked away. He needed a moment. To breathe. To think. In his life he had taken so much for granted, so much of what was now proving to be an illusion, and the process of seeing all that he'd seen—hell, demons, angels, universal powers working behind the curtains like so many gears and levers—was beginning to make him feel sick with the feeling of inadequacy.

When he spoke next it was softly and evenly. The words measured and scripted by his heart. "I'm too human, Gray. I can't do this. It's all too much."

The Gray Man waited a moment before he replied. "Yes you can, Kyle."

"I'm not sure I want this."

"Of course you're not."

"I'm not sure I can handle it, Gray."

"I believe you can."

Kyle put his hands on his hips.

"Regardless," The Gray Man continued, "there will come a time when you will have to choose."

"Choose?"

"Between this life and the next. Between earthly existence and a heavenly destiny."

"When?"

The Gray Man shot him a sympathetic look. "Only the Lord knows that."

Kyle smelled something in the air. "What is that? It smells… like iron, or hot metal."

"Blood. You smell blood."

Kyle turned and walked to the hotel room door. It opened, seemingly on its own, but Kyle knew better. "Neat trick," he said, glancing over his shoulder at The Gray Man as they both walked in.

The sensation of walking into a room now painted with evil struck Kyle immediately. To the naked eye it was nothing but a motel room, cleaned and ready for the next guest. But layer after layer of it, fumes of darkness, filled his nostrils. The feeling of being slowly suffocated crept over him.

"Kyle!" The Gray Man shouted. "Leave the room at once."

But it was too late. Kyle felt the evil and traced it immediately to its source: the mirror over the dresser.

In the mirror was nothing but a reflection of themselves and the room around them, but that too was a lie. Hell was there, on the other side, looking out at them forebodingly.

Instantly, Kyle thought of The Shaman. But this wasn't him.

This demon had a different calling card. A different name. Kyle focused, intently, for a moment, and then it came to him. "The La—"

"Do not say its name!" The Gray Man commanded.

Kyle shut his mouth.

The mirror shuddered for a moment, then held still. A few seconds later, the images it reflected began to melt and coalesce. Then, without warning, they snapped back into place; the lamps, the bed, the hanging picture of a pond beneath a bridge on the wall over the headboard, all returned back to their true forms.

"What was that?" Kyle asked.

"An attempt to reach us, I think."

"Reach us?"

"Yes. To transport us there... or something from there to here."

Kyle looked around the room. It was unremarkable. There were no major defects, no glaring pieces of evidence that pointed to a struggle or punishment of any kind. "There's nothing else here. We need to move faster to close the gap."

"I agree. I've already gathered the information we need. When they left, they went back out onto the highway. Headed east again."

"You or me this time?" Kyle asked wearily.

"Me. It's your turn to rest."

When the orb around them formed this time, it was the one Kyle was used to; the same one that had formed around him that first fateful night outside the LA Hilton, when this all had begun. The same orb that had transported him to the 76 station in Torrance too. Only this time Kyle recognized that the orb distinctly belonged to The Gray Man. It was made of *his* force, *his* power, not Kyle's.

He was evolving. The Gray Man was right.

But it was a lonely feeling.

* * *

"So, you used to be his partner?" the woman with the red hair asked calmly. Parker had introduced her earlier as Trudy and she had an edge to her.

Napoleon nodded. "Still am. Technically, I think, anyways."

"You as scared of ghosts as he is?" Trudy said with a smirk as she shot a sideways glance at Parker.

It was just past eleven, with midnight up next. The kids were finally asleep in one of the beds, two small lumps huddled close together beneath an over-sized comforter. Napoleon chuckled at Trudy's question and raised his eyebrows before he answered, "*More*, actually."

"You're kidding, right?"

"No. I don't think he is," Parker chimed in.

She sighed. "So, is anyone going to tell me what the hell happened in that parking lot?"

Napoleon noticed that Trudy's edge seemed to go butter-knife-dull whenever she was forced to think about what was *really* happening now.

She'd gotten nervous when she found out that Napoleon was going to be staying in their room too, but she hadn't said anything. Then, when he and Parker had discussed sleeping in shifts for the night, a concerned look rented space on her face before she evicted it and looked off into the distance.

But these were all second cousins to the look of stunned dismay that had appeared on her face earlier in the day, in the 7-Eleven parking lot, and the pure shock that followed when she'd asked for an explanation of what had just happened and instead only been hustled to the car with the kids and told to keep her head down. Danger was good at shutting people up. Even people like Trudy. But Napoleon had seen the resentment there, flashing in her eyes, at her question being ignored. Napoleon knew it would eventually come back around, and now it had. Really, how could it not?

Looking at Napoleon, Parker shrugged and asked, "You or me?"

"I got it," Napoleon replied. "Ms—"

"Trudy."

"Okay. Trudy. What I'm going to tell you is going to sound crazy, but in a way, I'm kinda happy you saw what you did. I think it'll make it easier for you to accept it."

Sighing heavily, Trudy rolled her hand impatiently. "Accept what? C'mon. Spit it out."

"The two men in the parking lot were demons. From hell."

Trudy blinked, and then looked Napoleon directly in the eye. "Quit fucking around."

Napoleon said nothing and Parker matched him.

A moment of silence passed before Trudy laughed and said, "You're serious?"

Napoleon simply nodded. It was no different than telling a mother that her son has disappeared, or a father that his daughter has been raped, or a wife that her husband had been killed in a car crash. The approach was the same: you kept it short and treated the words like pins in hand grenades.

Parker, as always with the etiquette, picked this moment of all moments to yawn.

"Oh. I'm sorry. Is this *boring* you?" Trudy whispered angrily, snapping Parker so hard he actually sat up straight, which made Napoleon instantly like Trudy more.

Parker shrugged at her and replied, "Hey… I've heard a lot of it already, is all."

"Not really," Napoleon said. "You haven't heard what color the sky in hell is—it's not red, by the way—and I haven't told you about The Shaman, either. Just so you know, he's this Indian guy who rides around on a horse, looking for souls that are trying to escape. Like a fucking officer from Animal Control or something."

Parker's eyes grew narrow and he leaned in across the small dining table. Trudy did the opposite; she leaned back, an incredulous look on her face. Some people take the bad news on the chin, others do it on the back pedal.

Napoleon looked at her solemnly. "So, Trudy, all cards on the table, okay?"

Trudy said nothing. She didn't move at all for a second or two. Napoleon wondered if maybe she was thinking that she was in a hotel room with two men who had completely lost their minds. Probably. Whatever. This was no time for the soft sell because Napoleon knew that the idiots in the 7-Eleven parking lot weren't the only ones. More would be coming. Soon, probably.

Finally, she nodded.

"I don't know what your religious or spiritual beliefs are, but heaven and hell are real. I've heard of the former and, as I said, been to the latter. Angels and demons are real too. I've seen them," Napoleon said quietly, hearing the reverence in his own voice. Then he nodded towards Parker. "And he has too."

Trudy looked from Napoleon to Parker and then back again.

"Now you have too," Parker said. "At least, you've seen demons. Those two guys in the parking lot. I hope you get to see the angels as well."

As usual, when a person goes into shock they ask the questions you don't expect. Trudy was no different. "Why?"

Parker rubbed his chin and looked at Trudy. Napoleon noticed it was a look filled with tenderness, and he smiled to himself as Parker replied to her, "Because I think it helps to see that the demons aren't all there is. That good is out there too, fighting the fight."

"You guys are crazy," Trudy murmured with a nervous giggle. Her eyes darted back and forth, an outward reflection of her mind at work, right there behind her skull, sorting through all the alternative explanations covered in the dust of reason. Finally, she found one. "It was a mass hallucination. That's all."

Napoleon countered immediately. "That no one else in the 7-Eleven or on the sidewalk or driving down the street happened to see?"

"Just us and the kids?" Parker piled on.

"Look..."

"You saw what you saw, Trudy. Why don't you tell us what it was?"

Trudy began to shake her head tightly, back and forth, as if her head were in a vice. "No. I won't."

"They had animal faces..." Parker said gently.

"No. Stop."

"What about the teeth and claws?"

"It was a hallucination. It wasn't real."

"Mm-hmm," Napoleon joined in, "and when we shot them... what happened to them after we shot them?"

"I don't know," Trudy replied tersely.

"There are bullets missing from my gun, Trudy, and from Parker's gun. Where did those bullets go?"

"Off into the trees, or into that brick wall maybe, that was behind the big guy."

"You mean, the big guy that wasn't there? That was a hallucination? They were both there, they both transformed, the world came to a stop, we killed them and then—poof!—they disappeared. How in the world—"

Trudy held up her hand for them to stop, so they both did. After all, this wasn't an interrogation. If it were, then it would've been the perfect moment to break her, right when she'd clearly had enough.

Napoleon marveled at her strength. She was in a weird situation, in a weird setting. Alone with her friend's kids, determined to protect them, now being confronted by the people she trusted as police officers with ideas and explanations that had to be horrifying, if not downright ridiculous. She looked overwhelmed. Still. No tears. No look of panic. Not even a quivering lip.

That's when it hit him: she knew already.

"What happened?"

"What?" Trudy replied.

"You know something. Something you're not telling us."

The visage of self-control finally cracked; she began to chew softly on her lower lip. Like a little girl with a secret to tell. Instead, she shook her head.

It was Parker's turn to press. "Look. The three of us are into something big here, and those two little kids need us to get our shit straight. Right up front. If you know something? You need to tell us."

"I don't know anything."

"Then… what is it?"

She rolled her eyes to the ceiling and took a deep breath. Exhaling through her nostrils, she seemed to come to some sort of an agreement with herself. "When I was young, about fourteen or fifteen, for fun, well, I guess for fun, whatever, I got into witchcraft a little bit."

Parker looked at Napoleon. It was a look that said what Napoleon was thinking: *Oh shit.*

"It was nothing serious," she continued. "Some Wiccan stuff. I fancied myself a white witch, if anything. Harmless stuff. At least I think it was."

"Yeah. I'm not so sure about that," Napoleon said warily.

"Well. Anyway. I got out of it once all the pentagram stuff started; first with marbles on the floor of my bedroom, then later with paint on the floor of an abandoned house in our neighborhood."

"Just you?"

"Shit no," Trudy said with a laugh. "My friend Cindy got me into it, along with her friend Megan."

Parker rested his forearms on the table. The bags under his eyes were huge. "And?"

"Anyway, one day, Cindy decides she wants a 'familiar,'" Trudy continued, making quotation marks with her fingers, "and so we got into some spell shit. It didn't work. She said we needed blood. So, next day, she comes with a can of blood. I asked her where she got it. She said it was from some packs of venison in the meat locker in her parents' garage, but I never really believed her."

"Yeah?" Napoleon asked.

"Yeah. Later on we found out she'd gone down to Chinatown and bought some live chickens with her saved allowance. I guess she had them killed and cleaned there and asked for the blood too."

"Odd request," Parker said glumly.

Napoleon scoffed. "Not in Chinatown. I've heard of pig dishes with blood. Not chicken. But who knows. Maybe she paid extra."

"She was a kid, man."

"Poor don't know age, Parker," said Napoleon. "The workers down there are mostly indentured servants. At best, they're making a quarter the minimum wage. Go on, Trudy."

"Anyway, so we drew up the pentagram in the house with the blood this time, then began the spells and incantations… and some weird shit started to happen."

"Like what?"

"Nothing Hollywood," Trudy answered with a shrug, but her eyes looked far away now. Way far away. "But, ya know, the door to the bedroom we were in just closes. All on its own. We nearly jumped out of our pants, then we blamed the wind. Then Cindy tripped out, for just a second, her eyes got… whacky."

Parker cleared his throat. "Whacky?"

"Yeah. They rolled back for a second. And she stared blinking really, really fast."

"What'd you do?"

"I thought she was fucking with us, ya know? I was like, 'Knock it off, Cindy,' and I threw something at her, a small rock I had in my pocket that I'd picked up the day before for no particular reason. Then it got weirder."

"How's that?" Napoleon asked.

"The rock… Shit, this is gonna sound totally ridiculous. I can't believe I'm telling you guys this. I've never told anyone. Not even Tamara."

"Try us," Parker pressed.

Trudy reached up to sweep aside some hair that had fallen over her eyes. "Okay. Fine. The rock… it just…

froze. It would've hit her in the chest. I didn't throw it hard and she was wearing a puffy jacket that day because it was cold. It wouldn't have hurt her, but damn it, it just froze, right there in mid-air."

"Froze?"

"Yeah," Trudy said. "As if something had… caught it."

"Then what happened?"

"It dropped to the ground after a minute or two. Megan flipped and ran out of the house."

"And Cindy?"

"She opened her eyes and just stared at me. Like, really intently for a bit. Then she snapped out of it. We left the house together, but didn't say a word about it. None of us did. At school or anywhere else. But, and this is really gonna sound whack, you know what?"

Parker and Napoleon answered in unison. "What?"

"After that? A black cat, no shit, it starts showing up everywhere with her from that day forwards. She carried it around with her like Paris Hilton does one of those damn little Chihuahuas. Megan was never our friend again, and when she saw that cat hanging around school every day, waiting for Cindy to get out, she flipped and went hard core Christian. Me, I just didn't want to believe it. Any of it. Then? One day, right before graduation, I went by Cindy's house to borrow some earrings and that cat… You know, looking back now? It always, always, always looked at me weird whenever I was over at the house. But that day it didn't just look at me."

The motel room was quiet except for the blunted sound of traffic through the window and the small hum of the heater. Napoleon waited and so did Parker.

Finally, Trudy continued. "It… tried to do something to me. Possess me or something. I felt it, ya know, just pure evil there in the hallway, while I stood waiting for those damn earrings."

"Yeah?"

"Yeah. I never saw Cindy again after graduation. She moved off, with the cat, to college. But I never forgot that feeling. Of evil. Never felt that feeling again. Until today. In that parking lot. The guy with the beanie on? He looked at me the exact same was as that damned cat. So you know what, Detective Villa?"

"What?"

Trudy sighed and wiped her eyes quickly with the back of her hand. "Push comes to shove? I believe you."

CHAPTER 21

BACK IN THE TRUNK. Back on the road. But it was different this time. Tamara climbed right in—let him tie her up with no struggle and no study of how to escape. She simply took up residence again with the musty rag and can of WD-40 that was in a small net bag just inside the lid, the "Instructions for Use" listed there like the shortest story ever. It was her only reading material, and it helped pass the time, the road bumping and rolling along beneath her head for hours on end. She read and re-read it with an eye of how it could have been written better, or what it might look like if it were in Spanish or German, or why they hadn't just cut to the quick and in big, bold letters written: POINT. SPRAY. YOU DIPSHIT. End of instructions.

When she was bored with the WD-40 can, she would begin reading her heart, taking notes on the state of her belief that she was not, in any way, resigning herself to any sort of fate. What she was doing was coming to terms with the idea that she would have a *part* to play in that fate, maybe big, maybe small. It didn't matter. If she were to believe Troy the Monster, then Kyle was coming and that meant he'd survived hell, which probably also meant The Gray Angel was coming with him.

She took comfort in that. Help was on the way. Maybe her part, her job now, was to stay alive until it could arrive.

Right about now, though, Tamara felt like the Vegas odds on that weren't so good. The way he was up front, behind the wheel, screaming and yelling and crying between spaced out sections of silence that were almost worse to listen to, it could break either way, at any moment. His… master, or whatever the hell that thing in the mirror was… could decide any second that it was time for him to pull over and slit her throat, and she had no doubt Troy would do as he was told, like a good little servant.

She wondered, for the thousandth time, where he was taking her, except this time she let the thought percolate a bit. When they had left the house she had the sense they were headed north. Yet, first time out of the car they were in the desert. She'd seen no freeway signs or numbers though, but really, out of Los Angeles the main corridors east were Interstate 15 to Vegas or Interstate 10 to Arizona. The former would be north-east, the latter a bit south-east.

The other morning when he'd fed her Donettes she'd watched the sun rise in the east, then took note of the road they were near. If he made a left turn upon leaving they'd be going west, right meant east. After he'd packed her back up to continue their journey she'd felt the car turn right.

There was just one problem with that idea: they'd stopped three times, once briefly and twice overnight, with a couple of hours or so of driving each time in between. Now they'd been on the road again for at least an hour, more likely longer. It didn't take seven or eight hours to get to Vegas from her home. It took four on a good day. Five tops.

Which meant they'd already passed *through* Vegas.

So where the hell was he headed?

She was ashamed to admit it, but well, she had no idea what was after Vegas. She'd never gone that way. Lake

Tahoe? Maybe. Salt Lake City perhaps? But that was Utah. Denver? After all she'd been through the last few days she could cut herself some slack for having a hard time with her States map right now. Try as she might to recall it, there was no seeing it in her mind.

She blinked against the darkness of the trunk. Soft moonlight gave just enough illumination for her to see her knees, one on top of the other, legs half curled to her chest, and her bound hands stretched out in front of her, the fingers of her right hand playing absentmindedly with a loose thread in the carpet.

She chastised herself for not listening more intently to any of his ravings earlier. Had he given a clue? Mentioned a state? A city? Shit, even a landmark of any kind? Reminding herself to calm down, Tamara arched her back and craned her neck from side to side. Her headache was gone. Her muscles felt alive again. Her exhaustion had finally overtaken her, and she could at least feel the benefits of a good sleep, still lingering there, across her body. Her eyelids were still a bit heavy but her mind was firing away with new resolve.

He would have to pull over soon. Maybe she would get a good peek at a road sign. Or maybe she could get a good look at the night sky? The stars could tell her something, but not much. She was never much for astronomy. There was the North Star, but in the desert all the stars were so big it wasn't so easy to pick out.

Shit. Why did you fall asleep? You may have lost…

Then she realized it would be very unlikely that the car would've come to a complete stop, or been turned off, without waking her. More than unlikely. It would have been impossible. Because even in the deepest of sleep every cell in her body was well aware that the next stop could be her last.

No. He hadn't stopped. There was no way.

So. Soon then. Unless he was pissing in a bottle up there—something that was, sadly, a distinct possibility—he would need a bathroom break.

Then, without much fuss, she realized it was probably futile anyway, a last-ditch effort to exercise some sort of control over her situation. She was headed where she was headed. She would get there when she got there. Who really cared anyway?

Something inside her heart rejected this last thought immediately. Someone did care. Her Lord. He cared immensely. She knew it in her bones. And something in her told her that the very worst thing she could do, ever, but especially right now, was to lose her faith in that. But why?

Because that's how they're tracking you. The stronger your faith, the stronger the signal.

The voice in her head was her own, but the words were not.

A faint smile stretched out over the dry skin of her face.

So that was it. She could help her own cause by staying firm in her faith and by… praying.

What had her dad always called it? "The Morse code of the hopeless." Yes.

So she closed her eyes and began to tap away.

* * *

In the morning, with the kids only briefly immersed in cartoons on Nickelodeon before they began to complain about being hungry, Parker made the decision to go out to get breakfast. Trudy was barely awake, the eyeshadow of sleep still dark in her eyes, when Parker told her of his plan: over to the corner, across the street and down a block was a McDonald's. He would load up on grub and, more importantly, coffee and be back in twenty. She looked a bit reluctant to agree at first, then they both looked towards Napoleon, who was deep asleep on the floor beneath a blanket, his head buried under a pillow, breathing as if he hadn't slept in years. Parker and Trudy appeared to share the same thought: It wasn't like Parker was leaving them alone; they'd be safe with Napoleon still here.

He stepped out into the brisk morning air as a light fog meandered over the motel parking lot and the street beyond, the sun casting a half-light all around.

Grabbing his cell phone from his jacket pocket, he saw that it was 7:47 a.m. He made his way across the lot, noting the spaces between the parked cars as he advanced, realizing that old habits died hard. Be it the Taliban or demons, you kept an eye out. All the time.

The coast, as the old movies said, was clear.

Once out on the street he was comforted by the morning traffic, not yet heavy but still frequent enough to shatter the feeling of isolation that fog always brought with it.

He figured now would be a good time to check in, so he called the station house. Klink answered on the third ring. "What up, *guero*?"

"You're just as much a white boy as me, Klink."

"More so, actually, to be honest."

"Don't I know it. One trip to King Taco would prove that." Parker chuckled, thinking of the restaurant they both used to frequent as foot patrol officers where they would have hot sauce duels with their carne asada tacos, the contest getting so extreme at one point that they were literally dipping them into cups of the stuff.

"Someday, man. Someday I will best you."

"Dream on."

"How we looking?"

"So far, so good. Got the kids on lockdown with the aunt. Getting them breakfast now." Parker had no sooner spoke the last sentence than he regretted it. Klink was no dummy. Not by a long shot.

"You left them alone?!"

Shit. Parker weighed the idea of mentioning Napoleon and knew immediately that would be a disaster. So he improvised. "She's got my gun and there's a McDonald's right across the street. I can see the room from here. I won't be long."

"Still. You shoulda called for backup."

"I know. I got this, though. Don't worry."

"When ya wanna rotate out?" Klink asked.

Parker figured this was coming, sooner or later. As with any witness or person under police protection, the officers usually rotated in shifts. Sometimes eight hours, sometimes twelve. Again, he had to improvise. "I don't."

"What?"

"Yeah. The aunt is pretty adamant that I stay with them around the clock. She's freaked out bad."

"So? What? You just gonna get the cap to pay you a hundred hours of overtime?"

"Klink. Look. I don't care about that. I got no one waiting at home for me, nowhere to go or be."

"Still, man."

"And between you and me? I know what this guy looks like. I've seen him." Parker paused. It was another lie. He'd only seen the same pictures of Troy Forester that everyone else had, but he didn't care anymore. "He comes at them? I'm the one person who will know it first."

Klink was silent on the other end of the line for a bit, then said, "Okay. Fair enough. Not sure the cap will see it that way but I'll let him know and—"

"He's so damn busy he won't even think twice about what shifts I've worked, man."

"They okay? The kids I mean?"

"As okay as can be expected."

"Yeah. Man. The shit they must've seen. This guy's a real bastard, I'll give him that."

"Any leads?"

It was Klink's turn to chuckle, but it was completely absent any humor. "Hell no. We pulled all his info, yanked his DMV file and put an APB out on the car. Nothing yet. We also dumped his cell phone records. He either doesn't have it or it's turned off. Or he has a 'throw away.' So… nothing there, either."

"Friends, family, fellow psychopaths?"

"Nothing. The guy was a regular Ted-fucking-Kaczynski, minus the cabin in the woods and the manifesto."

"No. This sick bastard had a manifesto too," Parker said bitterly.

"How's that?"

Parker didn't want to answer. He didn't even want to picture the image, but it came to his mind regardless. "You shoulda seen all the strings of hair on the wall in his garage, Klink. Like a ponytail collection, one from each of his vics."

"Yeah. Murillo told me what you said about the ravine, too."

More bad images: sunken eyes sockets, rotting flesh, tattered clothes wet with maggots. "Yeah. Let's not go there, man."

"Gotcha. Well. We're gonna keep pulling what we can off the wire. I don't think there's a cruiser in the state not looking for a black Chevy Camaro."

"Guy like him is smart enough to avoid any highly populated areas."

Again. Silence. Then, "Yeah. I know."

"And you can't pull over every black Camaro in three or four states, 'cause I'm guessing Arizona and Nevada are in on this too?"

"And Washington."

"Man. The department must be just getting laced over this. I mean, first we put out an all call for Kyle Fasano, then Nap, now this guy."

"If I'm not mistaken, the word 'inept' is pretty much being used by all the news stations, and the story has gone national."

"What?"

"20-20. Two nights ago. Word around here is that a lotta heads are gonna roll."

"The cap?"

"Almost for sure. Ya gotta figure an early retirement announcement is coming pretty soon, just a matter of time."

"I'm not in his fan club, Klink, but this gig has been a massive cluster bomb since day one. Doesn't seem fair."

"Yah. And it's probably good that Nap isn't around to see his name getting dragged through the mud."

"By who?"

"Everyone. The department. The media. They all need a scapegoat."

"That's bullshit."

"Yep. But they can only take it so far because, well, he's a possible victim in this too."

Parker realized how wise his decision not to bring up Napoleon moments earlier was. "So what's the story?"

"You know: the cop who made a misstep, the guy that got away, maybe killing him in the process, now still running around loose killing others."

"And?"

"And how Kyle Fasano might somehow be linked to Troy Forester, because that's the only way to explain how Tamara Fasano has now been kidnapped, right?"

"No."

"Right. But speculation needs to be fed and anyone's theory is as good as anyone else's."

"And me?"

"You don't wanna know."

"Yes I do."

Klink sighed heavily. "Man, Parker—"

"Just spit it the fuck out."

"You're the war vet with a history of PTSD."

"From long ago, formally treated and cured."

"Who couldn't let the case go… and then obviously had a relapse and should still be suspended."

"Really?"

"They're saying it's because of you that Sheriff Conch in Beaury is dead. That you dragged him into an investigation he wasn't ready for."

"That's bullshit too."

"I know. To his credit, that's what the deputy there is calling it as well and…"

"Kendall?"

"Yeah. That's it. Kendall almost smacked some reporter in the ear hole for asking if you were involved somehow. It was classic."

Parker smiled. "Well, that's something. Evidently it's a good thing I haven't had any time to be watching the news." Parker made a mental note to make sure that the kids got only cartoons all day long. Neither he nor Napoleon needed to be seeing any of this shit, and there was a good chance it might shake Trudy's confidence in them too, which was the last thing they needed.

"Yeah. Cap is taking a lot of heat from the chief for reinstating you. So far the press has no idea you're the one guarding Fasano's kids, or they'd probably have a collective orgasm."

"Great. How's the lid been kept on that one?"

"Cap has kept it in the squad room. Strict orders. Funny thing."

"What?"

"He said the exact same thing you did a little while ago."

"What's that?"

"That you're the only one whose seen Forester up close, that you'd see him coming before anyone else."

"So everyone believes he's still a risk to come after the kids?"

"Not completely. But enough for no one to want to shoot their mouths off and get two children possibly killed."

"Hmm."

"But, ya know, Parker, when I talked to Kendall recently for some case file info?"

Parker felt his stomach drop. That was the thing about Klink, with his surfer boy attitude and smirky face, it was easy to see him as super laid back when in truth he was a really good detective. Parker didn't even want to respond, but he knew he had to. "Yeah?"

"He said you and he never caught up with Forester. Never saw him yourselves. Only the sheriff did."

Shit. Shit. Shit. Parker was stunned, then barely managed, "Imagine that."

"Yeah. Exactly. But here's the thing, Parker. I know you, man. Something's up. Something crazy. I don't know what it is, but it's got Murillo lighting religious candles up here at his desk and everything."

"Yeah?"

"No shit… and we went from Saint Michael to an entire posse of saints hanging from the rearview mirror in our squad car too. So here's the thing: give us a check in every four hours. In the meantime I'm gonna have a black and white go by the motel on a regular basis. I got a few patrol guys I'm pretty tight with who will do it and keep a lid on it, okay? Murillo and I will swing by whenever we can."

"Got it."

"And Parker?"

"Yeah?"

"Watch your ass, *guero*."

CHAPTER 22

KYLE WAS RESTING, HIS eyes half closed, while he and The Gray Man sped across the desert a mile above the black road beneath them, snaking through the desert hills that rose up here or there.

For some reason Kyle couldn't stop himself from thinking about, of all people, Caitlyn. Her innocent face, her bright smile, and the monster that had been hiding right there behind her eyes the whole time. "How could I have not seen it?" he mumbled. The Gray Man made no reply.

He wasn't sure how God and fate worked, not really. Perhaps the whole "millionth" thing was his destiny, regardless, one way or another. Had he been able to deny himself Caitlyn, then maybe he would've just been forestalling the inevitable. Perhaps he would've just done the same thing a few years further down the road, with some other woman who might've made it worse.

Then he mocked himself. Worse? How could it possibly be worse than his wife being abducted by a psychopath and his children now under police protection?

His lust had been a mountain within him that, once shook, had turned into an avalanche of chaos, pain and destruction, sweeping over everyone around him.

Perhaps it could've been avoided, if he'd been stronger. If he'd—

The Gray Man finally spoke. *Perhaps this, perhaps that. If this, if that. Can't you see, Kyle? All decisions are interlinked. Each of them is a ripple from the splash, spreading ever outward, in a pattern you simply cannot fathom.*

"Yeah? But how—"

No, Kyle. Do not add "but"s and "how"s to the "if"s. You're stringing together a shaky web.

"Then… okay, fine—"

Go back to your first question. That was the one not of yourself. That was the one you were meant to answer and did not want to answer so badly that you brought up all the other questions to forestall it.

Kyle nodded and looked out over the desert sands to the horizon, the sunlight partially discolored by the radiant glow of their orb. He'd been thinking about Caitlyn and… how he'd been unable to see the evil within her, the evil that almost killed him. Again he felt himself wanting to change the subject, especially when the answer popped up in his mind as obvious as a stubbed toe; he'd been unable to see her evil because he'd been blinded by his own.

"I had *become* evil," Kyle said flatly. "Isn't that right, Gray?"

The Gray Man nodded. "How do you think that is, Kyle?"

Kyle recalled the months before that fateful moment with Caitlyn in the hotel room, and they fanned out before him like a deck of cards, each day offering up to him a color, a face and a value to his shame.

The low cards were the first memories: noticing her in the break room and saying "hi," then at a staff meeting and joking with her about her note-taking, then one night in the parking garage, her leaving for the day and him arriving from a meeting to grab his things, and chatting it up with her. For ten minutes. Then twenty. Small talk, pregnant with the urge for bigger talk, which would come later, the discussion in the garage about favorite beaches or college classes morphing later into whether or not she was dating anyone, and why he was in no hurry to get home most nights.

After that, thoughts of her were like mushrooms, setting roots, growing in his mind: the mole on her right earlobe, the fullness of her breasts, the way her eyes sparkled when she said something flirty. Then, before he knew it, came the nights he wasn't able to sleep because he was burning up with desire. The fantasies of taking her away and being someone new, someone better than himself, through her, because of her, never thinking of how sad it was that he was at such a low point in his life that he'd come to believe that a complete stranger, seventeen years younger and fresh out of college, could help him find anything, much less himself. Then came the need for her body, the want for her sex that infested him, despite his best efforts to be strong, to be a good husband, to be faithful.

Don't lie to yourself, Kyle. We've been over this.

"What?"

You didn't try very hard to be any of those things. Not in the end.

"That's not true." But it was. It was true. In the end he'd started fights with Tamara on purpose, to justify his behavior. He ignored the kids, not helping them with their homework or reading them bedtime stories, because the guilt of his thoughts and intentions were more than he could bear.

And you stopped praying. And you stopped going to church too.

Kyle nodded.

You stopped talking to God in every imaginable way. You stopped wearing the little cross Tamara bought you one year for your birthday and—

"I stopped wearing me wedding ring."

They fell silent. Kyle was trembling a bit, but he had to finish. "I started taking it off when I'd get to work. When Caitlyn asked about it I told her things at home weren't so good…"

Yes. You lied. You had no intention of leaving your family. You just wanted to play, Kyle. With another human being. With another soul.

The blue in Kyle welled up forcefully, like a watery tear in the center of his chest, and then it was apparent what had really happened. Clear as day.

"We fed off of each other."

That's correct. And the one evil begot the other. She lusted too, for what she couldn't have. Then had fun with it, and then became enthralled by it. When she saw you willing to do evil, she was more willing to herself, and vice versa, things eventually building up to what happened.

"But she was the one who attacked me."

The Gray Man flashed a sad smile. *Really? Are you sure of that?*

"Have you forgotten that she tried to kill me?"

Kyle. The good in us, the bad in us, it tallies up over time. We all know this. When I walked this planet I knew it too. We know full well when we deposit or withdraw good, or evil, into our lives or into the lives of others. God is in that accounting, and so is the devil. But make no mistake about it: we are the one's working the equation.

"And?"

And when you took advantage of her, when you made her feel adequate and woefully inadequate all at the same time, you were the one doing the attacking, my friend. You were the one inflicting harm.

"But I didn't mean to. I just wanted to—"

Use her to make yourself feel better about yourself, about your life, for a little while.

"No."

Yes. And by that point she felt used enough, by you and the others that preceded you, that she turned fully and completely to the darkness.

"My God," Kyle sighed in suppressed frustration. "What have I done?"

A wrong that you're still trying to right, as best you can. Meanwhile, you know the scripture: "The Father works for the good in all things."

"The good? What good could possibly come from this?"

The man who has Tamara right now has killed nearly a hundred women, Kyle. That was nearly a hundred families tortured by the evil that this man wrought, never knowing if their loved ones were dead or ever coming home. Thousands of sleepless nights are now giving way to sorrow and mourning, yes, but also to healing, Kyle. Detective Parker found the bodies of those women in a ravine, where they had been lying in decay. Now, they will be put to rest, and in the process you cannot imagine how much healing is going to take place, how much love will escape into the world as mothers start support groups or families start foundations to help others in similar predicaments.

"So what I did…"

Was wrong. But there is always an offset, Kyle, always a balancing of the books. That's what we do. That's what I do. We work to offset things. We work to help people who want to be helped, because everyone can be, if they want to be.

"And if they don't?"

Then, as you have seen, there are plenty of agents for the other side working just as hard as we are to offset thing towards the darkness.

They were so engrossed in their conversation that they almost missed the dark speck moving on the road ahead, a small shimmer of sunlight bouncing off its rear window. They'd passed hundreds of cars on the road so far on their journey, and The Gray Man had taken note of each of them and then looked away.

But not this one. The Gray Man's eyes were fixed intently upon it.

Kyle squinted as they grew closer; it was a black Chevy Camaro. Or, just like the ghost in Ragtown had described, a "black wagon."

Shifting his weight to his hip, Kyle swiftly stood up and leaned against the wall of the orb. "Gray!"

I see it.

* * *

When Napoleon awoke, his eyelids scraped hard against his eyeballs, as if there was sand in them, and his body felt heavy with a sleep that did not want to be disturbed.

He heard SpongeBob first, and then the little girl, Janie, giggling over something her brother whispered to her. He blinked and looked around. From his position on the floor, just below the television, he could not tell if the two children lounging on the bed were watching him or the cartoon. He guessed it was him, as he had awoken with his head jammed partly under the dresser with his cheek meshed against the carpet and drool dried to his chin.

"What's the story, Morning Glory?" Janie said, giggling again.

Napoleon grunted. "Nothing new, Suzie-Q."

Janie's eyes widened. "Whatever you say, Mr. Jose."

It was way too early for word games. But even now, after sleeping for what felt like twenty hours and wanting twenty more, Napoleon knew his fatigue had nothing on a little girl whose mother had been dragged out of their home right in front of her. Whatever gave her even a hint of a smile, he would do. "Okay. Give me sec. Right now I got nothin'."

She laughed from the belly, a sweet sound.

"You were out solid," Trudy said from the sofa chair nearby, looking at him over the edge of a magazine.

"Don't I know it. Shi—" Napoleon stopped himself, remembering to watch his language in front of the kids. "Man. I needed that."

"Evidently. You didn't even snore. Just: out."

Napoleon sat up and rubbed his hands over his cheeks, trying to massage them awake, especially his right one, which was now creased with carpet outlines. He glanced over to see if Parker was awake and noticed his spot on the bed was empty.

Before he could ask, Trudy spoke up. "He went to get breakfast."

"Alone?"

"He figured we'd be safe with you here."

"Makes sense," Napoleon replied, and it did. What didn't make sense was the weird feeling he had. Why had his first concern been for *Parker's* safety?

"It's been awhile though," she said with a sprinkle of worry.

"Whatdya mean?"

"He said he was going to the McDonald's down the street. That he'd be back in twenty minutes or so. But it's been just over a half-hour now."

Napoleon tensed. "Are you sure?"

"Yeah. He left at about quarter to eight. It's twenty past now. I was gonna wake you in another five if he still wasn't here."

"Why not sooner?"

"I figured maybe he misjudged the walking distance or something."

"He walked?" Napoleon asked as he stood to stretch, but he heard how foreboding the question sounded as soon as it escaped his mouth and regretted it. A look of concern flashed across Trudy's face.

"Yeah. Why? Is that a problem? I figured he wanted to leave the car here in case"—she glanced nervously at the kids—"we needed it."

Backtracking, Napoleon tried to cover. "No, I'm not worried, just still half asleep. That makes sense."

But even the kids weren't buying it entirely now.

Janie looked straight at him. "Watchya thinkin', Abe Lincoln?"

He chuckled softly. "Nothing at all, Crystal Ball."

Sighing, he walked to the bathroom to take a piss and wash up. Closing the door, he thought about things: Parker had left and was out there on his own. That was not a good thing. Napoleon could feel it clear as day, hanging on his neck like a four year old. But why? The kids were the ones who were supposed to be the target.

Using cold water from the sink he splashed his face, head and hair. In the mirror he saw an entirely different man than the one he knew; his face that had aged considerably, the wrinkles at the corners of his eyes deeper, the bags beneath them more pronounced. The cold water felt unbelievably good, especially as it trickled over his scalp and down his sideburns, so he went all in on a head bath, even using the tiny bar of soap on the sink as shampoo. Once done and feeling clearer, he returned to his musings.

He couldn't leave Trudy alone with the kids. That wasn't an option… until it was. Napoleon had seen the McDonald's the day before when they were driving here as well. It wasn't that far away, even by foot. Call it ten minutes there and ten minutes back. No way had it got past thirty minutes round trip unless he was lucky enough to get there right after the local soccer team arrived on trophy day or some shit, and it was a little early for that.

Combing his hair with his fingers, Napoleon looked again into the mirror and realized it didn't even tell half the truth. He'd changed three times as much on the inside now. He'd tracked down a wanted man, seen angels, literally been to hell and back and was now here, still a nomad of sorts, not a cop anymore, still dead as far as the world knew and… what now? What was his role now? His place? Efren knew he was okay, and that was all that really mattered on a personal level. But here, in this motel room, there was a woman and two children that still needed him.

But your partner needs you more. Now. Go.

And that was the biggest change of all in him, he knew it full well: the propensity to listen to that little voice in his head when it said something, instead of questioning it like he used to. Gut over logic, every time, yes, he'd lived his life that way. Now? Now it was spirit over gut.

When he walked out of the bathroom it only took one look at Trudy to prove that she was feeling uneasy too, even before she said, "He gave me his cell number. I've tried to call it three times now but there's no answer."

With the kids looking at him, Napoleon unholstered his gun and handed it to Trudy. "You know how to shoot?"

"Yes."

"Good. No matter what, empty the whole clip if you have to… understand?"

She nodded firmly, looking afraid but resolute.

The kids? Not so much. Seth sounded especially concerned. "Where's he going, Aunt Trudy?"

"Just to go find Mr. Parker, honey" Trudy answered reassuringly.

"Why? What's happened to Mr. Parker?" Janie asked, her voice trembling with emotion.

Poor kids, Napoleon thought. *They can go from laughing hysterically at cartoons one second to crying hysterically the next. This is too much for them.*

Napoleon straightened his shirt and headed for the door. Once there, Janie called to him. "Mr. Napoleon?"

"Yeah?"

She hesitated, her face contorted with emotion. It was obvious she was trying not to cry. Ten years old and it was clear as day that she was trying to encourage him. "Watch your back, Jack."

Giving her a nod, Napoleon smiled. "No doubt, Scout."

Then he left the room and closed the door behind him.

They were on the second floor. Looking around he took it all in: where the walls and corners were, which cars were parked where, especially the cars that were backed into their spaces or that looked threatening in any way, checking for reclined silhouettes. He'd been on enough stakeouts as the "watcher" to know what the "watchee" should be looking for. None of the cars were occupied.

Nearby a guy stood by a janitor's trolley eating a banana, but he'd taken no notice of Napoleon. Still,

Napoleon went directly past him, taking note of the guy's crew cut hair and marine tattoo before dismissing him outright as a threat for one reason: he was wearing a very large cross on a leather string around his neck. Napoleon felt that was a deal killer if you were working for the other side.

Walking briskly and with purpose, Napoleon made his way out the driveway and to the street, then made a hard left onto the sidewalk, where he double-timed it to Los Feliz Boulevard. It was busy with morning traffic, but Napoleon paid the cars no mind as he made it to the intersection. There, to his left and a short block away, was McDonald's, where he assumed Parker was. It was the only one around, so it had to be. The lot was mostly empty and there were three cars in the drive-thru.

There was no way he shouldn't be back by now. Something was wrong.

Napoleon picked up his pace. By the time he reached the McDonald's he was almost out of breath. Seeing Parker nowhere in sight, he went inside.

He noticed Parker as soon as he walked in. He was sitting at a corner table, a half-dozen bags of McDonald's food in front of him, getting cold. And he was sitting with another man.

What the hell?

Parker glanced quickly at Napoleon, and then gave him a hard look before returning his attention to the man opposite him. He was in a beige suit. A normal Businessman Joe, but his posture was odd. Overly composed, he sat with both hands palms down on the table, his head fixed, staring at Parker intently.

Immediately, Napoleon canvassed the rest of the McDonald's. A woman with two children sat at one table;

two Hispanic men in Edison power company uniforms were at another, talking with their mouths open. Near them sat a lady in yoga pants and a hot pink top with a guy in jeans and white shirt. At the table nearest Napoleon was a man reading on his iPad.

Napoleon figured he could play this a lot of ways, especially without his gun. But he still had the .22 in his ankle holster.

Kneeling down, he tied his shoe, even though it didn't need tying, and as covertly as he could he pulled the gun out and palmed it.

If no one else in the room wasn't a problem, Parker would've called me over as soon as I walked in. But he didn't.

Which meant the guy seated with Parker was only part of the equation.

So… who else was in on the game?

Then Napoleon had a bad thought.

Shit. What if all of them are?

CHAPTER 23

As she lay in the trunk aching all over, Tamara forced herself to think of something, anything, that could take her mind off of her misery.

There was a legend in the small village in Bolivia where Tamara and her parents stayed during their missionary work, of the sun angel Manacua who roamed the forest. If you encountered him and you were a good person, he would warm you—a comforting sort of warmth, like a heavy blanket, would wrap you up and keep you from being cold for the rest of your life. But if you were an evil person, the sun angel would burn you, through and through, so that even the ashes of your bones were scattered like embers into the wind, up and over the tree tops, all trace of you gone forever, never to be seen again.

As Christian missionaries, Tamara's family tried to dispel such myths and replace them with stories of angels of their own—angels who only loved and comforted. Angels who guarded and watched over you and were a source of peace, not fear.

But to Tamara this never fully washed with scripture. Her Bible had a few references to angels, and though many of them were kind and loving, others were anything but. They were the ones that brought justice, or the wrath of God, or confrontation, much like the story of Jacob and the angel that he wrestled in the field, and whom he overcame, yes, but who also left him forever crippled. Angels could love, yes, but they could maim and destroy too.

Which led her to thoughts of The Gray Angel.

She'd only seen him a few times, but those few times were enough. The power that emanated from him was so intimidating that it was hard to encounter. There was that first time, in her bedroom at home, when that demon had come and sat on her chest; The Gray Angel had simply arrived, rescued her and then blinked away. That wasn't so bad.

But then later, in the bathroom at the rest stop in Barstow, with the demon woman and her child, it was much different. He had killed them, or dispatched them, whatever the proper term was, with little or no hesitation. Like an afterthought.

In that moment he was a warrior, at war, and he had been ruthless in the task set before him. It had been so horrible that he'd even asked her if she wanted him to wipe her mind clean of the memory, as if her brain was just a hard drive with partitions that could be formatted. She declined, but that image, that proof of good in full force striking out at evil, was sometimes too hard to deal with.

Then later, at the house in Monterey, where her husband had evidently been dragged into hell, the angel had stood outside glowing in the night air, seemingly taller this time, totally in command one moment then completely baffled the next. He'd seemed a little more human, and therefore a lot more dangerous. The battle had turned against him, but he'd still gone the warrior's way, even then, headlong into the front lines, all for—and this was where things really got weird—her husband. All for Kyle.

What was so special about Kyle?

Her husband was a good man, who, yes, had made a big mistake, but at what point had he become a person worthy of universal attention? Worthy of the protection of an angel or the wrath of hell?

She had been so busy, so overtaken by events since this all began, that she never took the time to ask this question, to try and figure it out. Just why *was* her husband's life, and subsequently her life and her children's lives, dragged into all of this? To what end?

She rubbed her eyes with the back of her hands, the twine from the rope at her wrists scratching against her cheek, and sighed.

Once she thought about it, about the business of heaven, she didn't want to know. She was too busy now with the business of being human, which she realized, with a small chuckle of irony, was pretty much how we all spent our lives. Maybe not stuffed in the trunk of a killer's car, but stuffed nonetheless into the tight spaces of other fears.

"What?" she heard Troy say from up front. "Where?"

There was a commotion and then she heard a power window going down. "Shit!" he yelled, and for the first time in days, hope, true hope, clanged around inside her. He was freaking out up there. Maybe it was the cops, because the car sped up instantly, the motor roaring and vibrating.

Because he'd punched it, she half rolled towards the back of the car. The initial rush swiftly gave way to a dangerously escalating rate of speed. Her hope was drowned in the panic now that he would crash the damn car. How ironic would that be? To survive this long only to die in a car crash?

He had "opened it up," as her dad used to say on the dirt roads back in Bolivia when he would take her for drives into town. But never at this kind of speed. This kind of speed felt like it was moving her insides around.

Jesus. Please.

More prayers, but this time the comfort they brought was short lived, as the car swerved hard to the right and then seemed to hit a bumpier road. The WD-40 can rattled loose and bounced across her face and into her chest. Everything shook violently as he backed off on the speed only a little bit. The car was not meant for this kind of road, at least not with the pedal so close to the floor. The rear end fishtailed, first left, then right, knocking her head to one side of the trunk, then jamming her feet hard against the other, her ankles crying out in pain.

"Fuck you! Fuck you, cocksuckers!" he screamed, and then he began to shout in some sort of gibberish.

The road smoothed out again. They were back on the highway, but now hitting speeds that meant almost certain death if they blew a tire or he lost control. "Where are you?!" Troy screamed again. "Where are you, master? I need you! Right now!"

They were being pursued. That much was obvious. And he was feeling awful alone up there. But the engine was so loud that she couldn't hear any sirens. Surely there'd be sirens. If the police were on his tail there might even be a lot of them.

She was helpless, either way, and she hated it. Tied up here in the trunk, this was between them and him. She was just a bystander. And that seemed so wrong and unfair. After all she'd been through, she felt she should have some say in the matter.

When the car was suddenly grasped by something, she screamed. Their speed slowed markedly and Troy began to shout and curse all the more, his rage turning to panic, his panic turning back to screams of rage. Tamara's senses were telling her that what was happening was impossible; inertia simply wasn't arrested in this away. But it was happening. The car was roaring away, the engine hard at work, and she could hear the wheels spinning against the ground below, screeching in rubbery wails. But they were hardly moving.

"Okay! Okay! You guys want to do this? Do you?" Troy shouted, his voice booming through the inside of the car. "Fine. Let's go then!"

Suddenly the engine and tires stopped and the car shut off.

There was a bang as he got out of the car and slammed the door, then, incredibly, the trunk popped open.

The first thing she saw was the hazy sky, littered with gray clouds. Then she watched as Troy walked past her to a spot at the back of the car. With great effort, she propped herself up on one elbow to look outside, and what she saw there nearly crushed her with joy.

The Gray Angel stood on the road facing Troy the Monster, his presence every bit as awe inspiring as she had just been remembering.

But it was who was next to him that left Tamara dumbfounded.

Kyle.

His hands were at his sides and his fists clenched, glowing brilliantly, a deep blue.

She was glad for that.

If it had been a yellow glow, she would've never believed that it was her husband. Instead she would've been sure it was someone else: the sun angel of Manacua.

Come at last to burn the evil clean out of Troy the Monster.

* * *

Parker sat at the table in McDonald's and stared at the same man who had stopped them on their way out of the Fasano residence just the day before. Ben? Yes. That was his name. Last name Weisfeld. He worked with Tamara Fasano. He had dark hair, stood about six feet two, and had beady eyes.

He'd walked into the McDonald's just as Parker was finishing his order. Nothing stealthy. No attempt at being discreet. Just walked in and waited until he caught Parker's eye, and then sort of smiled, like someone who knows something that you don't and just can't wait to tell you.

Los Feliz. La Canada. They weren't that far apart. Parker was willing to consider it as just an odd coincidence. Ben was in work clothes: a tan suit, with shiny shoes. It was possible that he simply lived nearby and was grabbing breakfast on his way to work.

But that stupid smile of his had ruined the odds of that. He was here for a reason, and that reason was trouble.

Parker didn't have his gun and wasn't carrying his backup. He'd accidentally left it at home when he ran off to Beaury to help Sheriff Conch and Deputy Kendall in their investigation. He knew that when he left the motel room, but the safety of Trudy and the kids came first. Ben looked fit, like a lacrosse player, but Parker was fairly confident that the odds were still in his favor; he could kick Ben's ass, with authority and probably quickly if it came right down to it.

But as Ben walked towards him and Parker scanned the room, it was apparent that the odds were actually going a long way in the other direction: there was a punk girl standing in the small hallway near the corner of the counter by the ladies' room staring at him, and two men in Edison power company jumpers sitting nearby doing the same.

He felt his phone vibrating in his pocket, but he didn't dare answer it.

At first he thought that was it, until he noticed the creature in the white shirt and tie, playing on an iPad. Unlike Ben, they all had red orb-like eyes, but the rest were at least trying to blend into their environment. This one didn't seem to care. His face was a tortured mask of melted flesh over black tar, as if his chin and cheeks were burned to a crisp and his blood had melted into wax layers over the wounds, to seal them somehow. On his forehead the process hadn't worked so well; a cut there was festering and oozing puss.

Parker looked around the rest of the place, stunned that people weren't running or screaming at the sight of him, but no. The rest of the people in the McDonald's, the counter staff, the cook who had wandered up to grab an overcooked Egg McMuffin from the manager in her bright blue shirt, and the manager herself, none of them, nor any of the other patrons, had taken note of the creature at all. That was when Wax Face opened his eyes wide in a spooky glare and sneered at him.

It was a challenge, old as time: *Go ahead, make your move.* And Parker was about to, until something told him to stall. Hold the line. Wait. Talk. So that's what he did. Turning his attention back to Ben, he said, "Hey. Don't I know you?"

Ben nodded. "Yeah. We met yesterday."

"At the Fasano house, right?"

Again, the nod. He locked eyes with Parker and wouldn't look away. Another sign of aggression. But it was one propped up by numbers. One on one, Parker sensed Ben wouldn't be so bold, not even on his best day. "Yeah," he said, "you're the guy who wouldn't let me see Tamara's kids."

"Hmm."

"You and that bitch you were with. The one you'd like to fuck."

The cashier who was sliding Parker's order to him froze in shock at what he said, the bags still partially in her grasp, as Parker turned to fully face Ben. "Hey. Ease up, man."

"Oh yeah?"

"Yeah."

Parker glanced out of the corner of his eye, waiting for the cashier to back away in case it all went down at the counter. But she didn't move. The manager didn't move either, while the chef was frozen in place, like a stressed mime, at her side. None of the other cashiers moved either, and the girl in the drive-thru window was locked in place as well, the drink she was filling still leaning against the dispenser handle, overflowing the lip of the cup and down onto the floor at her feet.

What the… ?

"It's just you and us, Army Boy," Ben said. "And here's how it goes: you got something we want. Normally we could just go right after it, but for some reason we can't this time. The master has us going through you to do it. Fine. So be it."

"Who the hell is 'the master'?" Parker replied bluntly.

"One and the same, dipshit."

"What?"

"Where are the children?"

Parker blinked and shrugged his shoulders. "What're you talking about?"

"Don't. Let's not play games, okay? You're going to die today. It's your time. The quicker you tell us, the quicker we'll make it. I promise."

It was Parker's turn to smile. "Oh, really? And why would you do me such a favor?"

"Because you're headed to where we're from anyways. And after the shit you've done? You'll probably rank higher than us right out of the gate."

Parker's smile spilled off his face.

"Nothing smart to say now, huh, tough guy?" Ben pushed.

"Look, man, I don't know what your problem is. I was doing my job yesterday."

"That's all you've ever done, Army Boy, but we're not here for that," Ben said, nodding at Wax Face and the two utility guys. "We're here for the kids."

Parker steeled his nerves. You go through enough confrontations in your life, you learn how they add up, or not. This one was best played straight, and it was probably the only way to buy time. Since it was a fight that they wanted, he wouldn't give it to them. Plain and simple.

"Fine. You want the kids, we'll talk."

"Bullshit."

"No. No bullshit. I'm hungry. I'm eating," Parker said firmly, watching as Ben tensed up and the utility guys stood. "At least until I hear what's in it for me."

The moment hung there, like a picture, for a ten second count before Ben nodded and chuckled. "Ah. Of course. What's in it for *you*? I should've known. Fine."

Parker had paid already, so he grabbed the bags of breakfast food, taking care when prying one of them from the cashier's hands, and made his way to a corner table, with Ben following close behind.

If any of them knew what they were doing, they would've never let him do so. Strategically speaking, being backed into a corner was usually not a good idea, but this corner had its benefits; it was furthest away from all three pockets of additional combatants and nearest to an exit. So if, or most likely when, the shit hit the fan, he'd have a good shot of at least getting outside if he could get past Ben.

They sat at opposite sides of the small plastic table as Parker reached into a bag and grabbed a McMuffin. He wasn't the slightest bit hungry, but he was holding the line on the playing it cool and buying time bit. For what, he did not know.

"You want my hash brown?" Parker asked, offering the bag to Ben.

Ben shook his head. "No. I don't. But what is it that *you* want, Mr. Parker? Let me guess. Women? Money? Fame?"

Parker shrugged.

"No? Hmm. Hold on a sec. Let me ask the master."

Parker stopped chewing the minute Ben's eyes rolled backwards in their sockets. Slowly, his head leaned back too before his mouth fell open and he breathed in deeply. The Edison guys began to murmur, as did Wax Man and the punk girl, who seemed especially giddy, there in the hall, her black hair spiked in all directions, her nose and lips riddled with piercings.

Before long the murmuring grew louder and became a chant. Parker was frozen in fear. He was willing to admit it to himself. This was not a situation he was prepared for. No human being could be. The forces moving through the air now were dark and deep and powerful, mutual conduits to a far-off place.

Then, suddenly, the chant stopped. Ben brought his chin down as his eyes rolled forwards back into their proper place. But their color was gone; they were jet black now, and his face was smeared with disappointment. "Really,

Mr. Parker? That's all you want? A second chance?" he asked incredulously. "That's pathetic."

Parker clenched his jaw. "Well… it is what it is."

The world outside the McDonald's had come to a halt as well, with cars and birds and even the postman, who had been walking his route, frozen in place. Parker was surprised when he heard the door open.

When Napoleon walked in Parker felt as if an entire calvary division had arrived.

Parker looked down and nodded, his chin bouncing against his chest, swagger working its way back into his bones. "Well, well, well."

But Ben was nonplussed. "Do you really think he can help you, Mr. Parker? Don't you see? He's out of breath. Probably ran the whole way here. And he's already made a big mistake."

"How's that?" Parker replied, returning to their stare down.

"He's missed my companion, there in the hall."

Looking over at Napoleon Parker noticed that the punk girl had moved off the wall and was now standing directly behind Napoleon, who seemed completely unaware of her presence. Making eye contact with Napoleon, Parker then completely looked him off, hoping he'd catch the warning. Then he returned his attention to Ben. "So? What now?"

"Now? Simple. This just got a whole lot easier. Fuck your wish list, Mr. Parker. Tell us where the kids are or my little girlfriend there will start this party by ripping your partner's throat out of his neck from behind, quick and simple."

CHAPTER 24

THE CAR BELOW THEM almost emanated with evil, erasing any doubt whatsoever that they'd found them, at last.

There was no hesitation in The Gray Man's approach, and Kyle respected that. They swooped down on the Camaro like a fighter jet, the force field bursting and leaving the air a bit misty as Kyle launched through it and took flight, tucking and rolling across the sand on the passenger side of the car. The Gray Man hovered down on the driver's side.

It was as if the man in the car sensed them or, more likely, whatever was helping him had, because the Camaro sped forwards, carving a wicked line through the sand-dusted road as it snaked from one lane to the next in an effort to keep either of them from getting too near.

The Gray Man lunged forwards in a dive that brought him right up against the driver's door window, his fist flashing backwards in an apparent plan to smash through it, but he was repelled by something around the car, invisible but strong, that bounced him away and off a good thirty yards towards the open desert.

Kyle didn't hesitate to call on the blue. From deep in his chest it coursed to his elbow, reverberated down his forearm and into his hand, where he opened his fingers and released it. A fine laser of it shot towards the car with lightning speed, striking it directly over the roof. The same shield that had just repelled The Gray Man now absorbed the blue, but not nearly as well. Part of the blast made it through, rocking the car and forcing the rear end to fishtail ever so slightly.

Kyle's heart jumped into his throat. Tamara was probably in that car somewhere. If he accidentally blew it up or caused it to crash and roll…

"Gray?"

I'm coming.

"Is she in there?"

I can't tell.

"Damnit!" Kyle couldn't take it anymore; the car had slowed and he saw his opportunity. He ran, faster than he ever had, alongside the car on the passenger side, at last able to see a shadowy figure within. The man wasn't right; he was agitated and bouncing in his seat, jerking himself back and forth against the steering wheel, engaged in a whole new level of road rage. After flipping Kyle off a few times, he made hand motions as if to say "C'mon, let's fight!"

Kyle almost took the bait, wanting nothing more in the world than to hurt the man who'd hurt his family. But then he felt the blue nudge his mind, refocusing it: to the passenger seat, which was empty, and then the back seat, which was empty as well.

No Tamara.

She's here, Kyle. I can feel her now.

Kyle paused. Breathed. Reached out with the blue. "Yeah, Gray. I can too."

Rage mounted in him as Kyle Fasano realized that his wife was in the trunk.

The son of a bitch had crammed her into the trunk like some sort of animal.

Kyle. Hold it in. Don't lash out yet, Kyle! The Gray Man urged as he closed to within striking distance of the car.

"I'm trying, Gray… but—"

Hold on! We've almost got the shield down. Give it another blast. I will time my attack to coincide with yours this time.

Kyle looked over at The Gray Man and nodded, but not before he took a split second to really see what he was looking at; The Gray Man, when fully unleashed, was larger somehow, like a force of nature, a pulsating shadow of power, his gray a stark contrast to the light blue sky behind him.

Kyle summoned the blue and shot forth another bolt, commanding a wider blast this time and getting just that.

It hit the shield around the car so bright and fierce that it crackled, like the sound of Pop Rocks in your mouth. A dome was revealed that stretched all the way around the car and into the road; after The Gray Man struck the top portion of the shield and it shattered, the bottom half of it simply rotated around swiftly from beneath the road to over the roof, again protecting the car.

Kyle didn't know if the damn thing could regenerate, but he didn't want to wait to find out.

"Gray?"

Do it.

Kyle shot another bolt at the shield, almost striking The Gray Man in the process. A large crack appeared and in a split second The Gray Man was on top of it, prying his hands into the crack, pulling in opposite directions, a fierce scream escaping his throat as he ripped the entire shield asunder.

The driver punched the gas again and the car sped off, away from them at a blindingly reckless speed.

The Gray Man accelerated after it and so did Kyle, as best he could on foot, and then, for no apparent reason, the car began to slow, before it came to a complete stop.

Kyle ran up next to The Gray Man, who had descended to the ground and come to a stop behind the car, not pressing the attack. "What's he doing?"

I don't know. But... something's wrong.

Nothing happened. They stood behind the idling car as it rocked slightly back and forth in unison with the raving madman inside, whose silhouette could be seen now through the back window, his arms and hands going off in all directions, as if he were directing an orchestra, his screams bouncing around inside the closed car like a bad song.

Kyle stepped towards the trunk but The Gray Man raised his hand. *Wait. Something's not right. I know it's hard, but wait.*

A few maddening minutes passed and Kyle was just about to toss The Gray Man's warning to the wind when all the screaming, bouncing, ranting and raving came to a stop.

Then, revealed in the sudden silence, Kyle heard his wife's faint pleas for help.

And that was all he could take.

He took two steps forwards, intent on ripping the trunk completely off the car, when the man inside the car screamed. "Okay! Okay! You guys want to do this? Do you?" he shouted. "Fine. Let's go then!" The engine stopped as the car was shut off.

When he stepped out of the car he was a tall, rail thin man just this side of being dead, with wild eyes and greasy hair, a battered face and blood on his shirt. There were scabbed-up cuts all over his body, as if he were a cutter who just couldn't stop hurting himself.

Kyle didn't know if Tamara had anything to do with that face or with that blood, but he sure hoped she did. It would make him proud. Then he had a sickening thought: what if that were Tamara's blood?

The man wobbled briefly, his eyes filling with hate as he looked with contempt at The Gray Man and then with pure disdain at Kyle.

Then, incredibly, he lifted his hand that was holding his car keys and punched a button on the fob; the trunk of the car popped wide open.

Kyle heard Tamara's cries again but he couldn't see inside the trunk from where he was standing. Without even thinking he sent the blue to his feet and felt himself rise a little off the ground, just high enough to look in and see her. He knew he was supposed to be horrified by the vision of the bruised and battered figure within, but that could come later. Right now he was just relived beyond all measure that she was still alive.

She was looking back at him in disbelief. "Kyle?"

He was just about to reply, to tell her "Yes, baby. It's me!" when the coyote-faced creatures struck him, one on each side, and began to tear at his flesh.

They growled with a ferocity borne of hell alone, and when he next heard his wife's voice it was screaming. "Kyle!"

"Gray!" Kyle yelled, but glancing over he realized he'd been far too focused on the car. The Gray Man had his own problems; two men in long black leather trench coats, with Nazi arm bands, had grabbed him and were holding him firm. But they weren't the worst part. No. The worst part was the creature with the face of an old woman but the body of a salamander, black with yellow spots, which had wrapped itself around The Gray Man's head and neck, its body squeezing in strong undulations, the muscles in its back rippling under the sun.

No wonder The Gray Man hadn't screamed. He couldn't. He was in the process of being smothered.

Kyle swiped at one of the coyote creatures, only managing to knock him off briefly before it was on him again. Stumbling backwards, the pain ricocheting sharply through his body, Kyle summoned the blue, but it was hard because the creatures were after his hands and arms, the one on his right biting so hard into Kyle's wrist that he heard his bones crunch like dry twigs. The blue had nowhere to go. No outlet. No way to target.

Then, slowly, ever so slowly, as if pleased with the scene before him, the crazy man stepped towards the car and closed the trunk.

"Tamara!" Kyle screamed, but it was no use. He couldn't defend himself against the creatures attacking him and get to the car too.

The crazy man looked intently at Kyle and smiled. "Silly, silly man." Then he turned around, walked back to the driver's door, and got in.

"No!" Kyle screamed in desperation.

The Camaro began to pull away, the motor roaring ominously before it sped off, the coyotes gnawing at Kyle's arms as the car slowly became a black speck on the road, growing further and further away.

* * *

One thing you could be sure of in a standoff: first one to blink, loses. It really was that simple. Nerves were the end of more than one good man, overmatched or not. That didn't mean you waited for the other guy to make a move. No. Not at all. Napoleon's grandfather had always taught him to throw the first punch in any fight. Always. Take the advantage, right away, when you could. Then? After that? Never let go of it.

The guy who blinked was the first guy to hesitate. That could be right out of the gate or sixteen punches into a totally even fight. Whatever. Eventually, someone was the first to take accounting of the beating they were getting, and then take a split second to consider it. That was the blink. That was when, for them, all was lost.

When Parker had come to him as a detective first grade trainee just a few months ago, right before the Fasano case shat all over them, Napoleon knew that the last thing he would ever have to train him on was how to fight. The guy was a war vet. Decorated. Solid. How he got into the department with a PTSD diagnosis just after his discharge, in this day and age, when most law enforcement agencies in the country would avoid such applicants, was anyone's guess. Maybe he knew someone who knew someone. Maybe, like Napoleon himself, hiding his gang friendships all the way through the academy twenty-five years ago, Parker had just gotten lucky. Whatever. Parker would have to be trained on good "detecting," and have a few instincts honed for the field, but on how and when to fight? Nah.

So when Parker simultaneously looked towards Napoleon as he swung wildly at the man sitting across from him, Napoleon knew something was way off. Parker would never do that. No man in his sane mind looks away from his opponent as he swings at them and leaves himself vulnerable, unless he's trying to protect the person he's looking at...

Someone was behind him.

Napoleon ducked.

A hand with bracelets whizzed through the air where Napoleon's head had been just a split second earlier. He spun and followed the hand to an arm tattooed with skulls and demons, then to a body dressed in all black, and finally to the face of a girl in her early twenties with black lipstick and… eyes that were not human. Red eyes, like all the rest of her kind, lit by the fires of hell.

Good, he thought. Hitting a woman was not his thing, though he'd had to do it a few times before, usually during domestic disputes when the person you were trying to rescue was all tears until you tried taking their boyfriend or husband to jail. But this? This was not a woman. It was a thing.

So, with no thought whatsoever, he punched her right in the nose.

Her head rocked backwards, and as blood poured from her nostrils, her lips curled back to reveal large shark-like teeth.

"You mooooother-fucker!" she screamed as her hands came up in front of her. In her left was a switchblade; in her right, just a good ol' steak knife.

"I had no idea McDonald's served fine cutlery with the Big Macs these days," Napoleon said with a smile. He charged her, but it was a feint, to get her to back up some and give him some space. Because it was apparent now who was also in on the rumble; the two guys in Edison uniforms were making their way towards Parker, who was wrestling with the guy in front of him. The fat guy with the iPad tossed it aside and began approaching Napoleon's flank, his face melting into a plump, fleshy mass.

Napoleon glanced his way twice. The first time was to verify that, yes, indeed, that was a mace—a freakin' *mace* of all things—in his hand as he came forwards, and the second time was to level his gun at him, take aim and fire.

It was a good shot.

The bullet struck the man directly between the eyes and blew the back of his head out like meat art on the entrance doors nearby. He dropped like a bag of cement, the mace clanging across the floor.

This only enraged the punk girl more, and she charged Napoleon with the switchblade held over her head and tried to stab him in the neck. He barely stepped aside, feeling her rib cage bounce off his elbow. He was just considering the idea of launching his body against her when, at the last second, he thought better of it. And that was a good thing, because as she passed him by, she crouched and spun with inhuman speed, her right arm stiff as a board as she swiped the steak knife through the air with vicious force. It barely missed Napoleon's right kidney, instead slicing an even line through his shirt.

Shit. That was close.

He stepped back. Napoleon could see that Parker was winning his fight with the idiot in the suit, but the Edison guys were closing in and—

Now it was Napoleon's turn to take his eye off of his opponent. She had the knives and wicked-fast reflexes, but he had the gun and she knew it. She wasn't advancing yet. He had her in his peripheral vision and for now that would be enough. Because right now all Napoleon wanted to do was watch Parker at work.

Seeing the Edison men closing in on him, Parker had evidently had enough with the man in the suit; he snapped his arm at the elbow. The man let loose a guttural scream and clawed at Parker's face, but Parker only snapped his head side to side to avoid the attack and then seemed to take aim before he smashed his forehead repeatedly into the man's face, the first time shattering the man's nose, the second time into his mouth, causing blood to immediately spill across the man's teeth, and then a final time to the sweet spot right between the man's eyes.

He collapsed, but that wasn't enough for Parker.

Evidently he was somewhere else now, perhaps in an Afghan desert, because he stood, picked the man up and chucked him through the window and out to the sidewalk beyond.

The Edison men came at him like twins of trouble, but Parker didn't retreat an inch. Instead he stepped between them, punching the taller one in the side of the jaw before he spun around and brought his elbow up and across the face of the shorter one, striking him flush against his temple. They flew in opposite directions, flashes of orange, before righting themselves against the cheap wooden McDonald's tables, which creaked beneath their weight.

Punk Girl was trying to be scary now, babbling in some foreign language as she whipped her tongue out of her mouth like a nymphomaniac and scraped the steak knife against the wall. Napoleon was unimpressed. Compared to the dude on the horse outside The White City, this bitch was a fucking Girl Scout selling boxes of Tagalongs. Napoleon smiled and waved his gun at her, holding her at bay, determined to see how Parker finished this.

When the tall Edison guy lunged at him, Parker went through a series of moves that Napoleon had seen before. There was a Jewish guy in their department, Meyer, who was very proud of the fact that he had taken Krav Maga classes for many years. Napoleon had seen Meyer use it twice in the field, once after a rock concert at the LA Coliseum that had gotten out of hand and another time with an assault suspect on LSD that had acted up inside the station while being booked. The fighting style consisted of short, succinct moves that swiftly incapacitated your opponent.

And Parker was using them now, in rapid succession, first on the tall man, who took the back of a closed fist to the throat before being spun around, kicked in the back of the legs, and, as he fell to his knees, an elbow to the back of the neck, right between the shoulder blades. He fell over face first, probably unconscious, maybe even dead. Then Parker turned his attention to the shorter one. Stepping into his lunging punch, Parker caught him square in the solar plexus with the heels of both of his hands. Air burst from the man's lungs as Parker pushed him backwards and went judo for a moment with a spin kick that caught the man cleanly on the right side of his face. He fell over like a chained and yanked tree stump, arms limp at his sides, his head thudding hard against a green and orange chair.

Napoleon smiled. Yep. Parker could take care of himself.

Seeing the rest of her group now fallen, the girl looked panicked, but made her move anyway. To Napoleon's awe, she ran up the side of the wall and launched at him with both knives out. Instinctively, he brought the .22 up and shot her in the throat mid-flight, the bullet ripping through her flesh as her eyes went wide with pain.

They were demons, yes. All of them. But it was evident that here, on this plane, they had to play by the rules. Physical bodies and limitations included. It was obvious she was neither used to this concept nor willing to accept it, because amazingly, she still tried to scramble to her feet as blood poured out of her. Numb, Napoleon shot her again, this time in the side of the head.

Sorry, honey. No brain, no body. No body? No fight.

Napoleon was just beginning to relax when he heard Parker's voice.

"Shit."

"What?"

Parker was looking out the shattered window and shaking his head. "Fucker's gone."

Shrugging, Napoleon tried to make the best of it. "One of them had to be smart enough to run, right?"

"Yeah," Parker said, "but I gotta feeling that outta all these idiots? He was the most dangerous one."

"Why?"

"He was in my head, man—or his master or whatever the hell. I was trying to buy time when you got here but I think he knows…"

"Knows what?"

Parker looked at Napoleon with deep concern. "Where the kids are."

CHAPTER 25

Elywood, Nevada wasn't a small town. With a population of 4,262 people it barely qualified as "tiny." It sat in the distance framed neatly by the massive mountain behind it, a single two-lane highway cutting through the middle of a series of red brick buildings and white plaster-walled shops. The tallest building had a sign that read "HOTEL" in big block letters, hand painted vertically on a wooden sign mounted to the facade. A single late-model white pickup truck drove down the road at a lazy speed among a half-dozen other cars that were parked at the curb, again, all late models.

The town itself was a late model, from another era. You didn't need to know anything else about it to know that. It wore its age like a timeless shadow. Tamara wouldn't be the least bit surprised if, at some point in its history, it had seen horses and gunfights. She tried to imagine them, imagine anything, really, to keep her mind off the water that was pouring over her body.

He was bathing her with a green rubber hose from a pumping station that looked to be abandoned. But, still, some folks in the distance could see him doing it, and every single one of them looked away and went about their business, even though she was almost naked, her breasts exposed beneath the sun. He'd only allowed her to keep her panties on because she'd begun to put up a fight when he touched them. "Doesn't matter," he said. "The master wants you clean for the sacrifice, but when he's done with you I'll have you anyway, you know?"

Tamara said nothing.

"It's part of the deal. I do what I do, and then I get to do *you*!" And, thrilled with himself for the word play, he giggled like a demented fifth grader.

She stood her ground and refused to acknowledge him as the cold water spilled over her sweaty, filthy skin and pooled beneath her feet.

"Don't worry," he added with a sigh, "you might be lucky. You might already be dead by the time I get to do it."

More laughter. He really cracked himself up.

She closed her eyes, feeling helpless and afraid.

If Kyle and The Gray Angel were dead, then she had no choice now. Her fate was in her own hands. In hindsight, maybe it was never meant to go down any other way.

As the water spilled down her neck and over her breasts, her nipples, responding to the coolness, grew hard, and she panicked, afraid that he would see them and take it the wrong way, thinking somehow that she was enjoying this. Unable to will the hardness away, she folded her arms over her chest and rubbed the water over the neck and face, to make as if she were washing, which was hard to do with just water.

As if reading her mind, he suddenly thrust a bar of Lava soap in front of her face.

It was like a rock made of sand paper that scratched away her skin as the lather built in tight, round circles. He noticed her chest but wasn't leering, at least not yet. She played along, not covering up entirely, which she felt would anger him, and her "shower" continued uninterrupted. Twice more she looked down the road, at a woman coming out of a tiny market with two bags of groceries, and another woman who was leaning against a red Pontiac and staring her way. Surely, they would help. They were *women* too and—

Incredibly? Each of them, in time, looked coldly away.

"Do you know why the master picked this place?" Troy said softly into her ear.

She shook her head as she rubbed the bar of soap through her greasy, matted hair, feeling bits of dry and brittle scab from the beatings she took come neatly off her scalp.

"Because it's a town full of secrets, Tamara. Piled high. Dark secrets."

She felt her lips trembling but held them still as he continued.

"No one here will help you because it might mean calling attention to themselves, and their secrets. The things they've done, or that have been done to them."

She kept her eyes closed as the soapsuds spilled off her head and down her face, sure beyond any doubt that if she opened her eyes the soap was so harsh it would scratch away her pupils, and prayed. *Jesus. Please help me. I don't know what to do.*

"In most places, the 'shift' would take place. But it's not necessary here. Do you know what that is? The shift?"

Tamara shook her head, and then forced herself to speak. Some silence was good, but too much of it was submissive. "No. I don't."

"It's how I got many of them, the other girls, I mean. There is a space between here and there—my 'there' or that stupid, weak 'there' that you worship."

"And?"

"And it stops things. Things like time and reality. It freezes them, so that the forces of the universe that really matter, that really influence things, can go about their business."

Tamara kept scrubbing, buying time. "What business?"

"Why, influencing all of our shitty little lives, that's what." He sighed as he turned the hose from a stream to a spray by folding his thumb over the opening. "We have no control over our lives."

She let the spray come over her and rinse her clean, even ducking her head beneath it and pulling her fingers through her hair a few times, allowing it to feel good for a few seconds, because it did. It felt good and it also felt... refreshing. Energy was filling the bones and muscles that were tight and weak only moments before.

"I don't agree with that," she said before she could stop herself.

He slapped her across the face, the spray of water now targeted off to the side of her as she yelped and stepped back.

"What did you say?" he murmured through clenched teeth.

Oh God, oh God, oh God.

He brought the back of his hand up, threatening to strike her again. "Answer me!"

"We do have a say, in who we are and what we do," Tamara said in a voice so firm it felt almost impossible at a moment like this; somehow it was composed and self-confident.

When his hand came down again towards her face, she reached up and grabbed his wrist with both her hands, the simple act of self-defense, of at last making a stand, all that she needed to bring herself alive. Alive and determined. She dug three of her broken and jagged nails as deep as she could into his flesh.

The look of shock that came over his face was the happiest thing she'd seen in a long time.

That happiness rose over her, hope unleashed, like a bird in flight. She waited for his bodyguards to appear, or that thing from the mirror. Nothing.

Then it dawned on her. It had been a good half-hour since they'd left Kyle and The Gray Angel behind, but his entourage had made no appearances since, which meant they either were still engaged in the battle or they'd lost it. Either way, it was good news for Tamara.

"You're alone, Troy. Aren't you?"

She released the grip of her right hand from Troy's wrist, balled it up into a fist, and took another shot at the base of his nose, like she had that fateful day in the foyer at her house, when she'd barely missed.

This time, though, she didn't miss. The bone crumpled up like tin foil, releasing a sharp crack into the air.

Troy screamed and stumbled backwards, yanking his wrist from her grip as he brought both hands up to his face, dropping the hose to the ground, the water streaming from it not nearly as strong as the gush of blood now pouring down his face. This was it: her moment. It was one on one, and as she stepped forwards and kicked him square in the balls, Tamara Fasano really liked her chances.

He screamed again and let out a deep moan as he dropped to his knees. He tried to scream at her but the blood was evidently pouring in both directions, out his nostrils but also down the back of his throat, because his words were garbled and bubbly.

Looking around, Tamara was stunned to see the townspeople, still no more than a hundred yards away, simply going about their business. Watching, yes, but minding their own, even as an almost completely naked woman fought for her life. *Their secrets must be pretty bad*, she thought as she picked up the hose and began to beat Troy the Monster relentlessly with it, her anger loose and running wild, the metal end hitting his scalp and gouging into it.

He lunged at her and slapped an open hand across her side and stomach, leaving a bloody handprint. But between his nose and his groin, he was done for. He fell forwards again, his right hand barely keeping him from falling face first into a deep hole in the road right in front of him, which was now nearly full with water.

It was her best, maybe her only, chance.

Stepping behind him, Tamara looped the hose around the front of his neck and straddled his back. Sitting on him, she watched as his right hand slipped in the mud and his left hand abandoned his nose to grasp at the hose as she ruthlessly crisscrossed it behind his neck and began pulling it tight with all of her strength. Every ounce of it. Every drop.

He gagged and tried to cough but she had him flush. His right hand gave way as he fell forwards into the puddle.

Tears filled her eyes. Tears of joy. Tears of horror. Tears of pure, unadulterated rage, as she pulled up and down on the hose viciously, screaming at him, smashing his face into the puddle as his arms flailed out sideways and tried to reach backwards, all to no avail.

Then, finally, he weakened, and she forced his face deep into the puddle, shifting her weight slightly forwards on his back for more leverage, and held him firmly in place, his entire head now almost submerged in the water, his screams gurgling as his mouth filled with water, and with absolutely no hesitation, she realized that she was going to let him drown to death.

As she did she thought of how she'd been praying to Jesus, just a little while ago, for help. Surely, Christ would never approve of this, of her killing him like this. Regret and sorrow filled her heart. She tightened the hose and gritted her teeth. No. She could do it. It would be okay. She couldn't be blamed for finishing him after all that he'd done to her.

Then again, what if that's what all that the monsters of the world ever wanted: to pass their evil on to the next person?

By murdering him, ruthlessly like this, with Christ front and center in her mind right now, she would never be the same again.

He was completely unconscious. Limp, his face slightly blue and swollen.

She loosened her grip and checked his pulse. He was still alive.

Fine. Let him face his master, that thing in the mirror, for failing like this. It wouldn't be pretty, but it wouldn't be on her.

She dropped the hose, grabbed her pants and top off a nearby post and ran in her underwear to the car. As she drove off in the Camaro, leaving a trail of dust and dirt behind her, she cried out with joy and relief.

She'd done it. She was free.

* * *

Parker and Napoleon took off on a dead run down the street with barely a glance between them, winding side by side down the sidewalk, splitting up to make their way around pedestrians or cars pulling into the driveways of the various businesses along Los Feliz Boulevard.

The early morning traffic was fairly heavy, but as they made their way to the intersection it was obvious to Parker that Ben not only had a good head start on them, he was also one hell of a fast runner. He was nowhere in sight. The traffic light worked against them too, turning red just as they reached the corner, unleashing a good fifty cars on either side of the road, drivers making their way to the freeway on-ramps nearby.

It was obvious that Napoleon was going to try to time the gaps, but it was suicide. Too many cars came off the line like typical Angelinos, as if they were in *Fast and Furious 28*, willing to risk life and limb to make it somewhere a whole two minutes earlier.

Looking up the hill, Parker finally saw him. Ben was halfway to the motel on a dead sprint.

"She has my gun!" Napoleon yelled to Parker as he backed off from the traffic almost all the way to the sidewalk again.

"Okay," Parker replied, as he looked up the street at the oncoming traffic again. The side nearest them looked hopeful. "We got a gap coming up!"

It wasn't a big one, but it was big enough to at least get them across all three lanes to the center divider, if they really hustled. To Parker's surprise Napoleon was off on a dead run right as a black Tesla whizzed by them. He was old, but he could still scoot.

Parker took off a few steps behind him and was promptly laid into by a chorus of honks by the next grouping of cars that were approaching. One of them, a yellow Prius, almost hit him. "Assholes!" the driver screamed at them, his voice trailing behind the car as it went past.

The center divider held them at bay for another five seconds, which felt like five minutes, as the little figure of

Ben reached the driveway of the motel up on the hill and ran into it. The light was beginning to change but he and Napoleon, again seeming to read each other's minds, bolted through a narrow gap in the traffic, forcing a black Mercedes to slam on his brakes momentarily as another burst of car horns ushered them to the other side of the road.

Napoleon looked worried, his face strained as he began to run up the hill.

"What is it?" Parker shouted, pulling up next to Napoleon and matching his stride.

"I use a nine," Napoleon grunted grimly between strides.

"And?"

"That's a big gun for such a small woman."

It was true. Parker thought of a standard nine millimeter hand gun and of Trudy's small hands. She would need both of them to fire it. She was a tough cookie, but recoil was recoil, and physics were physics. Parker had never thought she'd have to defend herself alone. He'd left her with Napoleon. And that's when it dawned on him why Napoleon was so stressed; it was he who had left her all alone with the children, not Parker, which meant he was going to blame himself forever if this didn't end well.

Parker had seen his partner suffer enough. That wasn't going to happen. No way.

Opening his stride, Parker gave it all he had, blowing ahead of Napoleon and up the hill, his arms pumping vigorously in time to his legs as his mind went tactical.

The problem was that Ben would have the advantage. Enraged as he was, dangerous as he was, he could just storm the room. Kick in the door, grab one of the kids, or he could—

Parker forced himself to stop imagining the negatives. *Just get there, dumb shit. Fast as you can.*

The driveway grew steadily closer, but as always in desperate situations, in war or in crime, things seemed to play tricks on you. Like some prop in an *Outer Limits* episode, the motel seemed to keep moving farther away the closer Parker got to it.

He glanced over his shoulder and was surprised to see Napoleon had nearly matched him step for step.

We'll get there. If Trudy can hold him at bay just long enough...

It was right when they reached the driveway that the first shot rang out.

Then another. And another.

They ran into the motel complex just in time to hear Trudy scream, a feral, murderous sound, followed by a fourth shot, and then one more.

As they approached the balcony, Ben stumbled backwards out of the broken door of the motel room, his hands clutching his chest. Somewhere along the way he'd shed his suit jacket, and now blood spots were blooming like roses across the back of his pristine white dress shirt. He held up one hand for a second, pleadingly, towards someone in the room. It had to be Trudy.

It's okay. She's okay. It's self-defense right now. That's all. Plain and simple.

When the next four shots rang out, screams began to echo through the complex as other guests ran out onto the balcony or entryway below.

Three of the four shots caught Ben in the upper torso; the last one clipped his neck and shattered a light fixture on the balcony across the way. He was propelled backwards, his lower back hitting the balcony railing at just the right angle to lift his feet and flip him up and over. He fell with a sickening thud to the ground below, his head cracking like a coconut on the letter "R" in the word "Reserved" painted on the parking spot below.

More screams.

So much for self-defense, Parker thought. *And a lot of people saw this.*

"Jesus Christ," Parker muttered as he came to a stop.

Napoleon pulled up next to him. "More like Mother Mary," he said between gasps before adding, "I guess I was wrong about her being too small to handle the gun, huh?"

Trudy came to view in the doorway, her forehead bleeding a bit, her eyes wide with shock.

When she finally looked down and saw Parker below it was with a look of utter relief and fear. Tough girl, yes. But she still began to cry.

Parker wanted to hold her in his arms and tell her that it was okay to cry.

You always do after your first kill.

CHAPTER 26

As the blue pulsed through Kyle's broken right wrist the pain was excruciating, but it had to be done. The Gray Man was losing his battle. It was obvious that he'd been assigned the three toughest of the group. The Nazi men were strong and vicious, each holding one of The Gray Man's upper arms with one hand as they beat on his body, ribs, stomach and throat in alternating waves and with stunning accuracy.

The salamander woman, meanwhile, seemed to be relishing his torture, tightening her tail around The Gray Man's face as his hands struggled to free himself from her grip. His hat had been knocked to the ground and was being stepped on by his own two feet as he stumbled backwards and forwards, swinging his body from side to side in an effort to shake her loose.

Meanwhile, the coyote creatures had continued wave after wave of bites and tears at Kyle's body. He would spin one off just long enough for the other to sink his teeth into his thigh, spin that one off just as the other returned to bite his waist. They were no coyotes of this world. They moved way too fast.

As the blue pulsed into his arms they again attempted to attack him there, but by blind luck, the unthinkable happened; he fell on to his knees. This was what he'd been trying to avoid all along, being dragged down to their level. Down here they could get at his face and throat. But, instead, it finally got him a bit of distance, for just a split second, and that was all he needed to bring his hands up and release the power within them. The aim of his right hand, being in such bad shape, was poor, but the blast still clipped one of them in the shin, blowing the limb to pieces as the demon teetered for a moment, still trying to advance on three legs, before it fell sideways and began to thrash around.

The aim of Kyle's left hand had been true, though; it caught the other one dead center in the stomach, its guts blowing out before it fell over dead.

Upon seeing his partner go down, the remaining creature snarled, righted himself and began a wobbly charge.

Kyle tried to retreat on his haunches but it was no use. The creature bit into his foot and started crawling up his leg. Without really thinking, Kyle reached out, grabbed it on each side of its head and, as its fangs snapped, into the empty air, Kyle pulsed the blue from his one hand to the other, straight through the creature's head, leaving behind the stump of its neck pierced by what was left of its spine, a sharp white bone charred black around the tip.

That was close. Man. Another four feet and it would've been at my chin.

Kyle was exhausted, but there was no time to rest. Lying on the ground, he realized that the three creatures attacking The Gray Man were unaware of what had transpired. That or they simply had their hands full with The Gray Man, who'd managed to pull Salamander Lady's tail off of his face, revealing one eye glaring out for help.

Kyle couldn't risk taking a shot at her, so instead he leveled both hands at the shorter Nazi. Noticing that his right hand was hanging limply, Kyle tightened it into a fist, the pain again less so now, as if he were going into shock or something. The double bolt that escaped his hands cut one of the men into threes, one bolt carving through him just below the armpits, the other one right through his hips. He fell, akimbo and lifeless, to the sand.

The tall Nazi screamed and turned towards Kyle. His eyes darted side to side as he seemed to debate on what to do next: relinquish his grip on The Gray Man to go after Kyle or hold his ground. It was the only delay The Gray Man apparently needed, because in that split second he reached up with his one free hand and punched a hole into the Nazi's chest, a white light bursting forth into the creature and imploding him in a starlight flash that sent meat and bone in every direction.

Gasping through a small hole beneath Salamander Lady's tail, The Gray Man stumbled forwards, but seeing that her comrades had fallen, the salamander doubled down on her grip, eliciting a scream of pain from The Gray Man as she once more engulfed his face in her dry skin.

Kyle rose to his feet and ran towards them, stumbling on a half-buried rock. Regaining his balance, he launched himself at them both and knocked them over. As they all fell to the ground, he scrambled to get a hand in Salamander Lady's face, determined to blow her head off.

Instead, she released her grip on The Gray Man and lashed her tail at Kyle, striking him upside his head so hard that he almost lost consciousness. The world blurred and spun, then snapped back into focus. She was on the ground between The Gray Man and him, spinning in tight circles as her eyes rotated sideways.

Salamanders weren't supposed to have large teeth. Kyle was almost sure of that.

But this one did. Oversized, sharp and jagged.

All her movement had kicked up the sand so much that a cloud had enveloped them, making it harder to see.

Kyle could make out motions through the cloud. Her tail came at him again and he ducked, barely in time, hearing its meaty weight swing over him, sensing that that blow most likely would've broken his neck had it connected.

Then she was gone, the sound of struggle off in the distance now, where The Gray Man had been, before she was back again, her head darting at him through the sand cloud, her teeth gnashing at Kyle's face. Instead, she caught his broken hand, which he'd raised to protect himself. He cried out in pain, and almost in reply the air around him crackled and vibrated.

Her eyes widened in terror as, behind her, the dust and sand was blown away by…

Kyle gasped.

The Gray Man stepped forwards in a light gray tunic fastened by a leather belt at the waist, his wings massive and glorious, his eyes glowing white and his chin set firm.

Salamander Lady tried to scramble off Kyle and get away, but The Gray Man had her by the tail and was pulling her, hand over hand, towards him.

She twisted onto her back, claws exposed and slashing, her teeth snapping in defiance.

Kyle could do nothing but watch, dumbstruck with amazement at the sight of his friend as The Gray Man reached forwards, grabbed the creature around its neck, and began to speak in a blend of languages that appeared to cause the creature far more distress than any blow ever could.

It screamed in hellish wails as, slowly, it began it fall apart. Back limbs first, then its right front leg, before its head popped open and its brains oozed down its back, a final hiss escaping its throat.

The sounds of heaven and hell, meeting in this little spot of desert on earth, receded as quickly as they had arrived. Kyle lay still as the blue ebbed away, a pocket of it pooling and throbbing at his wrist, healing him.

After a few moments, the cry of a lone hawk cut through the sky above.

"Gray?" Kyle said. "What's wrong?"

His friend, who'd been looking at the ground, perhaps in prayer, looked up at him. When he spoke his voice was his own, but deeper and more resonant. Of all things, he looked sad. "I am revealed," he said.

"What does that mean?"

"It means… Kyle, listen to me. You know how to find Tamara. You must now. On your own."

Then he simply blinked away, as if a switch was flipped and he had been turned off.

* * *

"Who's Efren?" Trudy said, looking first to Parker and then to Napoleon, her eyes still partially glazed over with shock.

Stunned, Napoleon could barely speak. "What did you just say?"

"I asked, who's Efren?"

Parker looked hard at her. "Why, Trudy?"

"That man. Ben. Right before I shot him, he was telling me that the kids weren't safe, that they'd never be safe, and to tell 'him' that neither would Efren. But I don't know who he was talking about or who Efren is."

Napoleon's stomach went sour. Now he felt like the one in shock. "He meant me. To tell me. Efren is my nephew."

"Shit," Parker muttered. "What else did he say?"

"Just that. But it was the way he said it that was weird."

"What do you mean?" Napoleon asked firmly.

"It was like, at the end there, when he knew he was going to die, he got really sad, ya know? Like maybe it was all a game until that point, and then it became real. He was like a scared little kid about to go on a roller coaster ride he wasn't ready for."

"And?"

"He wasn't ready. Not at all. He was terrified. It was like…" Trudy faded away into her thoughts as she looked out the window.

"Like what, Trudy!" Parker yelled, snapping her out of it.

She looked at Napoleon. "Like the Efren comment was an attempt to make amends, like maybe he was tipping you off to something."

Pure fear clutched at Napoleon. "Parker. Give me your phone, man."

"Yeah. Sure thing," Parker replied, reaching into his pocket.

Once the phone was in his hand, Napoleon froze again.

"What's the matter?"

"Parker… I can't remember the number."

"For who?"

"Efren's mom."

"Call the station, they'll—" Parker stopped short.

There was no way Napoleon could call the station, and they both knew it. And with sirens approaching from a distance, time was running short. He felt Parker take the phone back from his hand and call in himself. Murillo and Klink weren't in, but Dane, the Desk Sargent, was. Covering the mouthpiece quickly, Parker whispered to Napoleon, "What's her name?"

"Anita. Anita Villa. She lives on Boylston. Middle name Ana."

In short order, Parker relayed the information to Dane and was put on hold as the sirens loomed louder.

"Did you notice?" Parker asked.

Napoleon squinted at him as impatience began to rise like lava from his stomach into his chest. "What?"

"Nothing froze or disappeared this time. Like at McDonald's or the 7-Eleven."

"Yeah," Napoleon answered. "Nothing back at McDonald's now but a bunch of confused people looking at a shattered window and a bunch of overturned chairs that, last time they noticed, were whole and upright."

"But here, with Ben?" Parker pressed.

"He wasn't from there, I guess," Napoleon surmised.

Trudy's face wrinkled again with confusion. "From where?"

"Hell," Napoleon said bluntly.

Parker nodded. Trudy, evidently topped off on stress for the day, seemed to take Napoleon's words and file them away for a later time.

"Still nothing," Parker said, still on the phone.

"They're almost here, man. I gotta go. I'm just going to go to the house. It's not far."

"How? If you take the rental they're gonna wanna know where it went, especially if they want to head back to the station house for statements."

"The bus will take too long," Napoleon said, speaking mostly to himself.

"Plus, how will you know if I even reached her if you don't have your phone?"

Napoleon felt as if he were outside his body, confused beyond rational thought. These were alien feelings, and they were overcoming him when Trudy spoke up out of nowhere.

"Take my phone and take the car," she said bluntly, handing Napoleon her phone and the keys. Then, looking at Parker, she said, "They don't even know I have the rental, but if they ask, we parked it miles away and walked here to throw Ben off. We'll have them drive us all to the station and tell them we'll worry about the rental later."

Parker looked at Napoleon and nodded. "Go," he said.

Napoleon wasted no time. As he exited the room he looked down at the small crowd that had gathered around Ben's body. The facility manager was keeping most of them at bay, comically using a mop to do so. Someone in the crowd had a small white dog though, which had pulled its leash taught and thus far had gone unnoticed as it licked at a small trickle of blood that had made its way down the pavement. Trying not to be obvious, Napoleon went down the stairs at the opposite end of the balcony and thanked his lucky stars that very few people noticed him as he made his way to the car.

He backed up, pulled out of the driveway and was just making his way down the street when he saw in his rearview mirror three black and whites pull into the motel, sirens blaring.

He drove as calmly as he could, watching as random pieces of trash danced across the street, caught in the tug-of-war of the cars that were passing in opposite directions. He clenched his teeth, thoughts of Efren being in danger bouncing around in his mind like shards of glass. He wanted to peel out, but that would be stupid. As if to prove his instincts right, another black and white was making its way down the boulevard from the opposite direction.

There was nothing like a speeding car leaving the scene of a shooting to raise suspicion.

Instead, he calmly drove at the speed limit, down the street and to the freeway on-ramp. Then, once on the freeway, he punched it.

Traffic was moderate but the cars seemed to be spaced out intentionally to frustrate him, with no gaps to exploit. A green Altima blocked him in on the left, a Ford F-150 on his right. To make matters worse, the slow lane had been gobbled up by semis trying to make their delivery deadlines. He banged the steering wheel with his right hand and tried to think. What could Efren possibly have to do with any of this? How did they even know about him?

"Shit!" Napoleon screamed into the empty car, hoping to relieve some of his panic but actually doing just the opposite, only ratcheting it up another notch.

As he made his way to East LA it felt like hours, not minutes, until Trudy's cell phone finally rang. He reached down and punched the speaker button on it. "Yeah?"

"Your sister is a major fucking pain in the ass."

"Why?"

"She wasn't about to tell me anything. Not a thing. I was a strange man calling, saying I was with the police and asking where her kid was. I get that, but man does she have a mouth on her."

"Tell me something I don't know. So where is he?"

"He's at a little league game. Evergreen Park. His team color is—"

"Dodger blue. I know." Tears were filling Napoleon's eyes. How could he have forgotten. When he'd seen Efren last, his nephew had told him that he had a special double header, for Cinco de Mayo.

He wanted Napoleon to come and Napoleon had said he'd try to make it.

Now he had to make sure he didn't make it too late.

"Hey, Nap. I'm down the hall, sneaking this call to you. So I'll make it quick. I'm sorry."

"What? Why?"

"I couldn't get her to shut the fuck up. She wouldn't listen. I had to tell her…"

"Tell her what?"

"That you're alive. That you're the one trying to get to him."

"What?"

"I lied too. I told her that you're on your way there with a few units, so she wouldn't worry."

Napoleon laughed. "Are you crazy? She's not going to worry, man."

"Okay then. That's good, right?"

"No, Parker. Instead of worrying, you know what she's gonna do? Call every member of Cuarto Flats in the area and send *them* there. To a park full of Evergreen gang members."

"Screw it. As long as someone gets to him first, right?"

"No, Parker. Wrong."

"Why?"

"We know which side is after Efren. So let me ask you something," Napoleon said with the heaviest sigh of his life. "How many gangsters you ever met in your life that were right with Jesus?"

The other end of the line went dead quiet.

CHAPTER 27

It was when the people in Elywood froze in place that Tamara realized something was wrong. The world didn't just… freeze like that. She was driving right through the center of town, determined to get past it to a place she could feel safe, somewhere she could flag down a woman to help her get some clothes, some help, anything, when it happened.

The town, the world, locked in place.

Her brain immediately went through a series of rationalizations, one of them logical (she'd fainted, is all, from the exertion of the fight), the other terrifying (she was still in the trunk, asleep and having a bad nightmare). Something had to give. There had to be an explanation for why the world just got stuck like the bad second hand on a rusty watch.

But the images and the impressions weren't going away. The woman who'd been standing next to the red Pontiac was caught in a half-seated position, one leg straight, the other out, as she'd just been getting into the car when it happened, while the lady with the groceries had just finished loading them into the back of a pickup truck and now looked like a crouched mime, both hands open-palmed against the front of the tailgate, which she had been closing. A man down the street with a rake over one shoulder remained in a half-walk, his stride split, the backpack over his shoulder hanging out oddly from his body, as if it were mounted on a stick.

Tamara had the feeling that she was seeing something unreal... How could this be? There was no wind coming through the crack in the car window. No feeling of energy in the air, or warmth from the sun. Even a small flock of birds flying in the sky over the front windshield were locked in place. How was this possible? How did—

The dirt ahead of her, about ten yards away, began to shift. In a normal situation it would've hardly been noticeable, but now, in the silent cocoon of the world in suspended animation, it sounded like an avalanche.

When she looked to see what the origin of the sound was, her grip on reality only grew weaker. A man was rising from the dirt, as if ascending from beneath a stage of some kind, an invisible platform under his feet. At least she assumed it was a man; he had the build of one, tall and lean with broad shoulders, as the dust cleared she could see that he was wearing a black wool trench coat—grains of sand and dirt cascading off of it as he rose—and a top hat, of all things. It was the creature from the mirror.

He had one hand at his side, clenched into a fist, and his other hand behind his back for some reason, his forearm curving at his hip. His black shoes had scuffed tips, and his dark gray pinstriped slacks matched his vest. A gold chain hung there in a small loop, one end no doubt attached to a watch of some kind in his vest pocket.

She stamped on the gas pedal. The engine roared... but the car didn't move.

"No! How? How is this happening?" she screamed.

He cocked his head to one side, then to the other, then back again, as if he were studying her, as if he could see *her* just fine.

Then he nodded slightly, as if he were either impressed or accepting some sort of truth about the situation. So this was the creature that Troy the Monster had been talking to all this time, a creature that emanated murder and hate, as if that was all that it lived for.

"W-what do you want?" she finally managed to scream, her lips trembling.

In a wordless reply the creature brought its other hand around from behind its back, and extended towards her an old brass lantern.

Like the one Ben had given her.

Her body went cold with shock. Ben? He *had* been a part of all this.

"Dead now," the creature said bluntly, its voice deep and hollow, like rotted wood. Then, from beneath the cloth strips, it chuckled softly.

She was just about to speak again when the small door of the lantern swung open and the entire world collapsed in sheets of black, gray and white. She wanted to get out of the car to run, but that required a place to run to, and there was nowhere she could escape.

The glass of the windshield shattered. She hadn't taken the time to buckle in but she didn't imagine that, in the face of this kind of power, it would've mattered. She was levitated and jerked through the window like a toy.

Then they were off and traveling somewhere, at an insane speed, Tamara's eyes only seeing the world in dull-colored smears as her insides leaned hard against her ribs.

When they came to a stop she was in a cave.

Turning slowly, sensing that the creature was still nearby, she saw him at last, in the far corner, his arm still outstretched, the lantern still hanging there, but now swinging slightly from side to side.

"Where are w-we?" Tamara squeaked, panic stuck in her throat like a chicken bone.

The creature said nothing. Instead, a gray light flashed from the lantern, illuminating the room in the depressing color of a cloudy day. "You stay here," his voice rumbled again. "Learn. I'll be back as soon as I'm done killing your husband." He nodded. " You've been the perfect bait. And now? He's unprotected."

She blinked and barely had time to scream "No!" before the creature disappeared.

Able to move now, she began to pound on the rock wall. "Let me out!" she yelled. "Let me out of here!"

But the wall wouldn't give, and there was no exit and—

The faces emerged from the rock in tight but sporadic groupings, each in various states of decay; some still recognizable as human, others half-rotted and the rest as naked skulls. A few had hands visibly at work; one was scratching at his chin, another had its head turned to the ground with a hand covering one eye, middle finger on its cheek, index finger stretched out to its forehead, as if it were contemplating something or trying not to watch what it knew was coming next.

"Oh my God," Tamara said, stepping backwards towards the wall to her left, the only one without faces emerging from its surface.

As if reacting to her words, the faces all flashed expressions of shock and anger. One in the upper right corner of the wall in front of her screeched like a crow, and another let loose with a string of profanities.

Tamara's heart sank. What was the old saying? *Out of the frying pan and into the fire.*

Slowly, the other faces began to talk too, one by one, each telling a story of how Tamara had hurt or disappointed someone at some point in her life. Story upon story of things inflicted, people ignored, needs left unmet. She backed up to the opposite wall and covered her eyes, then her ears, trying to close out the voices, but it was no use.

They weren't speaking into her eardrums.

They were speaking inside her mind.

The memories like forceps digging deeper and deeper into her head, until her skull felt as if it were going to split clean in half.

* * *

Sometimes you make a bad decision and know it instantly. It hits you, like a punch. Other times it takes years or decades for the blow of realization to come, by then too late. Then, there are the bad decisions that glance off of you, like a misdirected jab, and when you think it's passed, it comes back, again and again, like a stinging nuisance. Parker was feeling that jab now, nice and solid, banging at his head with a precise sort of pain, barely five minutes after Napoleon had driven away: *You shouldn't have let him go alone.*

He tried to ignore it when the black and whites pulled up, and when the questioning began. He tried to ignore it when Trudy and the kids were escorted back into the motel room by Klink, who'd arrived in his usual blue OP jacket, with his thin blond hair combed back over his increasingly balding head. But when Murillo arrived, for some reason, he could ignore it no more.

"So tell me again, Parker, what—"

"Stop," Parker said flatly.

Murillo looked up from his notepad and they locked eyes. "What?"

"We need to get to Evergreen Park."

Now it looked like it was Murillo who'd caught a jab. His head popped back a bit on his neck in surprise. "What are you…"

"Napoleon is at Evergreen Park. He's gone there to try and rescue his nephew, Efren. He's ten, playing in a little league game."

"Rescue him from who?"

"Whoever, I think they plan on hurting the boy."

"And here?"

"I can't say that the kids or Ms. O'Hara are totally in the clear yet, either."

Murillo took a deep breath before he rubbed his hand over his face in a sort of magic trick, his face changing from confusion into a mask of pure exasperation. "What… the… fuck, Parker!"

"We still got the guy that grabbed Mrs. Fasano on the loose. For all we know he and this guy were working together somehow."

"Somehow? How?!"

"I don't know."

"I just knew this was some sort of satanic cult shit. I been tellin' Klink that from the beginning."

"Well…"

Murillo seemed beyond exasperated. "Answers, Parker. Do you have *any* fucking answers?"

"Does it matter? *Now*, I mean? Can we get to the answers later, after we get to the park to help him?"

Murillo whistled to Klink, who stepped into the open doorway of the motel room. "What's up?" Klink said, looking down over the lip of the balcony, his face twisted in curiosity. His blond hair and blue eyes said pure California surfer boy, except he was originally from Kentucky and had never surfed a day in his life.

"You stay here. I gotta jump on a lead at Evergreen Park," Murillo said, looking at Parker before glancing back to Klink. "I'm taking Parker and a few units with me. I'll leave a few units behind."

"Why would you need to leave units behind?" Klink asked, a look of wariness now crossing his face.

"Dude. Stuff's still poppin'. Can we leave it at that?" Murillo said, lowering his voice a bit and snapping his eyebrows towards the back room, indicating that the kids and Trudy were still within earshot.

Klink was about to press, but Murillo's cheeks stiffened in an odd sort of poker stare. Parker knew that Klink and Murillo had been partners for years. Like married couples, you get to a point where a look is all it takes. Klink nodded. "Alright. Got it."

Murillo looked around. "Duquense and Willie, Tapia and Mendoza. You guys follow us. Huante?"

A youngish looking Latino cop with a neat haircut stepped forwards with his hands on his gun belt. "Yes, sir?"

After a short sigh, as if he were bottling his stress, Murillo motioned him and the five other uniforms over. "Look. There may be another fucking perp, maybe gonna try to come back around and pop the kids. You got it?"

The quorum of cops shifted on their heels uneasily at the news. Two of them were female officers, both white, another officer was black, another Asian and the last guy looked like an honest-to-God Navajo. All of them had the same eyes, not in color, but in awareness. Awareness of possible danger. One by one, they nodded.

"Klink's got the lead. Down here I want Huante at the head of the driveway. The rest of you get this crowd to disperse. Yueng, you get upstairs and take the door. You other four split up, two at the stairs on this end, two at the stairs on the other. That way, no one can get up there unless he fucking drops in on the rooftop from a damn helicopter."

"Any idea what the guy looks like?" one of the female officers, Carlisle, asked.

Murillo glanced at Parker with irritation. Parker shrugged, not wanting to describe Troy Forester because after the cast of characters he'd seen already, he had no idea who might be sent next. Murillo rolled his eyes.

"Probably a lot like the boogeyman, Carlisle. Meaning you won't know who he is or what he looks like until he's up in your shit already, okay?"

They all nodded again. Their black uniforms were long sleeved and strictly creased, the edges not unlike their hair, which for the men was just below their black caps and for the women up in tight buns. It was a look the LAPD had gone back to—black on black, instead of blue on blue, as it had been when Parker first joined the force. The starkness of the black only highlighted the shiny gold of their badges.

"Everyone get to their posts. The ME's coming soon. Huante, you show them the body."

Huante had dark eyes and a voice too old for his face. "Got it."

Parker looked around at the city surrounding them; it was like a cocoon made of concrete, tinted glass and signage. From the professional, big corporate signs on the skyscrapers in the distance downtown to the ones around them here, cheesy and in loud colors, offering ten-dollar manicures, flat-rate cell phone plans or one-dollar tamales. It was like the big city dressed sharp, from the waist up, all metropolitan and fancy, but was one hundred percent Tijuana from the waist down, here on the outskirts, where

East LA and Hipsterville were locked in a sociological battle of wills and demographics.

The sky was a weak blue, the clouds tinged with shit smears of smog that blocked most of what the sun had to offer, which wasn't much today.

"How many you guessing gonna be there?" Murillo asked, startling Parker out of his head.

"Man. I got no idea. Hopefully not too many."

"But more than one, that much we can count on?"

Parker nodded.

"Which means Nap is already outnumbered."

The words fell like glass on the hard truth of reality. Parker could barely manage a whisper. "Yeah."

"You better be right about this, Parker. Only for Nap do I risk an ass tanning like I'm gonna get from the cap if you're wrong."

"I hear you, man."

And Parker did. But deep down, he wasn't worried. He'd done the right thing; he could tell because the jabs had stopped.

But not the feeling that maybe he'd reacted to them too late.

CHAPTER 28

The Gray Man was gone, and Kyle felt a certain terror in being alone, just standing there as the sky loomed overhead and the blue continued healing his wrist. The sounds of the desert were lonely and solitary, echoing in the chasm that had just opened up within him, and from out of this chasm his fear began to creep, one gripping finger at a time.

What do I do now? Where do I go? What am I supposed to do? How am I ever going to figure out where he took Tamara? Think. Think.

He took a few deep breaths and leaned forwards, resting his elbows on his knees as he looked out over the desert sands and Joshua trees.

He'd been here before. Not this place, but certainly this situation: when The Gray Man had left him in Carmel to go and protect Tamara, leaving Kyle on his own to get to Monterey and find Victoria. For some reason Kyle could still remember the cafe where they'd sat and argued, even though it seemed like it had been a billion years ago.

Kyle shook his head. This was his fault. All of it. From beginning to… whatever end was coming. If Tamara were killed, how in the world would he be able to explain it to the kids? And that's when it struck him. Going back to the beginning, when he'd knocked his life clean over, how did he ever think he was going to explain even having the affair with Caitlyn to the kids? How do you tell your babies that you've broken their mother's heart? How do you do that without losing a piece of yourself forever? And even if they didn't find out until they were older, how much more of their respect do you lose for keeping it a secret for years?

He thought of Tamara's face, of the pretty eyes and firm jawline, with the chin that always stuck out, just a little bit, with pride, and he shook his head. He'd barely been able to speak a word to her since this whole thing began, but he didn't need to, really, to know that the damage this had done to her was immeasurable. It baffled the mind that his affair could've caused this much damage. Now, he had to find a way to stop it from continuing.

He stood and rubbed his temples. He knew what to do; he had to reach out, he had to… sense… where she'd been taken.

Inhaling deeply, he felt the blue fill the bottom of his lungs, and when he exhaled he felt it, truly felt it, for the first time; all five of his senses began to merge together. Sight, sound, taste, touch and feeling orchestrated to another level within his mind until a sixth sense came marching forwards. He recognized it immediately, but was overcome by the strength of it: intuition. Until now it had been like a flitting bird whenever it appeared in his life, but not this time. Now it landed and nested.

The first thing it told him was to go east again.

Without thinking he told the blue to take him there and he took flight, lifting off the ground awkwardly, at first unable to divide his attention between his need to get to where he was going and the fear of trying this alone.

As he moved through the air it became obvious that with the intuition came a dominant sense. This time, it was smell. The smell of his wife. Of her skin and her hair.

How many times had he buried his face in the nape of her neck on a lazy weekend morning, there beneath the covers, and inhaled that smell and felt happy to have her? When had he stopped doing that? More importantly: why? Why in the world had he stopped doing that?

Tears filled Kyle Fasano's eyes as at last, at long last, the immensity of what he'd done caught up with him, there in the sky, splitting the atoms of a barely-there world. What kiss, what lips, what shudder of sinful gratification, could ever be worth the loss of someone who truly, against all the odds, loved you?

He was a fool.

It seemed that he was getting a glimpse of that final accounting that everyone had to do when they closed their eyes for the last time. He'd skipped it, that stern process of death, when he'd fallen through the portal with Victoria and down into the dark depths. But it was still waiting for him, that day: the day he would face his sins.

The air rushed past him as he accelerated, panic building in him as he traced the remnants of Tamara's smells—her Tree Tingle Shampoo from Trader Joe's, her perfume—all of them little, tiny dalliances of scent, barely there and evaporating more and more into the air by the second. He pulled left, following the highway, moving faster and faster, until he realized that if he went too fast he would lose the trail.

Before long he saw a little town, dry and worn. But the whole place seemed off, as if it were built on a graveyard of some kind, of bad memories and bad deeds, like a current-day Ragtown. His awareness expanded; a copper mine was nearby. Closed now. But it had claimed many a life, either directly or indirectly, in the literal cave-ins of its brittle and collapsing walls, or in the mental cave-ins it caused in men who worked sixteen-hour shifts, six days a week, and went home to take it out on their wives and children each night.

He didn't want to go there, to that town, or anywhere near it. It was a place, he realized, that few left, and those who did left with irreparable damage.

But before the town he saw something on the ground, near an abandoned gas station. A body. *Oh my God. No. No. No.*

Kyle descended rapidly and landed to a skittering stop. He ran to the body but recognized almost immediately that it wasn't Tamara but rather the body of a man, on his side near a puddle of water, a hose wrapped loosely around his neck. Stunned, Kyle walked over for a closer look. It was him: the crazy bastard who'd taken Tamara. He was still conscious, his eyes almost staring through Kyle as he smiled weakly.

"Where is she!" Kyle screamed as he stood over him, the blue pooling in his left hand.

The man shook his head, and then his smile disappeared. "I don't want to go there after all," he said in a frightened voice. "I really don't." Then his eyes opened wide with horror as his mouth tumbled open in a silent scream. He struggled briefly with a shadow that fell over him. His eyes filled with blood, and he rattled out one final breath, his neck arching sickeningly backwards.

Kyle thought of hell, just there on the other side of that final breath, and shuddered.

The citizens of the sleepy town in the distance were moving about in their mundane tasks. Again he reached out with the blue, but this time he got nothing. Her trail had gone cold.

But how? Had someone else taken her? Was this sick bastard working with others?

He no sooner asked the question than felt incredibly stupid for it. Of course he was. All along.

"Kyle."

The voice was a sharply echoing whisper across the desert floor, cracking off the boulders and rocks like a cue ball against a fresh rack on the pool table.

Kyle snapped his head to his left, then to his right. But it was impossible to get a fix on where the voice had come from.

Then it came again, dark and raspy. "Kyle."

This time Kyle narrowed his gaze to an area off in the distance, directly ahead and beyond the town. There he saw a large, gutted mountain, its top gone, as if it were a dormant volcano. He launched himself into the air and flew over the town.

As he closed in on the mountain's edge he was stunned to see that inside of it was ring after ring of circular roads that led down, deeper and deeper, to a canyon floor with a small green pool of tainted water, entrances to mine shafts here or there, all now boarded closed except for one, the boards broken and shattered to pieces on the ground.

The voice spoke directly from the depths of the mine shaft. "Did you really think, you little maggot, that you could escape hell without hell coming after you?"

It was in the mine, whatever it was. Kyle pulled up, momentarily fearful, sure beyond a shadow of a doubt that he wasn't ready for this.

That's when he sensed her presence, strong, and thankfully, still alive: Tamara.

Tamara was in there too, hurting and scared.

And that was all it took, really, for Kyle to launch himself forwards into that black hole. His wife was in there, and he would take on every demon that hell had to offer, if that's what it took to save her.

* * *

Napoleon pressed the Honda CRV rental to its limits. After he'd hung up with Parker he decided to throw most—but not all—caution to the wind. He was taking side streets as much as he could, where he stood less of a chance of crossing the path of a black and white on patrol.

He exited the freeway at Fourth Street and held his desperation by the throat, driving the speed limit and checking the rearview mirror frequently—something the average citizen never did enough of, which was why they mostly got nailed for tickets.

Paranoia knocked at his temples. The last thing he needed now was to get pulled over and have to bail out on foot; he was too far away from the park. An accident would be just as bad.

Other people were headed there too. Napoleon could feel it in his bones. His stupid-ass sister, determined to protect her boy, had no doubt sent them with violent intent. But that violence might very well be directed at the person she was trying to protect.

His darkening thoughts made his foot press the gas pedal down harder.

Don't. Don't go there. Don't think that way. Shut that shit out.

He eased up again and, seeing heavy traffic ahead, he made a left on Soto Street, then went two blocks up to Second Street and made a right. The park was now less than a mile away. He forced his mind to think of other things: of what inning the game was in, if Efren was playing shortstop or playing third, or if he had been working on his swing.

Passing Matthews Street, then Fickett, he accidentally bottomed out in a dip, the car bouncing a bit and causing an old man doing tai chi in his front yard to look Napoleon's way as he sped by. Once he saw the park, there in the distance, just past Saratoga Street, Napoleon simply couldn't take in anymore. He punched it.

Screw it. Let them chase me to the park. It'd actually help.

Now that he knew he could make it regardless of a pursuit, he actually hoped for a cruiser to appear, as if sent by God, and light him up with its sirens.

It didn't. There'd be no Hollywood, out of nowhere, bullshit Steven Spielberg ending this time, it appeared. Nope. It was going to be Napoleon and—

He saw them breaking across the park from the sidewalk to his left. There was no missing them—the shorts cut at the shins, the pure white t-shirts looking starched and practically ironed. Cholos for the cause; the cause with no pause. They were straight from central casting, the black sunglasses and flat-billed caps. Napoleon couldn't see their tattoos but he was willing to bet that each of them had a rosary, and a Mother Mary, and the obligatory "La Race" or "Trust No Bitches" stenciled in lowrider script on their biceps or necks.

Two of them were wearing baggy jeans, sagging to nearly below their asses. It was a warm day, which made the jackets they were wearing a big problem: because they made no sense, *unless they were carrying.*

Napoleon cursed under his breath. That's all he needed: a shootout at a little league game with kids everywhere, and his nephew caught in the cross fire.

He was getting his head around these seven, and feeling like he at least had a chance, when a black Nissan pulled up in front of him and screeched to a halt, the cholita who was driving peering over the steering wheel as five more cholos piled out. Whistling to the other seven, the tallest one in this group, skinny as a rail and easily six foot three, motioned with his hand that he and his group were going to circle to the baseball diamond from the other direction.

This was not good in so many ways that Napoleon stopped trying to count them.

Instead, as the Nissan sped off, Napoleon drove forwards and jammed the CRV into an empty driveway. Hopping out of the car, he chose a path directly between both groups, so as one curved around the first-base side and the other the third-base side, Napoleon took a straight line right through center field.

It was ballsy and brash and insane, but right about now those were the only three cards he had to play, and it was taken from the first chapter of *The Gangster's Handbook*: before chaos can be inflicted on you, inflict it on them.

The baseball game was in play, a batter in a white uniform just outside the box, another on deck. The stands were full with people—another bad break—and an ice cream vendor was walking his cart nearby, the little bicycle bell chiming with each rotation of the wheels. Efren's team was the Dodgers, and they wore Dodger blue.

Please let him be at third. I have a chance to move him off to the side if he's not—

Napoleon was stunned; Efren was on the pitcher's mound, too far away, his little frame beyond adorable, his hat a little too big for his head. He massaged the ball in his mitt, looking for the catcher's signal. Why was he pitching? He hardly ever pitched.

Little man. Big arm. They put you in the rotation. That's why you wanted me to come to your last game, isn't it? You wanted to surprise me.

Napoleon felt every fiber of his being flood with fear.

This can't happen. He's even further away from me now. My God… please. Whatever you ask of me, just don't let this happen…

He swallowed hard, stifling his emotions.

Even if I have to die, right now, to stop this, so be it, God. So be it.

The sky was hazy and a seagull, of all things, was slicing a path through it, looking lost and a long way from the sea. Napoleon figured there'd be bullets going all over the place very soon now, so it'd better start flying back to the damn beach.

Efren threw his pitch, a called strike and an out, the umpire stabbing his hand to the side and grunting the batter's fate. That's when the first parent in the stands noticed Napoleon. A mother—of course—pointed to center field, and the kid there—Napoleon knew him actually, Samuel Herrera, a bit of a punk with a dad doing twenty in Corcoran State Prison—turned around and saw Napoleon too.

"Hey, Mr. Villa! Whassup?" he said, smacking a large gob of his Big League Chew gum awkwardly in his little mouth.

The cholos came through the dugouts from either side of the field. A few parents, some cholos themselves, most likely from rival gangs past or present, stood in the stands and started to shout out questions and protests.

"Samuel?" Napoleon said as he marched past the boy.

"Yeah, Mr. Villa?"

"Get the hell out of here. Now," Napoleon said firmly. Samuel was a hood kid. He knew what was what. He took off out of center field as fast as he could.

Seeing that all twelve of the gangsters were heading towards Efren, Napoleon drew his gun and waited.

It was simple really. If they were truly there to protect Efren from an attacker, they would naturally assume Napoleon was that person as soon as they saw him, which would be any second now. They would turn to confront him.

Napoleon had been a little hard on them when he'd spoken to Parker. Not all cholos were evil through and through. Like most people, they were a cocktail of good and evil and capable of doing either on any given day. Just humans, trying to get by, in the environment they were born into. They went home and hugged their kids and loved them the same as anyone else. So, Napoleon was willing to hope against hope that most of the ones here today were not out to hurt Efren intentionally. But some were bad. And it would only take one of them to hurt his nephew.

The first cholo, in a gray flannel shirt, saw Napoleon first. He whistled, like he and his crew spoke it as a secret language, like a flock of birds.

Napoleon let out a deep sigh. He had to be the target, wide open and exposed with the gun in his hand, clearly visible.

Then he had to wait and see how many turned towards him and which of them ignored him completely and stayed on target. Because they would be the ones possessed and after Efren, probably ready to kill him right on the spot.

At Gray Flannel's whistle, the cholos turned, like dominos going sideways. Jackets flew up and guns came out.

Napoleon's little nephew saw him too.

"Tio!" he heard Efren scream.

Then, as expected, the chaos came.

CHAPTER 29

TAMARA FELT THE MEMORIES in her mind shuffling and reshuffling, loud and obnoxious, like music so loud that you couldn't understand what you were hearing anymore.

The creature from the mirror had come back.

Writhing on the ground, she clutched at the side of her head with one hand while reaching out for mercy with the other. On some level she knew this was futile, that the last thing in the world that this evil thing with no face and long, wicked fingers would ever give her was mercy. But she felt like her mind was just going to collapse, like a poorly built house. As if to prove this notion, one support beam was already giving way: her consciousness. The cave was spinning and the internal night of sleep, wanted or otherwise, was overcoming her.

"Stop. Please," she mumbled faintly.

Again, the voice of dead dreams and lost hope came to her. "Deny Him," it said, "and it will all stop."

On her knees now, only her upper body could sway, and that it did, first to the right, then a bit backwards. "What?" she said weakly. The mental doors in her brain flew open, and sad moments began to spill out: there was the time she had wetted herself on a hike into the back country, and the time she had planted an entire section of corn wrong in Bolivia and covered up her mistake, even though she knew that meant she was damaging a quarter of the crop and people would go a little hungry because of it that winter, and the time she'd kissed Timmy Burcher, a pastor's son from Idaho, behind her parents' camp tent in the middle of the night, and the time she'd given herself to a dark, handsome man on a drunken night in Mazatlán on a college trip, because she wanted to know, had to know, needed to know, what that felt like. Just once. Only one time.

"Deny Him. Deny Him now. It's that simple."

The darkness and dizziness pushed down on her. Pitching forwards, about to pass out completely, she thrust her left hand out to stop herself, fighting back one last time. "Who? Deny…"

Then it was clear, very clear, who he was talking about.

Of course. She should've known. This wasn't a creature. Not at all.

"You're the devil," she said.

It chuckled, the sound not unlike charcoal briquettes when poured out of the bag, a flat sound, like muted stones knocking together. "One of many," it replied, "but not the one of which you speak."

"Leave me alone. Get away from me," Tamara cried. In her mind she was scurrying backwards from it, to a corner somewhere in the cave. In reality her eyes were telling her she'd barely moved. Righting herself momentarily, she felt the spinning of the room increase. More memories. Of Ben now. Of what she'd almost done. Then the mental pictures blurred and changed to the time when Janie was a baby and wouldn't go to sleep, all night, crying and crying, until Tamara couldn't take it anymore and gave her Benadryl to knock her out. And how then Tamara still didn't sleep, because she was afraid she'd given her too much and Janie might stop breathing and never wake up.

The demon stood and waved at the cave walls, all the faces there like stone-encased prisoners, writhing in agony, eyes bulging, mouths falling open to scream into the emptiness of the cave, to add their sound to the screaming memories in her brain, taking her pain to a place that was miles past anything humanly tolerable. "Deny Him," he said again.

The world melted. The cave became a haze of browns and black. So this was it: her time to testify, to stand for her faith or to cast it aside as false. He wanted her belief. Anchored within her and connected to a point on an eternal horizon, it was something she lived for beyond the pleasures and distractions of this life—or perhaps in spite of them, because the opposite of pleasure was pain, and the real cause of distraction was almost always vicious little hurts. All she had to do now, to end this, to save herself, was to deny her Lord and Savior.

For Tamara Fasano it was the easiest decision of her life. "Deny Him? Never," she said. "Ever."

She fell forwards, turning her face sideways so that her cheek and not her nose bounced against the cave floor. It was cold and hard. Pain cracked in her temple, throbbing just hard enough to mercifully make her forget about the pain in her mind.

The faces in the walls began to scream in rage. She looked up at the fearful figure as he approached, his black leather trench coat from another time dragging along the ground in heavy strokes and painting the dusty cave floor in lazy swaths, his black boots, tall toed and with silver buckles, were covered in gristle, as if he'd been walking over dead things before this visit, or had walked over them to get here.

Her eyelids were growing heavy as the creature raised the lantern. She waited for fire to erupt from it, or for one of its small doors, framed in worn brass, to fly open and for a snake to slither out. After a moment, when none of this happened, it occurred to her that it would be nothing that fancy, her death. It would be cruel and crude; he was going to beat her to death with the lantern. He was going to cave in her skull with it.

"You simple, believing little whore," he said. "I'm so happy that I will be here, in person, to capture your soul, forever, when it tries to leave. You. Here. In my lantern. Forever."

His laughter was full bellied. "My newest pet," he said, swinging the lantern upwards. "My… little… angel."

The lantern was on the downward swing towards her head when Tamara noticed a pinhole of blue light in the cave that swiftly widened, first by a few feet, then by a lot more. Powerful and warm, it seemed to pour into the cave and ricochet in all directions, immediately rendering all the faces mute, some of them peeling of the wall in blown off bits of flesh, others melting like lava.

The creature with no face was bringing the lantern down right at her head and Tamara was almost ready to close her eyes for her end, when she saw it: a piercing, narrow blue beam, that carved a hole right through the left shoulder of the demon towering over her.

Tamara had no idea that she could take such pleasure in the pain of another thing. But when the demon screamed, she did.

Bewildered by what was happening, she thought for sure that it was The Gray Angel, come to save her again. It had to be.

When he walked through the light, his silhouette that of hope and salvation, the demon screamed in rage and spun to face him.

"You don't stand a chance," Tamara said, deliriously.

"Fuck you, bitch," the creature shouted over its shoulder.

The light subsided to a blue glow. "Get away from her," The Gray Angel said. Except his voice sounded different. Different and yet familiar.

"You're not ready, heaven spawn," the creature said in reply, the lantern in its hand beginning to hum with power. "I will kill you for daring to touch me, but I will tear this slut to pieces right in front of you before I do."

The silhouette moved with blinding speed, shifting like a chess piece in all directions. When he came to a stop Tamara saw that The Gray Angel had no hat this time. And no suit.

He grabbed the demon's left hand, the one holding the lantern, and held it firm, a blue snap of lightening making them both scream as the powers within them, of good and evil, grasped outward and gripped one another.

But now the man was no longer a silhouette, and Tamara could see that it wasn't The Gray Angel.

It was Kyle.

"Oh my God," Tamara said, her eyes filling with wonder and amazement.

Her husband waved his right hand in her direction and the world went into a rainbow of rushing lines and bursting wind. She was in some sort of bubble, iridescent and fragile—like the kinds kids blow out of wands on warm, summer days—and it was transporting her out of the cave and across the desert sky.

"No! Kyle? No!" she screamed.

But it was too late. The cave mouth was a slowly disappearing dot in the distance.

"No!" she screamed out in frustration. "Kyle. Why? Why?"

She'd finally found him.

And he'd sent her away.

* * *

"Detective Parker?" It was Trudy's desperate voice. "Where are you going?"

She had bull-rushed past Klink and out onto the balcony, where she now gripped at the guardrail. The cops froze for a second before Murillo motioned for everyone to get going. Parker looked at Trudy, up there on the balcony, and noticed her, really noticed her, for the first time. Even though she was wearing a faded Aeropostale baseball cap over her red hair, which poked out in all directions, no makeup—or little makeup, he'd never been able to completely tell with women—eyes all fierce and defiant, he noticed that she was simply the most beautiful thing he'd ever seen.

"Trudy, I have to—"

"No! You can't leave us. You can't leave me and the kids!" Her voice was firm, almost commanding. Klink tried to grab ahold of her but she escaped his grasp. Making her way down the walkway to the stairs, she encountered one of the two uniform cops who had just been sent there by Murillo. He froze and looked down at Parker.

"Let her pass," Parker said with a sigh.

"You got one minute while I go get the car," Murillo said.

She came down the stairs in a rush. Her tennis shoes were newish, and they squeaked a bit against the sealant on the steps. "Are you crazy?" she said, walking up to him and punching in the chest.

Parker recoiled a bit and put up his hands. "Hey. Take it easy."

"Take it easy? Are you fucking kidding me?" The Irish was up in her now; her eyes were watery, but her face was flushing red with anger and her freckles were disappearing by the second. "After what's happened here? You trust us to anyone else?"

"Not anyone, no. But Klink up there? You bet. And there's a lot of other good cops here too."

"And I don't know any of them."

"Trudy, you barely even know me."

"Yes, I do," she said, clenching her teeth.

"Listen—"

"You've gotten us this far. You're supposed to protect us."

Parker met her gaze and directed it to the body on the parking lot, covered with a sheet, barely twenty feet away. "Seems to me like you've done a fine job with the whole protecting thing."

He'd noticed that she hadn't looked in that direction the whole way down. But glancing that way now seemed to push her over the edge. "Jesus Christ!" she said, beginning to cry as she brought both of her hands up to cover her face. "I killed someone, Parker. Oh my God!"

She was only a few feet away, and she fell straight into him. Hugging her, he squeezed tighter than he normally would because, truth be told, he felt like falling too. "You had to. He gave you no choice, Trudy."

"Maybe I coulda shot to wound him or something."

"No. You didn't have time to think, and besides, you knew full well he wasn't coming in just to wound you or the kids. He was coming to kill."

She was quiet for a second as the breeze moved a wisp of hair over her cheek and then back up to her ear before Parker had a chance to brush it back for her. "You shoulda seen his eyes, Parker," she said, putting her hands on his chest. "They weren't… human."

Parker simply nodded.

"Does that make me crazy? Am I crazy that I said that?"

"No. You're not."

"Then tell me what's next, I mean—"

Murillo's tires squealed as he pulled around a car that had partially blocked him in.

"I can't tell you that right now. But I will. I promise, okay?"

He tried to pull away but she clutched at him and wouldn't let go. "Where are you going?"

Grabbing her gently at the elbows, he looked deep into her eyes. "Trudy. Please. Napoleon is in very real danger. I need to get to him. Now."

She let go of him and stepped back. "Okay," she said, wiping the tears from her face. "But you come back, or I swear, I'll kick your ass."

Parker nodded, gave a faint smile and turned to get into Murillo's car.

He noticed it immediately. The very act of turning his back on her. It hurt.

"We're about five minutes away after we light it up, so let's go!" Murillo barked, snapping Parker out of it.

"Thanks, Murillo," Parker said softly as he got into the unmarked gray sedan and buckled his seatbelt.

"Don't thank me for shit," Murillo said angrily. They pulled out onto the street with two black and whites trailing behind them.

Again Parker felt another jab. But this one brought a little bit of fear. "We gotta hurry, Murillo."

"Oh, man," Murillo said, shaking his head angrily. But he floored it as requested. The V8 of the Crown Victoria roared to life as Murillo turned on the sirens. A second or two later the black and whites behind them did the same. *Good,* Parker thought, *Nap needs to know we're coming. The cholos needed to know it too. C'mon Nap. The calvary's coming, man. Hang in there.*

"Murillo, listen…"

"No, Parker. You listen. You were new to the precinct when all this shit started, so I was willing to cut you some slack. But no more. You haven't been straight with us from the time we picked you up in Monterey, and I still don't think you're being straight with us now."

"I was trying to protect—"

"Protect who? Those kids back in that room? Who almost got killed?"

"I thought—"

"Or maybe their mother, Tamara Fasano? Were you protecting her too, Parker? Tell me, how's all this shit's working out for you?"

Parker looked wearily out the passenger window as the city blocks sped by, a random pedestrian reduced to a blotch of clothing and color.

"And now? Even your partner may be fucked to shit because you didn't want to tell us… right when we pulled up today… that he was alive and off to do some dirty work in the park!"

"We both shoulda—"

"No. Leave Nap out of it. He owns his own shit on this. You own yours. So tell me: what are you hiding from me still? Cause I got a wife and kids at home, Parker, and I'd like to go home to them, you know?"

"You're gonna think I'm out of my damn mind, Murillo."

"Try me."

Parker took a breath. "Nap's sister, she's connected. Cuarto Flats, I think. Or Evergreen. I can't remember. Anyway. She's already sent some help to the park—"

"What?" Murillo's rage was peaking. "Great. Again, I have to ask: how many?"

"I don't know."

Murillo grabbed the radio instantly and spoke into it. "Lincoln 10, requesting multiple units at Evergreen Park for possible armed gang activity." He hesitated for a second before taking the situation up ten levels. "Officer involved. Repeat. Officer involved."

Parker set his teeth. That was going to bring a veritable army of uniforms into Boyle Heights.

The dispatcher confirmed the request and before long the bark of her voice broke over the radio. "All units in the vicinity of Evergreen Park. Immediate assistance requested. Officer involved in situation with armed gang members."

The radio began squawking madly as one unit after another confirmed their intent to head to the park.

Parker sighed.

It was just like in the war.

When one brother was in trouble, the other brothers came.

Often with a vengeance.

CHAPTER 30

KYLE STOOD STILL FOR a moment. The creature before him was tall, at least seven feet, but more than that he had a mummy-like face, with black rags wrapped around his skull. He recognized him immediately.

"You? From The Lake of Loneliness? How?"

"I've been assigned to you since the moment you were chosen."

The blue was beginning to give Kyle something more powerful than bolts of light or miraculous healing abilities; it was giving him knowledge now, which was how he knew that this demon was from a particular sect in hell, one of the worst that existed, a sect that did not just feed on sin, but had the power to actually create it and use it to influence lives.

"Knowing from whence I came or what I will do will not save you," the creature said. He was ten feet away, standing tall, the lantern in his right hand extended in front of him, a small flame burning within it. Kyle was again hit with a sense of... knowing. The flame was not of this world; it was hellfire. It did not just burn flesh, but had the power to burn one's soul too.

He would have to be careful, because he was still human—at least he thought he was—and if he were struck by that fire, bad things might happen. Then another thought fluttered into his mind: no matter the rank or the power, no demon liked to be named.

"You are Homo Lanternae," Kyle said. "The Lantern Man."

The creature flinched, and then a cacophony of hisses spilled from it, the sound penetrating the cave, bouncing of the rocky walls and hard floor. A pulsating wave of evil began to fill the air.

Kyle suddenly realized that so much depended on seeing someone's face. With no way to see a mouth that sneered or smiled, or eyes that squinted or burned with rage, it was much harder to read the intent of a person. The rags that were wrapped around this creature's face were not skull tight—they were partially loose in places, just enough to read the set of its jawline or the bony outcropping of its cheekbones.

"You dare to name me?" he replied, taking a few sidesteps to the left and in the process blocking the cave exit.

Kyle exhaled gently. It didn't matter. He had no intent to leave. He was all about ending this now. He could feel it all the way through to his bones. Victoria had been stopped. He'd been rescued from hell. The monster that had gone after his wife and kids was dead. And now, the creature who had created that monster stood right before him, and he had to be stopped too. Because if he got away? He would do as he'd been doing for millennia: corrupting human minds to murderous deeds, and then watching the tragic acts that ensued, before feeding, like some sort of grotesque mosquito, on the horror that followed, like blood to its belly.

Kyle thought of The Gray Man. "So," Kyle said to himself, "this is what you meant when you said I was ready."

The blue came to Kyle and filled him full up, like he'd never felt it before, and as it did he could actually feel it crowding out his humanity, changing him, perhaps forever. When it rolled down his arms and into his hands he held it there, and waited.

The Lantern Man seemed to sense all of this. He nodded. "I want you to know that after I'm done killing you, Kyle... Your daughter... There's someone I know who lives not very far away from your house. He likes children. Young girls in particular. I will make sure he rapes her, more than once, and I will make you watch with me from hell, a guest forever in my cabin by the lake of fire."

Kyle Fasano smiled, because it felt good, at last, to be above it all. "Words," he said, and then he let go with a flash of blue from his core, from a spot right between his stomach and chest, a burst that illuminated the entire cave. Unseen things screamed from deeper in its depths, ghosts that had been dwelling there all along. A hundred and forty-three of them, to be exact, of people buried alive in 1938. The knowing just kept coming, with not just the facts but the harsh truths: most of them had been bad men, but not all. Many deserved to be remembered. But their families took the hush money from the copper company and the whole memory of it was buried with their bones. Right here. A cave of bones.

The Lantern Man had stumbled backwards, bringing his hands up to cover his face, which meant that he still had eyes behind those bandages. Then he took his lantern and swung it forwards, the hellfire within it shooting out it in a wide swatch.

Kyle moved to his right in a blur of motion, beyond all human means, leaving the hellfire to crash against the wall and across the floor. It was like oil and stayed lit and burning where it fell, casting their shadows across the cave wall like two moving stick figures.

They circled each other for a moment longer before a small rumble shook the cave. Kyle looked to the opening; it was small to begin with, but was now closing up.

The creature laughed. "What's the matter, Kyle? Afraid of the dark?"

There was a sound of shuffling behind him, forcing Kyle to glance quickly over his shoulder. He could barely make out miners' caps, the lights on them shattered and bent, as they approached, bobbing in the shadows. He turned back just in time to see The Lantern Man charging him, his lantern held back behind him as his left hand extended outward, not to grasp but to stab, his fingers growing into long pointy sticks. Kyle ducked and stepped out of the way, barely in time, feeling the air blow past him as The Lantern Man went by, his needle fingers striking the cave wall behind them and leaving deep gouges.

Kyle asked the blue to carry him to the other side of the cave, and it did. He levitated a good foot off the floor and moved out of harm's way, coming to rest against the opposite wall, his feet dropping lightly to the ground.

This time there was no mistaking The Lantern Man's shock. He snapped his head around in surprise, and then spun, holding the lantern out in front of him again, though now in a bit more of a defensive way, Kyle noticed.

They stood facing each other, the shuffling from the depths of the cave growing louder as the mouth of the cave closed completely.

Kyle brought his hands together and, pointing them at The Lantern Man, he released a double bolt of the blue, which the creature barely avoided as it scrambled to the side. Kyle saw him move, but for the moment, he couldn't have cared less. Instead, he was studying the bolts: they were solid and focused; a far cry from the wobbly lines that had come from his hands in Victoria's home back in Monterey, seemingly a lifetime ago.

Or maybe not seemingly. Maybe he was leaving that life, his life as a man, a person, a cheating husband and a sinner, behind now, at last and for good.

Those lines had been so weak and confused back then, as he himself had been. These bolts were strong and true, and they carved deeps line across the cave wall as Kyle kept them on full blast and swung them off to the left, into the dark, cavernous hole of the cave, where the ghosts of the evil dead were called to help this stupid creature.

Flesh, bone and screams erupted in the cave, bouncing off the walls with dull thuds, splatters and screeches.

The blue filled the hole, and one by one, struck them all down.

When the bolts receded at last, sucked back into his hands with a sizzle of electricity, Kyle looked back at The Lantern Man.

Kyle didn't need to see his face to know what it meant when The Lantern Man took a step back and turned swiftly to the cave opening he had just closed, as if regretting sealing off his own means of escape.

"Did you think they would help you?" Kyle asked flatly. "Dead men and the tales they dragged with them from the pit?"

"Shut up, you little worm," The Lantern Man said, stepping forwards. "You dare to challenge me?"

Kyle said nothing.

"I've been doing this for thousands of years, you fool!"

"And your thousands of years are about to tick to a stop," Kyle said.

The Lantern Man laughed. It was a laugh heavy with hate. "Oh, that's rich. You? You are to be my end?"

"No more tricks or games," Kyle said. "Just you and me now, okay?"

"Oh," The Lantern Man said ominously as the hellfire in his lantern began to glow brighter and a red light began to burn at the creases of the bandages on his face. "By all means, I concur."

* * *

The shouts were coming from all directions, the cholos' words coming at Napoleon alternately in Spanish and English, asking him what his problem was, what trouble he was looking for and telling him to put down his gun. Napoleon wanted to tell them that he had too many problems to count, and that the trouble he was looking for he'd already found, which was exactly why, despite their requests, he *couldn't* put down his gun. But he doubted that they'd understand.

Two of the cholos had stayed on target though, heading straight for Efren, and Napoleon took note. The first one was wearing a black jacket and shorts and was shorter than his companion, who Napoleon could see even from this distance had a long goatee and was wearing a Raiders cap and a short sleeve flannel shirt, checkered in large blocks of black and gray.

The two cholos had about a hundred feet or so to get to Efren, who was still frozen in place, still screaming at Napoleon.

Dammit, mijo! Please... "Run, Efren!" Napoleon screamed.

The ten remaining cholos fanned out across the field in front of him. Napoleon noted that the second, fourth, sixth, seventh, ninth and tenth had guns. The rest held weapons of a cruder fashion. But, truth be told, the seven that made up his left flank he couldn't have cared less about. There simply wasn't time to deal with them. It was the three to his right that mattered, because they were the ones blocking his way to a clear shot at the two going after Efren.

Napoleon heard a siren in the distance and thought, *Oh, the irony, that a crime is being committed nearby at this exact time.* Then he realized the siren was really a series of sirens, coming from all directions around the park, some police cars having already pulled up nearby, with others still on the approach.

The park became ringed with blue and red lights, flashing in danger, flashing with hope.

But the cholos kept screaming and advancing regardless.

None of it mattered.

His nephew… the only little boy he would ever have… was all that did.

And he still wasn't running. While the Raider fan and his homie closed the gap between Efren and certain death, he stood still, his confused gaze fixed on Napoleon.

Napoleon noticed figures bobbing in the distance. Shards of sunlight hit them and their badges shone against their dark uniforms. Like the one he used to wear, so long ago, walking the streets around here, the streets he'd escaped but never abandoned, the streets that he'd loved so much, his chest out, so proud.

How often a man finds his pride in things like a badge. What a stupid man he was back then. Esperanza was just ahead in his future, as was a broken heart that had stayed open ever since, waiting for someone, anyone really, to fill it.

"*Dios mio…*" he muttered beneath his breath, panic exploding in his every nerve. "*Por favor. Protegerlo.*" My God. Please. Protect him.

The uniforms were coming from everywhere. Five, ten, fifteen, then a good twenty of them.

The first shot came from Cholo Two, and missed wide. Instinctively, Napoleon sidestepped to the right, ignoring him and instead trying to get a clear shot on the two men advancing on Efren. Then a volley of shots erupted around him. A few bullets whizzed past him and a few more blew holes in the grass in front of him.

Another wave of shots came, now from the uniforms, these directed at the cholos. As the fire fight spread rapidly, five of the cholos to his left turned to engage the officers nearest them approaching across the field. The two in front of Napoleon were unarmed but running at him regardless, one with a knife and the other with a small club. He shot them both in the chest and they went down.

Cholo Nine and Ten, to his right, fired at Napoleon next, and one of them managed to clip him in his left forearm. The pain was searing as a chunk of his arm disappeared, the force of the bullet reverberating down Napoleon's arm and to his wrist. He screamed but couldn't even hear himself; there were too many gunshots going off.

A loud boom shook the air. A shotgun. Police issued. He'd know that sound anywhere.

When the second bullet struck him in the hip and a third in his left ribs, Napoleon faltered and almost fell.

Resigning himself to the fact that at least the police were here now, that maybe they would save the day, Napoleon looked again for Efren and saw that he was running now, so hard, to…

Of course.

Parker. He was there, just outside the dugout near third base.

The stupid rookie who hadn't been listening to him since day one. Thank God for that.

He was the one who'd brought the army to Evergreen Park. And why not? Who else but an ex-army ranger to bring reinforcements? Napoleon snickered, in spite of himself, as his head grew foggy.

That's when he noticed with horror that Efren wasn't going to make it. The bastard with the Raiders cap had pulled out a gun, and was firing it at him.

Trying to blow a hole through his ten-year-old nephew.

"Mother fucker." Napoleon grunted, coming alive again with full fury. Maybe it was adrenaline. Maybe it was God. But he felt a surge of energy like he'd never felt before in his entire life.

He dropped the unarmed cholo in front of him with three shots to the chest, which gave him a clear shot at the son of a bitch with the Raiders cap, but left him totally exposed to the two remaining cholos coming at him, guns blazing, bullets flying.

Some choices were so easy to make that you hardly even had to make them.

Napoleon stopped moving, got in his firing stance, leveled his weapon, and prayed again. "*Padre, tiempo. Por favor, dame el tiempo suficiente.*" Time, Father. Please just give me enough time.

He tracked the Raiders cap as it moved across the infield, sighting down the barrel with a determined eye. Then he squeezed the trigger. Calmly. With confidence. It was a perfect shot.

A puff of pink exploded from the cholos' head and he went down, a mass of bones and flesh no longer in control of itself.

Napoleon was just beginning to feel a small bit of relief when a bullet struck him in the chest, his entire body shuddering at the impact, his lungs forced to exhale against their will.

No. No, there's still one more I have to—

Pain cascaded through his lungs and he could barely breathe. A second bullet hit him in the left side of the neck, feeling like the biggest bee sting ever.

His body begin to betray him; his right arm went dead, forcing him to drop his gun, and then his legs began to buckle.

As he began to fall and the world went dizzy, Napoleon looked hard at his partner, watching Parker the whole way down, and he smiled as he saw him running at a dead charge towards Efren. Parker had drawn down on the other cholo, who'd produced a machete. Shot after shot rang out and the last thing Napoleon saw was the cholo going down fast, like a dead man goes down, with no longer any care in the world, just ten feet away from Efren.

Then? Efren dove safely into Parker's arms.

Efren was safe. It would all be okay. It would.

Napoleon sighed

The ground was soft but firm. The smell of freshly cut grass and earthy sod filled his nostrils, welcome at first, then nauseatingly overwhelming.

He heard the cholos who had just shot him scream nearby as more shots rang out.

Then Napoleon Villa couldn't hear anything anymore.

CHAPTER 31

TAMARA WAS TRAVELING AT a very high rate of speed through a tunnel of blue light. Too fast. Way too fast. Her mind began to go black and her eyes closed against the velocity. Kyle had sent her someplace, but someone had diverted her somehow. She was going somewhere. But she had no idea where. Maybe to…

The Blessing Pool was two miles deep in the jungle, to the west of their little village in Bolivia. Twice a month, on Sundays, new believers would be taken there for baptism services. It wasn't a pool, really, but rather a deep pond that had formed between sections of the river that cut through a wide rocky inlet about a quarter-mile upstream to the east and a gully that sloped slightly downward to the west.

Shallow at the edges, the pond was deep in the middle, and her father, who was six-three, would stand about ten feet from the shore, the water level just above his waist, so that he could fully immerse those about to proclaim their faith. Most of them were from their village, or one nearby; some were visitors who came in the summers mostly, on missions trips, from as far away as Minnesota and Puerto Rico, and who had finally realized that being was no substitute for serving, or that serving was no substitute for believing.

"Really believing," her father had told her one day, after the baptisms, as he dried his hair with a towel. The rest of the group had left to go back to camp, leaving them behind to chat a bit.

"What does that mean, though?" Tamara asked with a frustrated curiosity. At fifteen she had still not taken "the plunge," and her parents hadn't tried hurrying the process.

"Well," her father said with a soft smile, his blue eyes like opals against the deep green of the sparkling pool behind him. "A lot of people will say that real belief, true faith, is absent the need for proof. I'd take it a step further. More importantly, I think it's something that's absent the need for doubt."

"There's a difference?" she asked, playing with a small dark-brown rock speckled with black and white spots that she'd found near the pool's edge. She ran her index finger over its surface, which was mostly smooth but with a few rough spots. If not for those spots, the rock would be nearly perfect. She wondered how many centuries the rock had sat there, beneath the surface of the running water of the river, being worn smoother and smoother, before she carelessly plucked it out, ruining the process, so that now those few remaining rough spots would never be erased.

He nodded. "Yes. The demand for proof can't even take place without there first being some level of doubt. Or doubts."

"But doesn't everyone have doubts, Dad?"

"Sure," he said with a soft chuckle. "But it's what you do with them that matters. Do you let them linger, haunt you, drag you down? Or do you dismiss them for the distractions they really are?"

"But my science lessons don't say that."

Now he laughed fully. "Of course they don't, honey. Science is good stuff, necessary really, when dealing with the real world. It's important for all sorts of great things. Space travel. Medicine. But trying to use science to figure out the cause and purpose of our creation is like trying to use a rake to loosen a screw."

"Yolanda and Carmen say that God is in everything and everyone," Tamara replied, thinking of her two best friends from the village.

"I'd say they got that right."

"So if He's already in us? Why the doubt? Why the need to do all this?" she replied, waving her hand over the pool in reference to the baptisms.

Her father took a breath, looked out briefly over the jungle foliage and then back to her. It's what he always did when he was saying a quick prayer. He didn't know she knew this, but she did. She'd been studying her father's mannerisms for a while now, because she loved them, and him, so much.

"You know how you can be… I dunno, at one of the feasts or gatherings in one of the huts?" her father said, referencing the village socials that took place only a few times a year, often consisting of a few hundred people, guides, tribesman, and other missionaries alike, from across the region. "And how sometimes it's full of people you don't know?"

"Yeah."

"How does it feel?"

"I get nervous."

"Why?"

She thought for a second. "I guess because when I don't know anyone, I get scared."

"Right. That's this life, Tam, if you really think about it: you're mostly all alone in it, and surrounded by people you don't know."

She furrowed her brow at him. “Geez, Dad. That’s a little harsh.”

“No, not if you really think about it. Look at all the wonderful friends we’ve made here, all the families we’ve shared the gospel with, and who’ve shared their lives and ways with us. It’s been awesome, hasn’t it?”

Tamara shrugged. “Yeah.”

“Right. But someday we’re going to be leaving here. We’re going to take a plane and fly away, back to the States maybe, or wherever else we’re called. Then what do you think will happen?”

“I don’t know.”

“The Garcias, the village elders, your friends Yolanda and Carmen? They’ll write us, and we’ll write them. For a while anyway. Then? There’ll be fewer and fewer letters until we’re down to a Christmas card each year. Then? Maybe nothing.”

“It doesn’t have to be that way,” Tamara countered.

“No,” her dad said with a smile, “it doesn’t. With effort and dedication you can write or come back and visit more often. But it won’t be the same. We are a deep part of their lives right now, day in and day out, and they are the same in ours. But, eventually, a separation takes place, and distance sets in. It’s all a very normal part of human life, honey.”

“So? I still don’t get it.”

“Tam… someday you’ll grow up. You’re going to meet and marry a fine man. He will love you, I’m sure of it. You’ll have lots of babies—”

“Daaaaad. Please. Gross.”

He put his hand gently on her shoulder. It was a strong hand. She didn’t know it at the time, and neither did he, but it wouldn’t be strong for very much longer.

Laughing, he pushed on. "And your mom and I will play with our grand babies for a while. But nothing lasts forever, honey. Then? We'll have to go."

"What?"

"We'll pass. God will bring us home."

"I don't want to think about that."

"No. Of course not. And I'm not trying to make you sad."

She shook her head at him in frustration. "Uh. Okay. But you are."

"Stick with me here, pumpkin. I'm getting somewhere, okay? Or at least I'm trying to."

Tamara nodded softly.

"People. Your mom, me, Carmen, Yolanda. Even this world. It's all temporal, honey. None of it lasts. Worse still, a lot of life is conditional. The people in your life come and go under certain conditions; the world around you exists under certain conditions. When you're older, when you dig way deep down, you're going to figure out that mostly the only thing you're really, one hundred percent sure about? Is you."

A small flock of toucans flew through a nearby tree, squawking loudly, the sound fading as they disappeared into the distance. Then it was just her, her father and the sound of the river again.

Her dad pulled her over to a boulder and sat opposite her. "That place—you? It can be a lonely place. Sharing you, letting others in, breaking down that loneliness is beautiful and scary. It can also, at times, be painful. But, going back to that hut I mentioned, at one of the village socials?"

She nodded.

"How do you feel after standing there a long while when, finally, Carmen walks in, or your mom or I?"

"Happy."

"Why?"

"Because I'm not alone anymore. Someone there knows me."

His smile was broad and creased at the edges. "Exactly. You are known."

"Yeah?"

"Honey. When you have God in your life, there's nothing temporal about it. It's like being known. Forever. Known deep down, fully and completely, for who you are, and accepted without condition."

She'd been thinking about going into the pool for a long, long time, but hadn't told anybody. Maybe it was his words, nudging her, or more likely, something far greater calling to her. But at last it felt like it was time. "Dad? Will you baptize me?"

He blinked hard a few times, tears filling his eyes. "I'd love to, pumpkin."

The water of God was not cool. It was cold. So cold that you gasped when you were immersed in it and it brought your bones to life and your heart to song. Tamara trembled, feeling alive, as she fell backwards, her father's arms holding her lovingly as that cold water dove deep within her and combed over her, even filling the tiny spaces between the roots of her hair.

There was a refreshing peace in it and at some point, without ever realizing it, the rock that was still in her hand slipped from her grasp. When she came up, they embraced and he kissed her on the head before they made their way quietly to shore, packed up and began the hike home.

Along the way they reached a section of the path that was surrounded by a small forest of plumeria plants. There was a certain scent to plumerias, faint but deep, that did not insist on love, like the scent of a rose, but merely hinted at the possibility of it. Her mother used to love the smell of that path and the plumeria flowers in their varying shades of light blues, pinks and yellows. The little forest of them was dense here, and aromatic enough so that those walking to The Blessing Pool on baptism days would have the smell of their sins covered just before they were washed away entirely.

As she and her father made their way home, Tamara realized no great difference within herself. There was no magic fairy dust that fell over her, no sudden disappearance of all her pains, restlessness or sorrows. Just the cool feeling of the water as it dripped off her hair and down her back, each drop caressed by a soft breeze.

But her father was right. She did feel something else now, there inside herself: a new relief, borne of a deep-rooted assurance that she would never again be alone, no matter how "alone" she was.

When Tamara's eyes fluttered open the blue had gone away. She fully expected to be in heaven and to see her dad again, at long last.

Instead she was in her home, lying in the shattered remnants of the foyer, which was surrounded by police tape.

Kyle had sent her back home.

To an empty house.

* * *

As Murillo pushed the car through cross streets that went by in a blur, Parker saw the black and whites streaming in, sirens blaring and engines roaring.

I'd better have called this one right, or I'll be fired for sure now, Parker thought.

"Klink's gonna be pissed he missed this," Murillo said through clenched teeth, his hands gripping the wheel.

"How far we still have to go?" Parker asked.

Murillo looked sideways at him.

"Remember, man," Parker explained, "I was based outta the South Side. I barely had any time to research the streets in this precinct when I was brought over."

"A mile or so. We'll be making a right soon. That'll take us straight to it. I'm guessin' it's the exact way Nap woulda taken."

Parker nodded and took a deep breath.

"Before we get there you gotta tell me, though," Murillo said. "Where's he been?"

"You don't wanna hear it. I mean—"

"Spit it the fuck out, Parker."

"Fine. You a religious man, Murillo?"

Murillo's face contorted in confusion. "*¿Que?*"

"You believe in God. In angels and demons and all that?"

"Of course I do, dumb shit," he replied. "But what's that got to do with—"

"Napoleon was in hell."

"What… ?"

"An angel showed up, at the Brasco home. Fasano was in trouble and Napoleon offered to help. It took him there—to hell, I mean—to try and rescue Fasano."

Murillo slowed the car as they bounced through a dip and ran a red light, and then he looked over at Parker. "You on acid or some shit, man?"

"You asked."

"C'mon man, gimme a break."

"You wanna break? Fine. I'll give you one: a guy who's never believed in any of this shit, his whole life, is the one telling it to you."

"Angels and demons?"

"That or some absolutely insane fucking costumes and special effects."

"Man. I ain't gettin' my head around this." Murillo's face had gone from confused to perplexed to a mask of utter disbelief. "Okay. You were right," Murillo said as they pulled a hard right and sped down the street. The park was there, at the end of the street.

"What?"

"I don't want to hear it. At least not now," Murillo said, kissing his index finger and touching a Saint Thomas figurine that hung from his rearview mirror. He crossed himself and added, "Later, though, okay?"

"Fair enough."

Two squad cars were behind them and one had already pulled into a space ahead of them, unknowingly parking right behind Trudy's CRV rental. Parker felt instantly relieved. Nap was here.

He'd just opened the passenger door and gotten out of the car when the gunshots began ringing out. Two shots at first, like precursors. Then four more. Then a veritable birdsong of them, all just inside the park. Murillo and the uniforms all drew their weapons, but Parker, almost in shock, could think of nothing else but to run as fast as he could towards the gunfire. Towards where he knew Napoleon would be.

"Parker!" Murillo screamed behind him. But Parker could barely hear him. It was the same in the desert; men and guns were so loud that the rest of the world became a muted song.

As he knocked over a trashcan and ran into the park, he saw that the entrance was immediately adjacent to a small baseball field to his right. An old man had taken cover behind his ice cream cart and people were running from the bleachers. Parker scanned the field of battle, because that's exactly what it was. A dozen cholos were on the field; two of them chasing a little kid in a Dodgers uniform as another ten advanced, some from first base, others from third, all towards the outfield.

All towards his partner, who was standing alone, in a firing stance, firing at none of them.

Even though four of them were firing at him.

Instead, it looked to Parker like Napoleon was pointing past them, his gun moving cautiously left to right and then back again, as if he were trying to take aim at...

The two chasing the boy! That's when it hit Parker that the boy was Efren.

Drawing his weapon, Parker ran in long strides through the dugout to the right, heading towards Efren. If he could get to him...

There are some things you expect. In battle. In life. But what happened next, Parker could've never seen coming. Not in a million years.

One of the cholos chasing Efren produced a long machete from inside his jacket and the other, beyond belief, produced a gun and just began firing it.

At Efren.

He was firing a gun at a child.

One bullet missed and kicked up a tuft of dirt in the infield. Another missed and struck the backstop, shards of wood exploding into the air, as Efren fled the pitcher's mound, confused, running in a circle at first then stopping cold, frozen in panic.

"Shit! No!" Parker screamed. "Efren! Efren, over here!"

The little boy's head snapped around just as a third bullet clipped the front of his baseball cap and sent it spinning into the air. But he was unhurt. By some miracle.

"Thank God. Thank you, God. Get me to him, God," Parker prayed as he ran. Caring not one bit about it. His free hand motioned for Efren to run to him as more shots rang out. One of them a shotgun blast.

In the outfield.

Parker glanced quickly in that direction.

Two uniforms had fired at three of the cholos, who all went down. One of them hit the grass as he returned fire, the bullet catching one of the uniforms square in the center of the chest, thrusting him backwards from the force.

It's okay, Parker thought. *Vests are standard issue now. Best place to take a bullet. A foot or so higher and the bullet takes off his head.*

Parker's heart sank, though, when he saw Napoleon stumbling to his right, wounded, his left hand clutching his side while his right hand still held his gun, still drawn, still aiming...

Parker snapped his head back towards Efren. The kid could run. Like the wind. But there was no way he was going to outrun the cholo with the machete. He was closing, fast, the blade pulled back to deliver the deathblow.

And his buddy, the one with a Raiders cap and long goatee, had stopped to draw a bead on the boy with his gun, Parker close enough now to make out the fat, blocky barrel, leveled and steady.

The boy was done for. There was just no way...

The Raiders cap exploded suddenly—meat, bone and flesh spraying into the air. The goateed cholo took a small step forwards, dropping his gun, before his body realized that most of his brain was gone, and then he fell over onto the grass between second and third base like a dead tree.

Parker didn't have to ask. He knew. Napoleon. He'd taken his time, he'd even taken some bullets, to make sure that his shot would be true.

"Efren! Dive!" Parker screamed. And the boy, as he glanced over his shoulder and saw the cholo within closing distance, his machete on the down swing, thankfully did just as he was ordered.

The gun bounced in Parker's hand as he ran, but it didn't matter. Fuck aiming. The boy was down flat to the ground and he was going to empty the whole clip if he had to. One of them was bound to hit the son of a bitch. He squeezed the trigger, feeling the sweat on his index finger on the curved piece of metal.

The first shot ripped right through the cholo's stomach. The next two missed, but the one after that caught him in the upper left shoulder, jerking him back and at an angle that allowed for the next bullet to rip through his cheek and blow out his jaw. Parker stopped pulling the trigger as the cholo crumpled to the ground, his body landing with a thud, a cloud of infield dirt rising around him.

Parker scanned the area around Efren as he slowed to a stop. A dozen or so uniformed police officers, Murillo and a few other detectives had filled the diamond, weapons drawn. The remaining cholos were on their knees with their hands behind their heads. The boy was safe.

As he knelt next to Efren, Parker could see that he was crying. He assumed it was out of fear, until he saw that Efren was looking into the outfield, his eyes flooding with desperation.

"Tioooooo!" he screamed into the ground.

Parker didn't want to look. He didn't want to turn around, or even be here in this park anymore. Because he knew what he was going to see, and he didn't want to. He told himself not to look, that nothing good could come of it. But he looked anyway. A quick glance, just to confirm what he already suspected; Napoleon lay in a heap, motionless, his face turned away from them, blood pouring from multiple wounds, two in his side and a massive one that took off half of his neck. Parker had seen enough wounds to know which ones were fatal.

"No," Efren cried. "My uncle, mister! My uncle's dead!"

"Don't," Parker said, feeling small, feeling inconsequential and completely overwhelmed. He grabbed Efren, picked him up and held him to his chest. "Look away. Just look away."

Then, even though he wanted to be strong, even though he knew he needed to be strong right now, Parker just couldn't be.

Detective First Grade Evan Parker sat with the little boy from East LA and sobbed right along with him.

CHAPTER 32

THE CAVE HAD BECOME warm and suffocating. The Lantern Man was emanating the heat of hell. But to Kyle Fasano it was no big deal.

He'd been there. Done that.

They moved in semicircles across from each other, shuffling first to the left, then the right and then left again. Kyle heard a distant soundtrack of screams and profanities coming from somewhere, before realizing that they were coming from the small open door of the lantern, which burned alternating shades of red and orange.

"So, human? What will it be?"

Kyle's hands throbbed with the blue, which was aching to escape the confines of his skin. With such a tall, large target, it should have been easy. But Kyle knew, no, he *sensed* better. He was being baited to strike first.

But he wouldn't allow himself to. No matter how badly he wanted to do so. Instead, keeping his hands open in front of him, his fingers splayed as if he were gripping the air, he waited, shuffling side to side, mirroring The Lantern Man.

"C'mon. When have you ever waited for anything? When have you ever, in your entire life, *not* acted selfishly?"

The blue was filling Kyle up, flowing like a stream through his torso and down his legs, pooling in his heels, alive. Kyle felt almost drunk on it.

A moment of clarity came, again, except this time he took a break in wonder at himself.

He wasn't human anymore. Not fully. He realized now that he'd begun leaving that part of himself behind over that first slice of pie with The Gray Man, way back when, and since then he'd been gradually evolving towards this state. He had no idea what exactly this "state" was, only that he was now standing face-to-face with a creature from a very real hell to defend humanity and the heavenly realms, two things that only six months ago he would have dismissed as impossible.

But then he'd sinned, been rescued and been brought into the light. The light that lit up all the dark spaces inside you. For a second he fixated on his sorrows and pains, the damages that he'd caused in his life and in the lives of others, but the morbid reflections were short lived.

The blue, the spirit of the very essence that coursed through it, wouldn't let him continue.

When he was in hell it was all about suffering, but here, now, it didn't have to be. Here and now it was about life: both its potential and the fulfillment of that potential. Janie and Seth had entire futures ahead of them, and so did Tamara. And she deserved more than what he'd given her. If it was the last thing he did as a human being on this plane? It was going to be that: to give his family the future that they deserved, to make sure that they would be safe.

And the only thing standing in his way now was this miserable, pathetic bag of bones from a place where all that was wrong and evil dwelled.

His left hand shot a bolt of blue at The Lantern Man as he held the blue in his right hand in reserve. Just in case.

He needn't have worried, on two counts.

First, The Lantern Man deflected the shot with ease, his lantern coming up in a half-arc to block it. The sound of the blue on the metal of the lantern let loose a loud twang as the bolt bounced off and dug into the wall of the cave, sending rock shrapnel exploding in all directions.

Second, Kyle's left hand refilled immediately with more power. No delay. No weakness. Just instant power.

The Lantern Man charged forwards, throwing the lantern down on the ground between them like a bomb. It erupted in hellfire, flames and lava going in all directions, as a good half-dozen gobs struck Kyle. The pain was beyond belief.

He backpedaled desperately, away from the fire and the heat, only to feel his back crash against the wall behind him so hard that his teeth rattled.

Through the flame The Lantern Man came, his large frame silhouetted by the fire as his hands crossed over one another and reached into his jacket. When they reappeared he held long, curved knives with ivory handles, their blades as black as coal.

"These are what I use on them, on my servants, in the end, did you know that? Century after century they come to me with their wants, and I give them to them. They know the day of accounting will come, and yet still, you wouldn't believe how much they scream when it does."

He moved with unbelievable speed across the cave, a black whir zigzagging his way closer. Kyle fired a bolt from each hand but both missed.

The first blade came point first, right at Kyle's head, as if to spear it like a coconut. He ducked at the last second and the blade dug deep into the cave wall. The second knife was swinging upwards toward his midsection, and Kyle realized there was no way he was going to be able to avoid it. To save being completely disemboweled, he rotated sideways and down. The blade cut through his side, struck something solid, probably a rib, then was pulled out again with vicious speed, stabbing a half-dozen times more but catching only Kyle's shirt and more of the cave wall behind him as Kyle deflected the arm holding it, the blue in his right handing letting out a loud crackle as it touched the flesh of the demon.

Kyle screamed first, but The Lantern Man's wasn't far behind. They pushed off one another and then stood apart again.

That's when Kyle realized that, in stepping through the flames, the cloth had burned off The Lantern Man's head, revealing his face.

His eyes were a deep, burning red. Like tiny stones, they were set into a rotted skull covered in black and brown decay, cracks in the bone most prevalent around the eye sockets and in the chin.

"You struck me? Me?! You maggot!"

He charged again but this time Kyle was ready. He let loose with a double blast, and struck The Lantern Man square in the chest, the force lifting him off his feet and launching him across the cave. There was a loud "Hrumph!" as he went, his top hat flying off and one of the knives clanging as it fell to the floor.

Immediately, the flame from the lantern on the ground began to ebb.

Kyle waited. And waited. Surely The Lantern Man would rise from the back of the cave now, one blade left, filled with murderous rage. Or perhaps he would reveal wings covered in spikes and fly from the darkness with those burning eyes.

But… nothing.

The lava began to run down the walls and join the droplets that were on the ground, each blob flowing slowly back into the lantern.

Kyle stepped forwards cautiously and saw him there in the half-light of the remaining flame. He was on his back, his legs splayed out in front of him, his neck and head against the far wall, the teeth in his skull gnashing away at nothing as he waved the knife in his right hand helplessly before him.

The blue in Kyle relaxed and receded. He asked it to light up the cave and it did, making his body glow brightly.

The Lantern Man screamed again and brought his blade hand up to cover his eyes. Kyle now noticed that his left arm had been blown off at the elbow, leaving behind two sharp points of bone beneath the tattered, smoking bits of his jacket.

"Get away from me! Get away!" The Lantern Man screamed. His bravado gone, blown away like a wisp of smoke that had been caught in a sudden gust.

Kyle walked towards him, sure as he closed the gap that it was a setup of some kind and that The Lantern Man was just playing possum.

It wasn't until he was only about ten feet away and could hear the gurgling sounds of hell rattling to barely a murmur inside The Lantern Man's mouth that Kyle realized it was over.

At first he was surprised, but the blue would have none of it.

Kyle smiled and nodded. "I should've known," he said softly. "We should all know."

The Lantern Man shook his head weakly as the second blade fell from his hand.

"You and your kind? You're all nothing, except what we *make of you*. You have no power, except that which *we give you*."

"You know nothing," The Lantern Man spat weekly, his jaw snapping at the words, the rotted crack in his chin growing wider with the effort.

"All this time, you've bandaged your head together just so it wouldn't fall apart," Kyle said. The blue still coursed within him.

"Get away from me," The Lantern Man repeated before a sea of words in languages, both modern and ancient, exploded from him. Incantations. Curses. Profanities. Useless spells.

"Not a single word you say will work," Kyle said, nodding weakly. "I'm beyond your tricks now."

The lava was coalescing at the lantern and disappearing. The Lantern Man's red eyes burned brighter. Even demons have emotions, Kyle realized, and right now The Lantern Man was feeling betrayed.

"I wonder," Kyle said, "how you will scream when it's your turn. When whomever you made a deal with to have the power you've had meets you at the door when you get back there, to hell."

The Lantern Man turned to face him with a hateful sneer.

Kyle heard the blue in his heart and nodded his understanding. "So. You know that I have to ask you, right? Do you—"

"Don't," The Lantern Man spat. "Don't you dare."

Kyle stepped forwards as power again filled his hands. "Do you wish to repent?"

The red eyes flashed wide and bright, one last time. "I will never kneel to your pathetic, weak way. Your master is a piece of—"

Kyle blew The Lantern Man's head clean off his body, the blue burning so harshly that it melted his spine at the shoulders.

When Kyle turned to leave, he noticed that the lantern had disappeared.

He blew a hole in the cave entrance and walked wearily out into the desert sun.

Out into the light.

* * *

The tiny potion bottles were lined up like little soldiers. Herbs. Medicines. Condensed soups. Bone broth. Hearts of Flower. And, of course, the only medicine she said that *she* ever needed, a bottle of Chianti. "From Genoa," she would always say with a smile. "It's supposed to be a very nice part of Italy."

His grandmother sat on a small wooden stool in the corner of what looked like an old wooden cabin. She wore a white cotton dress and a baby blue shawl that was wrapped around her neck and chest in two separate folds, one end disappearing over her shoulder and the other end, dotted with a colored pattern, resting on her arm. Her eyes were still brown, but her hair was now all white and tied upwards in a tight bun with a small blue piece of wood stabbed through the middle of it.

But it was her smile that finally brought him around from the hazy fog of the deepest sleep he'd ever had. "Hello, *mijo*," she said.

Then her hands, those wonderful hands, reached out to cup his cheeks.

"You've grown up so much, Napoleon," she said. "Oh my." And happy teardrops hovered at the bottom of her eyes like tiny globes.

He was lying down, with his head on some sort of coarse pillow. Looking up at the roof of the cabin, he could see that it was old but sturdy. A few dozen plants hung on chains from the rafters, some decorative, like ferns and wildflowers, others fragrant, like jasmine. There were windows in the cabin but, on his back as he was, he couldn't see out of them. He tried reaching up to her, but it was no use, he was still too weak.

"Don't, *mijo*. You lie still for a bit. Take it easy now, my little troublemaker," she said, the last word forcing a big smile to erupt across her face.

He was a never a troublemaker, and they both knew it. It had always been their little joke. The boy who tried his best to get good grades and protect the kids that got picked on at school—the same kids who would grow up bitter and each join three different gangs, without ever letting Napoleon get jumped in somehow, as if he was going to be the last good thing they did before all the crimes they would commit—and the same boy who once organized a search effort for a lost dog in the neighborhood, because the little girl it belonged to wouldn't stop crying, yes, but also because it was what Encyclopedia Brown, the hero in the books he was reading at the time, would have done.

Ever the detective.

They never found that puppy, but the little girl never forgot Napoleon for trying so earnestly. Three years older than him, there was no room for romance. Instead, even better, there would be a good friendship. She would grow up, move away, do well in school and eventually join the LAPD. She would also be the one who got Napoleon onto the force.

Because she knew it too: Napoleon was anything but a troublemaker.

"Wh-where am . . ." he began to ask, then stopped. Not because his throat was dry, even though it was, but because he knew. Just knew.

He'd told himself when he'd first opened his eyes that this was a fantastic dream.

Then knew, instantly, that it was no dream at all.

Heaven. He was finally there. Like a sojourner unaware of his intended destination until, at long last, he arrives, and then says to himself, "This is where I wanted to be all along."

His grandmother said nothing. Instead she smiled again and then stood. "I'm going to make you some tea, baby boy," she said. "Okay?"

He nodded and smiled back.

The secret to all her "magic" was no magic at all. A massive assortment of crushed tea leaves, from all over the world, some bought in Chinatown, others in Koreatown or the small South American imports shop off Figueroa, were stacked in equal-sized glass containers on a series of shelves against a nearby wall, just as they had been back in Boyle Heights. The cabin was not a full reconstruction of their old home, just a partial replica. There were new things too. Like the hanging plants and the series of watercolor paintings on the far wall, resting over a rickety wooden easel. It didn't matter. Just by being here in this room, with her, in surroundings that were at least somewhat familiar, he realized just how much he'd missed her, all these years.

He looked again to the teas.

They would come to her for help and healing.

She would pour them tea. Sprinkle in some sage or cinnamon, or some habanero oil, maybe even some dust of frog leg. All hocus pocus into the hat, for the rabbit of faith to come.

Relaxed, filled with hope for healing, they would be ready. She would ask them about God. Share together. Be together. With them. With Him.

Then she would pray for them after they left, for days on end.

That was her real "magic"—God.

"And because I pray for them, in faith, without doubting, like James tells us to, God hears and he helps them. Simple as that. Sometimes that help means calling them home, so it's harder to see it that way for those they leave behind. But here's the thing, *mijo*: he always helps them," she told Napoleon one day after making him a packet of Top Ramen, which she thought was disgusting and only bought and made for him because he begged her to. Because, really, there came a point when you'd just had it with beans, rice and tortillas.

As he continued stirring awake, she returned with a cup of tea and placed it on a nearby table. She propped him up on a few extra pillows, then straightened his hair with her fingers and chuckled, pointing at his midsection. "It doesn't *look* like you got tired of beans and tortillas, *mijo*."

Napoleon felt a smile form on his face. "I didn't know I said that aloud."

"You didn't, *mijo*. Here you learn that there are more ways to hear than one. And see. And feel."

Heaven was warm and cool at the same time. He wondered how that was possible. Sitting up now, he eagerly glanced out the windows. There were rolling hills out there, lush and green, sprinkled with sporadic fields of wildflowers, and a stream of some kind. He hadn't heard it until he saw it. Water moving over land, gently, more a brook than a stream. He wanted to run outside and drink it, and splash it on his face and look up to see what the sky looked like in heaven.

"Here you go." She held the cup of tea up to his mouth and he sipped at it, meekly at first, then with relief. Peppermint. "Your favorite, right?"

The hot water loosened his vocal cords. "*Si, abuelita.*" He felt his heart stir in his chest and the joy in him want to burst out in all directions, in tears, in shouts, in proclamation. Instead he said, "Man. It is *so* good to see you."

"Yes. It is. You're all grown up now. I so want to hear what happened in your life, from the time I left that place to now. So much must've happened."

The memories were there to draw on and share, but Napoleon held them in check for some reason. The urge to do so bothered him.

His strength returning, he took the cup from her hands and held it in his own. It was ceramic, and the warmth spread into his palms.

"Hmm. Well, there's a lot to tell. Not sure all of it you'll want to hear," he said with a tilt of his head, "But for some reason—"

"For some reason… not yet. Right?" She smiled softly.

Napoleon was surprised. "How'd you know?"

"Because, *mijo*, it's in your eyes. You're not quite ready. There's someone you love still, and that's always the case. We always leave people behind that we love. Sometimes naturally. Sometimes tragically. It's the way things work, you know," she closed with a shrug.

"But…"

"But sometimes there's someone we love so much that we have to go back for them, *mijo*." And when she looked at him there was so much pride in her face that it nearly broke him apart.

"Efren," he said softly.

"Yes. You're own little *mijo*, not from you but *of* you."

"He wouldn't stand a chance if—"

"You didn't go back," she said with a sigh.

They were silent for a moment. Heaven waited as he finished his tea. Then, quietly, she took his hand and began to pray. It was the best kind of prayer: long, with soft pauses that left room for the Holy Spirit.

When she was done she looked up. "Go back for a little bit. Finish things up."

He nodded. "Will you—"

"Yes, *nieto*. Heaven is what we make of it, and a heaven without you someday would be no heaven at all for me. The Father is so gracious that way. I'll be here, waiting for you."

She kissed his forehead. He kissed her cheek. There was no sadness, just a wordless resolve that passed between them.

Then heaven opened up and spilled Napoleon back out into his body.

CHAPTER 33

KYLE ASCENDED FROM THE cave bone-weary and confused. What next? He didn't know.

What he did know was that he was done. The blue within him was fading, pooling back to that place deep within him, where his soul resided, halfway between his mind and his heart. As it did so, it finished healing his wrist and the wounds he'd incurred in the cave, the cuts and bruises disappearing as his nerve endings and flesh were mended.

The sun was setting like a giant, bright orange ball. Fading heat waves rippled slowly across the desert sands, warping the view of the horizon. It struck him that this was what was different about the deserts of hell: no heat waves. Just pure, vicious heat that punctured every pore of your body. He'd escaped that hell, hadn't he?

But now he was in a new one.

He felt sure that Tamara had made it out, that he'd transported her back to safety, even though he only had a rough idea of how he'd done it. It was like before, where he had to tell the blue to go where she last was, except this time he told it to take her to where he wanted: home, to the house, where she could then get to the kids somehow. He prayed that Napoleon and his partner had kept them safe, and that his children were okay now too. But were they really? Would they ever be "okay" again? The truth dwelled there, in the corners of his mind, but it could not hide.

No, they wouldn't be.

He'd made a decision in his life, not that long ago, and that decision had proved to be costly. Very costly. To everyone.

Feeling nauseous, Kyle stumbled over to a group of boulders near a small batch of cactus plants. A spider scurried over the rock face of the largest boulder as he leaned against it, his hands slipping a bit against the sandy surface. He'd come all this way, only to end up facing the same thing he'd been facing on day one.

He'd cheated on his wife, and that simple, selfish act had reverberated through the lives of so many. First of all Caitlyn, already in a dark place, who had been dragged down by his lusts. He should've been older and wiser. Instead, because of his flirting and advances, she would never have fun with her friends again, or get married, or have children. It was a two-person act, but had he not played his role, could she have ever played hers? And what of The Gray Man? Where was he now? Then there was Napoleon and his partner. What had they been drawn into, and gone through, because of him? He thought of them all so that he wouldn't think of the ones he was trying so desperately not to think of. But it was no use.

Tamara and the kids. What had he done to their lives?

It was too much. His guilt was upon him like a ravenous beast, tearing at the flesh of his heart. "Oh God."

He sighed. The battles were over now. He could sense it. All that remained was the aftermath… and a decision.

Kyle sat down on one of the boulders and began to cry, his eyes filling with tears and his breath growing shallower as the crying became sobs and the sobs became wails.

He was a domino that had triggered so many others, simply by his own fall. He had so many amends to make, so many wrongs to right, and no time to do any of it. He was changing. God was calling him, and he could hear Him; it was the loudest whisper you could ever imagine.

"I did it," Kyle cried. "But I don't know what to do now, God. What do I do?"

He had sinned, yes, but his greatest sin had not been his adultery with Caitlyn. It had been in taking his pains and hurts to someone other than Tamara, who had never really been given a chance to address them, had she? Why had he done it? Why?

You're looking hard, just in the wrong place.

Kyle was so stunned he wasn't sure if he'd really heard him: The Gray Man.

It began with your father, Kyle. On the day he died.

"What?" Kyle asked, confused. His vision was blurry from his tears, but when he looked up, he could see The Gray Man standing right over him.

Sin nature builds, Kyle. Until it crashes down. Then you all get another chance to get it right. But you didn't. A sad thing happened. You acted poorly, and from there you could've chosen to grow, but you didn't. You chose to focus, again, on you. It's why you turned your back on your family, on your life, and went chasing after your own end, step by step, in a few short years, right into Caitlyn's arms.

Weak. Boneless. Kyle fell to his knees and gripped at the desert sands. "Stop it."

No, my friend. I cannot. It is time. We must deal with this. Your focus has always been you, even at the sake of those you love. We could draw a line from Victoria, through your life, to your father's deathbed, and from there to your relationship with Tamara. But selfishness and love coexist uncomfortably, and at best temporarily, Kyle.

A moment of silence came between them as Kyle wrestled with his pain. Then, he let it loose. "He had no right to take him!"

Again, you look in the wrong direction. And this time you will even blame God? You're wrong Kyle; He had every right.

"Not before I had a chance to say goodbye! He didn't! I was at work. Closing a deal, of all things."

Where you chose to be, my friend. Please. Lean on the blue. Use it to look inward this time.

"No. It wasn't fair," Kyle said, stifling his tears. But the emotions in him, the shame, the guilt, the deep regret, were all writhing to get out. "I was at work. How could I do that? He was in the hospital and I knew… I *knew* it was the end. But I wasn't there! For my own father, who had been there for me my whole life; I wasn't there."

Yes. That's true. You didn't want to face his death, so you ran.

"No."

Yes. But, even then, after all you've seen, you still don't understand?

Overcome with emotion, Kyle shook his head and rocked back and forth, snot and tears running down his face and off his chin.

This life into the next: it is a process. And the Father works for the good in all things, Kyle. Even our mistakes.

"What're you saying, Gray? Please. I don't understand."

It was time for your father to go. But don't you see? He wouldn't leave, Kyle.

"What?" Kyle's voice was barely a squeak.

Kneeling down before him, The Gray Man wrapped his arms around Kyle, hugged him tightly and whispered aloud into his ear, "If you were there, in the hospital room, he would've never let go, Kyle. It was his time, but he would've turned his back… even on heaven… for you."

"Why?"

"Because it's what you do for someone you love, even if it hurts. You do what's best for them."

The words moved through Kyle like a poem.

He buried his head in The Gray Man's chest and slowly, softly, bit by bit, he let go, let it all go, at long last, all the pain. Each ounce of regret, shame and sorrow washed slowly away by the love of The Gray Man's embrace, which was rinsing him clean. Clean at last.

"You're waiting, aren't you?" Kyle asked, as he released The Gray Man. They stayed that way, on their knees, facing each other.

The Gray Man nodded softly.

"It's time for my decision now, isn't it?"

Again, a nod. Kyle had never noticed before, but looking at them so intently now, he could see that The Gray Man's eyes had speckles of white in them, like stardust.

"Would I be like you?" Kyle asked.

"At first you would minister to individuals. That would be your training. Eventually, you would be helping millionths, yes."

"I'm afraid, Gray."

"Of course you are."

"This is such an amazing opportunity."

"But it's still a *choice*, Kyle. You do understand that, right?"

Kyle nodded and took a moment to think… and to look. Hard.

All he could see was Tamara; her small chin and the way her eyes smiled right along with her mouth when something made her happy. He could see Seth's little hands too, held out in front of him when he would play hide and seek. And he could see Janie and her pigtails bobbing behind her as she ran across the soccer field, looking back over her shoulder at him the way she always did, to see if he was watching.

It was odd, really, but the biggest decision of his entire life was actually the easiest one he ever made. He was, after all, still his father's son.

Kyle looked timidly at The Gray Man. "I don't want to offend Him. By turning this down, I mean. What if He's angered or disappointed by my decision?"

His face looked a little sad at first, but then The Gray Man smiled softly. "Kyle. You're choosing love, aren't you?"

"Yeah. I am."

"Then how could He be anything but extremely proud of you?"

There were no more words. Just the two of them and a fading desert sun for a moment, before at last The Gray Man put his hand on Kyle's shoulder and said, "Goodbye, my friend."

Then everything went blue, one last time.

* * *

Napoleon gasped.

There was a shift, inside himself, inside his mind, as he felt himself separating from his body. Emotions, like hinges, snapped open: first sadness, and then happiness, resistance, then acceptance. *Time's up. Time to go,* he thought.

He saw Parker's face, desperate and afraid, looming over him. Poor kid. This was going to be hard on him. But eventually, he'd be okay. Napoleon sighed. There was a feeling of glee sweeping over him, like a cool breeze, and it was making it so much easier to let go. It was all going to be okay.

As Napoleon felt the weight of an entire lifetime fall from him like leaves from an autumn tree, he saw the world around him.

It froze.

Like it had before.

He stood, but his body remained on the ground and Parker remained kneeling, and all the cops, parents, gangsters and people were like set pieces on a stage.

Except for one: Efren.

He was still vibrating, ever so gently, with the raw emotions of sorrow, his face twisted in agony, his eyes dark and vacant.

The floating feeling within Napoleon was arrested. The glee? Erased.

"He'll have a hard time without you," a familiar voice said from behind him, "but in time I suspect that he will overcome."

Napoleon turned. It was The Gray Man.

"Yeah?" Napoleon replied.

"He has a strong heart, this one, and sound principles. Despite the home and the world he's grown up in."

A soft smile crossed Napoleon's lips as he nodded. "Yep. He's something else."

"He got that from you, you know."

"Oh. I dunno about that."

A few moments of frozen time passed. Finally, Napoleon spoke. "I'm ready to go now."

The Gray Man did nothing. Napoleon expected him to sprout wings and fly him off to heaven or something, or at least give him directions on how to get there. Instead The Gray Man said, "Are you sure? I mean, you just got back."

Surprised, Napoleon took a half-step. "Back?" he asked perplexed.

"Yes. You went, but returned."

"For what?"

Chuckling, The Gray Man looked into Napoleon's eyes. "I think your grandmother already answered that question, Villa."

Something crossed between them, in that casual place between life and the afterlife, a mutual understanding through a shared secret, an idea through that thin veil. Napoleon looked back at Efren.

"Yeah. I suppose she did."

"It's still your right to go. All you have to do is concentrate and go back to that feeling you were having, of overwhelming joy, and it will take you, all by itself, to that place you've spent a lifetime considering," The Gray Man said as he put his hands in his pockets. "Before you do though, I thought I should tell you—there are some of us who actually choose to stay behind, at least for a while, to help others."

Napoleon was curious. "Help others?"

The Gray Man looked at the frozen crowd around them, then to the neighborhood and streets beyond. "There are just so many who are lost, Villa. Who need help solving the problems of their hearts and the crimes of their minds. You'd be good at it."

"At what?" Napoleons said. But the question had no sooner come out of his mouth than a possible answer dawned on him. "Wait. Are you talking, like, guardian angel type stuff?"

The Gray Man smiled and bobbed his head from side to side, as if he were balancing the question on a scale, and replied. "Yes. Of a sort. At least at first."

"You mean that stuff's true?"

"Yes. And as it turns out, we have an opening."

Napoleon knitted his brow and looked up. "An opening? You mean…"

"Yes," The Gray Man said with a curt nod. "Kyle Fasano didn't want the job."

Napoleon thought for a second. "He stayed behind to make amends, didn't he?"

"Yes. And why not? After all, the love of a good woman is the closest a man can ever get to heaven in this life."

Napoleon thought of Esperanza. She who had broken his heart and left him forever behind, but this time *la desesperación* did not come, this time there was only release. Napoleon may have never found true love in this life, but Kyle Fasano had, and that's why it made all the sense in the world that he choose to stay. "Good for him," Napoleon said.

"Yes. I agree. Good for him."

There was a brief moment of silence between them before The Gray Man added, "So?"

The sky above was open and bright. But heaven wasn't going anywhere, and for the first time in his life, Napoleon knew it.

"Why not?" Napoleon said, looking again to Efren. "Will I…"

"Yes. You'll be able to keep an eye on him, from time to time, and especially now, as he deals with your loss. But know this: it will be this very loss that will make him forever turn his back on the world this neighborhood has to offer. And you'll even get to see how he turns out."

"Okay, then. I'm in."

"Excellent." The Gray Man smiled.

They walked side by side to the edge of the park, and as a soft blue light began to overtake him, Napoleon thought of something.

"Hey, Gray?"

"Yes?"

"Does all this count as extra credit or anything?"

Bemused, The Gray Man shook his head. "No, it doesn't."

Napoleon shrugged. "Then… what? Pass/Fail?"

The Gray Man laughed, put his hand on Napoleon's shoulder and gave it a firm squeeze. "You've already passed, my friend. With honors."

Then the world went all-blue… and Napoleon Villa felt a different kind of life come over him.

CHAPTER 34

Tamara Fasano splashed water on her face and looked at herself in the mirror. Beneath the harsh light of the bathroom she could see that she'd lost a lot of weight. Her eyes and cheekbones were a bit more pronounced, but besides that it was the same face, her face, staring back at her.

The hallway outside was dark. Night had come, slow and laborious, absent any stars and with only a sliver of a moon.

The kids were peacefully asleep, both in Seth's room, with the door open. She doubted that Janie would ever sleep in her room again, but for some odd reason Tamara wasn't worried about that anymore. There was something about the house now. It felt cleansed. Safe. Protected. She hadn't seen any angels wandering the halls or floating over the roof, but she didn't have to; she could feel them. Most importantly? She believed in them.

She'd called Trudy the minute she'd gotten up off the floor in the foyer, after Kyle had transported her home, and she'd never heard anything more sweet than her babies on the other end of the line, stepping over Trudy's voice to talk with her. Less than an hour later, Trudy showed up in a police cruiser, the three of them sitting in the back like bandits. Another car came, unmarked, with a detective inside. Arias was his name. Taller and more athletic than

Napoleon Villa, he'd watched their reunion, waited briefly and then stepped back to give them time to quit crying and catch their breath.

His interview with her was brief, at her request, with her promise that she would come to the station to give the unabridged version tomorrow, when she wasn't quite so exhausted.

Trudy was in the guest bedroom now, with the door closed. When Tamara checked on her earlier she was snoring gently, just like back in college, which made Tamara smile. She was probably dreaming of the young detective, Parker, who she couldn't stop talking about. She was smitten, it was obvious, but in a way that Tamara had never seen before. It was as if her friend had decided, at long last, maybe in spite of herself, to believe that someone could actually be that special without them having to prove it to her.

It was a good place to be, that ledge right before you step off and fall directly into love. Tamara smiled. Trudy deserved that. Especially after what she'd just been through.

Tamara felt worry and tension begin to creep back into her a bit, despite her faith. What was it her dad used to say? "Odd thing about faith—it's thin as an egg shell if it ain't hard boiled." *Yeah, Dad. It is. God knows, I just want some hope back, Dad. Can you tell God that for me? Just a little hope.*

She reminded herself to hold the line. To focus on her joys: her little ones were safe, her best friend was safe. Evil was gone. These were not small things.

She splashed more cold water on her face and brushed her teeth again, something she'd already done twice before, as if she couldn't get clean enough.

A knock came at the front door as she was dabbing her face dry with a towel, and she jumped. It was a solitary sound amid the peace and quiet of the house, and it seemed to echo around awhile. She wondered who it could be at this hour. Most likely a neighbor come to check in, or someone from church with a meal to drop off, second guessing their decision to come by so late. Maybe even the cops again, not willing to wait until tomorrow for more details. A second knock came, softer than the first, almost tentative now. Definitely not the police.

She walked across the carpet of the hallway and onto the floor of the foyer, blissfully aware and appreciative of the feeling on her feet, from the squishy cotton fibers of the carpet to the firm, cool tile. It was so good to be home, to be alive.

When she flipped on the porch light, opened the door and saw him, she caught her breath. He'd lost a lot of weight too, making him look younger, but his shoulders were still broad, and the rugged face and black hair spilling over his eyes called to a part of her she'd been guarding safely since this whole nightmare had begun.

He said nothing, but his chin was dropped and his eyes swam with nervousness.

Her hands came up to her mouth in shock, seemingly of their own free will, as relief awoke inside her and stretched out like a lazy cat. At first she couldn't believe this was happening. Something in her was afraid that the last time she would ever see him would be as she saw him in that cave: something not entirely human anymore, something destined for another place already, a place that meant leaving her far behind.

But now, here he was: a portrait in repentance, framed by the doorway, and waiting.

Tamara was so stunned she couldn't speak, so the two of them stood there in silence for a few awkward seconds, forgiveness hovering in their midst, waiting to be given and received. She felt it, and yet still hesitation gripped her heart. He'd hurt her so badly. They had a lot of ground between them. A long journey back to being right again. She wondered if she could do it, make that journey. It wouldn't be easy.

Then it happened: she smelled a scent, faint, barely there, maybe not really there at all except in her mind, but there nonetheless, as it came and filled the entryway.

It was the scent of fresh plumerias. Like the ones in the forest along the trail that led to The Blessing Pool. Hadn't she just asked for a little hope?

That's when Kyle finally spoke. "One?" he said softly.

She smiled. "Plus one."

Then she opened her arms as wide as she could.

ABOUT THE AUTHOR

Tony Faggioli began writing stories in the 5th grade and continued doing so until college, when he gave up writing to pursue a very short career in politics and a much longer career in business. One day, he finally realized that neither brought him anywhere near the amount of joy as writing. Born in Pittsburgh, Pennsylvania, he was raised in Los Angeles, California and graduated from the University of Southern California. He is a happily married father of two kids, two dogs and a pretty awesome goldfish.

tonyfaggioli.com

www.facebook.com/tfaggioli

www.twitter.com/steelertony

Books:
One In A Million (Book 1 of "The Millionth" trilogy)
A Million to One (Book 2 of "The Millionth" trilogy)
One Plus One (Book 3 of "The Millionth" trilogy)

Coming in 2017, "The Snow Globe", a psychological thriller.